A KING'S CHOICE

"I fear it is already too late for me," Parlan said. "If I cannot have you for my queen, then I, too, will be as a grieving husband, empty and broken without the love of my life. Is my heart any less worthy of protecting than yours, even though I am only a mortal man?"

He closed the distance between them and boldly reached for her hand. She did not resist, and with a deep sigh he cradled her fingers against his cheek.

Her arm turned rigid as an iron sword. She withdrew it and stepped back to look at him, and as his gaze met hers he held himself very still. Eriu glared at him with a look as cold as the harshest winter night.

"I have already made you a king," she said. "Do you mean to say you would turn your back on me, and on the Land, and on your people, and become as any other man when the Goddess of the Land, the Goddess of Sovereignty, the Goddess of Eire, has made you a king?"

Other *Love Spell* books by Janeen O'Kerry:

GODDESS OF EIRE

JANEEN O'KERRY

LOVE SPELL NEW YORK CITY

...for every man who ever loved a goddess.

LOVE SPELL®

February 2006

Published by

Dorchester Publishing Co., Inc.
200 Madison Avenue
New York, NY 10016

ISBN 0-505-52587-9

The name "Love Spell" and its logo are trademarks of Dorchester Publishing Co., Inc.

Printed in the United States of America.

Visit us on the web at www.dorchesterpub.com.

PROLOGUE

"The Ard-Ri awaits you, Lady Eriu," said Brighid, as she walked through the sunlit meadow, her red wool gown trailing over the lush green grass and the bright yellow primroses. "I wonder if your anticipation is anywhere near as great as his."

Eriu looked up from her seat on the sun-warmed boulder and smiled faintly at her sister-goddess. "He cannot be the new high king if I do not find him worthy. No doubt his apprehension is great indeed."

Brighid stood before her, and took Eriu's hands in her own. "My dear sister, I do not mean simply whether he will become the next high king or no. I am thinking of the ritual itself. Does it truly mean no more to you than the mere appointment of yet another leader for the world of Men?"

Gently Eriu withdrew her hands, and she gazed out over the meadow to the surrounding forest of oak and holly. As always here in the Otherworld, that mystical plane of existence where the gods and goddesses made their home, the season was summer and the weather

1

warm and pleasant. She stood up and took a few slow steps across the soft thick grass, smoothing her green wool gown as she paced.

"I have performed the kingmaking ritual countless times," Eriu said. "From the very first days, when the gods and goddesses began to teach mortals to live as humans and not animals, the task that fell to me as the Goddess of the Land was to confer sovereignty on the king—to show his people in the clearest terms that this man was worthy to be their leader."

Brighid nodded, taking a step toward her. "And since the king is no less than the husband and protector of the land, no other but the Goddess of the Land—the Goddess of Eire—should be the one to approve him."

"Indeed. I have never turned away from this duty. Each time a new king is chosen, I leave the Otherworld and step into the world of Men . . . there to test the man they have put forward and decide whether he is worthy of being a king."

"Yet you do this in the most intimate manner possible for any woman, Lady Eriu—for any woman, goddess or no. If the man passes your test, you take him as your husband for that night."

Eriu turned and smiled at Brighid, calmly meeting her gaze. "So I do. A goddess can show no greater approval for any mortal man than to take him as a mate, even if only for a night. No one can doubt that such a man is worthy to be king."

"But Eriu . . . I have often wondered how difficult this is for you. As you say, you have done this since the beginning, and that is a very long time. I know what a gentle and caring spirit you truly are. Is it enough for you to simply take a mate for one night and then coolly turn your back and walk away from him, never to see him again? Does this not affect your heart?"

Eriu started to answer, then paused. She glanced up at

the slanting rays of the sun as it began to rise high above the trees and mountains to the east.

"I cannot allow my heart to be a part of the kingmaking ritual," she said at last. "If I should allow myself to fall in love with any man, how could I ever lie with another to make that one a king?" She shook her head. "I vowed as the Goddess of the Land to do this thing for the land where Men live, and I will keep that vow."

"Yet it seems to me too much to ask of any woman to set aside her need for love and companionship in order to serve the world of Men. Perhaps you have done this long enough. Perhaps it is time—"

"I do not perform the kingmaking ritual only to help the *people* of the natural world," Eriu said quickly, her eyes narrowing. "I do it for love of the land itself, to make certain it always has a worthy guardian and protector.

"I am no warrior. A sword would cut me down as quickly as it would any mortal. I cannot protect the land myself. But I can find the men who will, and so I do."

"So you do. And I understand why," Brighid said. "But even a goddess has need of a mate and companion who will be there for more than just one night—of someone to whom she can give the love that is now saved only for the land. And a broken heart can be as deadly as any sword," she warned. Brighid took a step toward Eriu. "We have all spent time walking among the people of the natural world. We others, too, may be drawn by the beauty of the Men. We may well choose to spend a night or a year or even a lifetime with a mortal mate, and then simply re-turn to the Otherworld when that lifetime draws to a close—as it must for all mortal Men. Even a goddess can-not prevent that."

"Indeed she cannot," Eriu said quietly. "And you are right, Lady Brighid: I do hear the calling of my heart, and I do wonder what it might be like to have the love and companionship of one of those fine kings for more than

3

just one night. Yet to do so, I would have to turn my back on the land that also has my love. How could I do such a thing, my sister? How could I ever do such a thing?"

Brighid had no answer for her. Eriu lifted the hem of her dark green gown and began to walk toward the east, toward the rising sun and the world of Men.

I

THE KING

CHAPTER ONE

"Bring out the man who would be our next high king!"

The voice of the druid commanded Parlan to step from the house, and so he did, walking out into the twilight atop the great hill of Teamhair Breagh just as the western horizon turned to deepest blue and the first stars began to appear. Behind him, he knew, the full white moon rose above the distant trees.

Parlan's warrior men stood facing each other in two long lines that led from the door of the house across the top of the mountain. The men watched him in silence, holding snapping torches and waiting to see if he would pass the test that awaited him. Behind them, the gathered men and women from the many kingdoms throughout Eire watched and waited as well.

Parlan began the long solitary walk between the two lines of men. He was scrubbed and glowing from the ritual bath he had been given inside the house, and his long dark hair lay damp and unbound on his shoulders. Though it was cold and windy on this *Samhain Eve*—this first night of winter—his feet were bare and he was dressed only in plain brown leather trews. Yet across his shoulders swung a long woolen cloak of seven colors— purple, blue, red, white, gold, brown and green—a cloak so wide it was folded into five pleats over his right shoulder and held with an enormous, heavy, circular golden brooch. A cloak so large and many-colored that only a king was entitled to wear it.

He walked straight ahead between the lines of men, across the soft grass of the enormous earthen-walled enclosure that covered nearly the entire top of the mountain, until he reached the Mound of the Kings. This was a perfectly formed hill of earth that stood just in front of the great curving wall. The grassy mound was as tall as two men, one above the other, and its only entrance was a slit-like opening with torches on either side.

In front of the Mound of the Kings stood a magnificent pillar stone. It was as tall as a man above the ground and just as tall below, and its surface was plain and smooth and unadorned. Three aged, white-bearded druids stood in a row beside this, the Tanist Stone. All three men were dressed in six-colored wool cloaks and tunics against the Samhain cold. Their hands were folded and they peered out at Parlan from beneath furrowed brows.

The tallest and oldest stepped forward. "Parlan of Dun Glas," the chief druid said. "Already you are a king among your own people. Two years ago you were chosen by your uncle, King Dur, the high king of all Eire, and by all the other chiefs of Eire, to be the *tanist* of the high king—to be his successor.

"A High King can be no ordinary man. As much as he can, he must be like the god Lugh, who was good at not just one skill or who accomplished not just one feat, but who was a master of every art and craft, and who led his followers into battle whenever necessary to defend their homes and protect the land from any who would mistreat it.

"You, Parlan, have proved yourself to be a warrior skilled like no other with sword and javelin. You are an unequaled horseman. You can ease the hearts of your people with poetry and the music of the harp, even as you can earn their trust with the fairness of a king's justice. And there is no greater warrior at raiding for cattle and adding to the wealth of his tribe than you, King Parlan. This is why you were the one named to be the next high king.

"That time has now come. The bones of King Dur rest before you within the Mound of the Kings, and you have come to take his place as high king of all the people of this land of Eire.

"It is the task of the high king to unite the tribes and have them live in measured peace instead of in constant rivalry and war. Yet it is not enough that the tribes alone accept you. The Goddess of Sovereignty, the Lady Eriu, who is the heart and spirit of the land itself, must also find you worthy and accept you as her husband, for the high king is no more and no less than the husband and protector of the land.

"If you fail to prove yourself as a mate for her, or if she will not accept you—or worse, if you choose not to accept her—then the land itself will become as a widow, and as with any widow she will become barren and fall into grief and despair. No crops will grow; no animals will flourish; no children will be born. And with no husband to protect her, the land will be left open to ravaging and destruction from all manner of beasts and monsters . . . even the dragon. They will not fear to approach if they believe the king is weak or scorned."

The crowd was silent. The only sound was the snapping of the torches.

"From the beginning of time, it has been so. The land must have a worthy mate who will not fail to guard and protect her. We are here to learn whether you might be

9

that mate. Go now, Parlan, and place your hands upon the Tanist Stone, that the goddess might know that you are here for her and come to you if she wishes."

Parlan nodded to each of the three druids. The glare of the torches blotted out the sight of the tightly packed crowd, though he could feel their tension and hear their quickened breath. Ignoring them as much as possible, Parlan moved to the Tanist Stone, stood with his arms wide for a moment, and then closed his arms so that his hands were flat on either side of the pillar.

The stone was cool and rough beneath his hands. He closed his eyes and waited, his heart pounding.

For long moments he heard nothing but the night wind in the distant trees and the faint snapping of the torches. Then, it seemed that he could feel rather than hear a low vibration through the Tanist Stone and through his hands and fingers . . . and then it was gone, so quickly that he was not sure he had not simply imagined it.

"Remove your hands from the stone, Parlan. The Tanist Stone has called out to the goddess. Wait, now, and see if she will come to you."

Parlan let his hands fall and stepped back from the pillar stone, still facing the Mound of the Kings. The darkness fell complete, and the stars showed themselves here and there above drifting veils of cloud. The wind picked up, bringing with it the damp chill of winter, but no one moved within the torchlit gathering.

As Parlan watched, the wind blew out the two torches that burned on either side of the slender entrance to the mound. Within the entrance a small glow appeared, as though someone inside had lit a lamp.

"She is here. Go to her. She waits for you."

Parlan drew himself up to his full height, standing even taller than the great Tanist Stone. Throwing his cloak back from his bare chest, he went striding across the grass until he stood within the glowing, slit-like entrance.

The air inside was cold and still and damp. It seemed to close in upon him as he took one cautious step, and then another, within the narrow passageway.

"You have not been here before."

He stopped at the sound of the voice that came from deep within the mound—a whispery, rasping voice like that of an old and decrepit hag. "I have not," Parlan answered. "This place is only for the druids."

"Except on this night. The night that a high king is made."

Parlan took another step. "I am here that the goddess might accept me as high king."

Laughter this time, awful, hacking laughter. "Look about you, Parlan. You are surrounded by the ashes and the bones of a hundred kings. They once stood before me in this very spot, all as tall, proud, handsome and strong as you, and spoke to me in the very same way. Now they are no more than cold relics pressed into the earth, as you, too, will be someday."

The chill and closeness of the earth pressed in on him, with a heavy silence more ominous than any sound he had ever heard on the battlefield. Parlan drew himself up and took another step forward. "But I am here now, strong and alive. And I have come in the hope that you will find me to be a worthy husband."

One final step, and a bend of his head, took him within the close and low-ceilinged central chamber.

Soft light from the flames burning in shallow stone cups flickered over the stone-and-earth walls, over the ashes and bones that rested in crude niches scattered throughout. The air was cold and damp and musty, and everywhere Parlan looked he saw another heap of ashes, another skull, another pile of bones.

In the center of the chamber was a rectangular stone platform so large that it nearly filled the room. The platform was piled thick with soft furs and fleeces, and strewn with cushions of leather and wool. Sitting on the edge of the platform, leaning on a carved oaken walking stick, was a bent, crooked, and very old woman.

She seemed to be looking at him, but he could not see her face at all. She was dressed entirely in faded black wool with a heavy black veil draped over her face and head. Her long, tangled white hair spilled out in a wild mass from beneath the ragged veil.

As he drew nearer, Parlan could see that her gown was ragged, even filthy, and that her hands were gnarled and spotted. He frowned in confusion, and the old woman made a hacking, coughing sound.

"I can hear your question, Parlan," she said, in her awful rasping voice. "Is not the Goddess of Sovereignty a young and beautiful woman? Who is this old and hideous hag? Is this some sort of trick the druids have played, a test of some sort?" She swayed back and forth, as though slowly shaking her head. "I assure you, it is no trick. It is no test. I am the true Goddess of Sovereignty."

To his surprise she raised a trembling hand and held out a shining gold cup nearly filled with deep red wine. Quickly he moved to catch the cup before the liquid spilled, and took the cup from her gnarled and shaking grip. Looking closely at the thickly veiled face, he tried to search out the shape of nose or mouth; but there seemed to be nothing on the other side of the dusty, ragged veil except deepest shadow.

Parlan raised the cup to his lips and drank deep of the wine. Its heavy biting sweetness went straight to his head, it seemed, and when at last he drained the cup and lowered his arm, the small scattered lamplights swam in his vision and the ground seemed to sway beneath his feet. He staggered and took an involuntary step forward, and to his horror the gold cup fell from his hand and rolled across the dirt floor.

Parlan caught his breath. Surely it would be a terrible insult to drop the cup the goddess had offered him. He could see it lying on the ground at the base of the stone platform, right at the dragging, dirty hem of her tattered black gown.

But the old hag paid it no mind. Perhaps she had not noticed, if her eyes were as old and weak as the rest of her.

"Tell me, Parlan," she croaked, "why should I take you as a husband? What makes you think you are worthy of me?"

He peered down at her, at this small, bent and aged crone who had only thick fraying veils where her face should be. "You are the goddess, no matter your appearance. I am here to serve you, to guard you, to protect you, in whatever way I can."

The hag on the stone platform raised her head a little and seemed to stare hard at him, and then her body began to shake and jerk as though wracked with a paroxysm of coughing. Parlan realized that, once again, she was laughing.

" 'No matter my appearance?' Oh, that is so very kind and noble of you, Parlan, to make yourself stay in this chamber with me when the 'goddess' turns out to be an ugly old hag that no man would ever want to touch!" She settled herself again on the edge of the stone platform, leaning on her stick with one hand and pulling her black woolen cloak closer around her with the other. "Look at you, standing there so formal and stiff and polite and trying to conceal your disappointment. No doubt you believed the 'goddess' would be a lovely young girl, all full breasts and curving hips and welcoming arms and spreading legs, that you might freely spend your lust with her and then come out again and believe yourself to be the high king."

Her shoulders jerked as she laughed once more. "Do

you think it is so simple as that? You are not here to be the guardian of girls of easy virtue, nor the protector of bush-strumpets. You are here to be the guardian and protector of the land."

"I understand that," Parlan said, as the warmth of the wine rushed through him once again in the close and smoky confines of the chamber. "I know that."

"You know nothing!" the hag barked. "Nothing of being a king. Will you turn your back on the land when it, too, becomes barren and ugly, at the time when it most needs the care and love of a husband? The land is not always new and beautiful and fruitful, any more than women are always young and lovely and welcoming. If you plan to be a king only when times are easy and good, then you are no king at all."

She struggled down from the edge of the stone platform, leaned heavily upon her staff, and began taking short and hobbling steps toward the passageway. "There is nothing for me here. You have rejected me. Go and find your pleasure among the women whose thighs can be yours anytime in trade for some bronze trinket, and who can simply be replaced should they ever appear aged or ugly to you. I will return when your people send me a man who is a king."

"Wait," Parlan said, and reached out to catch her arm.

She halted, still leaning upon her staff, and turned her thickly veiled face up to him.

Parlan hesitated. The hag's arm felt like a fragile stick beneath the layers of ragged black wool, and he quickly released her. "Please do not go," he said. "I do understand. You are right. It is true that no man, no woman, no region of land, is beautiful and attractive all of the time. To love something is to love it always, in all of its forms, no matter how those forms might change over time."

Slowly the old hag nodded. "Well said," she whispered. "Those are the words of a king. But words are one thing and deeds are another. We shall see whether your actions match your words."

Chapter Two

Parlan reached out and gently took the aged and spotted hand of the old woman. He raised it to his lips and kissed the leathery skin, and smiled down at the heavily veiled face. "Please do not go," he said. "I came here to be the husband of the goddess, and that is what I will do, if you wish it." He bent and kissed her fingers again, and then drew back in surprise.

The hand that he held was soft and young, and as fair white as a cloud on a summer's day. Catching his breath, he drew back her ragged sleeve, and as he slowly ran his fingers along the withered and mottled skin of her arm he saw it, too, become warm and fair and alive beneath his touch.

Parlan raised his hand to the heavy black veil that covered the woman's head. He slipped his fingers beneath the dusty old wool and ever so gently caressed her cheek, and moved to her neck, and then pushed back the veil so he could look into her face.

A young woman raised her head and looked back at him, more beautiful than any he had ever imagined. Like her hand, her skin was white and fair, and there was also a touch of reddish color in her cheeks and lips. Her hair was now dark brown and shining, flowing over her shoulders like the wings of a bird, and her eyes . . . her eyes were the deepest green of the forest trees and shone with youth and life.

"Any woman becomes beautiful when she is loved and accepted for what she is," said the goddess. "Would that every man could learn this, as you have." Her voice was now as young and lovely as the rest of her. She closed her eyes, leaned forward, and kissed him on the mouth.

Parlan felt the wine swim through his head again, felt a rush of heat and lust and desire like nothing he had known before. He had held many women in his day, of course, many of them quite beautiful and desirable; but in a heartbeat they all became plain and ordinary and even dull in his memory, compared to this dark-haired beauty who had come to him as a goddess.

He took her in his arms and held her close, and kissed her in return. As he did so, his body was seized with desire. She lay back and melted into his arms, her hair falling soft and feather-light over his hands as he held her by her shoulders. The warm scent of her skin drifted up to his nostrils and intoxicated him more than red wine ever could do.

As he bent to kiss her again, he sought to push aside the rags she wore so that he might caress her body, and found the thin and rotted black fabric coming apart beneath his hands and falling away to the dirt floor of the chamber. Now she wore nothing but her own fair skin and falling hair, and she pressed up against him and kissed him as only a woman does who loves a man completely and accepts him without question.

Quickly he picked her up and swung her onto the furs and fleeces of the stone platform. The perfect curves of her body seemed to glow in the soft lights within the chamber, and her green eyes shone with cool confidence and perfect trust.

He stripped off his leather trews as fast as he ever had in his life and threw them aside, pulled the heavy gold brooch from his cloak and dropped both to the floor, then lay down on his side close to Eriu. Parlan forced himself to remember that this was not some ordinary girl come to please the king, or who hoped to become his queen, or who perhaps had come to him simply to get a handsome child; this was a woman who was here as his equal, here as his wife, who at least for this one night loved and accepted him as a wife loves and accepts her husband. He must do no less for her than to love and accept her completely as well, and so he first held her close in his arms to kiss and caress her. He closed his eyes as she did the same for him.

At last, when his aching, throbbing body could hardly bear to wait another moment, she lay back and invited him to roll atop her, and welcomed him deep within her—not simply with lust but with something like joy, and with something like triumph, and with something very much like deep and abiding love.

Some time later, Parlan awoke. The small stone lamplights in the chamber still burned; so he knew that not too much time could have passed. He turned and reached for the goddess once more, but she was not there. The fleeces and furs beside him were empty.

In an instant he sat up. "My lady! Oh—"

She stood near the passageway. Instead of the awful black rags, she now wore a lovely gown of deep green wool that was trimmed at the neck, hem and sleeves in intricate patterns worked in the finest thread. The interwoven leaves and flowers and birds and animals, all in gleaming gold, seemed almost alive in the dim and flickering lamplight. Parlan watched as she covered the gown with a dark green cloak and fastened it at her shoulder with a heavy golden brooch that looked like a circle of oak leaves and acorns, set with shining beads of amber.

"Must you leave me already? Please, do come back. This night is not over yet. Surely we can take a little more time for ourselves."

She glanced at him as she finished fastening the brooch, and smiled. "Get dressed, Parlan. My part in this ritual is over. Your people await their new high king."

He eased his feet down to the floor and then drew on his leather trews, hardly able to keep his eyes off of her. "I have never known any woman like you. I have no wish to see you go, ritual or no," he said, standing up to face her across the stone platform. "Please—at least tell me your name."

She paused, cocking her head slightly. "Of course you know my name. I am Eriu, for whom this land of Eire is named."

Parlan laughed. "Surely I dare not call you that. The ritual is over. What is your real name, beautiful lady?"

She frowned. "I am exactly as I told you. I am Eriu, whom you call the Goddess of the Land, the Goddess of Sovereignty."

He studied her. "It is true that your beauty and charm are nothing if not otherworldly," he said. "Yet it is hard for me to believe that a goddess would be anything but young and beautiful, especially for a ritual such as this. Surely no goddess would come to a kingmaking as an ugly hag." He took a step toward her. "How can you expect me to believe you are anything but a fair young woman, as I have always been told the goddess appears to be at a kingmaking?"

"Of course that is what you were told, and you will tell the same to all the others. It is for the king to learn this thing for himself at his own kingmaking, for it will surely make him realize what kingship is like nothing else will."

She must have seen the doubt in his face. "Parlan . . . did you not notice my transformation? Did you not see the hideous hag transform into a beautiful maiden simply at your touch? Do you believe that a mortal woman could do such a thing?"

He looked away. "I suppose I thought it must have been some kind of glamyr—some small enchantment placed upon you by the druids to make me believe you were old and ugly when of course you were nothing of the kind." Parlan shrugged. "The light is dim and flickering. Shadows dance over every surface. You were heavily veiled and hidden from view. The wine you gave me went straight to my head and might have made me imagine I was seeing anything you wished me to see."

She studied him for a moment, then smiled. "I am no other than Eriu, whom you call the Goddess of the Land, the one who has always conferred sovereignty on a king. But it matters not whether you believe me, Parlan, for I shall remain as I always have, and go on to create new kings long after you are gone."

"You find me worthy to be a king, even though I cannot agree with you on what you really are?"

She shook her head with a small laugh. "You will make a fine king. And one day, probably near the very end of your very long life, you will realize what I truly am and understand what has happened here this night. Until then, you may believe what you wish—so long as you serve your people and protect the land to the best of your ability at the same time."

"I will not forget this," he said, walking to her and reaching out to touch her face one last time. "To me, you will always be the *lady* called Eriu—a dream, a vision of beauty and charm that far surpasses all others."

"Call me what you like," she said. "It will not change what I really am." She turned toward the passageway, and glanced over her shoulder at him. "Go now. Your people wait for you. Go and let your people see who you really are."

He took a step, then hesitated. "Will I see you again?"

"You will see me every time you look out over your lands and see them growing and fruitful."

Parlan shook his head impatiently. "I do not mean the land itself. I will care for that every day, as I promised. I want to know when I will see *you* again."

"You will never again see me in this form. Once I ride away, I will not return to you."

A chill passed through him, and it was not from the cold air in the chamber. "But—"

"You will soon forget me. You will take a queen, as every king must do, and I will become only a memory to you, as I should."

"I will never forget you," he said, his voice low with tension. "There is no other woman who is anything like you. I want you for my queen. I swear I will take no other."

But Eriu only laughed. "If you intend to be a king, you had best go to your people right now. I am certain they grow weary of waiting."

In the silence that fell between them, Parlan could hear the faint restive voices from outside the mound. He picked up his brightly colored cloak and heavy gold brooch, pinned the great cloak over his shoulders once again, and with a last look at Eriu walked out of the Mound of the Kings and into the cold winter night.

The great crowd of people stood watching him in tense silence, their faces somber and pale in the torchlight. "Behold your king," said a clear voice from behind Parlan. "I have found him to be a worthy husband to the goddess and to the land. Now he is yours, to serve you all as the high king of all Eire."

Even as the people bowed to him in acceptance, Parlan turned to see Eriu standing in the softly lit entrance to the mound. "And so that all who see you might know this, Parlan, this mark of kingship was made for you to wear for all of your days." From beneath her cloak she took a beautiful torque, a near-circle of heavy twisted gold that was left open at one side so that it could be slid around the wearer's neck. This particular torque had gleaming gold spirals fashioned at each end. Eriu herself placed the torque around his neck, and then stepped back from him and glanced over her shoulder.

All of the gathering remained silent and still as the sound of galloping hoofbeats approached from behind the Mound of the Kings. In a moment a magnificent mare appeared, young and strong with an arching neck and bright eye and high step, her coat still the dark iron-grey of youth. She wore a bridle of softest black leather with a shining bronze bit and a saddle made of crossed wooden frames rising up front and back. The seat of the saddle was covered with the softest, thickest white fleece, and all of it was tied together with soft strips of black leather.

The mare stopped before Eriu, who swung into the saddle as lightly as a bird flying up to a branch. With a last look at Parlan, she turned and galloped the mare around to the back of the mound. There was no opening in the high earthen wall behind the mound, but Parlan knew he would not see this horse and rider again.

The hoofbeats faded away. Except for the snapping of the torches, the night was quiet once again.

"The high king!" cried the chief druid. With that, the crowd shouted out in relief and happiness as Parlan's own men stepped forward to surround him, all of them congratulating him and slapping him on the back. One of the druids finally called out, "Take him to the hall, where his feast awaits!"

Parlan walked with his men across the walled enclosure, away from the Mound of the Kings, until he reached the open gates of the far side. As they all walked through and then turned to follow the outside of the wall, Parlan could not help but listen for the sound of hoofbeats riding up the wide sloping sides of the hill. He heard nothing but the wind in the darkness, as he knew he would; but even as he approached the Great Hall, Parlan knew that he would—he *must*—find a way to look upon Eriu again.

CHAPTER THREE

The torchlight wavered in the night wind that blew through the wide–open door of the long, narrow, high-ceilinged hall on the top of the hill of Teamhair Breagh, just a few hundred paces or so from the Mound of the Kings. Surrounded by the laughter and conversation of the finely dressed men and women of Teamhair, Parlan sat on a fine grey wolf hide thrown down on the clean straw covering the floor. Before him, as he looked down the long, long hall, stretched squares of polished oak laid end to end and set with plates and cups of bronze and gold. Servants moved among the noble guests, bearing wooden bowls of pale white butter and thick golden honey, and wooden platters stacked high with hot wheat flatbread straight off the baking stones.

But Parlan had little thought for good food or good company, not even on this night that should have been the best of his life. He could think of nothing but Eriu.

The full Samhain moon had barely moved in the sky since he had lain with the goddess within the Mound of the Kings. But now, after the powerful, lusty and very loving bond they had shared, she had laughed at him and ridden away and told him she would never see him again.

He sat down at his place at the far end of the row of wooden squares, and Parlan looked down at a seemingly endless face-to-face line of men and women who constantly glanced and stared at him and offered him nods and good wishes. He smiled tightly and nodded in return, even as his gaze flicked about the hall in hopes of seeing Eriu's tall and slender form.

But, of course, she was not there.

Sitting closest to him were two of his warriors. Gavin was at his left hand, facing Cillian across the wooden square. The three of them watched the servants approach with the bread and butter and honey.

"Ah, look! There she is," said Cillian, leaning in and nudging Parlan with his elbow.

Parlan looked up, his eyes once again searching every woman's face in the Hall. "Where? Where is she?" He started to get to his feet. *Has she come back to me? She must! She must come back to me!*

Gavin caught his bare arm and pulled him back down. "Sit down! Let her come to you. That's the way of it when you're a king. Enjoy it!"

"May I offer you some honey, my king?"

Parlan looked up to see Ona gazing down at him. She was a smiling young woman with long brown braids, young and fair with a deliciously round figure. She leaned over to hold out her bowl of thick, dark honey, allowing the low, curving, heavily embroidered neckline of her blue plaid gown to dip and reveal the fullness of her breasts.

He smiled politely. "You are no servant, Ona. There is no need for you to offer me food."

She cocked her head, her dark braids swinging gently. Still bending down to him, she smiled again. "Oh, but I would be a willing servant to the high king, if he would but allow me to share his place at the feast."

Parlan placed his fingertip beneath the wooden bowl she held out, and he lifted it up, forcing Ona to stand again lest she get her chin dipped in honey. "I thank you. But this place beside me is only for one who is unlike any other."

Ona frowned. "Who?"

"You will know her when you see her. Until then, I thank you." And with that he turned his back on her to accept a piece of bread and a lump of butter from the servant at his elbow. By the time he finished. Ona had gone away.

Gavin glanced at him. "Well, now. Is this what happens when a man becomes high king? If it is, count me out. I'd rather herd pigs for the rest of my days."

Cillian set down his cup. "Parlan, are we to believe that you have no interest in having a woman like Ona sit beside you at this feast?"

Parlan reached for his own cup. "She has no interest in me. She is thinking only of the prestige that would come from sitting beside the king."

"And why should she not? She will not be the only one to think of such a thing!" Cillian shook his head. "Many more will come to you before this night is out. You will find one to your liking."

"If not more than one!" Gavin said, lifting his gold cup and draining it. He and Cillian both laughed, but Parlan only regarded them with a cold frown.

By the time Parlan had finished the bread and butter, the servants began bringing out the second course— wooden plates and bowls of watercress, dandelion leaves and clover roots, all steamed in the drippings from the roasting beef. He saw a very young and beautiful woman in a soft red gown, her long blond hair spilling loose down her back, snatch one of the serving bowls of greens away from a servant. She cradled it briefly with one arm while she straightened and smoothed her hair, and then took it carefully in both hands as she walked to the high king with her best smile on her rowan-reddened lips, and determination shining in her clear blue eyes.

"Oh, now, this one may do for you," Gavin said. "Maeve is young, but quite a beauty. And she is quite sweet and willing and most anxious to please. Isn't she, Cillian?"

Cillian shot him a cold look, and Gavin quickly grabbed his wine cup and raised it to his mouth. "I think you would do well to look to Maeve," Cillian said, and nodded to the young woman who walked up to the king.

But she had eyes only for Parlan. "I have brought you the next course, my king. It is my pleasure to serve you."

Parlan's eyes flicked briefly over her face. Young, fair, light blue eyes, pretty enough . . . once he would have been quite happy to have her sit beside him, but now she seemed only a pale imitation of womanhood compared to the mystery and majesty that was Eriu.

He glanced at the dish she held, and then shrugged and turned away. "The servants will bring me a portion. You need not trouble yourself."

"It is no trouble—"

"Thank you," he said abruptly, looking only at his own plate and cup. He could hear her swift intake of breath and feel the sudden swish of her garments as she realized she had been coldly dismissed in front of everyone. She quickly walked away.

A few of the diners nearest Parlan glanced up and fell silent, but a sudden cold stare from him sent them back to their conversation. Still, he could see their furtive glances and whispered questions.

"Do you mean to offend every woman at Teamhair?" Cillian asked. "Both of those would have been more than welcome to share your plate on any night before this."

"At least direct them our way, if you have no interest!" added Gavin. "However, if it is now your decision to reject all but the fairest, look to Riona. She is one of the most

27

beautiful women you will find anywhere. I hear she has kept from allowing any man to touch her." He winked at Parlan, then turned a steady gaze on the woman of whom he spoke. "She would like nothing more than to marry a king and live her life as a queen."

"And well she should," agreed Cillian. "She is from the very best of families. You would have to look very long and very hard to find any woman more suited to being a queen than Riona."

"You do not understand," whispered Parlan. "I have known the touch of a goddess this night. All other women are as . . . are as sparrows to a falcon after that. None will ever compare."

Gavin laughed. "So, you mean to go the rest of your life without a woman? A very boring rule yours will be!"

"I do not mean to rule without a queen. But mine shall be the Goddess Eriu, and no other."

Both men stared at Parlan. Then Gavin laughed out loud, and Cillian grinned. "That's good, King Parlan!" said Cillian. "It's all very well for a man to want the best for himself. But surely you are joking about—"

"Good evening to you, my king."

The feminine voice was low and regal. Parlan looked up to see a tall young woman with red-gold hair pulled back from her face into two slim braids, with the rest flowing over her shoulders. Her gown of gold and brown and cream-colored plaid wool was cut so that the neckline touched her slender collarbone, but was closely fitted so as to emphasize her rounded bosom, slim waist and gently curving hips. Her eyes were shining brown, her skin smooth and pale, and her manner calm and peaceful.

She held out a gold plate piled high with choice cuts of hot beef, steaming with heat and dripping with red juices, and stood waiting for Parlan's response.

Parlan forced himself to keep his breathing even. "Good evening to you, Riona."

"May I offer you some of this loin of beef? It is the very best cut, just now done."

"Thank you, but I do not care for beef just now. You may take it away."

"Oh, but I should be glad to sit beside you and finish preparing it." Riona set the golden plate beside Parlan's own and made as if to sit down beside him on the straw. "Here, I will just take this little dagger of mine and cut it into strips—oh!"

Parlan took up the plate of beef, turned around and threw it with all his strength against the far wall. It hit the wood with a tremendous bang that instantly silenced everyone in the hall.

"I *said*," Parlan whispered, through clenched teeth, "that I do not care for beef just now."

Riona's brown eyes opened wide with shock, but her jaw was set with rising anger. In one quick move she got to her feet, turned her back on the king and went striding away through the hall with her chin raised high. Not once did she look back.

The rest of the people in the hall remained silent. Some seemed to have frozen with their meat hanging off their daggers halfway to their mouths, or with their hands reaching for their cups.

Parlan got to his feet and clenched his fists. "I must thank you all for introducing me to some of the most beautiful young women at Teamhair Breagh," he said. His voice was tight and his courtesy forced. "But I swear this to you now, as your high king: There is only one that I will take as my queen, and that is the goddess who came to me this night and made me a true king. I will have Eriu for my queen, or I will have no one."

And with that he turned and strode toward the doors at

the far end of the hall, focusing his glare straight ahead of him as he walked, even though he was well aware that every person there stared wide-eyed at him as he passed.

The moment he walked out through the doors, he could hear the hall instantly fill with the buzz of conversation and questions; but he kept walking—right on out across the grass and into the windy darkness, alone at last with only the restless clouds and veiled moon for company.

CHAPTER FOUR

At last Parlan came to the very edge of the wide, flat hill-top that was Teamhair Breagh, and he looked out to the north where the faint shadows of the cloud-covered moon glided among the fields and oak trees far below.

A quick glance showed him that, as he had ordered, no one had followed. A few of his men were gathered just outside the doors of the hall, watching him, but that was all. Parlan turned back to look out over the plain.

"Eriu, hear me now. I speak to you as the man you have made high king on this night—this Samhain night, the end of summer, the start of winter, the night on which this world and the Otherworld may well overlap and come to touch each other, even as a man and a goddess touched each other. This night when a goddess may freely walk the earth and lie with a king . . ."

He paused and stood waiting, hoping to hear the sound of hoofbeats and peering hard at every moving shadow made by the clouds as they drifted over the glowing white face of the moon. There was no sound but the wind high in the oaks, and the shadows were only shadows.

31

"Eriu!" he cried. "I do not know how you think I could go from you and take an ordinary woman for my queen—not when now I know what it is like to bond with a goddess!"

As his voice echoed through the night, the wind rose and began to blow until the trees began to roar and hiss as if crying out to Parlan in return. Lashed by the sudden wind, the branches bent low and then raised up high again, as though bowing to the new high king.

The wind struck Parlan full in the face and nearly pushed him back a step, but he faced it down and cried out again. "Eriu! How can you think I could forget what has happened here tonight!"

The wind howled even more fiercely, forcing Parlan to stagger back. A great screeching and flapping erupted from the bent and groaning trees as birds were driven from their windblown roosts and forced to fly up into the night in great dark flocks.

"Eriu! Come to me and be my queen!"

He shut his eyes tight and flung his arms wide, gripping the cold night air with his fists, willing the goddess to come to him, to come to him, to come to him now. . . .

And then, even as an enormous dark shadow swallowed the moon and sent the land below into deepest blackness, Parlan heard the faint sound of galloping hoofbeats coming up the side of the hill.

Angrily he looked up at the moon, hidden now by some great slow-moving cloud. "Move, curse you," he whispered to the cloud. "She is coming but I cannot see her! Move, so the moonlight will return. Let me see her."

But as he glared up at the black night sky, it seemed that this was no ordinary cloud. For a heartbeat he thought he saw the outline of monstrous outstretched wings and a long, thick, coiling tail. . . .

Then it was gone. The soft white glow of the moon returned to show him a tall woman riding toward him on a beautiful iron-grey mare.

Relief flooded him at the sight. He had not realized how much he feared he would never see her again. Yet the tension remained with him, for she could just as easily ride away again and there would be nothing he could do to stop her.

Eriu halted the mare a short distance from him, and slid down to stand on the grass. She threw her long, shining dark hair over her shoulder, where it glinted faintly in the moonlight against her green cloak and gown and heavy gold brooch, and dropped the reins so that the horse could graze. Yet the mare seemed nervous, lowering its head just long enough to quickly grab a mouthful of grass and then throwing it back up to glance into the darkness all around, pointed ears flicking rapidly back and forth.

"Solasta sees it, too," Eriu said. "It is here. You saw it."

"Saw what?" Parlan walked toward her, hungry to take her in his arms again, feeling like a man starving—

She held up her hand, so he could not help but stop. "The dragon," she said. "It flew across the moon even as you cursed its presence. You must take care, King Parlan. Your words have drawn it out."

"Words? What words?" He had no thought for any strange beasts, not even a dragon. Not with Eriu standing near enough to touch, to smell—oh, the scent of her, a scent so light and warm and sweet that it seemed to him now that all other women reeked of smoke and sweat, and always had.

He tried to draw breath. "I feared I would not see you again."

Eriu sighed, and stroked her grey mare's neck. "Oh, you are not the first king who has dared to summon me this way." She, too, glanced around her at the darkened land far below, even as the restless wind lifted her hair and swept it back across her shoulders. "Not the first to suddenly believe that a mortal woman is no longer enough."

She took a step toward him, and though his arms and legs ached for the feel of her close against him, he stayed where he was. "You are a king now, Parlan. You must have a queen."

"I have found my queen," he replied.

"You have? Well, then! That is good news. I shall be going." She turned to gather up Solasta's reins.

"Wait!"

Eriu turned back to look at Parlan, as though waiting patiently for a child to speak. "I . . . I will have no other but you for my queen," he said, drawing himself up to his full height. "No other but you."

She let go of the reins again, and folded her hands. Parlan found that he could not take his eyes from her long, slender white fingers.

"It is not fair to your people that you should rule alone. Surely you know that no king can fairly rule without a queen at his side to remind him of the concerns of all women, for those concerns are easily forgotten when men are free to revel in the pleasures of battle and the hunt."

"I do understand this, my lady Eriu. I want nothing more than to have a strong and beautiful queen at my side—so long as that queen is you."

She seemed not to have heard him, but only looked up at the shadowy moonlit sky. "Surely there are any number of women here at Teamhair Breagh who would be pleased and honored to be the wife of such a strong and handsome king as you."

Parlan closed his eyes and turned his face away for a moment. "There were three who made it plain to me tonight." He fell silent, staring off into the windy, brooding darkness.

"You were not pleased by their attentions?" Eriu looked down at her mare, and shrugged. "Well, no matter. Tomorrow you begin your year-long journey around the coastline of Eire, that all might meet the new high king and give him hostages to peace. Surely, within that year, you will find a woman who pleases you well enough and who your people will accept as their queen."

"I care nothing for their attentions!" he cried, snapping his head round to look at her. There was savagery in his voice. "Not anymore. Not since—not since I have known you. There is no woman anywhere who could compare to you."

Eriu laughed, a gentle sound that reminded Parlan of the high sweet notes of a harp. "Of course no woman can compare to me," she said. "I am not a woman. I am a goddess, a daughter of those most ancient beings who live now in the place you call the Otherworld.

"Comparing a woman to me is like comparing a blade of grass to a new golden primrose. But is the grass any less valuable? It is worth more than flowers, most would say, for the grass protects the earth and nourishes the animals that sustain you. The flowers alone cannot do that."

"There is grass in abundance," Parlan growled, and with two steps he closed the space between them. "I would have the flower for myself, and cherish it always." He raised his hand and reached out for her hair, her flowing dark brown hair shining in the moonlight.

"And what makes you think the flower would have you in return?"

His hand stopped, and he lowered it again. He raised his chin and looked straight at her, straight into her green eyes. "I will stand here before you now and tell you that every other king, every other chief, and ever other warrior man on the island of Eire believes that I am worthy to rule them all. I earned their respect and their trust because of my many accomplishments, all of which I gained through my own honest sweat and my own freely offered blood. If any man could offer love and loyalty enough for a goddess, I am that man."

She laughed again, and paced a few steps away from him across the wind-driven grass. "Surely you realize that other kings have offered me this same love and loyalty. But what need have I for those? I already own the love and loyalty of all those who live on these lands, and who care for and nurture them."

Eriu turned to face him, raising her chin. A flash of lightning showed itself in the cloud bank far behind her. "I would never be any man's queen unless I loved him in return—and I will never allow myself to truly love any man."

Parlan took a step toward her. The distant lightning flashed again. "But why should you not have the love of a king? A king is a man who has dedicated his life to your honor and protection. Why should you not live with such a man for a time, and be his cherished queen?"

She smiled, but her eyes were cool. "Think of it, Parlan. If I allowed myself to love just one man—to bond with him and him alone, even as a wife bonds to her beloved husband—how could I ever go to another at his king-making and lie with him as I did with you?"

Parlan tried to smile at her. "Because, my lady, it is as you said . . . one day I, too, will be naught but ashes and bone pressed into the walls of the Mound of the Kings. When that day comes for any man, his wife is free to take another."

Her green eyes narrowed, and she shot a cold glare at him. "It is true that any other woman could take another man—but do you still believe I am like other women?"

She gazed at him even as the lightning flashed again. "You constantly forget that I am not a woman. I am a goddess. My love, once given, is given forever. It will never fade. It will never be forgotten. It will burn within me just

36

as intensely in the thousandth year as it does in the first. Were I to give that love to just one man, I could never give myself to another and make him a king. What would your people do then, with no king to defend them?

"And there is something else. As the years pass, a man might well grow weary—or even frightened—of having a powerful goddess at his side. But he could never abandon her and take a mortal woman instead, for the terrible jealousy of the goddess would destroy any other woman he looked to.

"And when the day comes that my mortal husband dies, I would become a widow—a widow forever in mourning for that which is beyond even my reach. The land itself would become the same, spending its long and endless years in the same state as the goddess herself—a grieving widow who can never be consoled. Barren and bereft, the land would no longer bring forth life, and all those who tried to live on it would perish as well."

Parlan gazed at her. His heart beat swiftly in his chest. Behind the goddess, lighting flashed again, briefly illuminating the heavy rolling clouds in purple-white light. The grey mare quickly swung its head around to look, brown eyes huge and glittering.

"It is a frightening thing to contemplate," Parlan said quietly. "But surely a goddess could heal her own heart if she wished. Surely she could allow herself to accept another man once her beloved went to his natural rest."

Eriu shook her head. "The love of a goddess is not like that of a mortal woman. If you would wish it to be so, you should go from here now and find a mortal to love you and be your queen and not approach a goddess with such an offer."

"I fear it is already too late for me," Parlan said. "If I cannot have you for my queen, then I, too, will be as a grieving husband, empty and broken without the love of my life. Is my heart any less worthy of protecting than yours, even though I am only a mortal man?"

He closed the distance between them at last and boldly reached for her hand. She did not resist, and with a deep sigh he cradled her long slender fingers against his cheek.

"I have known other women," he whispered against her palm. "Wise and beautiful women, but not one of them ever fired the sort of passion that I have found here this night with you." He pressed the back of her hand to his chest, over his rapidly beating heart. "And I speak not only of the body's passion, but that of companionship—of conversation—of friendship. Of finding the one that I know beyond doubt was meant to sit at my side, whether I am a king or whether I am not."

Her arm turned as rigid as an iron sword. She withdrew it and stepped back to look at him, and as his gaze met hers he held himself very still. Eriu glared at him with a look as cold as the harshest winter night.

"I have already made you a king," she said. "Do you mean to say you would turn your back on me, and on the land, and on your people, and become as any other man when the Goddess of the Land, the Goddess of Sovereignty, the Goddess of Eire, has made you a king?"

He raised his chin and looked boldly into her eyes. "I would," he said to her. "I would, if that would prove to you that my love for you is genuine. I cannot live my life as a king without the only woman I will have as my queen. If I am forced to do that, it is better not to be a king at all."

CHAPTER FIVE

For a moment, a deathly silence fell over the land and throughout the sky. The trees became still. The birds were quiet. The clouds merely drifted overhead.

"Fool!" shouted Eriu. In her rage she seemed to somehow become taller, until she looked down upon him with fury blazing from her face. "Unworthy fool! Ungrateful animal! The king is the husband of the land, sworn to protect her! What sort of king rejects his wife and turns his back on her, leaving her alone and unprotected? You are no king at all!"

She caught the mare's reins from the grass, gathered them up and swung herself into the soft sheepskin saddle. Parlan broke out in a sweat, even though he felt very cold.

"Eriu, wait—please—I meant only to show you that you are more important to me than anything. That I would be willing to be as any other man if it meant you would believe my love for you is real."

"How can you love me when you reject me this way?" She looked down at him from astride the mare, who danced and tossed her head with nervousness. "I have made you a king this night not for your own pride and pleasure, but so the land might have a champion and defender. You, in return, swore to protect the land the way a husband protects a wife. And you think to flatter me by offering to simply walk away from that?" She turned the mare around just as a tremendous roll of thunder shook the hilltop.

"Please, Eriu. Do not go. I was wrong to offer up my kingship even for a great love. I understand that now. I thought only to prove to you that—Please, do not go!"

"I must go!" she cried, as the mare danced from side to side and searched the sky with wild rolling eyes. "It's coming."

"What's coming? The storm?"

"Far worse than any storm. And you are the one who brought it."

Parlan's eyes narrowed, even as the feeling of cold flooded his veins once again. "What do you mean, 'I am the one who brought it?' Brought what?"

"The dragon," Eriu said. "You saw it fly across the moon. You heard and felt its presence in the strange disturbances all around us this night."

"Dragon," Parlan whispered. "I have heard the tales all my life, but never seen any such beast. I thought they were just tales."

"They are anything but. They are the history of this land."

The wind lashed the trees and sent up a tremendous hissing. Lightning rippled all around the hill of Teamhair, and the ground trembled with thunder. The grey mare snorted and half reared.

"How is it that I have brought the dragon to this place?" Parlan cried, struggling to be heard above the wind.

Once more Eriu looked down on him in anger—but this time, Parlan saw fear in her eyes, too. "I am the Goddess of the Land," she said, as her increasingly frightened mare swung first left and then right. "I am its symbol, its protectress, its mother. Like the land itself, I grant sovereignty and power to those who have my favor and treat me well.

"But I am the gentle and creative side of this power of the land. There is another side—the side of power that is cruel and destructive, the side of power wrongly used. Its symbol is the dragon."

"But why has the dragon come here now?"

She glanced up at the roiling sky once more. "You, Parlan, were granted sovereignty and supreme power by the Goddess of the Land, but you used your power wrongly. You offered to trade it for something that you, personally, wished to have. You offered to give it away to gain your own happiness.

"Being a king is not something a man *does*. Being a king is what a man *is*. I made you a king, Parlan, and that is what you are—or so I thought."

"I *am* a king," he whispered, as a great gust of cold wind struck him. "I am—"

"You are a man who would trade his kingship for a woman's favor!" she shouted. "Does a true man offer to trade his wife for the attentions of another? The land is as a wife to you, but you would trade that away to have the woman of your choice sit beside you! For that you have brought the Curse of the Dragon upon yourself, upon your people, upon the land, and upon me. Your power, wrongly used, has been unleashed. It searches for you now. And it will find you!"

She looked up into the wind-whipped sky just as a great black shadow glided over the moon—a shadow that was darker and more ominous than any storm cloud.

This time the mare snorted and stood straight up on its hind legs, pawing at the wind with its front feet. Eriu grabbed the thick black mane with one hand, and with the other reined the mare around as it came back down to earth.

"I must go! I must go now!" Eriu cried, and at last she allowed the mare to leap down the hill and race off at a panicked gallop. "It may already be too late!"

"Stop! Wait! Where will you go? Stay here! I will protect you!" Parlan raced to the edge of the hill and looked after her, but it was too late; Solasta was just a small grey spot in the heavy darkness, galloping down the long slope into the wide plain far below even as the storm clouds boiled all around and the lightning flashed again and again.

Then, as the cold wind scourged him and the first sharp drops of rain stung his face, Parlan saw moonlight fill the plain once more. He could easily see the galloping grey mare, its black tail flagged high as it ran, and could see Eriu's gold-trimmed gown streaming down the horse's sides. He could even see Eriu's long brown hair glinting in the moonlight and her white face as she twisted in the saddle to look at her pursuer.

Parlan cried out, but it was far too late. The huge black shadow that had covered the moon swooped down after the racing mare.

The shadow's black wings were extended as wide as the Great Hall of Teamhair Breagh, and its coiling tail was just as long. Its body, black and heavy and muscular, twisted and writhed as it flew. It had enormous clawed hind legs and short curving front legs with heavy talons—but most frightening of all was the beast's head. It was monstrous, terrifying, long and pointed, with sharp teeth that flashed in the lightning as it snarled and snapped at the galloping mare.

"The Black Dragon," whispered Parlan. His blood became ice.

The mare dodged and turned as it ran, frustrating the

dragon's attempts to grab it. The huge creature was stronger but not so quick. The beast circled once, high above the panicked mare, and then swooped down on both Eriu and Solasta. It opened its fearsome mouth and roared out a blast of white vapor that plumed over the plain like a heavy coat of frost—and caught Eriu and the mare in its sparkling cone.

The dragon roared in triumph, climbing high into the sky once more.

Parlan watched in horror as both horse and rider were covered with the frost. Solasta ran slower and slower, and fell back to a trot and then a walk. At last the mare stood motionless, its head low near the glittering white ground. Eriu sat very still in the saddle, bent down over the mare's lowered neck.

They looked like a horse and rider made entirely of ice, sparkling in the cold moonlight.

"Eriu!" Parlan shouted, and tore off down the hill to go to her—but strong arms grabbed him and dragged him back.

"Wait! Don't go! It will only get you, too." Cillian forced him back to the top of the hill, aided by Gavin and a few other strong warriors. "The men are arming now. We've got to face this together!"

Parlan wrenched away from them, and made himself look away from the frost-covered plain and back toward the hall. The grassy lawn was now filled with his warriors, all of whom were quickly pulling on their pieces of leather armor and catching up the javelins and slings brought to them by serving men.

"Bring torches!" he shouted, letting a servant pull off his brooch and cloak, slide a blue woolen tunic over his head, and strap his brown leather sword-belt around his waist. "Bring at least one torch for every man!"

He grabbed a pair from another servant. His men gathered round, each of them with a javelin in one hand and a flaring torch in the other, and their iron swords strapped to their hips.

"Shall I call for horses, King Parlan?" cried Gavin.

"There is no time for horses. And no need. This will be a different sort of battle. Follow me!" And with that he raised the torches high and tore off down the hill, keeping his eyes on the weirdly glittering figures of Eriu and Solasta on the plain far below.

His men followed closely. Parlan could imagine how they must look like a river of fire pouring down the side of Teàmhair Breagh hill. It was a sight certain to catch the eye of any beast—and sure enough, as Parlan craned his neck to look up at the sky, it caught the eye of the great Black Dragon.

"Come down here! Come down here!" he shouted, as they reached the bottom of the hill. "We will answer you with cold iron and scorching fire! Come down here and meet someone who can return your attack—and who will take pleasure in doing so!"

High above, the monster screeched its rage at them and began to circle, coming lower with each pass.

Still running, Parlan and his men spread out across the grassy plain. He heard Cillian shout out from behind him. "Why doesn't it just attack?"

Parlan glanced back. "It's watching its new enemy to see how strong we really are. All right, then—here is where we will make our stand!"

He stopped, still some distance from the sparkling, motionless figures of Eriu and her mare, and turned to face the hill of Teamhair Breagh. "Come down here!" he shouted again to the snarling beast circling over them. "Now it is our turn! We are ready for you! Bring your fight to us!"

The rush of wind from its huge leathery wings beat down over them. The dragon circled directly over

Teamhair Breagh hill, turned to face them, and then with another screeching roar spread its black wings wide and swooped down over the hill directly toward the waiting men.

"Stand together! Raise your torches!" cried Parlan. His men obeyed, standing in a close block behind him with their torches held high. "Stand together! Stand together!"

Parlan braced his legs and held his own two torches high, though his breath quickened as the dreadful beast bore down upon him with its horrible mouth wide open and its rows of teeth gleaming dull-white in the moonlight.

"Stand your ground!" he called to his men.

A blinding cold blast of vapor and frost shot down over them, the stench of the dragon's bloody breath coming with it. But Parlan's men stayed with him, and as he turned and the beast flew overhead, to his relief he saw that the deadly cold vapor was melted by the flames from their torches and fell harmlessly to the grass all around them. Frustrated, the dragon screeched again and turned back toward Teamhair Breagh.

"I do not think it can breathe ice again so quickly," Parlan called out. "This time, half of you hold torches and the other half ready your javelins!"

The men in the rear quickly handed over their torches to those in the front, and then spaced themselves out behind their king. With the flames in front of them raised high, the men readied their javelins and kept their eyes on the beast circling in the sky.

"Here it comes!" shouted one of the men.

"Wait for my order! Do not throw except on my order!" Parlan glared hard at them and then turned back to face the dragon.

Again it dove at them with its mouth wide open, but this time only a faint mist escaped. "As I thought!" cried Parlan. "We are safe from its breath for the moment!" He waited for the space of a heartbeat ... and another and another. The beast bore down upon them with his clawed forelegs flexing open and reaching out.

"Now!" Parlan shouted. "Throw now!"

A mass of iron-tipped javelins tore through the faint hanging mist and flew straight at the heart of the Black Dragon. Parlan clenched his fists around the sticks of the torches he held. But even as all of the men watched and held their breath ... the javelins struck the dragon and bounced off its hide without doing the slightest harm.

For an instant, the men stood in frozen silence as the beast roared down upon them. "Torches! The torches!" shouted Parlan, and at last the men holding them got their wits about them enough to thrust the torches out at the beast. It skimmed by right over their heads.

The monster roared and jerked back in mid-air, flapping its huge wings with such force that the men were forced to turn their heads and shield their eyes against the sudden gust of wind—such a blast that all of the glaring torches guttered and went out. The sudden darkness left them all blind. Blinking, with the wind from the beast's great wings still hitting him in gust after gust, Parlan turned away to shield his extinguished torches with his body, and shouted at his men over the buffeting of the monster's wings.

"Strike at it! The torches are still hot, even if they do not burn! Strike at the beast and drive it back!"

They were all fearless in the face of any natural enemy, whether man or animal, but none of them had ever dreamed of a flying frost–breathing serpent, and Parlan realized his men were all transfixed by the hovering beast.

The dragon's eyes dilated in the darkness. Its claws flexed as it realized the searing torch flames were gone. Its terrible head with its nightmare smile began to reach down to strike at Gavin.

Parlan leaped forward and swung his torches at the dragon, though they were out, actually striking its reaching front legs. "Drive it back! Drive it back!" he shouted, swinging the hot wood at the beast even though his blood ran cold at the closeness of the monster and the memory of the terrible frigid blast of its breath. "Even the toughest leather will burn if fire is held to it."

Finally his men found their courage and began thrusting the heads of their dead torches into the body of the hovering beast, pressing them in and letting the heat sear the tough hide. It roared in rage and pain, and with tiny wisps of smoke curling up from its skin, it beat its wings hard and rose up into the air once more. But each time the men used their torches this way, the embers went out, and soon Parlan and his men were left with weapons that were entirely cold.

"We must have fire!" Gavin cried. "Someone must go back and get more torches."

"There is no time," Parlan growled. "Someone must build a fire here, and the rest of us will hold the monster off as best we can!" But even as he spoke the words, he knew it would take far too long to do so on this cold and rain-soaked plain. He could only drop the useless torches, draw his sword and await the dragon's return.

"Parlan! Look!"

The man beside him pointed up at where one of Parlan's torches lay in the damp grass. There, at the end of the burnt-out torch, was a small glow of red.

CHAPTER SIX

Quickly Parlan sheathed his sword and turned away from the fierce gusts from the dragon's wings. He sheltered the torch's tiny spark with one hand while leaning in close to breathe ever so gently on the frail speck of fire. Behind him he could hear the shouting and cursing of his men as they continued to face the dragon with their rapidly cooling sticks.

"Get back from us, you filthy beast! Get back!" he heard.

"Flame, the sole weapon against this dragon . . ." Parlan muttered.

"It's getting closer! The cursed torches are cold! It knows!" cried another of his men.

"Come alive for me . . . I give you my breath . . . I give you my protection . . ."

"Draw your swords! Gather in close!"

"Come alive for me now, that I might protect my own," Parlan demanded.

The tiny spark flared up at his final words. The speck became a spot, which began to spread through the remains of the grease and dried rushes lashed to the end of the heavy green stick. Finally a small flame took hold, and it grew and spread until half the torch was burning once again.

"Here it comes! Here it comes!" his men called.

Parlan caught up his other torch and pressed its tip against the now–flaming head of the first torch. He forced himself to keep still even as the sudden gusts of wind hit him again from behind—forced himself to wait, to stand still, sucking in his breath and gritting his teeth as he held the heads of the two torches together and willed them to burn as one, even as the terrible rushing wind drew closer and more powerful.

"King Parlan! Turn around! It is upon you! Turn around!"

He whirled and thrust out his two fiery torches, shouting in rage at the dragon even as the beast roared in pain and frustration. It tried to stop its dive but succeeded only in flapping to a slow mid-air halt, then frantically beat its wings in an effort to rise up and back away from Parlan. Parlan took full advantage of the beast's struggles to jam his burning torches into its hide and wings and into its snarling mouth.

Finally the beast managed to get itself away, but it screamed and screamed into the air, for this time spots of bright flame were clear on its leathery wings and crept along the lines of its scales. And the harder it flapped its wings, the brighter those flames became, the more they swelled and grew.

The monster threw back its horned head as it screamed, and tried to bite at its burning wings, twisting its neck first to one side and then the other; but of course it could not reach the fire spreading over its body. It could only continue to climb into the dark night sky as the flames from its wings and scales lit the grey-black smoke rising from its hide and turned the smoke a hideous orange. At last, still screaming in fury and torment, it flew off across the great hill of Teamhair Breagh and was lost to sight.

Parlan lowered his torches. His heart pounded and his breath came in gasps as he continued to watch for any sign of the beast's return. He strained to catch the sound of its screeching cry or beating wings.

But there was only the crackling of the flames of his torches and the tense breathing of his men.

"Eriu," Parlan whispered, and turned away from the hill to look out over the plain. Far out in the darkness, he could see the motionless figure of the mare and rider sparkling beneath the cloud-veiled moon.

"This way!" Parlan cried, and holding the torches up in either hand, he started off at a run toward Eriu and Solasta. His men followed closely, and when Parlan glanced back he saw only a few of them still looking toward the hill for any sign of the dragon's return.

It was not far across the plain to the place where Eriu and Solasta stood, but it seemed to Parlan that he had never run for such a long time. Slowly he drew closer to the white figures, and at last he slowed to a walk, lowering his torches and handing them both to Gavin. His heart pounding, he walked up alongside the gleaming figures and turned to look at them both from the front.

There was no life in those frozen faces; only a smooth tracing of their features remained beneath the glittering coat of frost that covered both horse and rider. Even Eriu's long hair and the mare's mane and tail were perfectly coated in solid white.

"Eriu," Parlan said. He stepped up alongside the mare. "Eriu, you must awaken. The dragon has gone. Please, wake up now. You are safe."

There was only silence. The night wind stirred Parlan's hair, but Eriu and Solasta remained as still as though carved out of sparkling crystal.

Parlan reached out to the mare's shoulder and tried to

brush away the frost with his hands, but it was like trying to brush away the surface of a stone—a very cold stone. He tried again with Eriu's long trailing skirts, and with her slender arm beneath her cloak, but it was the same: The frost had formed a cold, thick, impenetrable coating that held horse and rider fast in its glittering grip.

He turned to his waiting men. "Light all of the torches! Light them all, and stand in a circle around Eriu! Hurry! Hurry!"

Before he finished speaking, the men had run up and formed a ring around horse and rider. Parlan began by lighting Gavin's own torch, and then moved from man to man until there was a flaring circle of light around Eriu and Solasta.

"Move in close to them! Move in as close as you dare! Bring the warmth of the sun down to them both, and melt this unnatural frost!"

Holding the flaring torches out before them, the men stepped forward until they were only a pace or two from Eriu and the horse. The plain where they stood seemed bright as day. Parlan could feel the heat rising off the circle of flames, so much so that a trickle of sweat ran down his brow in the cold night. He set his jaw and watched Eriu closely. Surely this would melt the frost and release her from its terrible grip.

But as the moments passed and the torches flared and snapped, the frost remained as cold and as hard as ever. His men stood sweating in the heat, but Eriu and her mare were still encased.

"Step back from her," Parlan whispered, and without a word his men broke the circle and gathered behind him.

Flickering shadows fell over the goddess and her mount as the men stepped back. Parlan walked up beside the small mare and reached up to take Eriu's bowed head between his hands.

"Hear me now, beautiful goddess," he whispered, as

51

near to her frost–covered lips as he could get. "I swear to serve both you and your people until my last breath, which I would use to warm you now if I could." He moved even closer, pressing against the frozen body of the mare, so close that his breath touched Eriu's face as he spoke to her. "Though I still want only you for my queen, I swear to you now that I will be the king you made even if it means I must rule alone."

He paused, and it seemed to him that the hard frost on her lips had begun to show a thin sheen of moisture. "I am here to defend you, and protect you, and keep you safe—now and always. Please, Eriu, open your eyes and awaken to life."

With all the gentleness he possessed, Parlan leaned in and kissed the terrible cold that covered her mouth.

When he drew back from her, his hands still on either side of her face, he watched—and he saw a slight movement of her eyelashes. A little powder of frost fell from them as she blinked, and then slowly, slowly, she opened her eyes and began to move, raising her head and sitting up straight in the saddle even as a shimmering white cloud of ice fell away and settled to the earth.

She turned to look at Parlan, her face pale from the cold but with life shining clearly from her deep green eyes. "Has it gone?" she whispered.

"It has," he answered. "It has gone for now. But I see that there is nothing the land can do against such a beast."

"Of course not. It is for a loving husband to protect his wife from such horrors. I am the land. I am not a warrior— you are. I can change my shape and exist seemingly forever, but I can only give life. I cannot take it away. This beast . . . it is a destroyer." She glanced up into the sky, her eyes narrowed.

"The dragon is gone," Parlan assured her, covering her

hand with both of his own. Relief flooded over him. "You are safe now.

"Not safe. Never safe," she said. "So long as Men are careless of their kingship, and do not respect and value it as they should, none will be safe from the dragon. That is its purpose." Withdrawing her hand, she leaned forward, swung her leg over her mare's back and slid to the ground, creating another glittering fall of frost as she did. "Help me to restore Solasta," she said, and she began brushing away the thick, hard crust that held the mare fast.

Parlan walked to the other side of the horse, and to his astonishment he was able to break away chunks and large shards of the frost. "I tried to do this before. It was no use. None of us could move it at all. Then we tried—"

"I know what you tried. And I thank you," Eriu said, clearing the frost from Solasta's face. "But nothing can stand up to the dragon's curse save the promise of a true king. It was that which set us free—but it is a promise you must keep, for the dragon *will* return."

Parlan's blood felt as cold as the frost beneath his fingers. "What do you mean? I set fire to the beast! It turned tail and fled into the darkness, smoking and screaming from the flames that burned all over its wings and scales! The beast could barely fly. I would be surprised if it lives for long."

Eriu finished clearing away the last of the ice from Solasta. The mare sighed deeply and shook its head, and touched its nose to Eriu's shoulder. Parlan was relieved to see that the horse, like its rider, ultimately seemed no worse for the attack.

Eriu turned back to Parlan. "It is true that you have driven off the Black Dragon and saved our people and me this night. For that I thank you. But I must also tell you, King Parlan, that your work has just begun."

He frowned, still looking at her from across Solasta's

saddle. "But . . . surely any creature so badly burned would die from its wounds."

"Any natural creature would die indeed, but this is not just any creature. It is a beast of magick, and it will take weapons made by magick to destroy it. Weapons wielded by a king who has sworn to protect the land as a husband protects a beloved wife."

Parlan frowned. "I have sworn to protect the land, and I will do so. But I do not know how to wield weapons made by magick."

Eriu glanced up at him, and gave a small smile. "You will learn, Parlan. You will learn."

CHAPTER SEVEN

The warriors walked on ahead with their torches still burning, all of them keeping one eye toward the black sky for any sign of the dragon's return. Parlan and Eriu and Solasta followed behind in the shadows. As they reached the foot of Teamhair Breagh, Parlan waved his men to continue.

"Go on. A few of you keep watch above. I'll be along."

"We will watch all night, my king," vowed Cillian. With a final nod for Parlan and a bow to Eriu, he turned and started up the hill with the rest.

As Parlan's men walked away, taking the glaring torchlight with them, the plain once again fell into soft semi-darkness as the high white moon came out from behind the clouds. The wind blew gently in the surrounding groves of oak and rowan trees, but other than that the night was quiet. The mare dropped its head to crop the lush grass, and Eriu sat down on a large rock to watch. Parlan stood close by, unable to keep from glancing worriedly up at the sky.

He made himself turn his attention to Eriu. "I am so relieved that you are both well," he said, nodding toward the mare. "After what the dragon did to you, I feared the worst."

Eriu smiled, still watching her horse. She seemed to draw comfort from watching the animal relax and enjoy the grass. "The land can always recover when it is protected and cherished."

"It will be from this night forward. I swear it to you." He looked up at the sky again, and at the top of the hill where a wall of torchlight showed that a row of his men kept watch.

Eriu glanced at him, and he met her gaze. "You need not look to the skies anymore this night. The dragon will not return."

He frowned. "Can you be so certain? You said that only magickal weapons can destroy it."

"That is true. But you did indeed manage to hurt it badly, and took it as near to death as it could ever get through ordinary means. It will go and hide itself away for a time, sulking and brooding and waiting for its wounds to heal."

"Then I must find it! I must go and find it, and destroy it."

Eriu shook her head. "It is not so easy. You are right—it will eventually return. After some months of healing, it will return, and it will be stronger and more enraged than ever before. But you cannot just go and find it. You will find, to your despair, that you will not be able to get near the beast. It will simply fly away from you, and each day it will destroy more and more of the land around you, and you will be helpless to do anything but watch from a distance. By Samhain next, all that will be left will be your kingdom here at Teamhair Breagh—and if the beast is not stopped, even that will soon be gone."

"But there must be something I can do. You said something about magickal weapons. Tell, me please: What must I do to defeat this dragon and lift this curse?"

Eriu folded her hands and looked up at him from her seat upon the stone, and the night breeze brushed her hair back from her face. "The dragon's power was evoked by a king who turned his back on the land and left it open for the dragon to take, which the dragon will not hesitate to do. The dragon, now awakened, will destroy all that Men have made. It will make the land into a place fit only for wild beasts, the way it was in the days before the gods taught Men to live in a civilized world. All we know will be lost if the dragon succeeds."

"But surely the gods could have long ago destroyed this dragon if they wished," Parlan said. "Why did they allow such a terrible threat to the world of Men to remain?"

Eriu regarded him for a moment, then smiled. "They are the ones who put the dragon in place, Parlan. They created the beast and set it on the edge of the world, where it would remain so long as the land was cherished and protected."

Parlan's eyes widened. He took a step toward her. "The gods themselves brought this monster into the world? Into Eire? Why?"

"For exactly a day such as this one. They set it here against the day that a king would turn his back on the land and reject the gift the Goddess of Sovereignty gave him."

Parlan closed his eyes. "I see what I have done. But now to make amends. How can I hope to defeat this dragon?"

Eriu smiled again, and settled herself more comfortably on the rock. "It is true that the gods left the dragon as the ultimate guardian against an unworthy king, but they did not leave Men without a means to fight the beast—if a worthy king should accept such a battle."

"I will fight it, worthy or no. But you said I must use

magickal weapons against the beast. Where can I find such weapons?"

Eriu shook her head. "You cannot simply 'find' them. You will have to win them."

"Win them?"

"To draw the dragon to you, and then to have a chance of defeating it in battle, you will need the four sacred objects hidden away by the gods against just such a need. Those objects are the Sword of King Nuadha, the Spear of Lugh, the Cauldron of the Daghda, and the Stone of Destiny."

Parlan took a few slow steps toward Eriu and sat down heavily on the cold grass at her feet. "I have heard tales of those very things since I was a boy, but I thought them to be just tales from the old days, when all of the gods walked freely among Men. Surely no man knows where these objects are now."

Eriu sighed, her face smooth and serious as she remembered. "Once there were many of us, walking amongst you at will to guide and teach you in the ways of the gods, so that you might no longer live as animals in the swamps and by the rivers and in the seaside caves. Most of those gods are gone now, drowned and destroyed as they fought each other in the Great War that brought about the Great Catastrophe so many ages ago. I was one of the few to survive, for I was safe here in Eire when it happened."

She fell silent, and looked away for a moment. "The Otherworld is a lonely place now. It is still as beautiful, but lonely. It was once home to all the gods and goddesses, but so many were lost . . . and we who are left must do what we can to safeguard our magickal home, so that it is not lost forever. If too few of us live there, it will simply fade away and be gone."

She turned back to Parlan and returned to the subject at hand. "When the gods knew that the Great War was upon them, and that all was in danger of being lost, they took the four sacred objects and hid them in the safest place they knew—here, on the island of Eire. They set a supernatural guardian for each, to make certain those treasures would never be found until the gods returned . . . or until a true king had need of them.

"It was well that they had the care to do so, for when the Great War came it brought in its wake the Catastrophe . . . and when the ocean waves closed over the Island to the West and drowned it forever, it took many gods with it. The last Great Battle was very fierce.

"Now most of those gods are gone forever, but their four sacred objects remain, so that a worthy man—a worthy *king*—might use them in time of great need, if he has the strength and the will and the nobility to gather them all together. That is your hope, Parlan. That is *our* hope."

"I have the will. I have the strength. And I will prove to you that I have the nobility. Tell me, now—where can I find these four hidden gifts of the gods?"

"You leave tomorrow morning for your high king's journey around Eire, to gather princes from each of the four provinces that they might be hostages to peace and help you as high king rule fairly over all. I can tell you that in each of the four provinces is hidden one of the four sacred objects.

"In the East is the Sword of King Nuadha, guarded by his Wild Hunt.

"In the South there is the Spear of Lugh, guarded by his firedrake.

"In the West there is the Cauldron of the Daghda, guarded by his *merrows*.

"In the North there is the Stone of Destiny, guarded by the *dullahan*.

"And if—*if*—you return here to the hill of Teamhair Breagh by the dark of the moon after Samhain next with all four of the sacred objects, you will be able to use them to draw the dragon to you and fight it."

Parlan turned to face her. "In the four regions . . . How can I find these objects? I recall no tales stating where they are, only that they were brought to Eire by the gods long ago. Now you say they are spread across the isle. How will I know where to look?"

Eriu considered for a moment, then looked away. "No man could ever find them alone," she admitted.

He took a step forward. "Then how could any man— even the worthiest of kings—ever hope to use them, should there be a need, as there is now? Why would the gods hide them so well that—"

"So that no man could ever stumble upon them accidentally," Eriu snapped. "And because . . . because if the gods had abandoned Men so that there were none to show a king where to search, perhaps there would be no need for such magickal weapons anyway: Men would simply be living again as the animals they once were."

"But that has not happened. And it will not happen while I have breath and strength to stop it. Tell me, Eriu, please, where I can find these four sacred things."

The goddess slid down from her rock, and she gazed up into the windy night sky. "Tomorrow begins your yearlong journey around the entire nation of Eire. It was to be just a formality, a new high king visiting the four provinces of the land and accepting noble hostages at each."

He nodded. "That is true. But it is far more than that now."

"So it is. Now it is also a quest to find these four magickal objects, and to persuade their guardians to let you have them."

Parlan's eyes narrowed. "These are supernatural guardians. Would they not give their sacred treasures to the Goddess of the Land, should she but ask?"

She laughed. "They would—and I could hand them to

you in turn—but you would find them to be nothing but shining, useless trinkets."

His eyes narrowed. "Why?"

"No man can use these objects unless he himself finds a way to win them from their guardians. That is where their power lies. No one else could use them but the king who wins them. No other man, no other king."

"No goddess, either?"

"I am no druid, any more than I am a warrior. I am simply the land. Only a king—a true and worthy king—can use the sacred objects of the gods."

He walked to her and took one of her hands in his. "Then we must do this together, beautiful Eriu. If you will help me to find these magickal weapons, I will do what I must to win them from their guardians. This I swear."

He lifted both her hands to his lips, and closed his eyes. "We will do this together, Lady Eriu, and you will see that I am the one man worthy to have a goddess as his queen—and who still dares hope that she might love him as he loves her."

Her fingers became rigid. She withdrew them and went back to sit on the rock again. "I do this only to help you lift the curse you have brought upon the land. You will not love me when this is over, Parlan, nor will I love you."

He moved to stand in front of her. "I will always love you, Eriu—as my wife, as my queen, as the goddess that you are." He knelt before the stone where she sat and looked up at her. "Think of it. I would be a king such as this land has never seen, with your wisdom and power sitting beside me! You would have a guardian to offer you devotion and protection such as you have never known. You are the land; you are the one who grants sovereignty. Would you not take pride in knowing that the finest, strongest king who ever ruled from Teamhair Breagh rose to such heights *because of you*?"

He reached out and took her hand again, holding it firmly in her lap. He stared up into those cool green eyes, which regarded him as though from a very great distance.

Then, to his surprise, she shrugged her shoulders and laughed. Parlan's grip on her hand sagged. "You are the one who has brought this challenge on yourself," she said. "No one can make you a good king, not even a goddess. I can grant you kingship and sovereignty—already I have—but I cannot say what sort of king you will be. Nor can I make you a good king or a bad king."

She lifted her fingers and let Parlan's hand fall away. "Do you think no other king has asked me to do the same for them? They have—oh, they all have. And they all had to learn that only they could make themselves great. Not even a goddess could do that for them."

Parlan got to his feet. "I *will* prove to you that I am like no other king you have ever known. I have always proven myself the very best at anything I've attempted—hunting, riding, battle, poetry, the courtship of women—and I will do no less in being a king. I will never settle for being merely the equal of a man who has come before me."

Eriu gazed meaningfully up at him. "That is a good thing, Parlan. You have little choice but to be better than the rest—for if you are not, you will have no kingdom to rule, only a barren and blasted land where men and women live in caves by the rivers and in holes by the sea, and glean what food they can from the shallows and the shrubs."

Parlan clenched his fists. "I will rise above them all, as I must. I will prove to you that I am the one man who deserves not just a mortal queen by his side, but a goddess."

Eriu walked toward her peacefully grazing mare, stopping one last time to turn and face Parlan. "I will go with you on this journey and help you find the four sacred objects, but I do not do this so that you might cling to your hope of having me at your side as your queen. I do this only to help you right the wrong you have caused, and to show you that, with the many young and beautiful mortal women you will meet on this journey, you will never have the strength to turn away from them and wait for me. I am doing you a kindness by not accepting your pledge, by giving you the chance to forget me, and to find the woman you can love and make your true queen."

She picked up the trailing reins. In a moment she was in the saddle and looking down at Parlan.

"One day you will be grateful to me for giving you this chance. You cannot and you will not have a goddess for a wife, for no mortal man can love a goddess and survive."

She turned Solasta and sent the mare galloping out across the dark plain, past the spot where the last of the land frozen by the dragon's deadly frost still glittered in the moonlight. As Parlan watched, Eriu turned the mare sharply to the right and galloped behind a gnarled and ancient oak tree, where she vanished.

And with that, she was gone. Eriu and Solasta had returned to the Otherworld.

CHAPTER EIGHT

Solasta galloped through cold darkness toward the ancient oak tree and swept past it into warm bright sunlight. Eriu sat up and reined the horse to a walk, closing her eyes and breathing deep of the soft sweet air. They had both escaped the dragon and come back to the Otherworld, the magickal place that was always just a step beyond the natural world if one knew how to find it. Here was the beautiful, peaceful home of all the gods and goddesses, where night and day were reversed from the natural world but where the season was always high summer.

Eriu slid down from the mare's back and unstrapped the sheepskin–covered saddle, resting it on end in the grass, and slipped the soft black leather bridle from the mare's head. Solasta sighed and shook herself, walked a short distance away, dropped to her knees and rolled over with great delight in the thick sun-warmed grass. Then the horse clambered to its feet and bolted across the plain toward a distant grove of white willow trees, head high and tail flagged, neighing out a greeting to its companions.

Eriu smiled and watched the mare go, even as a little

knot of fear remained around her heart. She had endangered both herself and her beloved Solasta by dallying too long with that mortal man; she was very lucky that they had both returned home.

Unfastening her circular golden brooch with the gold oak leaves and shining beads of amber worked into it, she pulled off her warm green cloak. "You would not need your heavy cloak if you would but stay here in the Otherworld where you belong," said a laughing male voice. "It is always summer here, always warm and fair."

Eriu looked up to see Ogma watching her from the oak trees at the edge of the plain. He was tall, broad shouldered and heavily muscled, as a great wrestler and champion in battle must be, yet he had the gentle eyes, sensitive face and long dark curling hair of a poet.

"So it is," she answered, smiling at him the way she would smile at a brother. "It is always beautiful here."

Ogma stepped out from the shadows of the trees. He wore only brown leather trousers, high brown boots and a linen tunic dyed in softest blue. "Why do you persist in going back there, Eriu?" he asked, walking toward her. "I know you must return whenever there is a new king to be made—but why would you go at any other time?"

She smiled, and gazed out across the distant plain where Solasta and the other horses ran and played. "You are a god of eloquence and poetry. You can play your music and sing your poems here in the Otherworld. But I am a goddess of the land, and I must see to it from time to time."

This time a woman's voice answered her. "Yet it is dangerous there. You nearly lost your life. This king you have made has unleashed the Curse of the Dragon on your beloved land—and on you."

Eriu glanced past Ogma to see a red-haired beauty wearing a dark red gown trimmed in the finest gold embroidery. The woman wore heavy gold ornaments at her wrists and around her neck and hanging from her ears.

"That he has, Lady Brighid. Yet he did protect me from that same dragon, and he has promised to undertake the quest to destroy it."

Brighid took a step forward. "And you intend to help him?"

Eriu shook her head. "I have little choice. He cannot achieve the quest and destroy the dragon without the four sacred objects, and he cannot hope to find those objects unless I show him where they are."

A third voice, this one the low clear voice of another woman, joined the conversation. "And why should you show him? He is the one who brought about the trouble. Let him solve it himself."

Eriu turned to look into the shadows of the oaks behind her. At first she saw only a soft-eyed doe browsing among the tender young leaves, but then a slow and graceful form caught her eye. "My lady Flidais," Eriu said. "Will you join us? I would have your counsel, as well as that of these two others."

A rippling laugh came from the shadows. "You have just received my counsel, my lady Eriu. Leave your Man to his fate, and live here in peace and beauty in the Otherworld where you belong."

At the sun-dappled edge of the forest, the doe bounded away, revealing a tall woman with long coppery hair bound in several slender braids, and leaning against an oak with folded arms. She wore a tightly laced gown of softest leather, of a color somewhere between moss green and wood brown, and it shone here and there with the fine cobweb of the gold and copper strands that covered it. The woman's feet were bare, as were her arms, save for the slender bronze serpents wrapping themselves around each biceps. A belt of deepest brown leather, tied to a ring of gleaming bronze, held a long bone-hilted bronze dagger.

"If I leave him, I leave all Men—and the land itself—to their fate."

Flidais cocked her head, and took a step away from the oaks. "I agree with you. But it is *their* fate—not yours, and not ours. You made him a king, and he tried to refuse it—and for what? He is no fit king, Eriu. He himself said as much. It seems that you were wrong to accept him."

Eriu gazed out across the plain. "He is worthy. I am sure of it. But he is also a man, and men can sometimes do foolish things."

"Yet this was far more than mere foolishness," Brighid said. "If he does not succeed at this quest—and if you do not find a true king who *can* succeed at it—there will be no more land for you to protect. And if the dragon destroys the land, it will destroy you, too."

"That is why I cannot abandon the world of Men. I must help them, or risk losing my life."

"But that is not true, Eriu," protested Ogma. "You need not risk yourself at all. You can remain here in the Otherworld, here in your true home. Even if the land there is lost, you will be safe so long as you stay here."

"If the land is lost . . ." Eriu closed her eyes, imagining. She could not raise her voice above a whisper.

Ogma lifted one of her hands and covered it with his own. "Dear sister," he said, "we know you love the land, for you have been its spirit and advocate ever since the time of the beginning. But all things in the world of Men do come to an end. That is their fate, and none can change that—not even gods or goddesses."

"But I do not know that the end is here for them now," Eriu said, and she withdrew her hand. "It may not yet be. He is a strong king and a powerful, determined man. He has sworn to do this thing, and I have sworn to help him."

"So you did," said Flidais, stretching lazily. "But what good are Men if they have only to beg the gods for help every time they spill a bucket of milk or neglect to prepare their supper? How are they to learn? It is not for you to clean up after them, Eriu, as a mother cleans up the messes of her children. These are not children; they are Men, and they know what will happen when they ignore the laws that the gods set them."

"The laws were a gift to Men from the gods," agreed Brighid. "They were not given to be a burden or a punishment. It was the task of the gods to raise Men up from the beasts and to teach them to live as humans—and the laws were a part of this. A king is supposed to be the strongest and best of mortals. Allow this one to prove it to you, and to his people and to himself. If he is the king you say he is, he will find a way to do this quest without your help. If you step in to help him, he will never have the chance."

"And do not forget," remarked Flidais, striding out from under the trees, her bronze knife glinting at her hip, "as soon as he meets the right woman on his journey— one who would do anything to be his queen, who will be as young and pliable and wide-eyed as a newborn fawn when the high king looks her way—he will forget his unattainable goddess. In the space of a heartbeat, he will desert you. Do not risk everything for him."

Eriu raised her chin. "I do not do this for him. I have told him he will not love me by the time his quest is over. I told him he should be grateful for the chance to find a mortal woman to be his queen and rule at his side."

Flidais raised an eyebrow, and smiled. "Well, then, my sister Eriu, I will wait for that day—and for your sake, I hope it comes soon. In the meantime, I will admit that King Parlan is indeed a strong and handsome man. If you do not want him, perhaps I will bring him here and enjoy him for a time."

Eriu felt a twinge of pain, though she dampened it. "The way you have with so many others," she whispered. "So many. Will you take him, too, and let him delight in

68

his time with you here, only to find that when you become bored with him and send him back to the natural world, a hundred years have passed and all of his family and friends are long dead? It is a cruel pastime, Flidais. I cannot prevent your doing it, I can only ask that you not do it to Parlan."

Flidais threw back her head and laughed. "All right, then. I will promise you this: I will not bring him here. I may go into the natural world and seek him out, but I will not bring him here."

Eriu closed her eyes. "I thank you."

Brighid came to stand beside her, and placed gentle hands on Eriu's shoulders. "The Otherworld is a lonely place now," she said. "So many of us are gone forever. I could not bear to see you drawn away from here, staying in the mortal realms for longer and longer times and finally forgetting your true home as some of the others have done—those who were not destroyed in the Great War. You must protect your heart, Eriu. You must protect yourself."

"Do not help this man too much," Ogma warned, shaking his head. "You must not forget who you are and what he is. Do not let him take you away from us."

Flidais agreed as well: "They are right. There are only a few of us left. And if too many of us wander away and forget the Otherworld, we will never find our way back, for it will cease to exist."

All three stood close to Eriu, but she only closed her eyes, which had begun to fill with tears. She turned away from the powerful and comforting presence of her brother and sister gods, and looked out over the grassy, sunlit plain.

"Perhaps you are right," she whispered. "Perhaps I am risking too much. Perhaps I was wrong about this man, who offered to give back the sovereignty I had just granted him. No man—no king—ever did that before."

She looked out again at the herd of white horses running over the thick green grass in the late afternoon sun. "Perhaps I should just leave them to their fate, and care for my own home. Perhaps it *is* for Parlan to right his own wrong, and not to beg a goddess to right it for him."

II

THE EAST

CHAPTER ΠIΠE

After the longest night Parlan had ever known, he stood alone at dawn on the sloping southern face of the hill of Teamhair Breagh and looked out over the plain. He studied every faint shadow cast by trees and the hills, and every small movement of bird and hare and windblown leaf; but there was nothing that looked like a lone woman on a horse. Instead he saw three riders—mere specks from where he watched—galloping across the plain as fast as their horses could go, into the new day and never looking back.

"Three good men on your three fastest horses. Now every man and woman and chieftain in Eire will know that the high king is on his way to see them, and will prepare their noble hostages accordingly."

Parlan turned to see Cillian standing just above him. "And their best hospitality, too, I hope."

Cillian smiled, and gazed out at the rapidly disappearing riders. "No fear of that. Once those three warn the chieftains that you are coming to their duns, they will call in their oldest sons and cousins to be your hostages to

73

peace and order their best young rams and bull-calves to be slaughtered for a feast. And they will be pleased to do it for you, the new high king."

"I do not care whether they are pleased or not—and they may well not be. Giving their grown sons to a new high king to grow fat off his hospitality for a year or two is one thing. Trusting a king who has been so blundering and foolish as to bring the Curse of the Dragon down upon his land is quite another."

Cillian stood a little straighter. "Then do what you must to rid us of this curse before the beast returns—though I have never heard of the same man bringing a curse and also lifting it."

Parlan tried to smile. "Perhaps that is how it *should* be. Perhaps the man who should lift a curse is the same man who brought it." He shrugged. "But I am not lifting it alone. The Goddess Eriu has promised to help me."

"Yes, well, let the goddess help you lift it, as she promised, and before we know it the men will all be back to arguing over beer and cattle and which woman has the best backside. And the sooner you start your journey, the sooner it will end. The men are becoming impatient to go."

Parlan looked out across the southern plain once more. The bright sun gleamed in the corner of his eye and lit up the gently rolling landscape, but there was no longer any sign of the three riders; they were well on their way to his first visit, several days ride away, at the fortress of Dun Ghee.

Abruptly he turned away and began marching up the hill. "You're right," he said, striding past Cillian. "So let us start our journey now."

As Parlan walked up the hillside, he flicked his eyes left and right, looking for any sign of a beautiful dark-haired woman on a grey mare, but there was no movement at all on the wide plain.

The top of Teamhair Breagh rose into view, bringing

with it the sight of some one hundred warrior men standing beside their horses along with some thirty servants and pack ponies. The men all wore their finest wool tunics and plaid cloaks, looking like a sea of bright blues and reds and greens and purples against the thick green lawn, all of them gleaming with heavy gold bands on their wrists and twisted torques round their necks, and enormous flat circular brooches holding their cloaks. Every man wore a good iron sword at his side, and a sharp iron dagger at his waist.

Their horses, like their weapons, were the best available. Most were stallions, with heavy heads and arching, high-crested necks, with only a few tall slender geldings or dainty mares among them. Each beast wore a saddle of crossed wooden frames in the front and in the back, covered with dark brown sheepskin. And each horse was a different shade of red or gold or brown, their coats grown long and shaggy with the cold days and long nights that came with the start of winter, their thick manes and tails blowing wild in the wind.

Behind the brightly dressed warriors and their fine strong horses stood the little crowd of servants, all plainly dressed in undyed brown wool trousers and cloaks, and in tunics of pale coarse linen. Their cloaks were held only with small dull brooches of rusted iron, or with heavy gorse thorns. The small but sturdy pack ponies stood patiently with their heads down and their tails to the wind, already loaded with woolen sacks of oats and salt and honey and dried apples, long slender wooden boxes of iron tools and extra weapons, and leather skins filled with barley beer and blackberry wine.

As Parlan approached, Gavin walked up to him leading Maorga by his heavy brown leather bridle. The bay stallion was the largest and strongest of all the horses of Teamhair, and though he was not always the swiftest, Parlan had never seen a horse as fearless. Taking up the thick leather reins, he vaulted into the saddle and swung the stallion around to face the gathering of men.

The conversation, laughter and the shouted orders all died down as Parlan looked out at his men from his place on Maorga's back. They all looked rather grim and tense, both from the dragon and from waiting.

"We leave this day to gather hostages to peace," Parlan called, "and I leave this day to gather, if I can, the four sacred objects of the gods, that I might lift the Curse of the Dragon that I myself have brought down upon this land."

He drew his iron sword and held it overhead, as Maorga threw back its head up and sidestepped. "Here and now, I apologize to you all for bringing this dreadful curse upon the land and upon all of you. And I swear, now, by my own heart, and by the love I bear for my people and the land itself, that I will do all I can, and more, to rid the land of this curse that I have brought upon it."

He lowered his sword. "If you accept this, and vow to aid me in my quest, then ride with me now, for I will need you all if I am to do this thing. Ride with me now!"

Parlan shoved his sword back into its wooden scabbard and swung Maorga around to the south so that his back was to his men. "I will ride so that my left hand is always to the sea, and return to Teamhair Breagh before the dark of the moon after Samhain next. Ride with me now!"

Looking straight ahead, he sent Maorga galloping down the long southern slope of Teamhair Breagh.

For a moment there was only silence behind him, only the wind in his ears and the pounding of Maorga's hooves beneath him. Parlan wondered if he might truly have to ride his circle around Eire entirely alone, and knew in a moment that he would, if he had to, for he would never turn his back on this quest so long as he had breath and strength to move. He would ride it alone save for Eriu, who had promised to help him, and whom he could only hope would keep her promise—but if she meant to do so, he wondered why would she be absent now, at the very beginning.

His grip tightened on his reins, but he continued to look straight ahead.

Maorga galloped on; in a moment he would reach the foot of the hill. And then from behind him came a rattling and a pounding and a great shouting as one hundred men galloped their horses in a tight pack down the southern face of Teamhair Breagh.

"King Parlan! King Parlan!" shouted the men, and though he never looked back, Parlan grinned and sent Maorga racing across the open plain as fast as he could go. Together he and his hundred men galloped into the new day, into the new year, into a new and entirely unknown quest.

After the excitement of their departure, the next fortnight went by slowly and tediously. It was fourteen days of slow, meandering riding through the tracks and traces of the oak forests leading toward the sea, constantly leaving the main road while Parlan searched unceasingly for any glimpse of a tall and beautiful dark-haired woman and her magnificent grey mare.

There was no trace of either.

On the afternoon of the eleventh day, Cillian rode up to walk his horse alongside Parlan's bay stallion. "It is a slow journey we make, my king," he said.

Parlan continued to watch the forest, the light dim under a heavy grey cover of cloud. "A new high king is meant to take one year to make his journey round Eire, so that any who wish to greet him or ask something of him might have the chance to do so while he is within their province."

"So he is. And we must not arrive too soon, before the outriders have warned the duns and given them a chance to properly prepare for the high king. But . . . the men assumed that we would ride for a time and then make camp for a time, giving them plenty of good days for hunting and fishing and resting. This back-and-forth searching of every last deer trace and cow path forces them to keep a slow and tedious pace. All of us grow weary, as do our horses. How long will you keep to this?"

Parlan set his jaw. A quick movement deep in the forest caught his eye and made him turn, but it was only a raven flitting through the bare branches of the oaks. "I must find her," he said, looking straight ahead. "It is not for myself that I do this. I must have her help if I am to find the sacred weapons. I cannot get them without Eriu to show me where they are."

"We understand this," Cillian answered, reining his small red stallion past a damp depression in the trail. "But surely a goddess will appear to you when she wishes. You could look beneath every rock in Eire, my king, and she would only laugh at you from her place in the Otherworld while you do it. Why put your men through this ordeal? What do you hope to accomplish?"

Finally Parlan looked at him. "I must find her. I must. I can only show her how determined I am to have her help. I know I cannot force her to appear, and I cannot go into the Otherworld and search her out. I can only look for her here—on the path that I must follow with my left hand to the sea."

Before Cillian could answer, Parlan lifted his reins and kicked his bay stallion into a canter through the cool forest, and in a moment he rode out of it and onto a wide grassy stretch. Just beyond lay the heavy grey sea, touched with whitecaps in the winter wind and covered with crying, calling gulls, endlessly diving and circling between the frothing sea and the rolling grey-white clouds.

Parlan trotted Maorga out onto the grass as the rest of the men galloped clear and swept past him, their horses glad for the chance to properly stretch their legs. But Parlan only turned his stallion to the south and cantered him along the grassy edge of the beach, holding his left hand open to the sea and searching, as always, for any sign of Eriu.

The next afternoon, Cillian and Gavin rode at the rear of the one hundred warriors and watched as Parlan became the first to send his horse splashing through the long shallow ford of the Ruirthech River.

"Ah, the River Impetuous," Gavin said, slowing his horse and falling into line as each man waited his turn to cross. "So named for its wild floods, but also an apt name for the man who is fording it now."

Cillian watched Parlan walk Maorga up out of the cold rushing water and onto the grass. "I would have to agree," he said quietly. "No man is more loyal to the high king than I, yet after what Parlan has brought down upon us, I am no longer sure that I—or any of us—should give our complete trust to him."

Gavin looked up to the sky as though half-expecting to see the Black Dragon descending upon him, but there was nothing above his head except rolling grey clouds. "What do you mean to do, Cillian? Will you turn away and ride for home? Will you tell the other men to abandon him, too? Do you think they would? Some of them were well and truly shaken by that dragon, and I don't mind telling you that I was, too! But I'm not sure I'm ready to turn my back on the high king. Do you think—"

"I do not intend to do anything but watch him," Cillian said, cutting off the nervous flow of words. "First he brings down a curse upon us all, and then he believes that the Goddess of the Land will help him to lift it—a goddess who has not shown herself to him or to anyone else since the night the dragon attacked. And why should she help? He greatly offended and insulted her. Why should she not just leave him, and all who follow him, to the fate that they deserve?"

Gavin stared off at the distant foothills of the southeastern mountain range. "Perhaps she already has. And if so? What will we do then? How can we hope to lift the curse ourselves? What will we do at Samhain next, when the Black Dragon returns and we are powerless to defeat it? What will we do—"

"If Parlan cannot lift the curse, perhaps another king can do so." Cillian continued to gaze steadily at Parlan, as horse after horse crossed the river's ford.

"Another king? But . . . unless Parlan is maimed or becomes infirm, or is killed, he will be the high king for the rest of his life!"

"You are quite right, Gavin," said Cillian calmly. Then he sent his horse trotting and splashing through the cold rushing waters of the ford to follow the others.

CHAPTER TEN

Parlan sent Maorga trotting out of the River Ruirthech, headed toward the rounded granite peaks of the mountains to the south. He kept his attention on the wide vistas around him beneath the soft grey skies, forever watching for any sign of Eriu.

They were close enough, now, to their first stop of Dun Ghee, that they could have arrived by nightfall even with the slow-going pack ponies; but as before, Parlan could not keep from searching every track and path for the goddess. Another eight days went by—days of walking slowly through the wide plains and valleys of the foothills, winding in and out of the thick gorse and bracken of the mountainsides, and stopping to refill their waterskins from the general waterfalls that tumbled down the granite slopes.

On the eighth night, Parlan led his men as high as their horses could go on the steep mountainsides, and had them make camp there among the rocks and thorny shrubs of gorse. "Put up torches everywhere," he said to the servants. "Surely she will see their light here in the darkness, as high up as we are. Ring the camp with them. I will keep watch from that ledge up there, up above the camp."

He climbed up to the rocky ledge and sat down in the cold darkness, watching the torches waver and gutter in the wind. The sky overhead was a cold black vault covered with a solid layer of cloud, and Parlan could see little beyond the ever-present glare of the torches. Yet still he strained to see any movement in the blackness, and listened intently for any sound of hoofbeats or of light and delicate footsteps.

Suddenly a slight movement off to one side caught his eye. It came again up above him, and then down in the valley below—and then he stood up as he realized what it was.

Snow. A light snow was falling from the black night sky, and as Parlan watched, it began to dust the ground and rocks and gorse and grass with a coat of sparkling white.

One by one, his white-covered men got to their feet, stood very still and looked up at him in silence. With a sinking heart Parlan realized that they looked the way Eriu and Solasta had looked when the Black Dragon had breathed down on them and encased them in paralyzing frost. His men were reminding him of what their fate would be if their king could not lift the curse that lay upon them.

"I will do all I can," he whispered. "But I cannot do it without her. She will come to me. She *must* come to me."

The men remained silent and still, and the snow continued to fall.

At long last, Parlan closed his eyes against the sight of the slowly falling white, wrapped himself in his heavy wool cloak, and allowed himself to sleep for a time on the cold hard ground. He sat up suddenly at the sound of quiet footsteps approaching over the rocks, blinking in the cold grey light of dawn, but it was only a young serving man approaching him with a wooden bowl. He was still alone; she had not come.

"I am sorry, my king," the man said, holding out the bowl. "Cillian sent me to wake you. He said he was sure you would want to arrive at Dun Ghee before nightfall."

"And so we will," Parlan said, accepting the bowl of steaming oatmeal and honey. "Ready my horse. We'll leave right away, and we'll ride straight for the fortress. There won't be any more waiting."

As he had promised, Parlan led his men straight across the grassy, open hills of the kingdom of Dun Ghee while the sun was still high in the sky behind the broken grey-and-white clouds. The great fortress itself sat on the crown of one of the low rolling hills, open and visible for a very long way, and was a huge closed circle of grey-white stone with many thatched-roof, clay-walled buildings inside.

As they approached the fortress, Parlan could see the sentries pacing along the steps and ledges that ran around the top of the curving stone walls. Suddenly the sentries stopped and looked straight at them, and then began shouting down to the others within the walls.

"Wait here," Parlan said to his men. "Cillian and Gavin, come with me."

The three men cantered their horses across the open hills until they reached the looming walls. Parlan ducked his head and rode through the narrow stone-lined tunnel that was the only way in or out of the dun. His two warriors followed close after him, and in a moment they were out of the low, damp tunnel and riding across the lawn within Dun Ghee.

Walking forward to greet them were King Ros, aged and grey-haired but still standing tall; three younger men who bore a close resemblance to him; and a large crowd of druids, warriors and many of the noble women.

Parlan slid down from his horse, as did his two companions, and allowed the horseboys to lead their three animals away. "Good day to you, King Ros," he said, as the old king nodded to him. "We thank you for your hospitality."

"And we thank you for your presence." King Ros tilted his head and looked closely at Parlan for a moment. "I am told that on the night of your kingmaking, a Black Dragon came down out of the sky and attacked you and your men. I am told that you managed to drive it away yourself."

Parlan raised his chin. "It is true. I offended the goddess with a bit of arrogance, and the dragon came down to challenge me."

"But you did drive it away?"

"I did. And if it returns, I will destroy it. This I have sworn, and here swear it again."

King Ros looked steadily at him, then nodded. "We have seen no dragon here. It is the task of the high king to protect us from it, should one appear."

"I have done so. And I will continue to do so." Parlan gazed at Ros, and smiled. "Will you introduce me to those who are to be my guests until Samhain next?"

King Ros frowned slightly, then turned to the three young men who were to be hostages. "Here are Anluan, Uaine, and Calvagh," he said. "They are my oldest sons. They will be your hostages to peace for the coming year, and will serve you as they serve me."

Parlan nodded. "I am honored to have three princes of Dun Ghee among the men of the high king. So long as they serve me, they shall be my honored guests." His eyes flicked to Cillian, who walked over to the three men carrying a flat leather bag.

From the bag Cillian took out three iron torques—three twisted iron bars bent almost into a circle, with a space left between the ball-capped ends. Cillian slid one of the iron torques around the neck of each man. "You are now a captive of the high king and a hostage to peace. Do not remove this torque until the day the high king comes to you and says you are free to go." Each of them nodded, and Cillian returned to his place beside Gavin.

King Ros drew a deep breath. "They are yours, King Parlan," he said. "And now I would make you and your men welcome here within these walls. Leave your servants to graze the horses outside on the hills, while the rest come inside to my hall for a feast and for music and poetry. We await you."

"Thank you. We will be there," Parlan said. And with that, Ros and his sons and men all started toward the long narrow building that sat across the center of the dun.

As the three hostage princes walked away, Parlan's eye was caught by a lone woman who must have been standing in the crowd behind them, but who had stayed even as everyone left. She looked across the grass at him and smiled, and Parlan could not help but take a step toward her.

She was tall, slender, young and strong, and had long streaming hair of shining red-gold blowing in the ever-present winds at Dun Ghee. Her perfectly fitted gown of delicate rust-colored wool, beautifully embroidered with gold wire at the neckline and sleeves, sat wide across her white shoulders, and around her waist gleamed a belt of heavy gold links.

"You are most welcome here at Dun Ghee," she said, stepping up in front of him. "We have been expecting you."

"I thank you, my lady." He knew he should walk away and go with King Ros and all the others to the hall, but this young woman with her delicate skin and gleaming hair and easy, noble manner held him in thrall. "This is the first stop on our tour around Eire, and I am pleased to meet you." He gave a slight bow. "Might I know your name?"

"Might I sit beside you at the feast this night?" The woman cocked her head and gazed steadily at him, smiling all the while.

A great feeling of apprehension rose up in Parlan. Normally he would have seized the chance to sit at the feast with such an attractive young woman who was clearly interested in him; but now there was Eriu and the promise he had made to her.

A look of sadness came over the red-haired woman's face. "Will you reject me, then, King Parlan? I wish only to extend the hospitality of Dun Ghee to the new high king, for this is my home and I wish to make certain that you feel welcome while you are in it."

Parlan sighed, and then bowed again to the young woman. "I should be honored to sit beside you at King Ros's feast, my lady."

The young woman smiled brightly. Picking up the hems of her long rust-colored skirts, she ran past him toward the hall. "My name is Aisling," she called over her shoulder, and in a moment she had disappeared around one of the many houses and was gone.

By the time the sun began to set, Parlan had bathed, shaved his face with his bronze razor and some steaming hot water, and put on clean brown leather trews and a good wool tunic dyed a deep red. He stood now atop the walkway of a stone wall, his multicolored cloak blowing in the winter wind. All of his warrior men had left their horses hobbled and grazing on the surrounding grassy hills, with the servants keeping a close watch on the animals from the camp; and the men walked now through the tunnel in the walls of Dun Ghee and made their way to the long rectangular building that was the king's hall.

Walking behind them, after the five servants who had been brought along, too, was the lovely red-haired Lady

Aisling. She looked up at the wall where Parlan stood, and smiled at him.

Parlan saw her, but he quickly glanced out over the wide open hills surrounding the fortress. In the fading light he saw only the shadowy shapes of grazing horses, and the small campfires of the servants who guarded them, as well as the gleam of a distant lake at the place where the hills met the forest.

Abruptly he turned his back on the sight. Looking down at Aisling, who was a vision in her blue woolen gown with heavy gold and cream embroidery around the wide neckline, he made his way down the stone steps that angled down the sides of the curving wall, and walked straight to her. "A good evening to you, Lady Aisling," he said, noting how her face glowed with pleasure at having him join her. "I am about to join King Ros at his feast. Is it still your wish to sit with me there?"

"Oh, it is," she answered, tilting her head so that her long, shining, red-gold braids fell across her shoulder. Her hazel eyes shone in the deepening dusk, and though for a heartbeat Parlan was held by her gaze, he quickly looked away.

"Come with me, then," he said, and went striding off toward the hall just as Aisling caught hold of his arm.

The inside of King Ros's hall was bright with torchlight, and the warm air was filled with the savory smell of roasting meat. The people all looked up from where they were seated on leather cushions and heavy brown sheepskins thrown down on the straw on either side of the row of polished wooden squares, and they fell silent as King Ros and Queen Slaine got to their feet and walked to the doorway to greet their guests.

King Ros nodded to Parlan, and glanced a little too long at Aisling. "Such a beautiful lady you have brought with you," said the king, looking closely at her face and briefly at the curving, gold-embroidered neckline of her gown.

"Beautiful as all the women of Dun Ghee are." Parlan's voice was cool and polite.

King Ros finally looked back at him, as though waiting for him to say something else, but finally gave him a tight smile. "Come and be seated, then."

Aisling placed her fingers on Parlan's arm and smiled up at him. Together they followed King Ros and Queen Slaine to their place at the head of the boards.

Parlan expected to be stared at as he made his way through the hall—he was, after all, both the high king and a stranger to these people—but he had not expected the eyes of every last man and woman in the smoky torchlit hall to follow him all the way to his new leather cushion in the straw beside Queen Slaine.

Or, he corrected, for their eyes to follow him and Aisling.

He hoped he had not made an error here. Surely she was not the wife of some man of Dun Ghee, seeking to embarrass her husband in front of everyone with the high king himself! But he did not believe any woman of this kingdom would have the audacity to behave in such a fashion, and surely not one he had just met. And Aisling seemed perfectly at ease as she sat down on the cushion a servant hastily brought for her, and she had eyes for no one but him.

Parlan told himself that the staring people were all simply envious of the very beautiful young woman who sat beside him this night. But in any event, one of the advantages of being high king was that no one would ask him any questions.

Throughout the feast—which was itself a warm and pleasant respite from the long days and nights spent out in the cold and damp of winter—Parlan shared his plate with Aisling and tried to engage her in polite conversation. The gathered men and women continued to watch and whisper—and he noticed that even the servants stole long glances at Aisling.

He frowned at the servants and they quickly moved away. Was it so strange that the high king should sit with an attractive woman at the feast? Parlan shot a brief glare at the diners who stared at him and Aisling, and finally all of them turned back to their cuts of roasted beef and joints of venison.

Aisling placed her fingers on Parlan's arm, even as she took a bit of meat from their shared plate. "You must be pleased to take time out from your long journey to stay in such a pleasant place as Dun Ghee," she said.

Parlan glanced at her. "It is most pleasant here. The good food, the good company—"

"And the warm air and dry ground," Aisling said with a little laugh. She leaned forward until her face approached his, and one of her long braids fell against his arm. "I hope that you are in no hurry to leave."

He sat back as the warm sweet scent of her skin and hair went straight to his head. Quickly he reached for another bite of beef. "We must be going soon. We have three other kingdoms to visit, and nine more hostages to collect."

"The hostages will wait. Surely you could take your rest here for a few more nights. We would welcome you." She ran her fingers over his wrist and hands, and before he could move, she leaned forward to kiss him gently on the cheek.

Her lips were hot, soft and lingering. Instantly his body was seized with tension. Getting to his feet, he tightened his hands into fists and made himself look down at Aisling. "I thank you for your companionship here at the feast, my lady. I will retire now." And before she could touch him again, he strode out of the hall without a word to anyone else, and he did not care whether anyone stared at him or not.

CHAPTER ELEVEN

Parlan walked across the lawn, breathing deep of the cool darkness, and headed straight for the stone wall of the fortress. He all but ran up the steps until he stood atop the ledge running around the inside, and looked out into the night. His breathing stayed rapid—a combination of anger and desire. He placed his hands on the top of the wide stone wall and looked hard into the darkness.

Behind the clouds, the half-moon approached the western horizon, only shining through here and there as the cloud bank drifted over the hills. But there was nothing out there but the campsite of his own servants and the dark forms of the grazing, hobbled horses.

"A lovely night, is it not, King Parlan?"

He turned in an instant. Aisling stood on the ledge just a few steps away, smiling up at him with warmth and desire in her clear hazel eyes. She took a step toward him and threw back her bright plaid cloak, and he saw that she now wore only a simple linen gown. As she faced the cold wind, the thin gown pressed in on her body and outlined the curves of her hips and breasts, and plainly displayed her nipples. Her long red-gold braids hung down her back halfway to her knees as the winds blew a few loose strands from her face.

Rigid desire surged through Parlan again. "It is another cold winter night in Eire, my lady Aisling. Nothing more." He made himself turn away from her and look out over the ledge again, but somehow her warm sweet scent still reached him where he stood.

He fought down the throbbing desire that coursed through his body and concentrated only on searching through the darkness once again.

"What do you look for, King Parlan?" Her young voice was filled with curiosity.

"I am looking for . . . I am looking . . ." He stopped and sighed in frustration. "I am not sure you would understand."

She laughed a little—a delicate, musical sound. "I will try my best to understand, my king. I can see that this distresses you."

"It does. I fear I have made a great mistake."

"A mistake? How could the high king make a mistake?"

Her voice was so young and innocent, Parlan almost laughed. "Quite easily, my lady. And his mistakes tend to be greater than those of other men, for everyone is affected when the high king errs."

She took another step toward him and placed her fingers on his arm. "But I have only a sympathetic ear. Please—share with me whatever it is that troubles you, so that you need not carry the burden alone."

He set his jaw at the feather-light feel of her fingers on the bare skin of his wrist, and he looked hard into the darkness once more. "I made the greatest mistake a king can make. I became arrogant. I thought . . . I believed that I loved a goddess, and in my arrogance I told myself that she would love me in return."

"Do not all men love the goddesses?" Aisling asked.

91

Parlan smiled, still looking out into the night. "They do. But this was different. She came to me on the night of my kingmaking, and she . . . that is, she and I . . ." He paused. "I came to love her that night. I loved her as I believed no man has ever loved any woman. I was determined to make her my queen—her and no other."

"You say you *loved* her. Do you not love her still?"

He closed his eyes, remembering the warm soft feel of Eriu beneath him in the Mound of the Kings, the intoxicating scent of her glossy hair and perfect skin, the keen look in her shining green eyes—and the feminine strength in her arms and legs as she held him close to her in the darkness and tested to the utmost his determination to be high king.

"I will always love her—now and forever. Yet I may as well love the brightest star in the sky and demand that it come down to earth and be my queen."

Aisling cocked her head. "This goddess must have given you some reason to believe she might love you in return and would agree to be your queen."

He started to speak, then paused. "That is the trouble. I believed at the time she did—that she might desire me as I desired her. She agreed to help me lift the Curse of the Dragon that I brought down upon the land, for she well knows I have no hope of doing it alone. Yet on every step of the journey I have watched and waited and searched, and there has been no trace of her. It is as though I only dreamed her presence at my kingmaking, only imagined that I helped to save her from the dragon's breath."

His lip twisted in frustration. "What I thought was love was, in truth, only strong wine and powerful ritual. I have been played for a fool. She told me from the beginning that she would never be any man's queen, would never allow herself to love a mortal. And when I insisted I would change that, she let me think that might be true. She let me make a perfect fool of myself in front of my people, and bring a curse down upon them that may well destroy all of Eire."

He slammed his fist down upon the wall and turned his back on the dark and empty landscape. "I should have been more than pleased to have the status of high king and not dare to think that I might have a goddess for a queen, when all other kings have been honored to have a wise and beautiful mortal woman sit beside them." He looked down at Aisling, and smiled. "It was enough for them. It should have been enough for me. And from now on, it will be." He reached out and gently caressed the stray locks of her hair that rippled back from her face in the wind.

Aisling beamed at him, her face even more beautiful as it lit with happiness. "Oh, my king, I feared you did not like me . . . that my own pale looks could never compete with your magnificent goddess."

Again he stroked her hair, and again his eyes flicked over her curving body beneath the thin and wind-whipped linen. "Better a woman who is here for me than a goddess who remains untouchable."

"I am here for you, my king," she whispered. "Will you walk with me to your bed in the king's house? I am so cold out here in this wind, I so long to warm myself beneath the furs . . ."

"I will walk with you," he answered, the tension rising once more as he looked from her young and eager face to her rounded breasts and delicate nipples outlined beneath the thin fabric of her gown.

He stepped back to let her go past him down the steep steps, trying to ignore the pounding of his heart; but as she swept past him with her long plaid cloak brushing his leg, he glanced out into the darkness one more time. There he paused, resting one hand on the cold stone wall even as Aisling hurried down the steps. He listened to the wind rustling through the grass–covered hills and stared out at the distant glowing spots that were the campfires of his serving men.

Parlan spoke softly to the darkness. "I said these words to her: I will always love you, Eriu—as my wife, as my queen, as the goddess that you are . . . I will prove to you that I am the one man who deserves not just a queen at his side, but a goddess. This was the promise I made to the Goddess of Eire."

"But surely, if she has rejected and abandoned you, you would now be released from your vow . . . wouldn't you?"

He whirled at the sound of Aisling's voice. She had returned to the top step of the stairs and stood watching him.

"If she has abandoned me, as you say . . . and does not want me . . . what else can I do but find another?" he agreed.

She moved forward on the stone walkway and stood close in front of him once more. "What else, indeed," she whispered, and reached to take his hand.

Parlan looked at her, seeing her youth and beauty and eagerness to please him—her simple pleasure at being the one chosen by the high king, even if only for a night. She was no different from any of the other women he had known, save perhaps for being the most beautiful and tempting of the all.

Except, of course, for Eriu.

I will always love you, Eriu . . . I will be the one man. . . .

He took Aisling's hand, and raised it up and placed it on his forearm, and turned to lead her toward the steps. "Come with me," he said, as they walked down the steep steps in the windy darkness, and together they crossed the torchlit yard toward King Ros's house.

But instead of stopping there, Parlan continued past it and walked straight to the doors of the Feast Hall. They stood together in the shadows of the windblown torches, and Aisling turned her face up to him with a question in her eyes.

"I will take my leave of you, Lady Aisling," Parlan said. At her look of surprise and disappointment, he smiled. "I made a vow to a goddess—a goddess whom I will always love as a woman as well as a supernatural creature. If my promise could be so easily forgotten, simply because she is absent for a time, I should not blame her for thinking I did not mean it. But I *did* mean it—and I will keep my promise to her now. I thank you again for your companionship, and I will bid you good night."

Parlan leaned forward and kissed her gently on the forehead. He drew back and smiled at her, intending to turn and walk away, but he found that he was no longer looking at the young features and wide eyes of Aisling. He saw, instead, the elegant face and shining green eyes of Eriu.

Parlan's breath stopped. He could not move at all. He could only stare at her and try to believe what he was seeing.

"Eriu," he whispered. He still held her hand in his own, and quickly looked down at it and then back up to her impossibly beautiful face. "It is you. It *was* you."

She studied him as though from a great distance, but he could see the smallest of smiles at her lips. "You did not know?"

"I did not. It never occurred to me that this 'Aisling' might be a goddess in disguise. I thought her to be simply one of the many women of Dun Ghee, no more and no less." He paused. "So, that is why everyone was so curious about Aisling—I thought she was from Dun Ghee, but they thought I must have brought her. None of us had ever seen her before!"

"So it was," Eriu said. Her face remained still, but now there was a small gleam in her green eyes. "You nearly forgot your vow when Aisling came to you."

"But I did *not* forget it. I did not. I will freely admit to you, Lady Eriu, that I was tempted by Aisling. What man would not be tempted by a beautiful young woman so anxious to do nothing but please him? But when the time came, I did nothing more than wish her good night and leave her at the door of the hall—after telling her of my love for, and my promise to, the goddess Eriu."

"So you did, Parlan. So you did."

A few more people walked out of the hall, glancing at Parlan and the lady who stood with him as they passed. Eriu drew her dark green cloak's hood over her head and walked away across the lawn.

Parlan hurried after her. "Where are you going?"

She continued on, heading straight for the tunnel in the wall. "I, too, will keep my promise. I will help you find the four sacred objects. When you need me, I will be with you."

He stepped around in front of her, and she stopped. "Please, Eriu. I need you now. Do not leave me alone this night," he begged.

She smiled a little, but avoided him and kept on walking. "I am sorry. Since you kept your word to me, I will keep mine to you—but that is all. Good night to you, Parlan." She turned and walked through the damp tunnel, and just before she reached the end of it, Parlan saw her beautiful young grey mare trot over the grass outside and stand waiting for her. Eriu left the tunnel, swung up on the mare, and galloped away into the night.

Parlan could only stand and watch her go, but a great sense of relief washed over him at the same time. At long last, she had come back to him. And he knew, as sure as his own heart continued to beat, that she would come to him again.

CHAPTER TWELVE

The next morning, Parlan took his servants, horses, three hostage princes and his hundred warriors and set out toward the lake to the south of Dun Ghee.

"This country is open, King Parlan," Cillian said, riding alongside him. "There is nothing here but wide grassy valleys and fields. Do you still mean to keep to this slow and wandering pace?"

Parlan looked straight ahead, toward the distant mountains beyond the lake. "I know that the men are frustrated again. I can see it in their bored, resentful glances as we walk and circle and backtrack across the country, instead of just covering ground at a bold pace and then making a comfortable camp for a fortnight's hunting and fishing before moving on again. But I am just as certain that I am doing the right thing. Such travel shows the lady Eriu that I have not forgotten her for a single step of this journey . . . and because I did not forget her, I was able to pass a test she set for me at Dun Ghee."

"A test?"

Parlan smiled. "Perhaps the most difficult test of all for

any man. But because I passed her test, she chose to return to help me." He stopped his horse and turned to face Cillian. "I do not do this for myself alone! It is true that I love this goddess and will never love another. It is true that I want her for my queen. But there will be no kingdom at all if I cannot convince her that I am worth helping!"

Then Parlan kicked Maorga into a canter and sent the stallion on ahead of the group, following a path that veered off around a set of boulders and took him out of sight of his party. He halted the stallion and sat looking at the rolling landscape in the grey light of noonday—at the wide hill sloping away from his feet and down to a long narrow stream, the water's presence clearly shown by the thick line of trees and shrubs on either side, and following the line of trees as they rose up again on the other side of the valley into the distant hills.

All of this was his, as high king—his to guard and protect. But as he gazed out at it, it seemed that the thick green landscape began to fade, the color draining from it as the sky darkened and lowered. All of the grass and leaves turned to dull grey . . . and as Parlan watched, the vegetation began to blacken and curl and crumble into ash, as though it had been set afire—or perhaps scorched by a terrible cold that left it withered and dead.

This was the way it would be, Parlan knew, if he failed in his quest.

Cantering hoofbeats sounded on the path behind him. Someone had followed and even now was riding around the boulders.

Parlan swung Maorga around to face the way he had come, scowling ferociously and intending to unload his temper on whomever had followed him—but he sat back and the anger faded as he saw who it was.

Eriu stopped her mare and dropped her black leather reins on the beast's arching grey neck. "Good day to you, Parlan. A lovely view here, is it not? The gently rolling hills, the clear stream at their feet with the white willows on either side—one may see something like this almost every place in Eire, yet I never tire of seeing the fresh beauty. Nor of hearing the singing of the water over the rocks and gravel, of the smell of the lush grass and cool stream and dry winter leaves."

"And of the earth that gives it all a home," Parlan said, sliding down from his stallion and leaving Maorga to graze as he walked over to her. He covered her hand with his own, and smiled up at her. "I knew you would come back."

She lifted one eyebrow, but otherwise sat very still in her saddle. "I told you I would come to you when I was needed. That is why I am here."

"There is never a time when I do not need you, Lady Eriu." He caught his breath as he gazed up at her perfect face, no less mysterious and magical even in the ordinary light of day. "I have ridden every step of this journey searching for you. It is true that I need you—that I must have you—to accomplish this quest. But it is just as true that I need you, that I want you, at my side throughout the rest of my life as well. It would be like a draught of cool water to a thirsty man to have you ride beside me in the daylight, and to rest beside me in the warmth of the furs at night. I am so glad to have you here—"

She withdrew her hand and picked up the reins once more. "I have come to tell you that you are near to the first of your challenges. In three nights time you will reach the place where the Sword of Nuadha can be found."

Instantly Parlan tensed. He took a step back from her. "The Sword of Nuadha," he whispered, and then raised his head. "I am ready. I have been ready to do this since we left Teamhair Breagh. You need only show me where the sword is hidden, and I will go and take it."

"In three nights time, if you ride at a steady pace, you will be there. Do not search for me any longer. Your men are weary of this crawling pace you force them to keep. I will see you in three nights."

She picked up the reins and prepared to go. "Wait," Parlan said, resting his hand on her grey mare's long black mane. "Surely you will not leave me now. Surely you will stay with me this night, and let me warm and protect you by the fire, and let us face this threat to the land together."

She raised her chin and looked down at him. The mare sidestepped, moving out from under Parlan's hand. "I *am* the land, King Parlan," Eriu said. "And I am not the one who brought a curse down upon it."

Parlan closed his eyes.

"I have come to help you when it was necessary to your quest—nothing more. I will not allow you to grow more dependent upon me than you already are. I will come to you only when you must have my help. Ride for three days at a normal pace, and I will come to you on that third night. Prepare yourself."

She turned her mare and cantered around the boulders. The sound of hoofbeats faded the moment Eriu was out of sight.

For a long moment Parlan looked after her, listening to the silence. He knew he should be thinking of the terrible challenge to come; but right now, he could feel only the emptiness in his arms and deep within his chest, and knew that it was going to be with him for a very long time.

For the next three days, Parlan and his men enjoyed the freedom of riding at a bold canter across the open plains and low rolling hills at the foot of the mountain range. Even when just walking or jogging their horses through the cold grey days, they rode straight forward with no more meandering or retracing of steps. Indeed, Parlan led them at such a hard pace that some of them began to complain of having no time to rest their horses or to stop and catch a few hares for the cauldrons at night—but Parlan would only ignore them and send Maorga cantering over the next hill.

At last, on the evening of the third day, they came to an open grassy plain scattered with tall silver birches, their branches bare in midwinter and their delicate fingers reaching up to the clearing skies. Parlan halted his horse and looked left and right at the plain. "Here. Here is where she will come to me. Here is the place to make our camp."

"How do you know she will come to you here, my king?" asked Gavin.

Parlan slid down from Maorga and handed the reins to one of the horseboys. "She told me to ride at a good pace for three nights. I have done so, and now we have come to this beautiful plain. Make your camp. I will wait for her here."

He nodded to Gavin and Cillian, and they followed him to a small rocky rise near the edge of the plain. Together the three men stood and watched as the sun disappeared beneath the southwestern horizon, and the deep blue-black sky closed in around them, touched only by a few high wispy white clouds.

"I should have known she would choose this day for the first of the challenges," Parlan said. "It is the shortest day. The longest night. The winter solstice."

"And the dark of the moon," said Gavin. "You'll have nothing but a few stars and some torches to light your way."

"Perhaps not," Cillian said, as the sky turned black. "Look there."

He gazed up to the north, and Parlan's eye was caught by a sudden faint shimmer of white light up in the sky. It waved like a drape of fabric in the blackness, the stars clearly shining through it. Then the shimmer of light turned from white to deep violet and unfolded wide across the northern sky, before turning to red and then fading from sight again.

Parlan felt a sudden chill, and it was not from the cold damp wind that had begun to rattle the bare limbs of the birch trees. "The Ride of the Sidhe," he said, still watching the sky. "I have heard of this, but have never seen it until now. It has not visited us for a long time, but when it does, any manner of strange and terrible things are apt to happen."

"The Sidhe lived here long before the coming of Men," said Cillian. "They were driven away to live Underground, so it is said. But when they wish, they can rise up and fly through the night on fiery wings. As they do now."

Gavin stared up at the sky, wide-eyed. More veils of glowing blue and green moved slowly across the starry blackness. "What do they want? Why are they here?" he asked, his voice trembling. "Why have they come? How do we fight something like this?"

"Not with a sword," Parlan said.

"But I know no other way to fight!" cried Gavin. "Show me something I can kill and I will defend you to the death, my king!"

There was a footstep on the rocks behind them. All three men turned, their hands on their sword-hilts; but to Parlan's great relief he saw Eriu standing there with her dark brown hair and deep green cloak blowing back in the cold night wind. He could have sworn he saw the shimmering white veils of light in the sky reflected in her eyes.

"Get your weapons. Get your three hostages. Get your courage. But leave your horses. It is time." She gathered her cloak around her against the wind and turned to step down from the rocks.

"Wait! Please!" Parlan cried, climbing to the top of the rise. "Where are you going? Where is the sword! You must show me where it is! I cannot hope to find it on my own!"

"It is here," she answered, her eyes sharp and her voice serious. "Do not ask me any more questions. Get your hostage princes and come with me now."

The wind picked up, sending the last of the dry dead leaves whirling past their feet. The Ride began to intensify, the sky flashing and rippling in bright waves of blue and violet and white. Parlan glanced up at it—but when he turned back to Eriu, she was gone.

"Gavin!" Parlan shouted against the rising wind. "Go and get the three princes of Dun Ghee. Bring them here now. Now!"

Gavin turned and stared at Parlan for an instant, his eyes wide and his mouth open; but then he turned and raced back toward the campsite, hurrying in and out of the widely scattered trees toward the glowing spots of the cooking fires.

"What do you mean to do?" Cillian asked. "She said the sword was here. How can that be?"

"I do not know. I can only take this as it comes. Right now, I must follow Eriu and let her show me where the Sword of Nuadha lies." He peered out into the darkness beyond the rise, and in the unearthly red and orange lights of the Ride of the Sidhe, he saw her walking out across the plain—a dark shadow beneath the bare silhouette of the birch trees.

Purple-white light flashed across the plain, but this time it was from the heavy white clouds boiling up on the northern horizon beneath the glowing veils of the Ride. The lightning flashed and flashed, sending earth-shaking rolls of thunder across the plain, and the wind roared as it whipped up dry leaves and dead grass and stinging dirt.

"Eriu! Wait for me!" Parlan shouted against the wind.

But she did not respond, and in the instants of darkness between the flashes of lightning and the eerie glow of the Ride he would lose track of her. He could see her walking among the trees, but he would see her first on one side of the plain and then the next rippling flash would show her far on the other—but always she was walking away from him.

He stood up straight and took a deep breath, and then began walking across the plain with long sure strides, trying to be just as calm and unconcerned as Eriu herself was.

The roar of the wind and the banging and rattling of the birch limbs filled the air. Parlan wiped the blowing dirt from his eyes and tried to look for Eriu . . . and realized she was standing right in front of him, facing to the north—facing the violent, boiling storm and the rippling veils of light just above.

She pointed to the clouds. "He is coming," she said, raising her voice against the wind. "He is coming for you."

CHAPTER THIRTEEN

"Who is coming?" Parlan shouted, above the raging storm. "And why? Why now?"

"The Wild Hunt approaches," said Eriu. "They are the guardians of the Sword of Nuadha. They appear whenever there is an evil in the land. The Master of the Hunt is especially drawn to leaders of Men—*failed* leaders—and searches them out that he might gather and keep them for himself."

"And I am the greatest of all failed leaders, for I brought down a curse upon the land," Parlan muttered. "They come for me this midwinter night. So be it! I am ready for them."

He drew his iron sword and held it high, facing both the storm and the shimmering veils of blue and green light high in the black northern sky. "Come for me now, Master of the Hunt! I am ready for you, if you dare to come to me! Come to—"

Eriu pushed his arm down. "You dare not meet the master with force or insult. If you want the Sword of Nuadha, you will have to find another way."

"Another way! But—" He struggled to get his sword back into its wooden scabbard, distracted by the intensifying lights of the Ride. "What other way could there be?"

He turned to Eriu again, but she was gone.

The storm boiled and raged on the northern horizon, just above the wide stand of dark trees. The heavy clouds flashed purple-white as lightning tore through them again and again, and the ground shook with repeated rolls of thunder. The wind roared, lashing the birch trees and setting their bare branches to rattling and screeching against each other.

"Parlan!"

Parlan and Cillian turned, and saw Gavin rushing back with the three hostage princes—Calvagh, Anluan and Uaine. All of them ran with their heads bent low against the blowing dirt, their cloaks whipping about them in the violent wind.

The six men stood close together and could not take their eyes from the brilliant, violent lights flying and shimmering overhead. The waves of color, reaching from the very top of the black night sky to the boiling white clouds of the horizon, flared wildly from violet to blue, from blue to green, and from green to yellow and orange and red. The shimmering veils almost seemed to sing in their brightness and speed.

Then a new and terrifying sound reached the six men: deep howling and barking and baying, like huge and terrible hounds coming straight at them. And to Parlan's horror he saw, silhouetted against the lightning-lit clouds of the storm, a whole pack of hounds flying down from the sky as though they had just made a mighty leap over the stand of trees.

The snarling hounds came to earth and began to run in a vast circle around Parlan and his men, who stood back-to-back in the center of the plain. There were nine hounds in all, five black and four dark grey, all with eyes that gleamed bright red like the shimmering red lights of the Ride of the Sidhe. The beasts snarled and snapped and slavered as they ran, and it was plain to see that all had the skeletal appearance of terribly starved wolves. They were nothing but hide stretched over bone, and some were even missing paws or ears or tails as though they had been through endless brutal fights with one another.

"Death hounds!" cried Gavin. "I've heard the tales of them, but by all the gods who ever walked, I never hoped to see them!"

The death hounds were soon followed by enormous horses, all black or dark grey and just as red-eyed and skeletal as the hounds, leaping down over the wind-beaten trees. There were seventeen in all, and each one carried a tall skeletal rider shouting as he rode, wrapped in long and streaming black cloaks fastened with rusted iron pins.

The riders' hands and evil, grinning faces were all just as black as the night sky, as were their swords and scabbards and saddles and bridles. And as the riders began tearing around the plain after the hounds, Parlan and his men could see that some of the horses were missing hooves or tails or even entire legs. Their riders, too, had lost hands or feet or arms, or had still-gaping wounds showing beneath their heavy black cloaks.

Most terrifying of all was the hideous sound of the bones of the horses and hounds as they ran, a clacking and rattling so loud it could be heard even over the roaring wind and howling dogs and shouting huntsmen, and over the creaking and rattling of the tree limbs.

"This is the Wild Hunt!" cried Gavin, his voice cracking with fear. "They take any man they can find, and he is never seen again!"

"Not quite," said a calm voice behind them.

Parlan turned to see Eriu standing directly behind him in the center of the shoulder-to-shoulder men. "The master has other goals."

"The master?" Parlan looked to the north again as a single last figure on a horse—a figure larger than all the others—leaped over the trees.

"The Master of the Hunt. He is here for you, King Parlan. He has what you seek. Go and meet him now." Eriu stepped back, taking the other five men with her so that Parlan stood alone.

The ground shook as the skeletal, stark white mount of the Master of the Hunt dropped to earth and took off at a thundering gallop around the plain, close behind his death hounds and his huntsmen. Parlan could only stand and stare at the shrieking frenzy as it circled the dark and windblown plain. Driving them on was the master, dressed entirely in shining white leather. His white cloak, held by a gleaming bronze pin, flowed out behind him. Covering his entire head and face was a magnificent white helmet with the bronze antlers of a stag rising up on either side.

At his side was a long red scabbard, with the beautifully wrought and heavy gold hilt of a magnificent sword rising up from it.

Like the other dreadful mounts of the hunt, the master's horse appeared starved and skeletal, and had burning red eyes like glowing coals. It galloped at the head of the terrible riders as the hunt circled, as the thunder roared and the death hounds bayed. Above it all, the rippling veils of the Ride of the Sidhe danced across the sky.

Parlan forced himself to stay still, in spite of the wild and terrifying sights surrounding him. He glanced at Eriu. "What are they hunting? What do they want?"

She stood calmly, and her voice was steady and cool. "In life, the master was a warrior and a king. Through his own arrogance, he failed some test of character and courage—so long ago it was, none know now what. It matters only that he did fail, and so now he rides the earth and searches out other Men—other kings—who have failed their own tests of courage or character."

"Yet he has the Sword of Nuadha! I can see it there, strapped to his side!"

"So he does."

"Why would the gods give such a treasure to a man—to this wraith—who has already failed in life? Would he be any more trustworthy in death?"

"The gods set him as one of the four guardians so that he might right the wrongs he committed in life. The master's wounded pride drives him now, just as he drives his hounds and his huntsmen."

"Who are those huntsmen? Did the gods set them as guardians, too?"

"They did not. The Master of the Hunt gathered them himself, to help him in his guardianship."

Parlan's blood began to feel cold. "He searched them out," Eriu continued. "He is always looking for men—especially chiefs and kings and leaders of all sorts—who have failed their own tests of courage and character, just as he did."

"Just as I did." Parlan tried not to shudder.

"The huntsmen belong to the master forever. Once he knew they were failed men—failed leaders—he rode to find them; and once he did, all it took was one touch from his hand to transform them into those skeletal wraiths, not dead and not alive, that you see before you now."

"Why not just frighten them into being better men? Why take them away forever?" Parlan asked.

"Better to serve the master and the land for all time, than to spend even a short time as a bad king. And so they now serve him."

Parlan glanced at her again. "You said I would have to get the Sword of Nuadha from its guardian. You did not tell me that it would be a supernatural test of life or death—though true death would be far preferable to becoming what they are." He looked again at the black-draped wraiths that galloped their hideous skin-and-bone mounts around and around the plain, screeching and chattering and lashing their steeds with knotted lengths of black leather so that bits of black hide and bone flew up into the wind.

"You must not let the master touch you. If he does, you will become like those wraiths before the sun rises tomorrow."

"And I will no longer be a man who thought he could have a goddess for a queen."

She turned to look at him. "If the hunt takes you, you will no longer be a man at all. As far as the world is concerned, you will be dead."

He paused. "But will my death not break the Curse of the Dragon?"

"It will not. If King Parlan dies, I will have no choice but to return to Teamhair Breagh and create another king—a worthy king who can lift the curse."

He turned to look at her, feeling as though she had struck him; but she merely gave him a cool glance and turned back to watch the hunt. "I told you that you would not love me when this is over."

Just then, the master forced his horse away from the wildly circling hunt and galloped straight toward Parlan. Eriu stepped back, and Parlan found himself standing alone on the plain as the Master of the Hunt approached.

He stared hard at the imposing master for a moment, clenching his fists, and then glanced behind him. His two warriors and three hostage princes had apparently taken to heart Eriu's advice about not meeting the master with violence or insult, for they offered neither; indeed, all five of them had thrown themselves facedown on the ground and were clutching the grass as though afraid they would fall from the very earth itself.

Eriu was nowhere to be seen. Parlan would indeed have to face the Wild Hunt alone.

He turned back to the master in time to see him drag his white, skeletal, red-eared mount to a halt. Though the front of his beautiful, horned white helmet was solid and faceless, Parlan could feel the eyes of the master—no doubt just as red and glowing as the eyes of his horses and hounds—glaring at him.

The huge white horse went still. Parlan stood his ground, fascinated to see that the violets and blues and greens of the fast-moving Ride of the Sidhe were playing across the master's white leather armor and over his horse's white coat.

"Why have you come to this place?" demanded the master. "Why do you interfere with my hunt?"

Parlan bowed low with all the courtesy he could muster. "I am sorry. I had no wish to interfere." He straightened again, and raised his head high. "I have come to ask you to give me your sword."

The master stood very still for a moment. The faceless white helmet turned in Parlan's direction. The white horse stomped one of its great hooves.

"Give you my sword?" The master made a deep and ominous rumbling sound, which Parlan realized was laughter. "Why should I give my beautiful sword to one such as you?"

Parlan cleared his throat. "Because . . . because I have need of it. I must fulfill a quest."

"And why should the Master of the Wild Hunt have a care for your quest, much less give you my treasures? I do not give. I take. Perhaps I will take you and your companions." Slowly, never turning the blank face of his helmet away from Parlan, the master stepped down from his huge horse and stood beside the beast.

Parlan stood as tall as he could make himself, and stayed where he was, though Eriu's warning ran through

111

his mind: All it took was one touch from the master's hand to transform them into the skeletal wraiths, not dead and not alive, that he saw before him.

"My companions are not worthy of you, Master of the Hunt," he said quickly. "I beg you to take only me—if I can prove myself of sufficient worth."

The master took a step forward. Parlan could all but feel the terror and frustration of the five men behind him as they clung facedown to the grass, as Eriu had ordered them to do if they wanted to survive. "I will be the judge of who is worthy and who is not," growled the master. "Those three are princes. They are leaders of Men. Yet what have they done in their lives?"

Parlan swallowed, but he did not move. "They are young. Their lives are before them."

"They are failures already! They are meant to be princes, yet they excel at doing nothing! Since that is what they do, then nothing they shall be!"

To Parlan's horror, the master glided forward on the air, floating toward him and the five men behind him.

"Wait!"

Once again the master stood on solid ground—this time just a few steps away from Parlan. "Ah, I see," the master said. "You wish to trade for them. My sword for your three hostage-princes. Very well, then. I will take them, and then I will tell you whether I agree to give you the sword or no."

A bead of cold sweat ran down Parlan's neck. "Master of the Hunt! I have a better offer for you than just those three young men."

CHAPTER FOURTEEN

"What is your offer to me, King Parlan?" asked the Master of the Hunt.

Parlan forced himself to stand still even as the white-armored wraith moved ever closer. "I am not just a king," Parlan answered. "I am a high king. And I am a high king who did not merely fail his people, but brought a curse down upon them—the Curse of the Dragon."

"So you have. I was drawn to you for that reason. You are a failed leader of Men. That is why I am here—to take you for myself." The master reached out with one arm and began to move forward.

Parlan took one step back. "But if you give me your sword, Master of the Hunt, you will have an even greater prize for yourself!"

Again the master paused. "What greater prize could I have than a high king who brings a curse upon his own people?"

"Just this," Parlan said. "A king who gains first the Sword of Nuadha, which you protect, and then the other three treasures from their guardians, and so must therefore face the Black Dragon.

"Think of it! What hope do I have of defeating such a beast, even if I should gain all four of the artifacts? I would become known as Eire's greatest failure! What a prize I would be for you then, O Master of the Hunt! How much better a guardian would I make for you then, instead of just one more shallow man led astray by some woman's backside, or thrown out of his tribe for thieving!

"Why, perhaps I would even become Master of the Hunt myself, as you once did, and ride at the head of them all! I'd take your place and release you from this duty. Just give me the sword, and think of the prize you will have next Samhain Eve!"

The master took another step forward. He was nearly within arm's reach. Parlan held his ground . . . and then the master threw back his faceless bronze-horned head and laughed his terrible laugh once again.

"Oh-ho! I will take your wager, King Parlan! I will return for you next Samhain Eve, that you might join my hunt as the greatest failure of all the kings of Men!"

The white-armored wraith moved to within a breath of Parlan, and then walked on past to his hideously beautiful white horse. He swung up into the white saddle as the horse arched its bony neck. Its red eyes glowed fiercely.

"Farewell to you, King Parlan! I shall look forward to our next meeting!" And the Master pulled the red-jeweled scabbard from his belt and sent it flying end-over-end into the air, just as his horse galloped away after the shrieking huntsmen and their death hounds.

Parlan stepped forward and caught the beautiful scabbard out of the air. He held it out before him in both hands, gazing at the heavy, smooth, lustrous red fabric that covered it—a fabric he had never seen before—and at the sharply cut red jewels set along its length, which sparkled like deep red stars.

He held tight to the scabbard and involuntarily stepped back a pace as the shrieking of the huntsmen and the howling of the death hounds grew even louder, as the hunt followed its master around the plain one last time. Parlan fell back, and the five others continued to cling to the ground as the entire hunt leaped up high off the plain as though leaping over the great stand of trees again, and then arced down far on the other side, just small black figures leaping off into the fading storm.

The hunt was gone.

The last of the lightning flickered and faded in the receding clouds. The Ride of the Sidhe slowed and calmed to gently rippling veils of soft color, with stars shining through from behind them.

Parlan glanced back at the men on the ground. Slowly they raised their heads. "Are . . . are they gone?" asked Gavin, his voice trembling.

"Gone," Parlan answered. "But not entirely."

All of them froze and started to duck down again. "Where? Where are they?" demanded Cillian, plainly shaken by the hunt and furious at himself for having such a feeling.

"As I said, they are gone," Parlan said, walking toward them. "You are safe. All that remains of them is this."

He stopped before them as the five men got slowly to their feet, and he held out his prize to them. "The master left this with me." This time he placed his hand on the beautiful bronze hilt curving down on either side of the scabbard like stag's horns, and drew the shining sword. The lights of the Ride danced along the gleaming bronze blade. As Parlan pulled it all the way out and freed the tip from the scabbard, the sword seemed to drop neatly into his hand of its own accord. It rose straight up to the sky, the heavy blade so perfectly balanced that it seemed light as a bird's wing in his hand.

"The Sword of Nuadha," he said, turning it over and staring at the beautiful lights of the Ride of the Sidhe reflected into his eyes from the gleaming, perfect bronze.

"So . . . you did get it? You have achieved the first part of your quest?" Gavin came close just as Parlan slid the sword back into the red-jeweled scabbard.

"I did," answered Parlan, and grinned at him. "The first—and, I can only hope—the most difficult of all four parts."

"I do not know how any of the other three could be more dangerous than this one," muttered Anluan, trying without success to brush the mud and grass and dead leaves from his fine plaid cloak.

"Or more frightening," added Uaine, doing the same.

"And I do not see how our presence here did anything but cause our own humiliation." Calvagh stood and glared at Parlan. "Is this how you intend to treat your hostages to peace?"

"It is not," Parlan answered, holding the sword's jeweled scabbard close against his chest. "I had you brought to me because Eriu instructed me to do so, and now I see why. The master was attracted to the three of you almost as much as he was to me alone. Eriu wanted to be sure he would find me—and find me he did."

"Bait!" spat Calvagh. But Parlan ignored him, and bowed to each one of them in turn. "You have served me well. I thank you."

All three remained silent and scowling. Finally Uaine spoke. "We will return to our camp now, if we may."

"Of course," Parlan said, and turned his back on the three. "Cillian. Gavin. Go with them. I will be there soon."

The two men looked sideways at him, and then glanced up at the skies and out across the plain. "It is safe here. Safe from any harm," he said, knowing they would welcome the security of the camp after the terrifying ordeal of the Wild Hunt—and also knowing that they would never admit their fear.

The three princes of Dun Ghee were already trudging across the plain toward the glowing fires of the camp. "Go with them, please," Parlan said again to Cillian and Gavin. "I will be along—"

"After she comes to you," muttered Cillian.

"*If* she comes to you," added Gavin.

"Go!" snapped Parlan, and he turned his back to walk across the windy plain.

He did not get far before a familiar voice spoke from behind one of the silvery and skeletal birch trees. "So, you have succeeded after all, King Parlan."

He turned to see Eriu standing beside the birch with the last of the white, blue and violet lights playing over her shining hair and her cloak, and turning the silver bark of the birch tree to pale green and gold.

"It seems that I have, Lady Eriu." He could not help but stand taller as he spoke, and he held out the beautiful sword in its scabbard. "I did indeed get the Sword of Nuadha from the Master of the Hunt."

"So you did," she said, stepping toward him. "You have achieved the first part of your quest. But there are still three to go."

He lowered the sword and looked away. "I know that, my lady. But are you not pleased that I was able to get the sword? I did this only by persuasion. Not one man was injured or killed."

"You did well, Parlan," she said.

"Then will you take the sword?"

"I will not. What need have I with any sword? I could never wield it. You have gained it, and you shall be the one to use it when the time comes. Strap it to your side and guard it well."

"I will," he said, and unfastened his leather belt to slide it through the scabbard. "Yet . . . I supposed . . ."

"You supposed what?"

"That you might be pleased," he finished, strapping the scabbard around his waist.

"Oh, I am pleased enough. Pleased that you were indeed able to do what most men could not. More than that, though, I am surprised."

"Surprised?" Parlan finished tying off his belt, and slowly stood straight to face her. "You are surprised that I could face the Master of the Hunt and—"

"I am not surprised by that. I am surprised that you still wish to have me at your side, after I left you to face a terrible test alone—a test that you did not fully understand when you entered into it."

Parlan smiled, and he took a step toward her. "I told you, Lady Eriu, that I was not like other men. There is no test I would not undertake to prove I am worthy to have you at my side."

Eriu returned his smile, but the look in her eyes remained cool and distant. "We shall see, Parlan. Never forget that the Master of the Hunt is still out there, a guardian of the land and a servant of the remaining gods, gathering to himself all those who would dare to lead without being worthy." She stepped back into the shadows behind the birch tree, and was gone.

Parlan slept only a short time that night. He lay watching the northern sky even as the first faint grey began to show in the east, as the last of the storm clouds vanished beneath the northern horizon and the Ride of the Sidhe faded away into the soft light of dawn.

It was just another day. Another normal and ordinary day—but Parlan's hand dropped to the beautiful red-jeweled scabbard at his side, and he smiled with great satisfaction.

For him, no day would ever be ordinary again.

Later that morning, Parlan rode at the head of his men

and servants at a comfortable canter across the wide, windy plains and scattered hilltops of the southeastern lands. Never had he felt stronger, or more at ease, or more confident. He had faced the terrifying challenge of the Wild Hunt and won the sword from the master, and he felt fully ready to take on the remaining three challenges.

And he had no further doubt that Eriu would come to him again. She had told him—admitted to him—that she was pleased and impressed by what he had accomplished.

The horses cantered on into the new day. All the while he thought, she will be back. She will be back.

Parlan and his men made their leisurely journey through the southernmost regions of Eire, here and there making an overnight camp among the many shepherds and their vast herds of half-wild, long-legged, dark-brown sheep.

Much to the delight of his men, after a fortnight of traveling, Parlan ordered that a semipermanent camp be made on a wide curving plain near the foot of a mountain where it swept down into a shining, tranquil lake. The plain was mostly open, but scattered with oak trees providing shade and shelter for horses and men, and though some of the grass was long and dry, Parlan knew it would not be long before the first new blades of spring began to show through.

The servants dug pits for roasting meat and boiling water. They cut branches and saplings to make wooden frames, and threw cowhides and sheepskins over them to create warm shelters. The horses were hobbled and left to graze on the grass and drink from the clear waters of the lake.

Here they would all rest and hunt and fish until it was time to meet the next challenge. Here Parlan would wait for Eriu to come to him again, and he had no doubt she would.

* * *

A fortnight went by. And another. The men enjoyed their leisurely days of hunting and fishing, but Parlan did not go with them. There was no sign of Eriu.

One morning, Parlan stood beneath the oaks alongside the lake watching the sunrise. Cillian and Gavin and a handful of other men came to him with their horses saddled and ready to go. Behind them, the servants pulled down the cowhide shelters and packed the bronze cauldrons and the iron utensils and the extra cloaks and tunics securely onto the backs of the patient ponies.

"It is time, my king," Cillian said. "We have been here for over forty nights. It is time to leave this place and travel to Dun Farriaghe. Your next three hostages await you."

Parlan turned to them. "First you complain that we travel too slowly and camp too little, and now you complain that we camp too long. Which is it?"

"It is neither, my king," Cillian answered. "But it is almost spring. The king of Dun Farriaghe expects you."

"You cannot make her come to you," ventured Gavin. "She is a goddess. She will choose the time and place—"

"Go, then!" Parlan snarled, pushing past the men. "Get on your horses and we will go now! I'll be waiting for you!" And in moments, the camp was abandoned and the hundred warriors and their king had set out toward the west, to travel across the southern end of the country.

III

THE SOUTH

CHAPTER FIFTEEN

On the evening of the third day, Parlan walked a short distance from the temporary campsite and looked out across the landscape. He watched the sun set and the full moon rise, and he searched as he never ceased to do for the sight of a tall and beautiful dark-haired woman and, perhaps, her young grey mare.

He caught his breath at the sight of a lone horse galloping in silhouette across the light of the setting sun, with a tall woman astride its back.

Instantly, Parlan turned and raced back to the camp. He grabbed Maorga's bridle from where it hung on a tree branch and quickly caught the stallion, unhobbled him, swung up on his back and took off after the woman on the mare.

He found her trotting alongside a wide and winding stream that ran beneath the shadows of bare apple trees. She slowed her mount to a walk as Parlan galloped alongside and quickly dragged his stallion to a halt.

"A good night to you, Lady Eriu," he said, gasping for

breath. He felt as though he himself had been running for days.

She barely glanced at him, and went on walking as though merely passing the time with a ride through the countryside.

"A lovely evening for Imbolc, the first night of spring," she said at last. "The moon rises, small and white and full, and the new grass begins to show, and the apple trees display their first buds. It is perhaps my favorite time of year."

"Mine, too," he said quickly, unable to take his eyes from her. She sat tall and straight on the beautiful grey mare, with her dark green cloak flowing out behind her and its heavy golden brooch gleaming in the twilight.

"I am so pleased to see you, my lady," he went on, reining his stallion away from her mare. "I have missed you greatly."

She glanced at him again. "I told you I would return when it was necessary."

He tensed, watching her closely. "Has the time come for the next challenge? I fear I am not prepared. I do not even have my saddle—"

She smiled, looking straight ahead. "Do not worry, Parlan. There is no challenge today. I only wish to show you something—and, perhaps, to make you an offer."

"An offer?"

"Come with me. I have something to show you."

She cantered the mare away, but Parlan kept Maorga right alongside. They followed the winding stream beside the newly budding apple trees, until the moon rose just above the branches. Eriu halted her mare and pointed into the shadows.

"There. Do you see it?"

Parlan peered into the darkness and saw a grove of widely scattered apple trees ahead—and within the grove, lit by the soft glow of firelight, was a high circular earthen wall with the tops of a couple of thatched roofs showing just above it.

"It looks like the home of a farm family—those who tend these apple trees and the beehives that serve them. There are many such in Eire."

"There are. But come closer. Ride up to the wall, and look over."

Parlan frowned. "I do not wish to startle them. Or intrude upon—"

"You will not. They will not see you. Go, and look."

With Eriu close beside him on her mare, he walked his stallion close to the earthen wall. Inside he saw a small, round, wattle-and-daub home, its sides smooth with pale new clay over the framework of woven branches, and a couple of rectangular sheds for their milk cow and their few head of shaggy brown ewes and newly born lambs.

"Look through the doorway." To Parlan's surprise, a soft gust of cold wind came up, caught the piece of cowhide hanging in the doorway and flipped it up against the front of the house. Within the curving walls of the little round house he could see the central hearth built into the floor with its flickering fire providing light and heat. An older woman stirred a cauldron hanging over the fire, and then ladled some of its contents into a wooden bowl held by a girl of perhaps twelve or thirteen.

The girl took the bowl over to a woman lying on a pallet of fresh clean straw with warm sheepskins tucked in around her. On another pallet near the woman's feet, a handsome man with red-gold hair lay back on another bed of straw, holding a small bundle against his chest—a bundle that could only be a sleeping newborn.

"A sweet picture they make," Eriu said. "The new mother rests and accepts a bit of food from her older daughter, while the new daughter sleeps on the father's chest."

"Quite peaceful, indeed," Parlan said politely, "and

quite common at this time of the year. So tell me, Lady Eriu: Why have you brought me here to see this?"

She turned her mare away. A second gust of wind blew the cowhide back down over the doorway of the house, and Parlan followed Eriu as she rode back along the apple trees beside the stream, the water shining here and there in the cloudy moonlight.

At last she stopped the mare and slid down to her feet on the grass, slipping the soft black bridle from the mare's head that she might graze and drink from the stream. Parlan did the same with Maorga, and then he turned to face Eriu as she stood beneath the bare twisted apple trees in the moonlight.

"Let me ask you a question, Parlan," she began. "Do you know the three stages of a woman's life?"

"I do," he answered. "I was well taught in all things by the druids. The three stages of a woman's life are maiden, mother, and crone. The maiden is the young woman, before she knows a man; the mother has children to care for, whether they are hers or those of someone else; and the crone is past childbearing but is respected for her knowledge and wisdom." He smiled at her. "Did I answer correctly?"

"You did. And yet there is one more stage."

"There is? You asked for the three, and I gave you—"

"You did, King Parlan. But there is, indeed, one other—one which everyone forgets and which is nearly always overlooked." She reached up and ran her fingers along the gnarled branch of an apple tree, over the tiny delicate buds. "The fourth stage is the one which you were privileged to see tonight. It is the newborn, the infant, the early springtime of every woman's life. Beginnings are very important, and must be given every chance to succeed."

She turned to look at him, her hand still resting on the branch of the tree. "Perhaps I will give you a chance to succeed as well."

Parlan looked up at her, holding himself very still, feeling a great surge of warmth within his chest in spite of the cold damp winds of the first day of spring. "I thought I had succeeded, my lady," he said quietly. "I did gain the sword from the Master of the Hunt."

"You did succeed there. And I am not ashamed to tell you that I did not believe you would."

He watched her carefully as she stood beneath the apple branch. "If you thought I had no chance, then why did you encourage me to go? Why did you bring the huntsmen to me?"

"Because you deserved at least one chance to succeed—or fail—on your own. You had brought a dreadful curse down onto your own lands. It was for you to lift it if you could. I could only do what I am able—and what I promised I would do. I would show you where to find the Sword of Nuadha and let you succeed or fail from there."

"And I succeeded," he whispered, "where you believed I could not."

"Where I once believed no man could."

This time he closed the distance between them, and reached down to take one of her hands in his. "And I will say to you again: I am not like any other man." He leaned forward, slowly, gently, his eyes half-closing as his lips approached hers, breathing in the sweet scent of her skin, almost tasting her now, just as he had done on the night of his kingmaking—

She withdrew her hand and lifted the top of her cloak up over her head to hide her face, and stepped away as though Parlan was not there. She walked over to the stream and stood in the moonlight not far from where her mare grazed on the silvery grass.

"I came to you this night because I have decided to make a new beginning with you. You have done what I thought no man could. Perhaps it is time for me to be of more help to you."

He studied her for a moment, unable to believe what he was hearing. "My lady Eriu—why should you want to be of more help to me? I rejected you, though I did not mean to, and in so doing I brought down the worst sort of curse on the land itself—upon you, the goddess of that land. Why should you do any more than you promised, which was simply to show me where the four sacred objects could be found?"

She smiled, though she continued to gaze out across the swiftly flowing stream. "Because any man can succeed when all things go his way. If you are willing to persevere when things are difficult—even hopeless—then I can do no less. I told you that the curse was yours to lift, and you have done more than I ever expected."

She turned to gaze straight at him. "From this day on, I will ride with you throughout your journey and help you where I can. There is nothing I want more than a king who can lift this curse from me and the land. If that king is truly you, then so be it."

He stepped forward, starting to reach out for her even from the first step. "I knew you would come to me. I knew we would be together, now and always—"

But she faced him head-on and raised both hands. He stopped in his tracks. "Do not misunderstand me, King Parlan. I did not believe you would ever succeed against the Master of the Hunt. I intended to give you your one chance and then, when you failed, I would retreat to my place in the Otherworld, believing the time of Men to be over and their fate beyond the hands of the remaining gods."

"But did you not say it is lonely for you in the Otherworld, beautiful as it is?"

"The Otherworld is now a lonely place, I will agree. But more importantly, I have seen—for you have shown me— that perhaps the time of Men is not over yet."

"Not as long as I have breath and strength," Parlan

whispered. "And even if I did not have those things, I would find another way."

Eriu turned away again and looked toward the place where Solasta and Maorga grazed. Parlan thought he heard the soft call of the skylark, though no such bird would be out and singing in the dark of night. The mare soon came trotting across the stream to Eriu with Maorga following closely, and in a moment, Eriu had slipped the soft black bridle back onto the beautiful head and swung up lightly into the sheepskin-lined saddle.

"I will ride with you during the day, though you will not see me at night. Do not misunderstand, King Parlan— I do not come to you out of love. I come to you because I believe you might truly have a chance to lift this curse, and I wish it to be lifted, too."

She turned Solasta toward the moon, and the mare leaped over the shining stream and galloped away into the night. Parlan rested his hand on Maorga's neck. The stallion lowered its head and nickered softly.

Riding out the next morning, sitting straight and tall on Maorga as the stallion danced beneath him, and with the red-jeweled scabbard bearing the Sword of Nuadha strapped to his left hip, Parlan had never felt stronger or more confident. "It is strange," he said to Cillian, who rode alongside him, "but I won the challenge not with strength or arrogance, but with the utmost in humility—by presenting myself as the poorest of men and not the best."

"And this makes you proud?"

"It does!" Parlan threw back his head and laughed. "I no longer fear the remaining three parts of the quest."

"You mean the remaining four parts. You will still have to face the Black Dragon again, if—*once* you get the other three artifacts."

Parlan laughed again. "Today I could face the Black Dragon alone, and his father and all his brothers, too!"

But Cillian remained serious. "From this day on, the challenges to come can only be more difficult," he warned.

"Make them as difficult as you like! I am ready for them! I have the Sword of Nuadha, and I have the utmost in humility, and I have—I have—" Parlan stared straight ahead. "I have her," he whispered. "I have her!" And he sent Maorga galloping eagerly ahead to meet the tall and beautiful woman cantering toward them on her graceful grey mare.

From that day on, as she had promised, Eriu rode at Parlan's side as long as the sun was in the sky but was nowhere to be found once it set. The party rode steadily for several days, fording a wide river into the southwestern lands and then making a semipermanent camp as before so that the men could hunt and fish and make sport and rest. Eriu disappeared during these days, too, but Parlan was not so distressed by her absence as before. He was sure she would reappear once they were on the move again, and so she did, riding up to him each morning and vanishing into the shadows as soon as the sun was gone.

Though he longed to take her in his arms as he had done on their first meeting, and his body ached for her each night as he lay alone beneath the furs, he fiercely reminded himself that she—a goddess—was here for him each day and had pledged to help him any way that she could during the ordeals to come.

He had succeeded in bringing her to his side for the days. Soon he would begin working on bringing her to him at night, as well.

Humility had brought him Nuadha's sword. It would bring him his goddess, too. It was only a matter of time. He was certain of it.

CHAPTER SIXTEEN

At last, after another twenty-five nights of riding and camping, Parlan and Eriu and the hundred warriors arrived at the southern end of a large and beautiful lake that ran along the foothills of Eire's southern mountains. They stopped late in the afternoon to make their temporary camp in a wide field overlooking the lake. As the servants built fires and dug pits for roasting and boiling meat, the men hobbled their horses, left them to graze and then started down the rocky, boulder-strewn hillside that led to the flat, grassy, rock-strewn fields at the level of the water.

Eriu walked to the top of one of the great granite-and-limestone boulders and sat down on it, gazing out at the lake far below as the sun approached the horizon. Soft grey clouds rolled lazily across the sky, pushed by a cold spring wind from the west.

Parlan came striding up with his seven-color cloak blowing wide behind him, and sat down beside Eriu on the rock. "A beautiful view," he said. "In just two nights time, we will arrive at Dun Farriaghe and I can collect my next three hostages to peace. I will be that much closer to the next challenge, and I would give much if you would tell me when—and where—that might be."

She seemed not to have heard him. She turned away, facing the western wind so that it lifted her dark brown hair away from her shoulders. "There is something strange on the wind this day. I can smell it. I can taste it. It is coming this way," she said.

Parlan looked to the west, and shrugged. "I can tell nothing out of the ordinary. To me it is just the western wind, cold in early spring and damp with the promise of rain." He turned back to her. "What is it that's coming? Is it the next of the challenges, the next of the objects that I must win?"

Eriu shook her head, still looking to the west. "It is not. That will come only after you gain your next three hostage-princes. This is something far different."

She turned back to him. "Keep watch, Parlan. Keep torches lit. I can only tell you that there is something on the wind this day."

"I will not leave your side," he answered, and with a wave of his hand summoned a servant. "Light torches. Post guards around the circle of the camp. Keep watch."

"Torches now, my king? The sun is still high. Should we wait until—"

"Light them now! Post the guards, too! If you wait, it could be too late!"

The frightened servant hurried away. Parlan leapt down from the boulder and stood at Eriu's feet. "I will bring a torch, and I will stay in this spot until whatever it is that approaches shows itself." He looked up at her. "Will you stay beyond the sunset this night, Lady Eriu? I promise you, I will do no more than wait here beside you and—perhaps—ask you for your counsel."

At last she turned back to him. "I will stay, King Parlan," she said. "But I do not know what counsel I can offer."

* * *

With agonizing slowness, the daylight faded. The sun was swallowed up first by the soft grey clouds, and then by the horizon. As he had promised, Parlan stood beside Eriu high up on the boulder overlooking the lake, holding a torch in one hand while the other one rested on the gleaming bronze hilt of the Sword of Nuadha. Parlan glanced all around him in the heavy twilight, but saw only the torches and fires of his own campsite and the faint gleam of the distant lake tucked away within the grey-white rocks and dark stands of trees.

Suddenly Eriu stood up on her rock and turned to face the west. "It is coming," she said, and took a step back, her deep green cloak brushing Parlan's side. "It is here."

A heavy burst of wind struck them from the west—and then another, and another. Eriu leapt down from the boulder and stood with her back pressed against it, looking out over the lake. Parlan followed her gaze . . . and then he saw it.

Almost beyond the lake, riding the thick grey clouds from the distant sea and beating the cold air in bursts with its terrible wings, was the Black Dragon. It made a ragged screeching sound as it circled once above the lake and then swept down toward one of the rocky hills.

Parlan gripped his sword's hilt until his fingers hurt, but he could do nothing more than stare in fascination at the beast. He saw instantly that it was not, now, as powerful as it had been on the night of his kingmaking. It landed heavily on the rocks, its head and wings dropping as it hit, and sat for several moments as though exhausted.

Parlan took a sideways step toward Eriu and held the torch out away from her. "What's wrong with it? Why does it look so weak?"

"You injured it badly," Eriu said, still hiding within the shadow of the boulder. She never took her eyes from the dragon. "Any other creature would have died. This one is just now beginning to recover."

In the last light of day, Parlan could see that many of the thick black scales covering the dragon's sides and belly and wings were dried and cracked and even missing. Its entire body looked thin and drawn. "It is only now able to fly again. It has been unable to feed, and so has spent its time in the high mountains of the southwest, thin and weak and hungry. Now, at last, it has come down for the first time since being so badly injured."

"Then, now is the time for me to strike! Now is when I should try to destroy it, when it is weak and off its guard! I will get my men and we will strike immediately!"

He started to turn back toward the camp, but Eriu stopped him with a surprisingly strong hand. "You cannot. Do you not remember what I told you on Samhain last, when the beast first appeared?"

"But if it is not destroyed, there will be nothing left to save. The Time of Men will be over. It will never be weaker than it is now. We must go now, for we may not get another chance like this one."

She shook her head. "Perhaps the cruelest part of this curse is that you can never get close enough to the dragon to engage it in battle at all. It will not attack you again, much as you wish it would. You will not be able to get near it at all unless, or until, you can lure it to you by having all four of the sacred objects in your possession at the dark of the moon following Samhain next." Eriu released his arm. "Put back your sword. Come with me to the top of this rock. There is something you must be made to understand."

He walked beside her to the top of the grey-white boulder, where she pointed to the dragon. "Look at this beast. What do you see?"

Parlan shook his head. "I see a monster—a terrible creature that must be destroyed before it destroys the Land."

"A monster, indeed. But is that all you see?"

134

He drew a deep breath. "You told me that the gods were the ones who set the dragon in place, as a safeguard against an unworthy king."

"And as a way of guaranteeing that a worthy king would be found—one with the strength and cleverness and courage to gain the sacred weapons and wield them against the dragon." She shook her head. "The gods wished Men to know that no Man rules with impunity—that there would always be justice, even for a king. And there it flies: a king's justice."

They watched as the Black Dragon spread its burned, scarred wings, jumped off the distant hilltop and laboriously beat its way into the air. For a few heart-stopping moments it started to come toward the campsite, but wheeled away as soon as it saw the glare of the torches. It returned to the hilltop where it had just rested, and made a turn to the west; and then the newly fallen night was made bright with a violent, brilliant spray of frost from the mouth of the cruel Black Dragon. Then the beast dove down, following the same path as the spray of frost, and was lost to sight behind the rocks and hills.

"I can only wonder what sort of damage the monster is doing to the lands and the cattle of Dun Farriaghe," Parlan said. "And I can only hope that those are animals it is killing and eating, and not—and not the people who live on this land. The king of Dun Farriaghe would never give hostages to me, were that to happen."

"That will be for the high king to manage," said Eriu. "And you will find a way if it does." Holding her cloak close about her as though she were cold, she turned away and looked out into the night, where the Black Dragon once again climbed up into the sky and dove back down. Its torrent of killing frost was a bright white slash in the darkness.

CHAPTER SEVENTEEN

Two nights later, Parlan sat with Cillian and the three hostage-princes within the long, rectangular king's hall of Dun Farriaghe, listening to the sounds of crashing waves echoing from the rocky cliffs that fell away from the curving stone walls of the great seaside fortress—and to precious little else, crowded though the hall was.

King Morrissey had gathered his warriors and their wives to the boards set on the clean dry rushes on the floor of his hall. His servants moved around with generous offerings of boiled eel and oysters, and with wooden plates piled high with flatbread and fresh butter.

A poet sat in a corner with a harp in his lap, playing and singing gentle songs of welcome. The fresh sea breeze found its way in through the heavy thatching of the roof. But the atmosphere inside the king's hall was anything but friendly.

At the head of the long row of boards, King Morrissey bent low over his golden plate as his wife sat silently beside him. He ate steadily of the oysters and bread, and peered out at Parlan from time to time from beneath his thick grey brows, scowling fiercely but saying nothing. His two nephews and his youngest son—Tadhg, Daithi and Bearach—sat along the sides of the boards and kept their attention firmly on their own plates. They hardly glanced at Parlan or Cillian or at the three young noblemen from Dun Ghee who already wore iron collars around their necks.

Finally the meal was over. Servants took away the golden plates and brought out more skins of good blackberry wine with which to fill the golden goblets. King Morrissey sat back at last and stared hard at Parlan.

"There is a dragon attacking my lands," he said. "A hideous Black Dragon, the likes of which has not been seen by any man for a hundred generations. Perhaps you have seen something of what it has done to the fields and to the beasts and to my people."

"I have not," Parlan said quietly. "I saw the creature make its first attack two nights ago—the first attack since it was drawn to me on the night of my kingmaking."

"We heard," growled King Morrissey. "We heard that there is now a curse upon this land because the high king rejected the goddess—and that this curse has manifested itself in the form of the Black Dragon." He took a long drink of blackberry wine and glared at Parlan, waiting for an answer.

Parlan met his cold glare and gave a single nod. "You are right. I was foolish. I was arrogant—for a moment. And now I spend every moment I have making right my poor decision and working to lift the curse."

"My lands were ravaged these last two nights," King Morrissey said. "On the first night, the beast unleashed its foul breath on wild pigs and deer and ate them the way a boy would eat a handful of snowflakes. On the second night—when twenty of my strongest men went out to drive the beast away—it destroyed half their number and swallowed them whole."

Parlan closed his eyes.

Across the boards, Tadhg raised his head. "We cannot help but wonder what sort of high king would be so arrogant—and so selfish—as to take he wants when it means that other men suffer."

Parlan stood up. Staring Tadhg hard in the eyes, he pulled the Sword of Nuadha from its scabbard and held it out over the boards. The huge bronze blade gleamed in the torchlight.

The three princes of Dun Farriaghe jumped to their feet and fumbled for their own swords, but Parlan never moved. "No need for your own weapons," he said. "I mean only to show you this beautiful blade, which none could have made but the gods."

Daithi glanced at the shining sword. "We see only that you are a man of arrogance and violence, King Parlan. Not only do you bring a monster to kill our men and ruin our lands, you draw your sword in our king's own hall."

Parlan raised his chin. "I did not defeat the Master of the Hunt with arrogance—or with violence. I met him only with the utmost humility, and that is how he was persuaded to give me his sword."

"Perhaps you did get the sword that way," said Bearach. "Though a man who brags about his humility is hardly humble."

A rumble of laughter made its way around the boards. Parlan glanced to the side and saw that all of the men and women were indeed laughing at Bearach's joke, but also hanging on his every word.

He turned back to the men across from him. All three were slowly sitting down, their weapons back at their sides. Parlan replaced the Sword of Nuadha in its scabbard and sat down again on his leather cushion.

King Morrissey leaned toward him. "I am also told that you are a man who believes he deserves a goddess as a consort." The old king shook his head. "Until you can prove to us that you are not merely filled with arrogance and recklessness, with no care for the consequences of what you do—until you can show us that you are a civilized man and a king who respects the laws the rest of us must live by—neither my son nor my two nephews will take one step out of Dun Farriaghe with you."

King Morrissey got to his feet, and the rest of his men and their ladies did the same. They all began to make their way outside through the large wide door at the center of the long side of the hall, and in a few moments Parlan stood alone with his own four men in the enormous hall—alone with his men and with the servants.

And with the harper.

Parlan hurried over to the poet in the corner. "Please," he said, reaching out and taking the beautiful harp from him. "I must have this. I promise you, I will return it."

Staring up at him, wide-eyed, the poet released his tight grip on the delicately carved willow frame. "Her name is Amhranai," he whispered.

"*Amhranai.* I thank you. Right now I have great need of Amhranai." And with that he hurried outside into the darkness, after King Morrissey and his departing guests.

Cillian ran after him. "If these hostages will not go, we will have to take them by force," he warned in a low voice. "You cannot let any man refuse to give the high king the hostages he is owed! I will go and get the men—"

Parlan caught him by the arm. "You will do no such thing!" he whispered fiercely. "This king and his three princes already believe I am a wild and uncivilized man. I must try another way."

He released Cillian and walked a short way out to the center of the great stone-ringed fortress that was Dun Farriaghe. The scattered torches cast spots of glare on the worn grass and round houses, but a quick glance above the curving walls showed Parlan the vast darkness of the sea on one side and the rocky hill with its crown of willow trees overlooking the fortress on the other.

He thought he saw the figure of a tall cloaked woman standing up there beneath a lone willow, and for an instant he caught the reflected gleam of a beautiful golden brooch.

The sky itself was heavy and black, for the waning half-moon had not yet risen; but Parlan could feel the damp and heavy clouds rolling slowly through the air above them. The people were making their way over the grounds and scattering in all directions as they headed back to their homes.

Parlan cradled the harp in his left arm, and with his right hand began to play. He no longer had the fine long fingernails he had had as a youth, when the druids first taught him to play the harp; the endless sparring and hunting demanded of a man of the warrior class had seen to that. But he found that there was enough left of his nails to coax a few singing notes from the bronze strings, and then a few more, and then Parlan began to play a lively tune that he remembered from his boyhood.

The people stopped. They turned to look at Parlan. A few of them began to smile.

Parlan's fingers danced merrily over the strings, playing the light and simple melody over and over, sometimes faster, sometimes slower. Sometimes he would rap out the song with his knuckles on the willow frame, and sometimes he punctuated the song with deep vibrating notes that sounded like rude noises.

Now nearly all of the people had gathered round and were clapping and laughing at the music played. Even King Morrissey, standing with his smiling queen, seemed pleased. And it seemed to Parlan that the tall cloaked woman who watched from the hill raised her head and smiled at the laughter and celebration rising to her on the notes of the harp.

As he played, he became aware of the lively freshness in the cool sea breeze, and of the sweet smell of the damp grass underfoot as the people danced, and of the bright gleam of the stars up above as the clouds flew apart and revealed the dark sky. Far in the distance, a little lightning danced harmlessly at the edges of the clouds. Even the trees seemed to raise their branches in a merry dance as the fresh wind caught them.

Parlan paused for a moment, letting the quick ringing sounds of his playful notes trail away, then placed his hand against the bronze strings to silence them. Then he lifted his hand, drew a deep breath, and began to play a different kind of song.

Now his fingers plucked more slowly at the strings, and moved to the shorter strings with their higher, more plaintive sound. The music became slow and keening, sounding for all the world like a heartbroken woman's lament for her child or lover.

The people slowed their dancing and stopped their clapping, and they stood very still as the high quavering notes moved through the great fortress. High up on the hill, the woman in the cloak bowed her head and did not move as drops of water fell down on her from the slender leaves of the white willow tree.

The wind from the sea became quiet and heavy and wet, and as clouds moved in to cover the sky, a few large drops of rain fell to the grass like tears. The tree branches drooped in the still, thick air, and here and there dripped water to the earth. Everyone stood with eyes closed and faces somber, sometimes leaning their heads together or even holding one another as their own sad and tragic memories, awakened by the music, ran through their minds.

Finally Parlan paused, and allowed a short silence to settle over the fortress grounds. Then he began to play a soft and soothing melody, as gentle and sweet as a mother singing to calm her children into sleep. After the liveliness of the laughing music and the poignancy of the weeping music, Parlan would now give them sleeping music to soothe their feelings and allow them a peaceful rest.

In twos and threes the people moved slowly to their homes, quietly and calmly, where they would find welcome sleep. The woman in the cloak left her place beneath the willow and walked slowly down the winding path toward the gates.

The wind became soft and gentle, and the trees moved calmly in its grasp. A few clouds drifted overhead, and here and there a star shone through. To the east, just above the willow tree on the hill, the half-moon hung in the sky like a faithful watchman looking down on the fortress.

As the last of Amhranai's soft notes faded away and the people closed the doors of their houses, King Morrissey and his son and his two nephews walked over to Parlan. "A lovely performance, King Parlan, I will admit," he said. "Worthy of a civilized man. If you do intend to destroy this dragon and lift the curse that lies upon this land, then I can see no reason why these three princes of Dun Farriaghe should not go with you."

"I *will* lift the curse," Parlan said, cradling the harp in one arm. "Of that, you need have no doubt." He turned to Bearach, King Morrissey's own son, and held out the harp to him. "Please return Amhranai to your poet for me, and give him my gratitude again."

Bearach met Parlan's gaze, and his face remained serious. Finally he took the harp without a word and walked off toward the hall. King Morrissey watched him go, then shifted his gaze back to Parlan.

"All three will be waiting at the gates for you at sunrise. Good night to you, now."

"Good night to you, King Morrissey," Parlan said. And when all of them were gone, he walked across the quiet torchlit yard to the fortress gates.

Chapter Eighteen

She stood in the shadow of the hill, just beyond the fortress gates, with the faint silvery light of the moon outlining the hood of her dark green cloak.

"I am glad to see you, Lady Eriu," Parlan said. "I am always lonely when I am without you, no matter who else might be present."

She took a step toward him. "Your music was beautiful. I have never heard any man play so lovingly."

He smiled. "As I said, I was taught very well by the druids."

"But this was far more than just teaching. You put your own love for the music, your own spirit, into the notes you played. And you saw the effect it had on the people."

He took a step toward her. "Yet I wonder how my music affected *you*, my lady."

She smiled a little. Her face remained hooded by the dark green cloak, and he could see only her curving mouth. "Your music first made me smile, and even laugh a little," she said. "And then . . . then your second song moved me almost to pain."

144

"Pain?" Parlan gazed at her, and then frowned. "The last thing I wanted was to cause you pain."

She shook her head. "You did not. Your music did as it was supposed to do—it brought up those memories of mine that would move me to tears."

"And what is it that would move a goddess to tears?" Parlan asked.

"The same things that cause any woman to weep. The greatest of those is loneliness."

"Loneliness?"

She nodded, still looking down. "The world is a different place now—both the world of Men and the world of the gods. The world of the gods, the Otherworld, has long been nearly empty since so many of us died in the Great War and the Great Catastrophe. Our world has long been fading. Now the world of Men may well be ending, too. And I can do naught about either, save try to help the one man who might be able to save both."

"Save both? I understand what must be done if I am to save the world of Men—but how could I possibly hope to save the Otherworld?"

Eriu raised her head and looked straight at him, and he forgot all else at the sight of her luminous green eyes. "Because if the world of Men—this land with which my own spirit is inextricably linked—does continue, perhaps I can find the strength to continue in the Otherworld as well."

"And if this world is lost—if your land is ravaged and destroyed—it would take your spirit with it," realized Parlan. "And no creature—no animal, no man, no woman, no goddess—can hope to live without its spirit."

"I am glad you understand, King Parlan."

He closed the distance between them and reached down for her hand. It was cool and damp in the moonlight. "Do not be lonely this night, beautiful Eriu," he whispered, leaning close beside her hooded head. "Come with me to the shelter of the trees, high on the hill in the moonlight, and let me show you what love and care a mortal man might offer. Do not be lonely again this night. Not when you do not have to."

He thought she would turn away. He thought she would walk back up the hill and disappear into the night, as she always did. But instead, she raised her head and let her dark green cloak fall back so that the moonlight shone down on her rippling hair. "Perhaps this is one night when I will, indeed, not be lonely."

Parlan held her hand close against his chest, and when she remained gazing up at him, he leaned down to claim her perfect lips. To his great joy, she returned his kiss.

He took her in his arms, where she relaxed and allowed him to hold her close. In an instant his passion was fully fired, and it seemed that he could not hold her closely enough, could not kiss her deeply enough. At last he reached down and lifted her in his arms. He carried her up the winding path to the top of the hill, past the lone white willow tree where she had stood listening to his music, and into the grove of oaks and willows beyond.

Here, the quiet darkness welcomed them. Here the branches of the trees folded down over them like the protective roof of the finest of homes. Here the earth itself provided a soft cushion for them to lie on, a bed fit for a king and for his goddess, where they embraced each other and took comfort and strength from each other until the eastern sky began to lighten and the first of the seagulls began to call.

Late the next morning, Cillian and Gavin rode a few lengths behind Parlan, with the rest of the men and servants and the three newly collared hostage-princes following along. Beside Parlan rode his goddess on her grey mare, and the two of them talked and laughed together and even, from time to time, held hands.

"Look at them," Cillian muttered. "You would think there was no one else in the world but those two."

Gavin glanced up at Parlan and Eriu. "I think she must have stayed with him last night, instead of riding off as she usually does. What do you think?"

Cillian grunted. "I think he is so distracted and beguiled by her that he hardly gives a thought to this monstrous, impossible quest he is supposed to be fulfilling, or of how his failure would affect every last man, woman and child in Eire. She is the reason for this terrible quest in the first place!"

"But—she didn't cause it. Parlan made the mistake of saying he'd lay down his kingship if she would be his wife. The goddess took that as a rejection of the kingship she had just given him."

"And rightly so! Now we are all in the greatest danger, and they ride together like two young lovers without a care in the world."

"But . . ." Gavin shifted in his saddle. "He has no hope of gaining the sacred objects without her. Maybe it's best he stays on her good side so she doesn't disappear into the Otherworld and leave us to face that dragon alone—isn't it?"

"Perhaps he can play his harp for the beast and charm it as he did his audience at Dun Farriaghe last night."

"Did you not like his playing? I thought it was the best I'd ever heard!"

Cillian scowled. "A trick. A glamyr, done by her no doubt. A small deceit to turn the heads of those who might have reason to doubt him."

Suddenly all the horses halted, for Parlan and Eriu had halted theirs at a spot overlooking a valley. They stood very still, just staring out into the distance. Cillian took his horse forward and stopped a short way from Parlan, with Gavin quickly riding alongside.

"What are they looking at?" asked Gavin, peering down into the valley. Then his jaw dropped. "Oh . . ."

The once-beautiful valley now had wide black scars crisscrossing it—scars where nothing grew and where nothing would grow for a very long time. Dead cattle lay here and there in the midst of the scars, wet and blackened and bloating, and further contaminating the frost-bitten land.

"See what your high king has brought down upon us," Cillian whispered bitterly. "Parlan may well have more accomplishments to his name than the great god Lugh himself, but this dragon has shown us what sort of man Parlan really is."

They all stood together in silence, as the sun moved slowly through the sky and the stench of dead cattle rose up to meet them on the wind.

For the next three days, the high king's party traveled north through forests of oak and rowan, skirting the mountains that lay just to the east and enjoying the signs of spring that were now in full bloom all around them.

Here and there along the way were groves of apple trees, each branch covered with delicate white blossoms touched with pink. Whenever a brisk wind blew in from the sea, the trees gave up a beautiful pink-white rain of flowers that eventually lay scattered over the thick mat of three-leafed clover that covered all of the world, it seemed, and gave their horses a soft cushion to walk on during the day and sweet nourishment at night.

Parlan knew he would never forget the sight of Eriu cantering her grey mare through the rain of blossoms, her long dark green cloak sprinkled with pink-white flowers.

They forded one small river, and then another slightly larger one, until at last they reached a plain overlooking the greatest river in Eire. This was the great wide waterway known as the Abhainn Mor.

From the plain where the riders lined up, the river looked more like a vast lake. It stretched out of the east as far as they could see, and continued on to the west until it disappeared below the horizon, and eventually, they knew, poured itself into the sea. It glittered in the afternoon sun, calmly traveling into the west.

The plain itself was thick with green clover, and dotted everywhere with the bright yellow flowers of spring—dandelion and cowslip in the clover, along with delicate primrose, of course, always the first to appear, and the little marsh marigolds lining the rivers where the water met the bank. Eriu looked to the west, toward the high cliffs that sat beside the river and overlooked the plain where they stood. A few tall white willows grew near the river, while the rugged cliff itself was covered with the coarse, thorny outgrowths of fragrant white-flowered blackthorn and tough patches of gorse with its masses of sweet-scented tiny yellow blossoms.

"There is the place where you should make your camp. And over there, at the base of the cliffs—tonight, the dark of the moon, the midpoint of the season of spring—there is the place where you must build the bonfire to mark this night, so that all who see it will know what night it is."

Parlan frowned in confusion. "Then should the bonfire not be built on the top of those cliffs, so it can be seen all over this countryside?"

Eriu shook her head emphatically. "The bonfire must be built exactly there at the base of that cliff. And when it is, be prepared, Parlan, to win the next of the sacred treasures."

Parlan's head snapped up. "I should have known. The last test was at midwinter. But I will be ready. I have never been more so!"

He reined Maorga around and set the stallion off at a gallop toward the cliffs. "Come with me! Come with me!" he shouted, to his men and to his servants. "We have work to do, and but a short time to do it in! Come with me to save our land!"

While the servants built the camp on the plain by the river, Parlan's men set to work climbing the cliffs, cutting stacks of thorny, yellow-flowered gorse and tossing them to the plain below.

Eriu watched from beside one of the willow trees by the river, with Parlan beside her. "The gorse will burn hot and fierce," she said. "Have them gather all they can and put it at the base of the bonfire.

"Next, tell them to cut the branches of just one willow and place those atop the gorse. Willow wood burns slow and cool. It will help to contain the fierceness of the gorse, and direct its power downward into the earth."

"Into the earth?" Parlan's apprehension rose. "Why would we want to—"

"Last of all, have them cut a single flowering blackthorn and lay the pieces atop the willow," she continued. "It is the tree of cursing—or of lifting one. The sweet white flowers will help to outweigh its dark and thorny nature, and bring out its positive aspects."

"Cursing—"

"Go, Parlan. The sun has already set. Go and direct your men. When darkness sets in, you will light this fire with your own hand."

CHAPTER NINETEEN

Before long, the moonless night swallowed up the river and the plain and the campsite. Heavy clouds from the sea covered any light from the stars. It was so dark that no man could see his own hand in front of his face. Then, near the base of the cliff, a tiny light flared in the darkness.

Parlan sat back from the little twig he had been rubbing into a piece of dry gorse, and blew gently onto the glowing spark. The ember brightened a little, and began to take hold of the broken gorse twigs and bits of dry dandelion fluff used for kindling.

Parlan lifted a twig of gorse, now burning with a bright yellow flame, and carried it to the big stack of gorse, willow and blackthorn waiting near the base of the cliff. He said, "On this night of mid-spring, when night and day occur in equal measure, let this fire be seen by all in this countryside—king and cowherd, queen and servant—that all might know what night this is."

He threw the fiery bit of gorse high into the air, where it flipped end–over–end in a high arc and then dropped with a clatter into the center of the great stack of wood.

Right away the hungry flames ate into the blackthorn sticks, releasing a cloud of dark smoke faintly tinged with the fragrance of the white flowers. Then they reached the softer, damper white willow wood, sending up a thick, heavy fog of smoke lit from beneath by the orange glow of the flames.

But the dripping sparks and embers soon found the dry gorse waiting beneath. In an instant the entire stack of wood flared into brilliant yellow light. The men surrounding the bonfire quickly fell back as the low roar and terrific heat of the flames filled the air.

Parlan stood with Eriu and watched the fire burn, squinting in the glare of the fierce yellow flames. "It's going to burn itself out in moments. Let me send the men to bring more wood. I'll have them bring more willow, to slow down the flames—"

Eriu placed her hand on his arm. "Wait here. Let it burn. That is its purpose. Let it burn all the way down to the earth, and then see what it shows you."

Parlan turned back to face the flames, gripping the bronze hilt of the Sword of Nuadha at his hip and watching the glaring fire rapidly consume itself to nothing.

It was not long before the inferno burned down to hot red ash. Soon the ashes faded into the dark earth—all except those in the center of the bonfire site, which glowed a fierce yellow-red in the outline of a spear—a spear in the shape of a trident, with three terrible barbed points.

"Here is the Spear of Lugh," Eriu said. "It never misses its target, and it returns of its own accord to the wielder's hand. Yet it is a terrible weapon, for once it strikes, its barbed hooks prevent it from being withdrawn. It will tear any creature to pieces before it can be pulled free."

"The Spear of Lugh," Parlan breathed. "I know of it, as I did the Sword of Nuadha—but I never hoped to see it."

"Go and get it, then," Eriu said. "It is the second of the four treasures that you must find."

"Is it so easy?" Parlan murmured. "Is it as easy as building a fire in the right spot?" He glanced all around him, but saw only darkness. He looked at Eriu, her face softly lit by the glowing outline of the buried spear, but she remained silent and impassive.

Parlan turned back to the spear. Its outline remained hot and glowing on the surface of the dead ashes. Parlan walked to the far end of the spear, away from the three barbed heads, and cautiously began to brush away the red-yellow coals from the end of the shaft.

Instantly the plain was filled with a glaring yellow light. It came from above his head, Parlan realized, and was followed by a thick wave of heat. It was as though a hundred torches had just been thrown down from the cliff. Parlan turned around and looked up at the overhanging rocks, shielding his eyes from the glare, and in the heartbeats before the light died, Parlan saw a winged beast like a small white dragon. It stood tall on its powerful hind legs, its beating wings supporting its upper half, roaring down at him from the cliff and breathing flame as it cried out in rage.

"Eriu! Get back!" Parlan shouted, drawing the Sword of Nuadha. The heavy bronze blade gleamed in the low light of the glowing spear, though the weapon felt featherlight in his hand. He strained to see the monster, or hear it, in the darkness, but instead heard only the shouting of his startled men and the loud snorting of terrified horses.

At the edge of the light he could see Eriu still standing calmly while his men came forward with their weapons drawn. "Eriu! Get back! What is that beast?"

"It is a firedrake," she said, her voice carrying to him even over the shouting of the men and the clanging of their swords and shields and javelins. "It is the guardian of the spear."

"Guardian!" Parlan cried. He turned this way and that as he searched for the beast in the darkness. "I can see there will be no persuasion this time, no battle of wits as with the Master of the Hunt! Come to me, then, guardian! I am ready for you this time! I have the Sword of Nuadha!"

"Killing is not always the best course, Parlan," she warned. "Things are not always what they appear. Have a care—"

But Parlan heard no more, for just then the beast roared again and leapt straight at him from the top of the cliff, a torrent of fire streaming from its jaws.

Parlan jumped out of the way just as the firedrake landed across the glowing outline of the spear. The light from the spear revealed the creature in half-shadow, and Parlan stared in fascination as it turned on its four legs—the hind legs huge and powerful, the front ones small and delicate—and snarled. It was perhaps as long as a very tall man, not including its equally long, whipping tail. Its head was heavy, its eyes small and gleaming black, and its jaws were filled with long sharp teeth. Its hide was gleaming and almost transparent white, and the wings on its shoulders spread wide and beat hard to help lift the front end high off the ground. The firedrake roared at Parlan, and then lashed out again with another torrent of flame.

Parlan dodged the flame as his men shouted out and fell back with him. He readied his sword and prepared to strike. His men urged, "Now! Get it now! Surely it cannot breathe flame again so soon—"

He ran forward and raised the sword. Several of his men moved with him. But, to Parlan's horror, the firedrake instantly whipped its head to the side and breathed a gout of flame straight into three of the charging warriors.

The trio was instantly engulfed in fire. They flailed blindly and fell writhing to the earth, and their comrades struggled to help them but were driven back by the flames.

Parlan ran to the other side of the firedrake. "Here, beast! Leave them be. Face me! I have the weapon to match you!"

The monster turned to him and breathed its terrible flames again—but Parlan held out the Sword of Nuadha and used it as a shield to drive off the fire and direct it straight back at the eyes of the drake. The beast shrieked and threw its head up, cutting off the torrent of flame, and when it did, Parlan threw the shining bronze sword directly at its chest.

Again, the monster screeched in pain and fury. It tried desperately to claw at the heavy sword that had buried itself in its shoulder, but it could not reach the tormenting weapon. Blood began to run down its white hide. Parlan was fascinated to see the blood smolder and flare into flame, until a line of fire ran and dripped down its shoulder to the earth.

"Its blood turns to fire when it meets the air," he whispered. And to his great relief, the firedrake's black eyes rolled up in its head and it fell hard to earth, lying across the glowing red outline of the spear.

Light came now from torches carried by the running servants—and, horribly, from the cloaks and tunics and skin and hair of the three men who had been caught in the firedrake's breath.

With the beast subdued, the men finally managed to put out their companions flames with their heavy woolen cloaks and with a bucket of water brought from the river. But now the three burned warriors lay on the grassy plain with reeking smoke curling up from their bodies. One lay silent, either unconscious or already dead; the other two moaned and cried in unspeakable agony, one arching his back up off the ground and the second reaching out with his hands in a desperate search for comfort that could never come.

Eriu moved quickly to look at each of them. She looked at Parlan and shook her head.

He closed his eyes.

She walked to stand beside him, and whispered quietly but urgently, "They are finished. I cannot save them. Even among the gods, there are none left who could. But I can ease their way."

"Do so," he said quickly. "Do not let them linger in such pain."

She moved back to the badly burned men, her long green cloak sweeping over the grass. She crouched down beside the first—the one who'd reached out with his hands as he gasped in agony—and let him take hold of her fingers as she rested her other and on his charred forehead. His wailing faded and then stopped. Slowly his hands lowered, and then fell back to the grassy earth.

Eriu moved to the other writhing man, and she placed her hands on his forehead and chest. In a moment, he too, relaxed and fell silent.

The third man still had not moved, but after Eriu laid her hands upon him, Parlan could see an almost imperceptible relaxation. Then this man, too, was clearly gone from the world and from his pain.

The only thing moving now was the smoke rising from their bodies.

Parlan started to go to Eriu, to thank her for this last mercy she had shown his men, but her attention had turned to the white firedrake, which still lay writhing feebly across the burning outline of the spear. As he walked up to her, she caught his arm and led him quickly to the other side of the beast. The gleaming bronze Sword of Nuadha still protruded from its shoulder, moving up and down with each labored breath the creature took. Spots of flame still ran and dripped from the wound.

Eriu moved close beside him. "Pull out the sword."

"What? Pull it out? The monster is not yet dead! This sword kills whatever it strikes once blood is drawn, whether the wound itself is mortal or no! I may push it in the rest of the way to the hilt, to hasten the end, but I will not pull it out!"

"You must do it quickly. There is still time. Pull out the sword."

Parlan tried to catch his breath. "Did you not see what it did to those three men? A more horrible death I cannot imagine! I will not—"

"You do not understand, Parlan. I told you that things are not always what they seem. I will ask you once more: Pull out the sword."

Parlan set his jaw, looking hard at Eriu, then walked over to the fallen beast. He took hold of the quivering sword, but it would barely move in the thickly muscled shoulder. He was forced to place his foot against the creature's chest and pull on the weapon with all his might.

It finally wrenched free. Parlan staggered backward and nearly fell. The firedrake made a thin keening cry, threw its head back, and lay still.

"It's dead," Parlan breathed, with a sigh of relief. He turned to Eriu and reached for her hand, intending to lead her away from the gruesome scene; but she stayed where she was and turned him to face the firedrake once more.

"Watch," she whispered.

Though it lay very still and its eyes were closed, the creature's sides still rose and fell. And as Parlan stared at it, in the uneven glare of the torches it seemed that the body of the beast began to collapse and shrink . . . but how was that possible?

His warriors took a few slow steps forward, holding

out their torches to get a better look. The shriveling remains of the firedrake began to turn from white to grey and then to black, and then fell apart like ash. All that remained was the glowing outline of the spear—with a young, naked, ash-covered man lying on his side across it.

CHAPTER TWENTY

The men all blinked at the sight, and looked at each other. "How is this possible?" Parlan asked, staring at the unconscious man—unconscious, not dead, for as with the firedrake his chest still moved. One ash–covered arm slid down to the earth, and he gave a small moan.

Eriu stepped forward and crouched down beside him, brushing away the thick layer of soot that covered his shoulder. She eased the young man onto his back. "Parlan! Come here. You are needed."

Parlan hurried to her side. As she continued to clear away the ash, he saw that the man was young—not twenty years of age, he guessed—and had a terrible wound in his shoulder. There was a brief glimmer of flame at the wound, and then it faded and there was only dark blood flowing in narrow lines down his pale skin. The man's eyes rolled up in his head, and he gasped for breath, his skin turning pale as death.

"The wound is bad, but it does not look fatal," Parlan said. "Why is he dying?"

"You struck him with Nuadha's own sword," Eriu said, continuing to clean away the ash. "As you said, its bite is always fatal."

Parlan looked at the young man. "You cannot save him?"

"Perhaps. Perhaps not. But I will try. Go, now, down to the river, and bring back the clean water that flows where the river meets the earth. Bring it to me with your own hands."

Parlan got up and hurried to the river edge, stepping carefully in the darkness through the tall grass along the banks. He crouched down, dipped up some of the water in his two cupped hands, and hurried back to Eriu and the dying youth.

The man lay still, his head thrown back and his eyes closed. Eriu scooped up some of the newly burnt ash and earth from the bonfire site and held it out in her two hands together. "Here, Parlan. Pour the water on the ash. Quickly."

He did as she asked, soaking the ashes until Eriu could fashion it into a smooth cohesive shape. She turned back to the fallen youth and carefully pressed the poultice of wet ash and earth into the still-bleeding wound on his shoulder. She held it tight, looking at the young man's black-streaked face as she sang to him in a low voice. Parlan could not make out the words. But in a moment the young man's eyes opened, and he tried to focus on the dark and flickering world around him. He raised his hand up to the wound on his shoulder, and Eriu slipped her fingers out from around the poultice and pressed his own hand down upon it.

"Lady Eriu," the man whispered, his voice rough and hoarse as though he had not used it for a very long time. "I never thought to see you again."

"Nor I you," she replied. "But I am glad to know that you will live—and live as the man you were meant to be."

Parlan stood up. "Will one of you please explain this to me?"

Smiling, Eriu smoothed back the young man's ash-dusted hair and got to her feet. "You know that each of the four sacred treasures has its guardian."

Parlan nodded. "The Master of the Wild Hunt held Nuadha's sword. This firedrake protected Lugh's spear."

"They did. But as you have seen, the firedrake was not really a beast at all."

"Indeed. The monster was a man. But how did this come to be?"

She continued to watch the fallen man. He seemed to be in less pain as he held the wet poultice to his shoulder. "This is Rian," she said. "He was one of Lugh's most loyal servants. Rian was not a god, but a young and beautiful mortal, and he devoted his life to the most skilled and accomplished of all the gods."

She turned to Parlan. "When the final war came and the treasures were being hidden away to protect them, Lugh rewarded Rian for his devotion—and saved him from the battle—by making him an immortal guardian. And so he has been here for all these countless years, guarding his master's weapon even though the master can never return."

"Lady Eriu—do you mean that Lugh is truly gone? Gone to the Otherworld?" Rian asked.

She crouched down beside him again, and helped the man raise himself up on one elbow. "I am sorry to tell you, Rian, that Lugh and many of the other gods and goddesses are now far beyond even the Otherworld."

"How?" he whispered.

Eriu smoothed his hair back again. "When the gods

make war upon each other, few of them survive. I am only glad to know that you survived, and with you the treasure you guarded."

Rian closed his eyes. "It is a terrible thing to know that he is gone—that so many are gone." He looked up at Eriu, and at Parlan, and his eyes widened at the sight of the sword. "So, if you seek Lugh's spear . . . and you already have King Nuadha's sword—there must be a great trouble in the land once again."

Eriu nodded. "There is."

"But if the ruling gods are gone, never to return . . . what could have brought about an event so dire that the sacred treasures must be found?"

Eriu paused. Parlan raised his head. "There is a curse on the land," he said. "Without thinking, I made light of the kingship I was granted by the Goddess of the Land. Now the Curse of the Black Dragon corrupts all of Eire, and I have need of the four treasures that I might destroy it forever."

Rian sat all the way up. Though he was naked, and still filthy with ash, the look in his eyes was clear and he no longer seemed to be in pain. "Then you are trying to make it right," he said, looking at Parlan.

"I am."

"And Eriu found you not only worthy to be a high king, but worthy of her help in lifting the curse." Rian glanced at Eriu, then back at Parlan. "If she believes you to be such a king—such a Man—then I can do no less. I will go with you, and serve you as best I can on your quest, if you will have me."

Parlan could not help but smile. "I will have you, Rian, if you will have some clothes—and a bath."

Rian carefully took the damp poultice away from his shoulder. The skin where the poultice had rested was smooth and whole, with no sign of an injury. "I will have them, my king. I will have them."

Parlan drew a deep breath and walked away from the gathering, into the heavy darkness outside the torchlight. Eriu followed him. "Will you not go and take the Spear of Lugh from beneath the earth? You have certainly earned it."

He looked up, first studying Rian and then looking over at the still–smoldering bodies of his three fatally burned men. "Perhaps I will ask Rian to carry it for me," he said. "He has guarded it faithfully for all these many years, and it almost cost him his life through no fault of his own. He deserves to carry the Spear of Lugh, if anyone does."

"I am sure he will do so if you ask him—but *you*, Parlan, must go now and take it from beneath the earth, if you want to be able to wield it when the time comes."

Parlan looked back toward the gathering. Two of the servants slowly helped Rian to his feet and led him away toward the campsite. The outline of the spear remained where he had fallen, but its glow was becoming fainter, as though it were settling deeper into the earth.

Parlan walked back to the spear, and as before began to dig through the ash from the end of the shaft moving forward. He uncovered the beautiful reddish-brown shaft, made from the heartwood of the rowan tree and polished so that it was perfectly smooth and absolutely straight.

He took hold of the shaft near the head of the spear, and with some difficulty lifted the weapon free. The ash fell away and left it shining and clean, its three barbed points gleaming bright in the light of the torches.

Eriu came to stand beside him. "You have done well, Parlan. You have gained two of the four sacred objects, which you must have to complete your quest. You should be pleased."

Parlan stared down at the shaft of the spear without really seeing it. "I have gained the spear, it is true. But at what cost?"

He gazed out into the darkness toward the spots of firelight that dotted the campsite. Out there, he knew, Rian was being bathed and dressed by the servants. "I nearly killed him," Parlan said. "He is an innocent man, and I all but killed him."

Eriu shook her head. "I do not understand. He accepted the role of guardian when Lugh offered it to him. He knew he might be called upon to lay down his life to protect the sacred spear, should he be met with a magickal weapon. He knew this. You had no choice but to face him if you wished to gain the spear."

Parlan gripped his sword. "I thought the same when I faced the Wild Hunt—but it was not necessary; I was able to outwit the master. No one died—not one of my men. I should have found a better way to deal with this threat. You tried to tell me that killing is not always the best course, that things are not always what they seem. But instead . . ."

He looked toward the gathering of torches where the three badly burned men lay dead. "I do not even know who they are. I could not recognize their faces, or their clothes."

"I can tell you their names, my king."

Cillian stood beside him, a few paces away. "They were Siadhal, one of your own men from Teamhair Breagh—and Uaine, one of the hostage-princes from Dun Ghee—and Tadhg, another hostage to peace, from Dun Farriaghe."

Parlan turned away, wanting to see only darkness. "I am charged with protecting my own men, but especially am I charged with protecting hostages to peace. I have failed these three men. I did not even try to find a better way to cope with the guardian of the spear. I simply charged straight into battle, and there lies the charred and stinking result."

He made himself look back toward the bodies. Even now, faint wisps of smoke rose from them into the darkness and disappeared.

When the sky lightened again the next morning, it showed a wet and sodden world drenched with rain—a world that included three new rock-lined graves beneath the wet and dripping overhang of the cliff. The camp had been dismantled. Cillian waited beside his horse with the other men and servants as Parlan swung up on Maorga and reined the stallion around to face them.

"We have done all that can be done for Siadhal and Uaine and Tadgh," Parlan said. "I have already sent two men back to Dun Farriaghe and Dun Ghee to tell them what happened to their sons. And it is by my order that Rian, a loyal servant of the gods who has now sworn fealty to the high king, rides Siadhal's horse."

Parlan turned his stallion to face the east. "We will get to Abhainn Aille as soon as we can. We will collect our next three hostage-princes and we will continue in search of the remaining two objects. I want this quest finished as much as you do. We leave now."

He sent Maorga jogging through the wet grey morning, heading inland as the river beside him flowed on to the sea. Eriu cantered out of the misty field ahead and swung her mare around to join him.

Riding near the back of the line, Cillian barely glanced over as Gavin trotted his horse up alongside.

"Well, Cillian," Gavin said, "Parlan got the second treasure, and he defeated a fearsome beast. Do you feel any better about him now?"

Cillian slowly turned his head and scowled. "Not only are we embroiled in this wretched curse of his, we have to watch good men die in agony. He was right—he should have found another way to subdue the firedrake. It was

165

no stag or wolf or boar. None of us had any hope of facing down a supernatural beast! Those three men did not have to die—not like that."

"But I don't know what else he could have—"

Gavin stopped talking as another man rode up. It was Seamus. "I do not believe they had to die, either," he said, in a quiet voice. "I do not believe that a man who calls down a curse will also be the one to lift it. That task should lie with someone else."

Cillian nodded. "That thought has troubled me ever since the start of this." He looked at Seamus and spoke softly. "A new king is needed. A king who did not bring about this curse, and who will lift it without wasting any more lives."

Gavin urged his horse a little faster to keep up. "But won't the goddess be displeased if Parlan . . . if he should be . . . if there is a new king?"

"The goddess will help whatever man is king and can lift this curse from her lands. She cannot choose the king—but we can."

"And we must." Cillian looked hard at Seamus, and the three men all continued on in silence through the wet and drizzling morning.

IV

THE WEST

Chapter Twenty-one

They rode for two more days, following the enormous river that was sometimes so vast they could not see the other side. Gradually the river narrowed until it was not much wider than any other, and finally they could see a ford. Parlan wanted to pull his heavy cloak up over his head against the driving wind and rain of this particular day, but he and Eriu and the men who followed had nearly reached the place where they would cross the great river, and he would need a full view when attempting it.

He halted Maorga near the first of a set of two stacks of large stones, each half as tall as a man, which marked the entrance to the ford. Even here, Abhainn Mor was wider and swifter than the main flow of any other river. Parlan halted near the edge, and he looked out at the wide grey river, its surface strongly rippled by the wind and thickly dotted with raindrops. The grey skies arched over him as he kept his eyes on the distant open plain, lined with reeds far on the other side of the river.

Cillian rode up beside him. "This storm has made the ford fast and treacherous, my king. Perhaps we should wait until the skies clear and the current is not so swift, the ford not so swollen—"

Parlan shot him a hard look. "The king of Abhainn Aille awaits. All the men are tired. Many of them are still shaken by the battle with the firedrake. I want to get them to a place of comfort and rest as soon as I can. I will not wait on a little rain, which is as common in this land as birds singing in the spring." He turned Maorga away and walked him over the sodden, grassy earth to where the hooded Eriu sat waiting on Solasta.

"Do you wish to make the crossing now, Parlan?" she asked. "It would be easier for your men—certainly for your servants and their ponies—to cross at a calmer time."

He looked straight ahead, out across the windblown water. "I am sure that I can lead them safely across. They deserve the comforts that Abhainn Aille can offer."

"You cannot reach Abhainn Aille for another two fortnights. What difference will it make to wait here for another afternoon, another day?"

Parlan raised his head and looked at her. "I failed them during the test of the firedrake. I must do something now to restore their confidence in me."

She raised one perfect dark eyebrow, and smiled a little. "Leading them all to drown will not raise their confidence, I think."

"I will not lead anyone to drown! I have been crossing storm-ridden fords since I was born. This is but one more."

Eriu shrugged. "You must do what you must do, Parlan. You are the high king—not I." She started to turn the mare away.

"Wait. Wait!" Parlan looked into her dark green eyes. "Lady Eriu—should the men, any of the servants, have any difficulty with the crossing, you could help them, could you not? You could calm the waters if you chose, turn the mud and silt to firm gravel beneath the feet of the horses? I can do anything—anything at all—if I know you are there beside me."

Instantly she turned her mare to face him, and anger flashed across her face. "I will do nothing of the kind. I could do those things, but I will not. I never will."

The mare snorted and danced sideways across the soaked grass, sending up little sprays of water from beneath its hooves. Eriu said, "I am the Goddess of the Land, King Parlan. I am not a tool for you to wield, that you might make your work easier. Such ease would not help you; it would only weaken you and make you dependent upon my powers instead of upon your own. I am not here to make you either weak or dependent."

He drew a deep breath, and finally looked away from her. "I beg your pardon, Lady Eriu. I do understand. I will lead them across myself, without assistance, which is as it should be."

Eriu turned her mare away, and she cantered along the river until it curved around a distant hillside and she was lost to sight.

Parlan set his jaw. He swung his horse around to face his men and called out, "We will make the crossing now! Follow me!" And he kicked Maorga's sides and sent the beast leaping into the fast-flowing river, even as the rain continued to pour down all around.

Maorga was almost immediately belly-deep in the cold rushing water. Parlan pulled his own heels up and rested them high on the horse's sides in an effort to keep the heavy leather of his tied-and-folded boots from soaking all the way through.

The wind in his ears and the rain slapping his face made it difficult to hear, but after a moment Parlan heard the unmistakable sound of a few horses splashing through the water a short way behind him—but then the sounds stopped. He heard only an irregular floundering and splashing, as though the horses were turning back.

He twisted in the saddle to look, while still keeping Maorga moving straight ahead—but just as he turned, he felt the stallion shudder and crouch and leap. In an instant Parlan found himself falling toward a rippled grey sheet of water as Maorga hurtled forward and sideways.

Parlan hit the water with a huge splash. The river swallowed him up and shut out the sights and sounds of the world, biting him with cold and roaring in his ears and dragging him down by his heavy, sodden clothing. He struggled to get back to the surface, but now the storm-driven current had him in its grip. Parlan reached out with both arms in an effort to swim upward, but his fingers found only the soft mud and sharp gravel of the river bottom. He managed to get his feet down, even as the current continued to drag him, and with all his remaining strength pushed off hard and drove himself upward.

Parlan broke through to lashing rain and howling wind, and to the frantic shouting of his men. He gasped for air, once, twice, and then continued struggling to keep his head above the cold nothingness of the water. Frantically kicking his feet to keep himself up, he twisted the circular gold brooch holding his heavy woolen cloak at his shoulder until at last he got it free. He pulled the long pin out of the thick folds of wool and then dropped the brooch.

The cloak swept off his shoulders. Instantly Parlan felt lighter, but the Sword of Nuadha dragged heavy at his left hip. It grew heavier with each passing moment as the wooden scabbard filled with water. Parlan reached down, drew his dagger from his belt, and with a terrible effort—battling the river each time it pulled him down, certain each gasping breath would be his last—he worked the blade of the dagger under his belt and began to cut it loose.

The wet leather was heavy and thick. Parlan hacked at it between gulps of air at the rushing surface of the water. At last the belt snapped, and in the same instant he dropped the dagger and grabbed the belt before it could sweep behind him.

Keeping hold of the heavy sword, he worked his arms to stay afloat and tried to make sense of where he was.

A quick look showed him that he was already far away from the ford. He could just make out Maorga's black form returning to the men, and other horses still waiting on the land—and he also saw that the current had carried him far out toward the center of the river.

Struggling, gasping, using all his strength just to keep his head above the surface, he caught sight of one of his men coming toward him. It was Rian—tall, strong, long-legged Rian, who yesterday had worn the shape of a fire-drake and now was trying to race on foot to save the high king—but it was too late. The river had Parlan in its mighty grip, and he knew it would only let him go in its own time. He could only watch as the ford and his men were lost to sight.

After a seemingly endless time of being carried along in the cold dragging current, the river began to push him closer to the opposite shore. His feet ran up against mud and rock and the half-submerged stalks of tall reeds. Finally, exhausted with long and terrible effort, and stiff with bone-chilling cold, Parlan climbed out onto the shore and collapsed on the wet ground with the Sword of Nuadha still in his fingers.

He was not sure how long he lay there on the bank, just gathering breath after breath into his lungs, but when at last he opened his eyes and raised his head, the sky had cleared to blue with only a few puffy white clouds. The sun shone down, warm and welcoming.

He got to his feet. He stood on an open plain just like the other side had been, with only a few scattered willow trees growing near the water. The cold winds of spring seemed to blow right through his drenched clothes, driving a chill all the way through him right down to his bones. The sun was only about halfway between its zenith and the horizon, so he might at least have a chance to dry out somewhat before the darkness set in—but he was going to be very cold this night with no fire and no cloak.

He placed the Sword of Nuadha, still in its dripping wet, bloodred scabbard, against the trunk of the nearest willow tree. He stripped off his leather boots and his linen tunic and woolen trews, and hung them one at a time from a low branch of the willow.

He had no food and little hope of getting any. He was chilled and exhausted. He had no dagger or sling, and no hook or line or net. He did have the fabulous, magickal, and extremely powerful Sword of Nuadha standing up against the willow tree, but it was hardly a useful tool for preparing food.

The best course, he decided, would be to rest in the sun for a short time, allow his clothes to dry a bit, and then start walking back the way the river had brought him. The walking would help to keep him warm and, perhaps, take his mind off the hunger that was sure to come.

At least there would be no shortage of water.

He stretched out in the sun for a time, trying to soak up every trace of its thin springtime warmth; but soon the grey clouds came rolling back and brought a damp chill wind with them. Parlan got up and dressed in his still-damp clothes and boots, picked up the sword, and turned to begin his trek the way he had come—and then stopped before he even took the first step.

There, on the plain—which he was certain had been open and empty a moment before—stood two trees. One was an apple tree, its branches heavy with ripe yellow-green fruit, and the other was a hazelnut, so laden with fully ripened nuts that a few were falling to the ground in the light wind that blew across the river. And resting on the grass between the two trees was his own neatly folded woolen cloak and shining brooch—the same he had discarded in the river in an effort to save his life.

For several heartbeats, he could only stand and stare. He was certain these two trees had not been there before, and equally certain that hazelnuts and apples did not ripen in mid-spring.

Nor, he was quite sure, had his cloak come ashore with his brooch of its own accord and then politely dried itself out for him.

He smiled to himself, and walked slowly toward the trees. Setting down the sword on the grass beside his cloak, he ran his fingertips over the ripe hazelnuts and sweet-smelling apples. He would not be hungry tonight.

He took three of the largest hazelnuts, and three of the ripest apples, and placed them neatly in the grass beside the sword. "These I would share with you, Lady Eriu, as very small thanks for this great kindness you have shown me. You were right not to help me across the river, but I am so glad to know that you will help me when I am truly in need. Again, I thank you."

He sat down to eat, wrapped in the warmth of his dry cloak, glad to be alive and grateful for Eriu's care—and trying not to think of what could have made steady, fearless Maorga take a sudden violent leap out of the water.

Parlan passed the night in the soft grass beneath the apple and hazelnut trees, kept warm and dry by his cloak and protected by the Sword of Nuadha lying close at hand. When the morning came, grey and damp, he picked up the sword and slid its scabbard through the leather belt that went around his tunic. He placed his two hands on the trunk of the hazelnut tree and stood quietly for a moment with his eyes closed, once again thinking of his gratitude to Eriu. He did the same with the apple tree, and then picked up a few more nuts and one more apple and started walking along the river, back toward the ford.

Though a light rain still fell, the storm of yesterday had passed. The river had subsided to its usual place below the banks and ran slow and quiet as though it had never been violent and raging just yesterday. Parlan knew that his men would have already crossed the ford and would be riding toward him even now—it would only be a matter of time before he met up with them again.

As always, he scanned the distance for signs of horses and riders, and especially for one green-cloaked rider on a lovely grey mare. But it seemed that Eriu was intent on letting him find his own way out, for there was no sign of her.

Parlan ate the apple as he walked.

The day wore on. He finished the hazelnuts and tossed the shells aside. The river must have taken him farther than he'd thought, for he walked and walked but saw no one at all.

He would not allow himself to believe that they would go on without him, that they would have left their high king for drowned in the river and never even searched for the body—that they would have left him there and gone on to find another king, a better king, a king who could lift a curse and not one who brought curses down upon them and got them killed in agonizing ways. . . .

Then, far ahead, came the faint sound of hoofbeats.

Parlan kept walking toward them. He did not want his men to see him merely standing around and waiting, as though he was too tired to go any farther. He carried himself tall and proud, and kept one hand on the hilt of the Sword of Nuadha, expecting his horde of warriors and loyal servants to ride into sight.

But all he saw, galloping toward him on the wet open plain beside the river, were two horses side by side.

Parlan frowned and walked a little faster. As the horses approached, he saw that only one—a heavy bay with front legs white to the knees—carried a rider. The tall young man on the bay horse's back led a black stallion with a crooked white blaze on his face, and drove both horses as fast as he could get them to go.

"King Parlan! King Parlan!" Rian shouted. "I am here for you!"

"So you are," Parlan said, as the two horses trotted over. "And I do not mind saying that I am glad to see you."

Rian halted the horses and leapt to the ground. His eyes were wide and his face pale with relief. "I feared never to see you again. I feared the high king was lost to the storm and to the river."

"As you can see, I was not lost. I am well. I am fine."

"And you even have all your possessions about you," Rian marveled, studying him. "Only your sword-belt and dagger are gone. How—"

"I do not know," Parlan said. "I simply went with the river until it took me to its bank, for no man can fight such a current. That way lies exhaustion and drowning."

Rian nodded. "Sometimes, it's better not to fight," he agreed. He grinned, and his young face lit up. "Your men are coming this way. They sent me ahead to search for you, and I was ordered to bring you back whether—" He looked away.

"Whether dead or alive," Parlan finished for him. He smiled. "No matter. I am indeed alive, as you can see, and glad to see you—and very glad to see Maorga again."

Parlan stroked the stallion's neck, and took the reins from Rian. But before swinging up into the saddle, he walked around to the back of the stallion and ran his hands over the horse's broad rump. There, just to one side of his thick black tail, was a small deep gash that still oozed blood.

It was as though a vicious small stone had come whipping out of the sky to bite the horse deeply and send him leaping out of the water, dumping his rider into the storm-lashed river, presumably to his death.

But stones did not fly of their own accord. Someone in his troop of men and servants had struck Maorga deliberately—and since his plan to kill the high king had failed this time, Parlan knew that he would, without fail, try again.

Chapter Twenty-two

Parlan and his men camped along the river that night, not far from the spot where he was sure there had been a single hazelnut tree and single apple tree the day before; but when they passed it today, they saw only a few scattered willow trees on the wet grass.

He could still taste the sweet ripe apple.

They rode on for many more days, fording two quiet rivers and riding through high rocky hills lightly scattered with oak and willow trees. Twice they camped for several nights near the rivers while the men enjoyed the slowly lengthening days and spent them in hunting and fishing and swordplay and wrestling, forever testing themselves against nature and against each other.

Parlan sometimes joined them in the hunt, for it was a pleasure to gallop after the smooth-headed stags and watch his men bring them down for the cooking fires. But always he watched for Eriu on her grey mare, for she only came to him now once every several nights, and did not ride with him during the days as she once had. She offered no explanation for her lengthy absences, but Parlan suspected she was continuing her lesson of not allowing him to become too dependent on her.

On the nights when she did come to him, he welcomed her into his embrace and asked her for nothing, grateful for the unearthly smoothness of her skin, the unbelievable warmth and strength of her body, and the sheer magic of her green-eyed, dark-haired presence.

During the days, Parlan rode always at the front of his men as they cantered through fields and splashed through the rivers. Maorga did not offer to leap out from under him again, and all of his men and servants were nothing but polite and respectful to him. Perhaps it had been just some rare trick of nature that had caused Maorga to unseat him, and some other ordinary thing that had caused the small injury to the horse.

Yet, what else could it have been?

Parlan tried to put the incident out of his mind and think of what must be done now—the distance still left to travel, the unimaginable tests that still awaited him. But always his recent failures nagged at him: the horrific deaths of three men when he'd chosen to battle the firedrake, his carelessness in arrogantly crossing the storm-driven river that nearly ended in his being drowned like a weakling pup.

The high king had to do better. He had to repair the damage done, or risk losing the loyalty of his men—and he would have to come up with something soon.

One morning, some thirty-five nights after Parlan had been swept into the river, he stood atop one of the low rocky hills that surrounded their campsite. As the servants worked to break down the camp and the men prepared their horses for another long day's ride, Parlan stood with his back to the rising sun and gazed out at the lush green land that here began to slope down to the cliffs and beaches of the nearby sea. A stream ran across the land not far from where he stood, but it would be no obstacle even to the pack ponies.

They were so near to the ocean, he could almost hear the sound of the waves. Then a movement caught his eye—the movement of something white beyond the stream, along the low grassy hills where they led down to the water.

At first his heart leapt, for he thought it must be grey-white Solasta bringing Eriu towards him. But as he watched, he saw another white form, and another, and another, all galloping toward the stream just in front of him . . . beautiful, grey-white, riderless horses, ten or twenty or more, floating toward him on the wind like a herd of beautiful clouds.

Parlan caught his breath. These were not ordinary horses. These were the mares of the gods and goddesses themselves, the impossibly tall and beautiful steeds kept for their use alone, the way Solasta was reserved for Eriu. Rarely were they seen by men, for these creatures roamed the lushest of the green pastures and drank from the clearest of streams and hid in the deepest forests should any man draw too close.

It was rare to catch a glimpse of even one, but right now the land was disrupted and tormented by the presence of a dragon, and in such times even the horses of the gods would have to chance drinking where they could. And so a whole herd of them was coming across the dew-laden grass to the stream to drink.

In an instant, a daring thought crossed Parlan's mind. The servants had everything packed. His men were already beginning to swing up on their horses in preparation for the day's ride. Even now, a servant led the saddled Maorga toward him.

Parlan ran to the horse and grabbed the reins. As he vaulted into the saddle he shouted out, "Ten men, stay with the servants! The rest of you ride with me! *Now!*"

The men glanced at each other and then wasted no time galloping after Parlan. He knew that they had no idea what they were chasing or why; they just did not want to be one of the ten left behind with the servants!

As they thundered toward him, Parlan waved his arm wide. "Spread out! Spread out in a single line! Do it now!" And by the time they joined him and he swung the snorting, plunging Maorga around to gallop with them, more than eighty men rode abreast straight up over the rise to the west.

A shout rose from the men as their quarry came into sight. Drinking from the tumbling rapids of the stream were some twenty mares—horses they had heard stories of, but unlike any they had ever seen. Most were white, white as cloud, white as frost; but the younger ones showed frosty grey coats as Eriu's mare did, as they faded from the black they had been at birth to the pure cloud-white of their older sisters.

"These are the horses of the gods, but the gods no longer have need of them!" shouted Parlan. "Catch them and they are yours! You have earned them! You deserve them! And I will be the one to help you get them!" The white horses instantly swung around and galloped away, flinging bright drops of water from their muzzles as they did. "Keep your lines! Do not let them turn back! Use your slings! Drive them to the sea, where we can hold them at the shore!"

The white mares swept down the plain together in a tight herd. Leading them was a tall mare with faint streaks of silver-grey in her mane. At the back, driving them on and keeping them all together, was the single stallion in the herd, a powerful creature with an arching neck and a thick white mane and a bright fierce look in its hazel eye. But the stallion had to slow his great stride a bit, for nearly all of the mares were either heavy with foal or had small black colts running at their sides. The horses of the gods, normally the fleetest and strongest the world had ever seen, were slowed now by offspring both new and unborn.

Parlan knew this gave him and his men a chance they would otherwise never have. He grinned as he thought of how pleased his men would be when they received their gifts of the magnificent horses of the gods! The herd abruptly turned hard to the south, and Parlan could quickly see why. Rising into view was the wide and sparkling expanse of the sea, stretching as far as anyone could see in either direction. The mares continued to run along the grassy hills above the sharp drop-offs to the rocks and ocean below, and Parlan felt certain that this line of men could keep them going in this direction. But coming up ahead was an outgrowth of the forest, very near to the hillside where the white herd galloped. If they managed to turn and run into the woods, Parlan knew they would never be found.

"Slings out!" he shouted. "Don't let them turn!"

Three men riding nearest the front took out their flat leather slings and began the delicate and difficult task of reaching into the leather bags at their belts, drawing out a stone, and folding the center of the sling around it—all from the back of a wildly galloping horse. But they had not become the high king's warriors for nothing, and one by one they sent their stones flying toward the fleeing mares.

Three of the mares nearest the forest flinched and threw their heads up as they ran. Red spots of blood appeared on their white necks, but they continued on—and then the stones flew again. This time they found their marks in two of the little black foals who galloped frantically alongside their mothers.

The foals tried to leap away from the fierce and frightening bite of the stones, but they stumbled and staggered and fell hard to the rocky ground, sliding and rolling with flailing legs as the mares behind them made wild and clumsy leaps in an effort to avoid the fallen foals.

But not all of them succeeded.

Flying hooves struck one foal hard on the side and knocked it down again, where another mare could not avoid stepping on its front leg. One foal managed to get up and go skittering after the racing herd, even as its mother called out to it, but the other was left struggling to stand on only three legs and hold up one that was broken and bleeding.

The injured foal let out a high and terrified whinny, but in an instant found itself surround by the galloping horses of Parlan and his men.

"Surround it! Surround the foal!" Parlan shouted. "Its mother will come back for it. Some of you stay and catch her! The rest of you keep going!"

Even as five of his men surrounded the terrified foal, the rest of the warriors ran headlong into the white mare who had turned back to find her screaming foal. Her ears flattened with rage, she plunged past her pursuers and snapped and kicked at them. The warriors' horses quickly swung out of her way, in spite of their riders' forceful attempts to turn toward her.

The mare finally reached her foal, neighing to it in a deep and urgent voice, and the little creature pressed close to her side even as it and its mother touched noses. Then the mare led it away, glaring and biting at the mortals' horses and lashing out at them with a swift hind foot. The other horses stayed well away from her, no matter how much their riders shouted and beat them, and in a few moments the mare and her foal walked free.

Parlan ground his teeth. "Forget them! Get the others! Look, they are slowing!"

And so they were. The chaos caused by the injuries to the two foals, and the confusion as their mothers turned around to find them, had caused the herd to slow and turn back on itself. The stallion arched its neck and bared its teeth and shrieked its defiance at the horses of Parlan's men; but though they stayed well back from the white herd, it was not long before the men had the mares surrounded on all three sides.

On the fourth side was the roaring sea.

"We have them! We have them! Keep your slings out, to hold them here! Three of you ride back and get ropes. They are ours!"

It seemed that the white horses were indeed now the property of Parlan and his men. Though Parlan regretted that the two foals had been struck and that one seemed to be badly injured, it seemed a small price to pay. "Look at them!" he whispered, as Maorga danced beneath him.

The herd of some twenty-five cloud-white and silver-grey mares, along with six black foals and the powerful white stallion, stood with their tails to the sea and watched Parlan's men closely. Anytime they thought they saw an opening between the mounted horses, they started to run toward the dark forest just beyond the men; but instantly the slings would come out and a couple of well-placed stones would fly, and the white horses would be driven back again.

Suddenly Maorga swung around hard to one side and ran backward for several steps. Parlan kicked hard to get the stallion back on line, afraid the white herd would escape; but as Maorga tucked its tail and leapt again, Parlan finally looked back to see the white mare with the injured foal walking through the line of mounted men to rejoin the herd.

The mare moved slowly so that the hobbling offspring could keep up. Parlan's heart sank at the sight of the black foal's badly broken foreleg—he could see bone through the torn skin and black hair, and blood trickling down to the little dangling hoof—but he vowed that once they had the herd in captivity, he would do all he could to heal the unfortunate creature. "Eriu will care for you. Eriu will know what to do," he whispered as the horses walked past. "As soon as we get you home, she will help you."

The white herd gathered around the returning mare, with all of them moving in close to greet the mother and its injured baby. Parlan saw the other foal that the sling-stones had struck. It was not crippled, but half the soft black hair and hide was scraped from one side of its body where it had slid along the rough rocks. It moved slowly with lowered head, as if stunned and in pain.

Then, almost as one, the white horses raised their heads and stared at the forest behind Parlan's line of men. "Slings ready!" Parlan shouted. "They're going to charge for the woods! Don't let them get past you!" But as all the men watched and raised their slings, the herd of white horses turned around and ran straight into the sea.

Parlan caught his breath. "Stop them! Stop them!"

But there was nothing he or his men could do. The mares and the foals and the powerful stallion galloped and lunged into the crashing waves. The black foals were soon lost from sight against the dark surface of the water, and the white coats of the mares and the stallion next became one with the flashing whitecaps of the breaking waves. In a moment, all were gone.

Parlan and his men sat on their horses and lowered their slings, staring out at nothing but an empty sand beach and the never-ending waves of the sea.

CHAPTER TWENTY-THREE

Slowly, with low grumbling amongst themselves and furtive glances at Parlan, the men rode their tired, sweating horses at a walk back up the coast to return to the camp. Parlan sat on Maorga and watched them go, and then stared out at the sea.

He saw no swimming horses, nor any floating bodies of dead mares and foals. He saw only the smoothly rushing waves and whitecaps, as always.

At last he reined Maorga around and trotted across the sand toward the grass—and there, walking out of the forest, was a grey mare ridden by a dark-haired woman in a green cloak.

Eriu halted her mare as Parlan rode toward her. "Eriu! Please tell me where they are. Please tell me they are safe."

She turned and gazed at him, her face very white and still and her green eyes very cool. "The horses were safe here, King Parlan, until your men chased and terrified them and hurled stones at them—and badly injured two of the foals."

He looked away. "I am sorry. I did not mean to harm them. Please—where did they go?"

She gazed out at the ocean. "They fled to a place of safety. They returned to the Otherworld, where no man will chase or harm or capture them. The sea, of course, is one of the doors to the Otherworld."

Parlan let out a sigh. "Then they are safe. I am glad to know that. I thought only to capture them, and . . . and . . ."

"And what?"

He raised his head. "And to give them as gifts to my men, for their loyalty and courage."

Eriu smiled a little. "Those are the horses of the gods, Parlan. They would not serve your men unless one of the gods asked it of them—and that, I assure you, is something we will not do. You have horses of your own. You had no cause to torment ours."

"I am truly sorry, Eriu. I thought only to reward my men."

"You cannot buy their loyalty. It is foolish for any man to try to do so, and far more foolish for a king."

He frowned. "Why do you think I try to barter for their service? Do I not have to bribe them to keep their loyalty?"

"That is for you to answer, Parlan. I am not the high king. But I do know that your men are shaken from their battles with the Black Dragon and with the firedrake—and that some of them have their doubts about a high king who has brought this terrible curse down upon them, however inadvertently."

He looked directly at her. "I am aware of that, Lady Eriu. I wished only to encourage them on the most difficult journey they will ever face."

She nodded, and looked out at the sea again. "Go back to your men, King Parlan. Do not forget that wound on your horse's rump—and hope that he does not sustain another."

She reined her mare around and trotted back into the woods, disappearing almost immediately into the deep shadows beneath the oaks.

Parlan found his men waiting for him at the place where they had camped. None of them said a word, but simply followed him as he continued on his way to the north with the sea to the king's left hand, as always.

The days were lengthening now and growing milder. Soft spring rains alternated with warm sunshine throughout each afternoon, and everywhere the world was bright with wildflowers—deep blue-purple spring gentian amongst the rocks and boulders, bright yellow dandelions and the fiery crimson bells of the mountain sorrels in the open grassy meadows, and blue, pink and purple violets in the shade at the edge of the forests.

Yet after just a few days, the earth around them began to change. The fields of grass and stands of oaks and willows and rowans gave way to an open region as far as any man could see—bare open ground, sometimes of solid stone but sometimes wide flat stretches of ridged and shattered rock, which seemed to have been crushed and folded by the hand of some giant.

"The Place of Stone," Cillian said, halting his horse beside Parlan. "It will cut the horses' feet to ribbons. We'll have to go around it."

Parlan nodded. "I have heard of this place, this *bhoire-ann*. No trees, no rivers, and hardly any grass—surely the strangest place in all of Eire."

He reined Maorga away from the long flat outcrop of limestone rock at the horse's feet and edged past it in the grass. "Tell all of the men to have a care for the sharp rocks. We'll get past as much of this as we can before nightfall." Cillian nodded and turned his horse back, while Parlan continued on ahead.

The bare and tortured landscape went on and on. Once

Parlan would have considered the place a mere curiosity, but now it gave him a very disquieting feeling—almost a feeling of dread.

"It seems an unnatural place, does it not, King Parlan?"

He turned his head to see Eriu riding beside him. He had not heard any hoofbeats, nor had Maorga reacted in the slightest to her sudden presence, but that did not matter; she was here.

He took a deep breath and looked out at the cracked and barren landscape. "It does seem unnatural," he answered. "I wonder why the Goddess of the Land would not heal such a place and make it whole and green like the rest of Eire."

"It has its own beauty. It was once covered by the sea, and it still keeps the shapes and carvings that the water gave it, even though it is now dry land."

Parlan looked away. "It is a place where nothing grows. It looks like it has been destroyed by . . . by . . ."

"By what?"

He set his teeth. "By the foul cold breath of that black beast that threatens to destroy every blade of grass and every leaf and every flower in all of Eire. I fear that all will look this way the bhoireann looks—and that the fault will lie with me."

Eriu glanced out at the parched and broken land, then looked at Parlan again. "Perhaps you are right. Perhaps I have always left this place as it is so that it might serve as a warning—a warning to all that the land and the life that exists on it should not be taken for granted."

"I can assure you that I do not take it for granted. Not any longer."

"Yet this place is not entirely dead. Look again. Here and there you will see that a little grass has found purchase in the long narrow crevices in the rock surface. And all throughout the cracked and shattered rocks you will see small and beautiful wildflowers that grow no place else in Eire."

He glanced at her again. "I already know that life will find a way. But this land I swore to protect deserves far better than a few blades of grass and a few tiny blossoms, no matter how rare and pretty they might be."

Eriu gave him a small smile. "I am glad to know this, King Parlan," she said, and she rode away again, disappearing over the crest of a nearby hill.

For several more days, Parlan and his men rode beside the desolate *bhoireann*; and Parlan felt as cold and empty as the barren stone landscape. Eriu had again vanished from his life, leaving him to ride alone past this empty reminder of the curse that might soon destroy his entire world, and to sleep each night on a cold stand of grass with only his heavy cloak to keep him warm.

At last they left the Place of Stone behind, and reached the deep and beautiful oak forests near the western coast of the island. The tall and ancient trees welcomed them into their cool shadows, and the men rode onto the sun-dappled paths and felt something like relief at the sight of tall sturdy trunks and free-flowing brooks, and most of all, rich damp earth with clumps of green grass and clusters of blue and purple violets.

The forested land began to climb up into the hills, and by the time the sun approached the horizon, Parlan and his men had reached the top of the highest hill. They rode out of the dense oak forest onto a wide rolling expanse of open grass-covered hilltops, rising above the forests that crept up on all sides.

Parlan halted his men at the edge of the open hilltop fields, for out on the centermost hill were a number of men and women hard at work.

Two teams of men dragged heavy logs and fallen

branches out of the deep forest and took them to two enormous stacks of wood perhaps twenty paces apart, rising at the center of the highest hill. The women picked up dead twigs and sticks from the forest floor and tossed them into the growing stacks of logs, and gathered violets from beneath the trees, and wove them into strings with the bright yellow primroses that grew freely on the grassy hilltop.

Parlan heard a low buzz of excited conversation spread through his men. "*Bealtaine*. This is a Bealtaine celebration! We didn't miss it after all!" They began jumping down from their horses and shouting out to the servants: "Make camp here! Hurry! Hurry! It's Bealtaine!"

As Parlan slid down from Maorga's back, three men from the hilltop left off their work and walked over to him. "Good day to you, King Parlan," the first of them said. "We've been expecting you. Your messengers have been and gone. We feared you would be too late for the ritual."

Parlan smiled. "No one wants to miss the Bealtaine fires. We will join you at moonrise."

The man grinned back. "Moonrise, then," he said, and the three strangers started back to their work.

As the sun made its way down below the hillside, and then down below the trees, Parlan's servants set up camp as quickly as they ever had. His men went into the forest and came back with a fair number of trout from the clear rushing streams. And when at last they sat down to eat their earth-baked fish and steamed watercress and hot flatbread, the men and women on the hilltop had completed their work and gone back into the forests.

"Who are these people, King Parlan?" asked Gavin, taking a huge bite of thickly buttered bread. "There is no large kingdom fortress anywhere nearby. Would it not have been better to celebrate Bealtaine with a king and his many highborn people?"

"Are you afraid there won't be enough women here for you tonight?" Parlan asked, reaching for another chunk of trout.

"Well, there are nearly a hundred men among us— away from their wives, away from any woman, for how many fortnights now?"

"About twelve, I should say. But never fear. This particular Bealtaine celebration is for those who live in the fields and forests and so are the closest to the ways of nature. Not for them the rules and formality of those who live behind the high walls of a king's fortress."

"Ah, I see," Gavin said, grinning even wider.

"But that is not the only reason." Cillian took another piece of flatbread from the wooden plate as he spoke up. "A king—a high king—is supposed to be a king to all of his people, not just to those who live in fine houses with feather-filled cushions to sleep on and who wear gold jewelry and embroidered clothes. The women here will have plain linen gowns and their hands will be roughened from work, but they are the high king's people just the same."

"And they expect the high king to serve them just the same!" Gavin laughed out loud at his own joke, but Parlan only stared at the ground.

"Eat while you can, Gavin," Cillian remarked. "The sun is all but gone. The moon will rise very soon."

Moonrise—and then it would be Bealtaine, when the people would of course expect the high king to participate fully in the rite. But, Parlan wondered, what would the king's goddess think of that?

CHAPTER TWENTY-FOUR

At last night fell over the hilltop, and in the east rose the enormous full yellow moon. From the forests came first a few scattered torches, and then a line of them, and then another, until the hilltop was filled with the light of hundreds of torches carried in both hands of each man in the crowd.

The women all carried heaps of long woven strings of white violets and yellow primrose, and wore plain linen gowns with simple leather belts. Their jewelry consisted of only an armlet or brooch here or there made of copper—the most ancient of metals used by men.

The men, too, were dressed only in simple linen trousers and tunics. All of them, men and women, were barefoot.

These were the folk who lived not in great fortresses but in small earth-ringed homes among the fields. These were the people who tended to the fields of rye and barley and oats and wheat, and to the herds of the red-and-white cattle and the shaggy brown sheep.

As the great crowd gathered around the stacks of waiting wood, with the light from their many torches casting a bright yellow glare all across the hilltop, Parlan and his men walked to the crowd and stood together a short distance away.

Though the huge crowd fairly trembled with excitement, and people could not stop themselves from whispered conversation and peals of laughter here and there, they kept themselves as still as possible and waited—just waited. Before the revelry of Bealtaine could begin, there was a ritual to get through.

Finally, three men made their way through the crowd. Their progress was easy to mark, as the torchbearers fell back to let them through. The trio came to stand together between the two mountains of wood. Unlike the others, they wore soft leather boots, woolen trews, tunics in bright shades of blue and red and yellow, and colorful plaid cloaks fastened at the shoulder with heavy golden brooches.

Druids. Come no doubt from Abhainn Aille, the nearest king's fortress to this remote place, to conduct the Bealtaine ritual for the high king. The three raised their arms and the crowd instantly fell silent.

Parlan could not help but smile a little to himself. He knew it was not entirely out of respect for the druids' authority that the crowd gave them its attention. The people just wanted the formalities out of the way so they could get on with the revelry! Parlan could not blame them. His own tension rose with every heartbeat. He had been to the Bealtaine fires every year since becoming a young man, first as one of his king's many warriors and later as a king himself. Now he was here at Bealtaine as the high king of all Eire, the ruler of all the rulers of all the tribes, and he well knew that every woman here would be seeking him out.

"People of the scattered kingdoms, High King Parlan, people of the fields!" cried the first druid. "You have come together this night at Bealtaine, the night of the second full moon past the spring equinox—a night like no other night of the year.

"The gods instructed us, uncounted years ago, that on this night all men and women who were willing should take whatever partners in love that they might like . . . for any of those partners might well be one of the gods or goddesses come to walk and revel amongst mortals this one night of the year."

A quick movement in the forest caught Parlan's eye. He glanced toward the spot, but the glare from the torches remained in his eyes and he could see nothing at all.

"Now!" said the druid. "All who wish to dance around the Bealtaine fires and take part in the ritual, adorn yourselves with the flowers the women have gathered."

With laughter and flirtation, the women quickly draped their flower strings round their hair and went from man to man placing the long threads around their necks, taking full opportunity to take in each man's appearance and to smile at and touch the ones they found most appealing. They seemed to find it especially amusing that the men all carried a torch in each hand and so could not touch them back—not yet!

Many of the women went straight to Parlan's men, flocking to the strangers who were, they knew, the favored warriors of the high king and therefore the strongest and most skilled in the land—and the most handsome. And many walked straight toward Parlan himself, with flowers in their hands and smiles on their beautiful young faces. But before they could reach him, another woman stepped directly in front of Parlan.

He blinked. She seemed to have come out of nowhere. For an instant he thought it must be Eriu, but a second look showed him it was not.

She was very tall, taller even than Eriu, and had her knee-length coppery hair pulled into many tight slender braids. Her soft linen gown, the color of cream, was snugly belted around her waist and clearly showed her tall strong body. And her face—her face seemed shaped by perfection itself, smooth as milk and just as fair, with a cold look in the pale hazel eyes that flicked up and down his body as she looked him over.

"You have no flowers," she said, lifting up one of the strands she carried. Her voice was low and smooth. "Surely a man as strong and handsome as you will not skip the Bealtaine ritual."

Again, the movement beneath the trees caught his eye. This time he thought he saw a white hand drawing a dark hood up over a white face—but then his attention turned back to the tall woman with the braids, for she had draped a string of white and yellow flowers around his shoulders. "There. Now you must take part. You would not reject me on this Bealtaine night, would you, King Parlan?"

Her voice was as cool as her face, and just as enchanting. "None should be rejected on Bealtaine night, my lady," he replied.

She tilted her head and gave him a lazy smile. He stared, fascinated, at the fine strands of copper that draped her hair, and the shoulders of her gown like some gleaming, near-invisible cobweb. He had never seen anything like it.

"Then I will see you when the ritual begins," she said, and turned and walked away.

"You didn't even get her name," said Gavin, looking down at the string of flowers around his own neck.

"No one requires a name on Bealtaine night."

Gavin grinned. "So right, my king! With that, I will leave you to the ritual." He walked away, disappearing into the crowd.

"Her name is Flidais."

The voice came from behind him—a voice that was soft

and feminine and familiar. But when he turned around, there was once again only the briefest glimpse of a white hand in the darkness before it disappeared again, as though drawn beneath a cloak.

He took a step toward the forest. "I know you are here," he said quietly. "I hoped you would come to me on this Bealtaine night, Lady Eriu. I want you first of all."

"First, King Parlan? You mean to honor me by taking me first?"

He could not meet her gaze. "They will expect it of me, Lady Eriu. Surely you know that."

"I do know well what the Bealtaine ritual involves. The gods instructed mortal men and women to set aside one night of the year—the night of the second full moon after the spring equinox—when all could take any sexual partners they wished, no matter what their commitments. Men love this time of free indulgence with no consequence, while women often use it to get a child by a strong and handsome warrior or a king. Perhaps, if they are lucky, a high king."

"Or a god."

Eriu nodded. "Even the gods have a desire for companionship—and to know that their own blood will not be lost to the world of Men forever."

"Then you will take part," Parlan said. "Surely you must have done so many times."

She shook her head, and gave him a cool stare. "Never have I taken part in any Bealtaine ritual. My interactions with mortal men are confined to the kingmakings. That is the only time that any man ever touches me. That is my place. That is my purpose."

Parlan reached for her hand. "I understand. It is your place, as the Goddess of the Land and the granter of sovereignty, to hold yourself apart from the lust and license of Bealtaine. Yet it is my place, as a king—as a high king— to involve myself in it to the utmost."

"To mate with as many of the women as want you—with as many as you *can*."

He closed his eyes. "That is the way of it. That is the way it has always been. Eriu, that is what the gods and goddesses themselves instructed mortal men and women to do at the celebration of Bealtaine."

She turned away from him. "So, Parlan. I see that you are only an ordinary man after all."

He raised his head, and set his teeth. "Of course I am a mortal man. I am not a god, nor have I ever claimed to be one."

From several steps away she turned to face him, and he looked directly at her tall slender form and cold green eyes and impossibly fine and beautiful face. "Oh, but you did claim to be one, Parlan. You claimed to love a goddess. You claimed to be worthy of having a goddess as your queen—and that makes you the equal of a god. Do you disagree?"

Parlan opened his mouth to speak, and then closed it again. He drew a deep breath. "I never said I was a god, Lady Eriu—"

"But you did say that you were the one man worthy to love a goddess. You said that you would do what no other man could do, or was willing to do, to prove that you were worthy of such a thing. Did you not swear that to me on the night of your kingmaking?"

He looked away. "I did swear it, Lady Eriu."

"Then we shall indeed learn this night whether it is true or not." She melted back into the darkness, and Parlan was left alone once again.

He clenched his fists, and then turned away and walked back out to the open hilltop and the light of hundreds of torches. The women had finished handing out their strings of flowers to the men, and now the women surrounded the easternmost stack of wood while the torchbearing, flower-draped men surrounded the westernmost stack.

Once more, the three druids stood between the stacks. The first turned and cried out to the crowd: "Each man, go and give one of your torches to a woman, then return to your place. Go, and do it quickly now, for as soon as you return the music can begin!"

With a shout of joy the men broke ranks and ran to the shadowed circle of women, handing over the flaring torches and then running back to their own circle. Now there were two circles of bright light on the hilltop.

"Let the music begin!" shouted the druid. "Let the revelry begin!" The three then turned and ran out of the circles of light. As the druids left, the insistent sound of the drums filled the hilltop, pounding through the forest and sending the men and women into a frenzy of leaping and dancing.

The trio of druids continued to move away from the circle, toward the edge of the forest, and as they did they saw Parlan standing beside the trees and watching the dancers.

"King Parlan! What is this? Why does the high king not join in the Bealtaine ritual?"

Parlan glanced at the first druid. "The high king may do as he wishes on this night. If he wishes to watch the people dance, that is what he will do."

The two other druids, younger men than the first but no less self-important, looked at each other. "The people will be very disappointed if the high king refuses to join their celebration . . ."

"Disappointed and confused," added the third druid. "They will wonder what their ritual lacks that the high king would turn his back on it."

"They will be far more than just confused and disappointed," said the first druid. "They will be sorely offended, and rightly so. Does the high king object to simple surroundings, preferring only the comforts of some great fortress? Does he find the women here too plain and rough-handed for his taste, and would rather wait for soft-fingered, highborn ladies?"

He shook his head. "If you wish, King Parlan, when we return to Abhainn Aille we will tell the king about all of those things. When you arrive there in another fortnight or so, you yourself may explain to the king—and to his people—why you found the Bealtaine ritual that they, and we, prepared for you to be unfit for High King Parlan."

The three druids stood in stony silence, staring at him while they waited for his answer. Parlan ground his teeth and glanced into the forest again, but saw only darkness. Finally he looked his accusers in the eye. "I will go and join this very fine ritual, with the very beautiful women who live in these hills and valleys." And with that, he went striding off to join the dancers.

CHAPTER TWENTY-FIVE

The rhythmic beat of the drums filled the air, for the musicians had left the forest and moved to surround the two circles with drums and harps and whistling wooden pipes. Parlan walked straight to the circle of men and fell into step with them, having no trouble allowing his feet to follow the rhythm of the drums.

The men circled round, as did the women, throwing each other inviting glances as they passed between the two stacks of wood. Finally, with a great shout of joy, one of the women threw her torch high into the air so that it fell into the center of the great mountain of wood, and on seeing this all the rest of the people threw their own torches into the waiting piles. As the fires caught, snapping and biting and flaring from the wood, the music grew ever louder, and soon the pounding of the drums competed with the roar of the flames.

With the two great fires in full bloom, the male and female dancers were forced close together as they passed between the flames. Soon the circles were entirely mixed as men and women chose their first partners and danced with each other instead of alone. Before long the heat became too intense for anyone to pass between the flames, and the two circles became one large circumference encircling both great fires.

Parlan found himself caught up in the power and excitement that was Bealtaine, in the playful dance around the fierce flames, in the joy that infected every dancer and made him forget any troubles he might have had before moonrise. But most of all, he was caught by the many, many beautiful and desirable women who danced here in the circle with him, and whose blood was fired by carefree desire like his own.

Though he could see that many of these women had already found partners among his own warriors and among the other men, many more of them began to dance near him. They were the youngest and most beautiful of all, with flashing eyes and laughing smiles and long, long hair of red or gold or brown. All of them were flushed and glowing with a sheen of sweat over their skin from the heat of the flames and the exertion of the dance, and from the desire and anticipation that pounded through them all like the pounding drums.

For a time Parlan saw only a blur of curving bodies and flying hair. Then he became aware that one tall woman matched him step for step on the wild dance, circling wide around both fires—and when they passed nearest to the forest, she took him by both hands and led him toward the darkness of the trees.

Parlan, breathless and laughing, allowed himself to stumble after her. Pulling one hand free to steady himself against the rough bark of an oak, he looked up to see that same tall woman with the very long braids who had placed the string of flowers around his neck. Her now-damp linen gown clung to her breasts and outlined her hips and her very long legs. A spider web of copper filaments gleamed in her braided hair.

"I do not always attend the Bealtaine ritual," the woman said, her voice low and steady, "but I knew that High King Parlan was to be here this night." She ran her long slender fingers down the side of his face, and onto the damp skin of his neck. "It seems it was worth my trouble to come here."

Parlan shut his eyes as tension and desire surged through him at her touch. He was already aroused enough by the flames and the dance and the many beautiful women all eager for his touch; and now, as she stepped toward him and the warm musky scent of her filled his nostrils, his entire body was seized with desire and he could not help but catch her in a hard embrace and pull her close.

"Ah, now that is more to my liking, King Parlan," she whispered, pressing the length of her body against his and fitting the softness of her curves against his rigid desire. "I am glad to see that you are a man after all, not just a king who would hold himself apart from the women who desire him as though he were too good for them."

The blood pounded in Parlan's ears. He took hold of both her arms and pulled back enough to look into her gleaming hazel eyes, his breath coming fast.

You said you were the one man worthy to love a goddess . . . the one man who would do what no other man could do, or would ever be willing to do.

He forced himself to take his hands away from her arms, and took another step back. "But I swore an oath that I would not live as an ordinary man, for the one I love deserves no less."

The woman looked him up and down again, and gave him a kind of half-smile. "She is a cold and demanding mistress, is she not, King Parlan?"

He caught his breath, but said nothing.

She went on, "I know you mean to win her . . . but look at you on this night. She is not here for you at Bealtaine,

yet she expects you, the high king of all Eire, to hold yourself away from the ritual and not touch a single woman
here." She stepped in front of him again, once more close
enough to touch. "You are weary of it already, are you
not? Do you think it will ever change? You say you will
make yourself her equal, but will she ever consider herself
to be *your* equal?"

"I . . . I love her," Parlan said. "I love her like no other. I
swore an oath to her."

The woman laughed. "No one will hold you to such an
oath—least of all the Lady Eriu. Go back to being a king.
Go back to being a man. And start now, on the very night
when you should open your arms to all the many women
here who want you."

Parlan blinked, and looked away from her. The two
great fires billowed and flared and would be seen for a
very great distance. He realized that there were no longer
any dancers in the fields, and no more music; the only
sounds were the roar of the fires and the satisfied groaning and lusty cries of the Bealtaine revelers in the darkness of the forest all around.

"Lady Flidais is right," said a soft feminine voice. "You
should do as she suggests. It is no different from the advice I myself have given you."

Parlan turned around. Standing behind him, shielded
by the low-hanging branches of the oaks, was Eriu.

"My lady, I swore an oath to you and I will not break it.
Not now, and not ever."

"But you have never wanted to break it more than on
this night—and none would blame you." She shook her
head. "You are a mortal man, Parlan, and that is what
you are meant to be. I hereby release you from your oath.
Go, now, and be the king that I made last Samhain
night."

Eriu gathered her deep green cloak close around her. "I
will not stand here and wait while you choose between

two goddesses. You are released from the oath you swore to me, Parlan. Go and be a king. Go and be a man."

He bent down and pushed beneath the low branches to go to her, but by the time he could stand upright again she was gone. He found only empty darkness beneath the oak branches.

"So, King Parlan, you see? Eriu feels as I do. You may choose whatever woman you wish. And if one goddess has abandoned you, you still have another—at least, for tonight."

She stood before him again, and her long legs and curving form and swelling breasts beneath the damp and clinging linen gown were almost enough to make him forget all else, but he forced himself to turn his back on her.

"You are indeed a goddess, Lady Flidais, and at any other time in my life I would have taken you the moment I saw you. But understand this: Though Eriu may have released me from my oath, I do not release myself from it. I will never do that. I will always love her and I will always want her—and if I must wait forever to prove that to her, then that is what I will do."

Her eyes narrowed. "And to think Eriu told me that I was cruel when it came to the way I dealt with mortal men." She sighed. "No matter. I will simply go and find another, and take him back to the Otherworld with me for a time. Perhaps I will choose from among your own."

He waved her away, still not looking at her. "Go from me. Please. Go and leave me in peace."

"As you wish, King Parlan. May your oath bring you much happiness—though I do not think it will this night." He heard the sound of long-striding footsteps over the forest floor, and then she was gone.

He sighed deeply, and shut his eyes. All around him came the laughter and whispers, cries and moans of men and women deep in the throes of sexual passion. He looked out toward the brightness of the fires and started to walk toward them, determined to return to his own camp, but before he could take a single step he found himself surrounded by laughing voices and strong feminine hands.

"Now you are ours!"

"Now Bealtaine can begin!"

"No man has touched a one of us this night."

"We have been waiting for the high king!"

"We have been waiting for you!"

Five of them. Five beautiful, young and very mortal women. They pressed in close and ran their hands over every part of him, giggling and whispering even as they did. It was torment.

With his last trace of willpower, he wrenched himself away and fled into the forest, staggering through the darkness as fast as he could go, feeling his way past the low branches and stumbling over roots and rocks.

"Eriu!" he cried. "Eriu! You are right! I am only a man after all. Soon they will get the better of me, and I will not be able to resist them! I know I do not deserve a goddess as my queen, but my oath to you still remains. If you have any trace of love for me at all, Lady Eriu, come to me now, and give me some comfort this night!"

He dropped to his knees and steadied himself with one hand against the cold damp earth. "I am only a man, no different from any other. I will always love the goddess Eriu, the way that a man truly loves a woman. And that will always be so, no matter what else happens on this night or any other night."

Parlan allowed himself to collapse to the earth. It was silent out here, and dark and cold. He had left the warmth and light and raucous cries of the Bealtaine celebration far behind.

Then it seemed that the darkness began to fade, and a

soft yellow glow found its way down into the forest. Parlan looked up to see the huge Bealtaine moon pushing the clouds out of its way and shining down upon him.

"You are a king, Parlan. And you are indeed a man—though I do not know any man, whether mortal or god, who would have kept to the oath he made on a night such as this."

He started to get to his feet, but Eriu took him gently by the shoulders and eased him back down. "It is the night of Bealtaine," she said, "and I choose the high king."

He pulled her close, and held her tight and hard, and buried his face in the soft and dark of her hair. And as Parlan had so many times before, he found comfort and release again and again in his time alone with Eriu. He also found, as always, love and acceptance that was total and complete, both in body and in spirit, of a kind that he knew he would never find if he took every other woman at the Bealtaine fires—that he knew he would never find with any other woman at all.

Chapter Twenty-six

The following day passed in a haze of dampness and sleep for all of the Bealtaine revelers. They curled in heaps, wrapped in their heavy cloaks in the soft grass beneath the oak trees and blackthorn shrubs.

Away from the others and deep in the forest, Parlan lay close to Eriu, conscious only of the warmth and sweet scent of her body as they lay together wrapped in his heavy cloak. Finally, thirst and hunger roused him and forced him to get up. Eriu rose when he did, and together they walked back to the campsite, passing a number of straggling revelers also making their tired way back.

He could not help but notice that though he himself was exhausted, damp, muddy and pale—as were the others he saw—after the very long Bealtaine night followed by nearly an entire day without food or fire, Eriu looked as fresh and fair and beautiful as though she had just stepped out of the Otherworld.

They walked in the late afternoon across the open hilltop field, past the cooling ashes of the Bealtaine bonfires. Parlan drew himself up a little straighter as they approached his own campsite at the edge of the trees. His men would see him walking with his goddess as he returned to camp after Bealtaine night. All would know that this magnificent creature had chosen to spend the night with him and only him.

As he had expected, all was quiet at the campsite, with the men merely sitting around the fires and dozing on the grass within their cloaks. Practically the only movement was the lazy rising of smoke from a few fires scattered throughout the camp, though he did begin to hear a few orders barked to the servants.

"Wake up! Put on the food! Lots of it!"

"We ride out today, and I'm starving!"

"I've never been so hungry. Get the meat and the bread and butter, and the boiled oats and honey, all you can carry!"

Parlan smiled. It was always so on the day after Bealtaine, with the men sleeping late into the afternoon and waking up ravenous after spending themselves completely at the Bealtaine ritual. For many days their heads would be filled with the thoughts and memories of the many women they had lain with under the trees and beside the roaring bonfires. Normally, Parlan would be enjoying the same thoughts.

This time, though, it was different. Instead of remembering only a collection of nameless, faceless women in the glare of the Bealtaine bonfires, he now saw only Eriu's beautiful green eyes looking up at him as he lay with her, and only her, on the soft forest floor.

Before Parlan could speak to anyone, Cillian hurried out to meet him and barely spared a glance for Eriu. "Where is Daithi?" he asked, looking closely at his king.

"Daithi? The hostage-prince from Dun Farriaghe?" Parlan shook his head and frowned. "I do not know. Perhaps he is still sleeping in the forest. Many of them—"

"Daithi is the only one of our men who has not returned. I thought that perhaps he was in the company of the high king, but I see now that is not the case." Cillian looked briefly at Eriu before glancing at Parlan again. "Did you see him at all last night?"

"I did not. I was . . . farther out in the forest. I do not recall seeing any of our people last night."

"Well, I saw him," Cillian said. "Very late. The moon was halfway past its height. He walked in the company of an extraordinarily beautiful woman. She was very tall, and very long-legged, with long braided hair the color of gleaming copper. It should not be difficult to find such a magnificent woman among the herdsmen's daughters of this place. I know I would recognize her if I saw her again."

But Eriu raised her chin and looked at Cillian. "The woman you describe was Flidais. She resides in the Otherworld with the remaining gods and goddesses, and often amuses herself by taking mortal men back there with her—and keeping them until long past the time when all of their own people have lived out their natural lives and died."

Parlan glanced at Eriu. "She offered to take me back with her last night, and when I refused, she laughed and said she would simply find another." He shook his head. "I thought nothing of it at the time."

Eriu drew her hood up over her head. "Then the man you seek is in the Otherworld with Flidais. You will not see him again."

Parlan set his jaw. "She has taken a man whom she knew would cause us great difficulty. She has taken not just any man, but a prince of Dun Farriaghe and one of their hostages to peace."

Again Cillian stared hard at Parlan. "The safety of those hostages is for the high king to guarantee, yet now three of our hostage-princes have been lost forever. What will you say to the king of Dun Ghee and to the king of

Dun Farriaghe, to explain what happened to their son and nephew?"

Parlan returned his hard glare. "I do not know what I will say to them, except that both men served well and bravely before they were lost."

"I am sure their people will understand—just as the people of these lands will understand why the high king held himself apart from their Bealtaine ritual and kept himself to just one woman."

Parlan caught Cillian by his cloak, just below the throat, and held him fast. "The high king does what he must do. He does not have time to ask his men each time he makes a decision."

Cillian raised his chin, but did not try to free himself from Parlan's grip. "It is true that he does not have to ask them—but one day, he will have to answer to them."

Parlan let go of the warrior's cloak. Cillian remained still. "I will return to your camp now, King Parlan, if I may."

"Go. I will take my leave of Lady Eriu."

Cillian glanced past Parlan's shoulder, and smiled faintly. "As you will, King Parlan." He turned and strode back to camp.

Parlan took a deep breath and forced his fists to un-clench. He thought only of turning back to Eriu again and finding comfort and strength in the warmth of her embrace, and as the memories of last night's Bealtaine rit-ual flooded through his mind he turned and reached out for her.

She was gone. All he saw was the grey sky and open field, with the two enormous circles of dead ash the only remaining traces of the warmth and life of Bealtaine.

The next day, the group followed a pleasant river to the north and made a leisurely ride while taking in the beauty of the first days of summer. The earth was covered in lush green grass, with dandelions and violets scattered everywhere, and the trees seemed to stand taller and more graceful with their newly grown covers of fresh green leaves and delicate buds. The wind was softer and warmer now, especially as the riders left the last of the seacoast and continued north even as the land jutted out west for a great distance and its high mountains sheltered them from the colder winds of the sea.

Rian came up to ride beside Parlan, well at the head of the procession. "A question for you, King Parlan, if I may," he said.

"Of course," Parlan answered. "What is it?"

"I am told," Rian began carefully, "that though the high king danced at the Bealtaine bonfires, he held himself apart from every woman there save one. Can that possibly be true?"

Parlan smiled. "It is true, Rian, strange as it might seem."

"But . . . why?"

"Why, indeed." Parlan drew a deep breath. "It is a strange feeling, and I can only tell you that I cannot explain. Normally a man proves his worth and strength by the number of women he can get to lie with him, especially at Bealtaine. Yet now . . . now I find that a new feeling stays with me. It is the feeling that I have received a great gift, and indeed have given one in return . . . a gift that could never be equaled, much less surpassed, merely by counting up female partners conquered beside the Bealtaine fires."

Rian laughed a little. "I am not a man who deserves a goddess, King Parlan, so you are right—such an idea does sound strange to me. Yet I am not unable to understand it."

Parlan glanced at him. "I believed as much. I would never speak of this to any other of my men, for I have no doubt they would only mock me as a weakling for settling for just one woman—even if she is a goddess."

213

"You are not the only one who has been given a gift. I have received the gift of the high king's trust and confidence, and for that I am grateful."

"I am grateful for your loyalty and companionship as well, Rian. I well understand that it was once given to Lugh, the greatest of the gods, and it is my privilege to have it now. I am very glad you are here. I feel certain I will have great need of you before this quest is over."

"We—*you*—are halfway through it, my king. Two of the sacred objects are yours."

"So they are. Halfway through, with half still to go." He gazed out over the green and gentle summer landscape. "And I have learned that even my own true love for a goddess—or hers for me—is not enough by itself to lift the terrible curse that love brought down upon my people in the first place."

Parlan closed his eyes for a moment. "Look at what is still to come. There are still two more tasks to get the next two artifacts, and then the unthinkable battle to come with the Black Dragon, *if* I manage to get them." He sighed. "There is something else that I will admit to no one else but you, Rian. I often think of how wonderful it would be to just lay this impossible quest aside and go and live in peace for the rest of my days, either with Eriu if she will stay with me, or simply loving her from afar if she will not."

"None would blame you for such thoughts. What man does not doubt himself at some point in his life?"

Parlan shook his head. "Now that the distraction of Bealtaine has passed, I find that a cold and creeping doubt grows in the pit of my stomach. And it is not fear of the tasks themselves, Rian, but fear that I will do all I can and it will still not be enough, will never be nearly enough to save my people and save my land. I sometimes awaken late at night and think of how it all seems futile, and hopeless, and far more than any man could hope to handle, and I do not know where I will ever find the courage to complete such an impossible task."

"If any man has the courage, King Parlan, it is you."

He smiled. "Those are kind words, Rian. But it is nonetheless true that three good men are dead and one is lost forever in the Otherworld—all because of my own failure to protect them. All because I allowed my arrogance and overconfidence to cloud my judgment."

"You fear you cannot trust yourself," said Rian quietly.

Parlan rode in silence for a few moments, and then slowly nodded his head. "You are right. But no matter my own dread of what is to come, I will not turn away from this quest. I will complete it or I will die in the attempt—and if I die, then perhaps some man more worthy can succeed where I failed."

One afternoon, after a few more days of riding along the narrow river, they left the forest paths for an open grassy plain on a gentle slope where the river widened somewhat and went tumbling and splashing down a series of little waterfalls.

"Make a camp here," Parlan said, as Cillian halted his horse alongside. "We'll spend some time in hunting, which I know the men crave, and stay here for a time in comfort."

Cillian looked down the sloping plain and out at the river and lakes that lay beyond. "Abhainn Aille is just down there, on one of those lakes. We could reach it tonight," he said. "Why do you wait?"

Parlan avoided looking down at the lakes, and instead peered out at the inviting forest surrounding the plain. "Set the servants to building the camp. Have the men meet me here. Tell them we're going for a hunt."

"A hunt. Now?"

"Now. For red deer. We need meat for ourselves, and I want to make a gift of it to Abhainn Aille as well."

"A gift, King Parlan? You need not give them any gifts. They owe allegiance and hostages to the high king. It is for them to offer *you* hospitality. You need not—"

"Bribe them?" Parlan shot him a cold glare. "It is not a bribe. Can I not give them a gift if I wish?"

Cillian sat a little straighter on his horse. "They will respect the high king no matter . . . no matter what difficulties he has encountered."

"You mean, 'No matter what curse he has brought down on their heads, or how many hostages to peace have been lost while in his care.' I cannot forget what has happened, much as I would like. Now, go and tell the men to gather for the hunt."

CHAPTER TWENTY-SEVEN

A short time later, with the sun still high overhead in a mostly blue sky, Parlan and most of his men left the servants hard at work raising the camp and digging the cooking pits. The hunting party rode west across a knee-deep section of the sparkling river, and then headed toward the deep and shadowy forest beyond.

All three pairs of their tall, wiry-coated hunting dogs came with them. The animals immediately became excited when their masters took them off their leads and they saw the spears at the ready in the hands of the riders; the six dogs knew right away that this was not merely another part of the journey; this was a hunt, and they immediately raced ahead of the riders and began searching through the dappled paths for any sign of game.

It did not take them long. The seventy men spread out through the forest side by side in a very wide line, and quickly flushed out a deer.

Though the dogs kept silent as they ran, concentrating on keeping their heads up and their quarry in sight, their crashing race through the brush echoed freely through the forest. The men had no trouble following, especially when the sound of a large and panicked animal tearing through the woods was added to the noise of the dogs.

Very soon the sound became localized and even more violent. There was the tearing of brush and trees, the fierce growling of the dogs, and the frantic deep bleating of terrified prey.

Parlan rode at the head of his men and saw, to his delight, that the dogs had not one but two young red-tail bucks in their grasp, with four dogs on one animal and two on the other. All six dogs were doing their best to bring down their frantic prey.

"Go," Parlan said, reining the snorting Maorga to one side, and two of his men eagerly urged their horses out to the struggling deer. In a moment the creatures were down and twitching, a spear thrust through their hearts, and then it was over and they lay still.

"Five of you stay here and get this meat back to camp," Parlan ordered. "Houndmaster, send the dogs out again. There is still plenty of daylight left and plenty more meat to be had. Send them! Go!"

At a shout from the houndmaster, the six long-legged dogs left their dead prey and tore off again to the west, racing through the forest in eagerness to find another red deer and drag it down for their masters.

Parlan trotted Maorga through the forest as the men once again spread out across the woods, feeling pleased at their success. He and his men would enjoy the meat they had just harvested, and it looked like there would be plenty more to take to Abhainn Aille. It was no bribe, he told himself fiercely; it was just a gift from a generous high king.

He kept his attention on the satisfying sounds of the hounds tearing through the forest after another deer. But suddenly the noise stopped—nothing but silence floated back to him through the woods.

Parlan looked hard in the direction the hounds had

gone. He could see that the dappled sunlight filtering through the forest ahead of them was growing brighter, as though the forest were ending, but it should not be ending. It should go on for a day's ride or more in this part of the island.

And then Parlan and his wide line of men burst out of the forest to a sight that left all of them cold.

They pulled up their horses. The hounds kept going after the wildly leaping buck, but none of the men had any more thought for hunting. Instead, they sat on their snorting horses and stared at the landscape before them, hardly able to comprehend what they were seeing.

Rolling hills lay at their feet. But where the hills should be covered with thick forest—where, indeed, until just a few days ago they had been—there was now only bare and blackened earth as far as the men could see. There was nothing but cracked and broken land covered with blackened shreds of grass, with cold, dead, broken sticks that had once been mighty trees.

"What has happened here?" asked Gavin, staring out at the ruined landscape. "Where is the forest?"

Parlan grabbed hold of the bronze hilt of the Sword of Nuadha, but he did not draw it. Instead, he only gripped until his knuckles turned white. There was no use in drawing it, for there was nothing here that any sword could help. Instead, he merely glanced over his shoulder at Gavin.

"Don't you see?" he asked, through clenched teeth. "The Black Dragon has been here. The creature scorches huge regions of land with breath so cold it burns, in order to get a few poor cattle or sheep or deer to feed upon." He looked out at the blackened hills once more, feeling a cold sense of dread rising in his chest. "And it is working. The beast grows stronger. Now it is destroying whole ranges of hills at once in its search for food. We were lucky to find any deer here at all."

He turned Maorga back toward the forest, back from whence they had come. "Call the dogs. Bring them back. We've seen enough. We'll go back to our camp and make straight for Abhainn Aille in the morning."

Five men rode past him, skirting the blackened hilltop as they followed the boundary of the forest to bring in the dogs and their prey. The buck had feared to cross the blackened earth and swung back toward the woods, and the dogs had instantly swarmed upon it. Parlan looked at the cool dim forest behind him, thinking only of how quickly they could get to Abhainn Aille and collect the hostages, and get back to the journey and the remaining tasks—

"King Parlan!"

He halted abruptly as Cillian swung his horse in front of Maorga. "Look there!"

The warrior pointed down the hill. There, emerging from a section of the remaining forest, was a small group of people. They were all on foot and dressed in the simple tan and brown woolen garb of farm folk, their plain cloaks pinned with worn copper brooches or sharp thorns from gorse bushes. Parlan saw men and women and children, some of them with their cloaks drawn up over their heads as if wary of showing their faces.

One man took a step forward to meet the high king. He was grey-haired and bent with age, but wore his rough garb as proudly as any of Parlan's men did their own gold and brightly dyed wool. He carried the tall oaken staff at his side pointed up to the sky, as though it were a fine iron-tipped spear.

Parlan rode Maorga forward to meet the man, who stood waiting with his followers still largely within the shadows of the forest. "Good day to you," Parlan said to him. "I am Parlan, created high king by the goddess Eriu last Samhain Eve."

The man nodded. "I am Baur. These are the last of my family."

"The last?"

Baur glanced behind him at his little group. "A fortnight ago, there were twice as many of us. Then that cursed beast came—that flying black monster—and we could only grab our children and dash out of the way while it killed the earth and ate the blackened sheep and cattle at its leisure."

"Did it . . . did it also kill those of your family? You said you were twice as many a fortnight ago. What happened to them?"

The man shook his head. "We saw it coming. We ran for the deepest woods." He paused and studied Parlan for a moment. "If you will, I will show you where we lived."

Parlan nodded. The man turned and walked along the forest edge, down the hillside until he could point down into a valley below. "There," he said, and stepped aside so Parlan could see.

Down in the valley, the earth was scorched and blackened just as it was at the top of the hill. But down there, Parlan could make out the widely separated remains of three circular stone walls.

Cold dread gripped him once again. These had been three *raths*—the homes of farm folk and their families, each one a collection of homes and sheds surrounded by a high circular stone-and-earth wall to keep the livestock in and wolves and thieves out. But now the walls were half fallen through and completely gone in spots, and the little buildings inside were heaps of blackened clay and sticks with chunks of brittle burnt straw scattered over them. Looking closer, Parlan could see the bloated forms of what had been cattle and sheep now black and frozen from the breath of the beast.

Parlan looked away from the scene of death and destruction, and turned back to Baur. "Where are the rest of your people? What happened to them?"

"Most of us escaped the beast's attack, but many were lost to the sickness that followed . . . the food, the water—all was tainted by the poisonous breath and the blackness and death it brought. The oldest and the youngest among us are all gone now."

"Where will you go? Where will you live?"

Baur glanced over his shoulder. The others stayed within the cool green shade of the forest, as if fearing to leave its living shelter to set foot on the cursed ground. "We will live deep in the wood, though we can grow no oats or wheat there. We will live on what we can hunt and gather. And we will hope that somehow the Goddess of the Land will be able to heal the damage done, that we might live in the open as we did before."

A few steps from Baur, a tall slender woman adjusted her woolen cloak where it hung over her face. Parlan caught a glimpse of a slender jawline, soft full lips and a few wisps of dark brown hair.

"The goddess walks among you this day, Baur, as she always has. When the high king has destroyed this evil beast, as it is his task to do, then she will heal her lands so that her children might live on them once more."

The man bowed. "Then we can only hope this task is finished soon. Good day to you, King Parlan." Baur and the others turned back toward the forest and began walking inside, into the deepest shadows.

"Wait!" Parlan cried. Baur paused and turned around, as did the hooded woman with the dark brown hair. "We have taken three deer in our hunting this day. Come back with us to our campsite in the field by the river, and we will prepare them and give them to you."

Baur raised his hand as if to protest. "There is no need, King Parlan."

"There is need, and it is the least I can do. And I promise you, I will do much more when I am able."

"Then we thank you." Baur nodded to him again. "You are a generous king."

Parlan shrugged, but muttered to himself, "I sometimes think I am no king at all."

The hooded woman raised her head and looked full at him, and when he saw the quiet confidence in those shining green eyes, Parlan felt ashamed. He looked up at Baur again. "It is my privilege to be the king of such brave people as you and yours. I have no doubt that you are blessed by the goddess, who draws strength from you even as you draw it from her. Now come with us, and we will prepare the deer for you."

Baur made a bow to Parlan once more, and then he and his people walked through the forest alongside Parlan and his riders. The hooded lady walked among Baur's people all the way to the campsite. All of them stayed close around her as they made their way through the dense forest, but when at last Parlan and his men and Baur and his people walked out into the grassy field by the sparkling river, the lady was gone.

None of Baur's people seemed distressed by her absence, or indeed even seemed to notice. They accepted the pieces of the butchered deer carcasses from Parlan's servants, and then prepared to return to the forest to find what shelter they could.

"We thank you again for your generosity, King Parlan," said Baur.

"I wish I could do more for you," Parlan replied. "Yet I should not be surprised if you should come across a tree of ripe apples in your search, even so early in the year, for a goddess does what she is able to do, even as does a king."

The next morning, under soft grey skies, Parlan swung up into Maorga's saddle. He turned the stallion and led

223

his men and servants out of the open field beside the river and back into the forest, following the track that would take them to Abhainn Aille before sunset that day.

Cillian rode alongside him, with Gavin close behind. "Where is your goddess this day, my king?" Cillian asked. "None of us have seen her for some time. Will she meet you at Abhainn Aille, perhaps, as she did at Dun Farriaghe?"

Parlan clenched his teeth and looked straight ahead into the forest. He had hoped she would come to him last night, after his sighting of her among Baur's people, but she had not. "Perhaps she will be there. Perhaps she will not. How can any man know what a goddess might do or not do?"

"Ah, I suppose you are right. Even a goddess is no less a woman, when it comes to predictability."

The horses snorted and tossed their heads as they jogged along in the cool spring morning, fretting at the slow pace that the winding forest trail forced them to keep.

"King Parlan!" called Gavin. "My horse wants a run. The beast is pounding my backside with his fretting. When we come to an open stretch, will you race me?"

Parlan glanced over his shoulder. "Race? Have you not had enough of riding horseback on this journey, Gavin?"

Cillian laughed. "Why not? Your own Maorga is just as fresh. And perhaps a race would amuse the king and ease his mood before we arrive at Abhainn Aille."

Parlan made no answer. But a short time later, when they came out of the forest and found themselves looking out across a wide valley with gently sloping sides and a small stream running down the center, he shot a quick glance back at Gavin and then dug both of his calves hard into Maorga's sides.

The stallion grunted and half-reared, then shot off at a gallop down the side of the valley, taking Cillian's and Gavin's horses with him. Parlan kept a tight hold with his leather reins in one hand and a grabbed handful of the thick black mane with the other, guiding the stallion in its wild plunging flight down the hillside while still staying securely in the saddle.

The sound of the other horses' hoofbeats behind him drove Maorga ever faster. Parlan held on and let the stallion go. Lighten the king's mood, would it? Well, perhaps it would at that. Perhaps he could let Maorga run faster and faster until he left this world behind altogether, this world with its quests and its curses and its dreadful Black Dragon—

Maorga swept down the hill and galloped straight toward the narrow stream, stretching his neck and flicking his ears forward at the sight of the fast-flowing water. He crouched down, dug in hard and then flew over the stream—and to Parlan's astonishment, the stallion's neck continued to rush away from him as he found himself sitting on the saddle with nothing beneath it but air.

Parlan crashed to earth just on the other side of the stream. He tried to roll to absorb the force of the fast-moving fall, but the saddle got entangled with his legs. His head slammed hard into the rocks on the far side of the stream.

CHAPTER TWENTY-EIGHT

Cold water splashed against his face; Parlan blinked and tried to turn away, but was stopped by the terrible aching in his head.

"King Parlan! Wake up!"

More very cold water on his face.

"Parlan! Get up! You must!"

Someone shook him violently by the shoulder.

"Open your eyes! Get up! Get up now!"

He opened his eyes enough to see a pair of hands just overhead, cupped together and dripping with water. He grabbed one wrist of the pair and shoved the hands aside before they could douse him again.

"I am awake," he said, slowly sitting up. "And I am alive." He looked around and saw nothing but the faces of his men gathered closely around him, all of them looking very worried. With a will of iron, he made himself get to his feet and stand at his full height with his hands clenched into fists at his sides. Slowly his men stood up alongside him.

"Where is Maorga?"

"There," said one of the men. "Seamus has him. The horse did not go far after . . . after you . . ."

"Bring him here. And . . ." He paused, remembering the fall, remembering trying to roll and being stopped by the heavy, wood-framed saddle. "Where is my saddle?"

"It lies where it fell," the man said.

Parlan walked over to the saddle, which lay in a heap beside the stream. He lifted it up and examined it carefully. When he looked at the wide, thick leather strap that held the saddle frame to the girth on the right side, he saw that the heavy strap had broken in two.

But a closer look showed that only a small part of the strap was ragged and torn, as though ripped under strain. Most of the break was clean—as though cut by a knife.

Parlan let the saddle fall to the ground. Maybe it was better this way. Maybe his men, and indeed all of his people, were better off with their cursed king gone so that another could take his place.

He turned and walked over to Maorga, took the reins from the man who held the horse, and vaulted onto the stallion's bare and sweat-roughened back. "We will be at Abhainn Aille by nightfall. Have one of the servants repair that saddle. And do not fear. If I fall from my horse a third time, perhaps I will not return."

He spun the stallion toward the forest on the far side of the valley and set him to a gallop, never looking back as the men and servants scrambled to keep up.

As twilight fell, Parlan and his men rode to the top of a hill and looked down on a wide river-fed lake, its waters soft and grey with dusk. Partway across the lake was a large island, sheltered by ancient oaks and twinkling with firelight from torches and hearths. This was Abhainn Aille, the waterborne home of King Diarmaid and the three hostages he would give to peace: his two sons, Seanan and Ebhear, and his nephew, Ronan.

The servants stayed on the grassy shore to make camp and tend the horses, while Parlan and ten of his men stepped into the waiting curragh at the shoreline. They all sat quietly as the small leather boats took them out across the lake to the torchlit island.

The people of Abhainn Aille greeted Parlan most politely. They took him and his men directly down the sandy tree-lined path to the Great Hall, where they served a fine feast of roasted haunches of spring lamb with boiled dried apples and honey—but the meal was eaten in dismal silence, with almost no conversation.

As soon as the food was removed, King Diarmaid called for the three hostage-princes to be brought to Parlan. As Cillian fastened the iron collars around their necks, Diarmaid said only, "Finish your quest, Parlan. Do what you must. I care nothing for all your many great feats that got you chosen as high king. Just finish it and bring my sons and my nephew home to me—alive, preferably."

And with that he got up from his cushion on the floor and strode out of the hall. All of the other men and women followed him, save Parlan and his men and the three hostage-princes.

Parlan got to his feet and looked at the hostages. They stood silent and resigned to their fate, and it was clear they would have no more to say to Parlan than King Diarmaid had. "Well, go then!" Parlan said, glaring at the three of them. "We will leave just after sunrise. Until then, do what you will."

The three nodded politely, turned their backs on Parlan and left.

Parlan was left alone with his ten men, but the silence was equally uncomfortable. He sighed. "You are to sleep here in the hall. I wish to be alone. I do not want to see anyone until sunrise, when we can leave and get closer to finishing this cursed quest." Parlan left, too, walking out into the cool spring night on the tree-covered island of Abhainn Aille.

The feast hall was nearly at the center of the roughly circular island. Parlan walked directly away from the hall, following the curving sandy footpaths past the many small rectangular houses, each with a torch set in front of it and glowing softly with hearth light inside, until he reached the edge of the island. There he crossed the stretch of grass and stood on the rocks that lined the shore.

He could not see the campsite of his men, for it faced the other end of the island; instead, he looked out at the vast dark lake as it stretched away from him into the darkness. The sky was soft and dark and lit only by the few stars that showed through here and there as the clouds drifted past. It was impossible to tell where the dark sky met the deep black lake, and Parlan had the feeling of floating in a place that was neither earth nor water nor sky, but something else.

"It is a lovely place, is it not? Probably more like the Otherworld than anywhere in the land of Men."

Parlan turned at the sound of that gentle familiar voice, and he saw Eriu standing in the shadows of the oaks, backlit by the soft glow of torches.

He sighed. "It is beautiful, and peaceful, and serene . . . sheltered and isolated from the rest of the land, which does not touch it in any sense."

She stepped out from under the trees and let her dark green cloak fall back from her head. The heavy gold brooch at her shoulder gleamed faintly in the starlight. "It is a fine place to rest, and to forget the cares of the rest of the world."

Parlan sat down on the soft grass, leaning back on one elbow and listening to the soft lapping of the water at the rocks. "Here—at least, at this moment—I could believe that I am not a king, and certainly not a high king. I could believe that I am just an ordinary man surrounded by nighttime and peace, with no one depending on me or looking to me for protection."

"And with no terrors hiding in the darkness."

He almost smiled. "No terrors. No horrific beast brought on by a curse of my own making. Only darkness and quiet and the ordinary things of nature."

"There is nothing wrong in wishing for such things, Parlan. I, too, love nothing more than to see the land and all who live on it existing in peace and serenity. Why should a king be any different?"

Parlan lay back on the grass and looked up at the cloud-veiled stars. "I sometimes wish I had been no more than just a king and not a high king—or even not a king at all, but just another warrior. Look what happened when I was given the power of a high king. Would it not have been better to simply be the king of some local tribe, to spend my days deciding disputes between farmers, and silencing arguments between warriors, and wearing plenty of gold while watching a battle of insults and shield-beating between warriors and the neighboring folk? Would it not have been better to be successful as a petty chief instead of failing as a high king?"

"You have not failed, Parlan. The quest is not finished yet."

He closed his eyes. "You do not understand, Lady Eriu. I am a failure precisely because there is need for such a quest in the first place." Parlan gazed up at the stars again. "One of my own men wants me dead. Or maybe several of them do. Those things that recently came near to taking my life were no accidents. Maorga would not simply leap out of a river like a salmon for no reason, and good strong leather does not break of its own accord.

"Someone has decided that the land is better off with a new king—and who could blame him? What high king worthy of the name would be so foolish as to insult the goddess and reject the kingship she granted him?"

There was silence for a time. The cool breeze off the lake blew over his face, and then he heard the soft sounds of Eriu sitting down beside him in the grass. "Perhaps the test is not whether a man makes a mistake. Perhaps the test lies in seeing what that man will do about it if he does make one."

Parlan sat up and turned to her. "But what if his best efforts are not enough? What then?"

"So, you have given your best effort already, Parlan? You have done all you can do to lift this curse?"

He turned away. "I have not. The quest is not over yet. There is much more to be done."

"Then how do you know if your best will be good enough when you have not yet given it?"

He swallowed, and looked out over the dark water. "Perhaps I fear to try. Perhaps I fear to learn that it will not be enough. And what sort of king fears to try?"

"A king who is a man, Parlan. As all kings are." She paused. "I can only tell you that you have already done far more than any other man could hope to do. If you do not try—if you give up now—you will always be tormented by not knowing what might have been had you not."

Parlan closed his eyes. "It was my own arrogance that brought about this trouble in the first place. Surely I can find the arrogance to try to end that same trouble."

"Have you nothing more to offer than arrogance?" she asked. She placed a gentle hand on his arm. "Yet I must agree that I can think of nothing more arrogant than informing the Goddess of Sovereignty that she has made a mistake and chosen the wrong man."

He turned to look at her shadowed form in the starlight.

"Was I wrong, Parlan? Did I choose the wrong king? Shall I let you remain here forever, disgraced and forgotten, while I go and find another while there is still time?"

She got to her feet and stood tall in the darkness looking down at him. "I neither want nor need an unwilling king. Neither do your people. The choice is yours. I hereby release you from the kingship. If you wish to go, you have only to turn and walk back to the Great Hall. Sleep in the straw this night among the servants and your men. In the morning you will awaken as just another warrior, and your men will return home to Teamhair Breagh in all haste to choose another king. You will live the rest of a long and ordinary life as just another good warrior among many, with no further demands made upon you."

She took a step toward him. "Choose, Parlan," she said gently. "You are not required to be a king if you do not wish to be one, no matter what the goddess thinks."

"Eriu . . ." Parlan got to his feet. "Eriu, surely all men have doubts . . . even men who are called kings." He took her hand. "Surely even I can be permitted—"

He stopped. The hand he held, normally as warm and vital as the sun, was now as cold as the frost on a winter morning.

He looked hard into her eyes. She tried to tighten her grip, but already he could feel the frailty in it. He turned her to face the torchlight from the island and pushed back her dark hair. Even in the dim light he could see that her skin, always fair, was beginning to show an unhealthy whiteness—a pallor that was something like death.

He caught her by the shoulders. "It has begun," he whispered. "The land suffers beneath the ravages of the dragon, and its goddess suffers with it. And it will only grow worse until something is done, or until the end comes." Parlan drew her close, and to his great relief she rested her head on his shoulder.

"I am sorry I doubted the choice of the goddess. Perhaps I will never stop doubting myself—but I promise you, I will never again give thought to giving up the task that is mine to do. I will carry it out and protect the land, or I will spend my last breath in the effort."

He kissed her gently on the cool skin of her forehead. "I will go now and sleep in the camp my men have made on the shore, so that we might leave at the earliest light and continue with the quest. Will you stay with me this night? I assure you, I want only to lie beside you and keep you warm and let you rest."

She smiled faintly at him. "I thank you for your offer. But I will stay here in the peace and beauty of Abhainn Aille this night, and send your men and your hostages to you before dawn. If you are now truly committed to your quest, I will remain committed to helping you finish it— at least, for as long as I can."

He held her close and closed his eyes, resting his cheek against the top of her head. "No man can be more committed than one who has truly doubted and then returned. I will finish the quest, Eriu. One way or another, I will finish it."

CHAPTER TWENTY-NINE

As Eriu promised, Parlan's five men and the three hostages to peace from Abhainn Aille arrived at the campsite at the first touch of grey in the eastern sky. Eriu did not come with them. While Parlan wanted nothing more than to go straight back to Abhainn Aille and search for her, he kept his word, mounted his horse, and led his men and servants northwest toward the coastline. He could only hope that she would meet him there.

"There are some twenty-four nights remaining until the night of the summer solstice," Rian said, as he rode alongside Parlan. "Are you ready for that night, my king?"

Parlan tried to smile. "I know I can expect the next of my tasks to come on that night—the shortest of the year—since the other two came on the nights of the winter solstice and the spring equinox."

"It would seem only fitting," Rian agreed. "Those nights are the markers of the year, the four corners that support it. They would be the expected time for such

234

powerful things to occur as the chance to recover the four sacred objects of the gods."

Parlan sighed. "Nonetheless, I would face the remaining two tasks at once if I could, just to set Eriu and her lands free from this curse—and so I would not have to live each day with the terrible knowledge, and no small dread, of what awaits me. I would much prefer to simply get it over with."

"Yet perhaps the tasks are spread out for a reason," Rian suggested, as their horses walked through the damp and drizzling morning. "Perhaps no man could do so much in a short period. Surely time is needed for recovery from each one."

"And to learn from mistakes that are made," Parlan murmured.

"Even so. And to sharpen the desire and readiness to take on the next challenge, no matter how difficult it might prove."

"In that case, then, I should say it is effective. I have recovered, I have learned something from the mistakes I made, and I want nothing more than to finish what is left of the quest."

"Then let us keep going, and continue to rest and think and plan. The night of the summer solstice will be here soon enough."

For over three weeks, Parlan rode with his men through the broad flat lowlands that led to the sea. Twice he made a semipermanent camp with them, and rode with them on their hunts for red deer, and every night he endured waiting and loneliness, for he guessed he would not see the increasingly weary Eriu until the night of the summer solstice.

When that night finally arrived—after a day that seemed never to end, for it was after all the longest day of the year—Parlan walked away from the comfortable campsite spread out in the open grassy plain, and walked until he could hear the sound of crashing waves. At last he stood on a gentle rise that gave way to a narrow rocky beach down below, watching as the last golden light of the sun shone on the foaming water that slid back and forth on the rocks and sand of the beach.

"You have come at just the right time, King Parlan," a voice said.

He turned to see Eriu standing a little distance behind him on the rise. She stood so that the last light of the setting sun could not penetrate the shadow of her cloak where it fell over her face.

"What other time could be right, Lady Eriu? It is the evening of the summer solstice. We stand on a beach, a place that is neither land nor sea. We stand here at dusk, a time that is neither day nor night. If ever there was a time for strange and magical things to happen, this is it."

Eriu looked out over the sea. "You seek the Cauldron of the Daghda," she said calmly, above the sound of the rushing waves. "It is the great golden cup of plenty, from which all who drink and eat are satisfied, and which never is empty of whatever one likes most. And it is right out there." She raised a hand and pointed out to sea.

Parlan frowned. "Where?" He looked out at the water just as the last crescent of the sun disappeared below the horizon. "I see nothing but endless surf. Where would I look for a cup?"

"It is just beneath the waves."

He sighed heavily, his frustration rising. "Does this cup lie on the ocean floor? Must I dive in and search among the seaweed?"

"You need do no such thing. You would never find it. If you want the cauldron, you must draw its guardians to you."

"Guardians." His fists clenched. "And what horrific

monsters await me this time? More dead who ride? More fire-breathing monsters?"

"Nothing like that. Not this time. This is not an enemy that you can fight with sword or spear."

"What weapon will I need? I will go back to camp right now and—"

"Just this." She handed him a wineskin from beneath her cloak.

"I have to fight them with wine?"

She smiled. "You already have all the weapons you need. These guardians are not drawn by power or strength or challenge or threat. If you want them to come to you, you have only to take off your boots, your cloak, your tunic and your trews, and stand facing the sea with your feet in the waves while the last light of the sun shines upon you."

"Take off my—what?"

"All of your clothes."

He started to laugh. "And what will that bring? Hordes of farmers from the surrounding countryside, come to laugh at the naked king?"

"It will bring the *merrows*."

"Merrows?"

"Perhaps you have seen them—oh, you have not? Well, no matter. The merrows are the beautiful ladies who make their homes in the sea. They are wild, alluring and quite dangerous. They prize nothing more than a strong and handsome mortal man whom they can lure to them, and once they have such a man, they do not give him back. And yet—"

"Yet?"

"If they can be coaxed out of the sea and onto the land, they become most timid and submissive. That is what you must do—persuade them to remove their cloaks, draw them out of the sea and have them willingly walk on land to join you."

"Surely it cannot be so simple!"

"Your beauty will draw them. They will not pass up a chance to take one such as you. But do not wait long. The light is fading, and a storm approaches."

"What storm?" He turned his back to Eriu and looked out across the sea—and sure enough, he could see heavy clouds boiling up in the northwestern sky. "What does this storm have to do with the cauldron? Will these guardians ride in on the lightning and thunder?"

He turned to face Eriu, but once again she was gone.

Parlan sighed, and turned to face the sea once more. Already the light was fading from the sky. "All right, then. Let us see what sort of terrors my nakedness can lure."

He pulled the heavy gold brooch out of his seven-colored cloak, wrapped it in the woolen folds, and set both down at the edge of the grass. Then, watching as the light turned from pale azure and soft pink to an ever-deeper blue, he unstrapped the Sword of Nuadha and placed it atop the cloak. Quickly he stripped away his leather boots and his woolen trews and his fine linen tunic, until finally he stood naked at the edge of the beach. The only thing he still wore was his golden king's torque around his neck, with the spiral-capped ends resting just below his throat.

Parlan strode across the water-smoothed rocks of the beach until he reached the edge of the sea, and the cold water washed over his feet. He held out his arms and let the last light of day envelop him.

"I am here!" he cried, walking along the edge of the foaming water. "Merrows! Guardians! I am here to meet you! Come out, if you will, and meet with the high king of all Eire!"

The sky turned black. He could no longer see that place where the heavens met the sea. The only light came from the brilliant river of stars overhead in the rare clear sky, and from the occasional silent flashes of lightning deep within the clouds to the northwest.

Except for the deep voice of the ocean as it surged forward and back over the rocks of the beach, all was quiet and he was very much alone.

Frustration rose up within him. "Is this some jest you play with me, Lady Eriu?" he shouted, looking back toward the land. "Are you and the other gods laughing at the foolish naked king from your place in the Otherworld?

"They are not laughing," said a raspy, high-pitched voice. "But I am!"

Parlan whirled around. The voice had seemed to come from the direction of the sea. "Who is there? Who are you?"

Hideous squeaking laughter was the only response. A small splash followed.

"Show yourself!"

A head popped up out of the ocean, just a few steps from shore. "Well, you needn't be so rude about it," said the rasping voice. "Look at me all you like."

The creature stood waist-deep in the water and grinned at Parlan, who started at it with both fascination and revulsion.

At first glance in the dim light, it appeared to be human, but as Parlan got a better look he realized the resemblance was only superficial. The thing stood no taller than his waist, he guessed, and had rough dark red skin, sickly green hair, little beady eyes and a nose that resembled a pig snout.

Parlan swallowed. "Are you a merrow? Are you the guardian of the Cauldron of the Daghda?"

The little beast laughed again. "Indeed, I am the finest and best example of a merrow that you will ever see, King Parlan!"

"But I was told that merrows were beautiful and

alluring—that no mortal man could resist them." His mouth twisted in disgust. "Nothing could be easier for me—or for any man—than to run far away from you!"

"Oh, but King Parlan! Surely you will not—"

The creature suddenly vanished, as though something beneath the water had seized it and pulled it down. Parlan could only stare at the dark place where it had been. Then another sound rose up from the rushing waves, a sound that was sweet and soothing like the delicate notes of a harp. Parlan began to realize that he was indeed hearing a song, sung by the most beautiful and gentle of women's voices—and not just one voice, but two, or perhaps even three.

He closed his eyes as the lovely voices sent a feeling of peace and warmth flowing through him. It seemed that he would be content to do nothing more than listen to their welcoming song forever.

He took a step into the sea . . . and then the singing faded and a gentle splashing made him open his eyes.

Instead of the ugly little creature that had been there before, Parlan saw a slender and beautiful woman standing knee-deep in the ocean waves. And as he gazed at her, another equally lovely woman stood up out of the sea behind her, and then another joined them . . . and Parlan could only stand and stare at all three as the shining starlight revealed them in all their beauty.

All three had skin pale as moonlight, and were covered with delicate scales, like every creature that lived in the sea. They wore gowns that appeared to be fashioned from the gold-white foam of waves, trimmed and belted with braids of red and purple seaweed. Over these shimmering gowns they wore fine cloaks, as any lady would, and theirs were of dark shining sealskin fastened with brooches of pearl. Around their necks and wrists were strings of delicate white shells, alternating with flakes of the iridescent lining of oyster shell.

And when he dared to look into their faces, he saw features delicate and beautiful and young, with eyes of deep and glittering green. Their long hair, the color of sand when the sun shines on it and held back from their faces by pins made of pearl, floated on the water behind them.

Parlan realized that the three were studying him just the way he was studying them. He stood a little taller, and ignored the cool night wind that blew freely across every part of his body.

"You are the merrows," he said to them. "You are the guardians of the Daghda's cauldron."

CHAPTER THIRTY

"We are indeed the merrows," said the first, and tallest, of the three strange women standing knee-deep in the ocean. Lightning flashed behind her, and Parlan realized that the storm was rapidly drawing closer. He watched, fascinated, as the rising wind lifted the long wet hair of each of the merrows until only the very tips brushed across the waves.

"You are the bringers of storms. You are the ones who drown men in boats when they become trapped in your storms."

"We sing to them, and they come to us, and we keep them forever in happiness after that. We would keep you in happiness, too, King Parlan. Will you not come with us, and let us sing to you for as long as you like?"

He closed his eyes. Their song rose up in him again, a feeling of warmth and love and acceptance, of beautiful women who would never turn him away . . . but when the cold wind struck his face and tore at his hair, he opened his eyes and raised his head.

You must persuade them to remove their cloaks, come out of the sea, and willingly walk on land to join you.

"Perhaps you will sing to me on the shore," he said, as the clouds rolled black over the sky and a cold rain began to lash his naked body. He could see the merrows only by their luminous white skin, like moonlight on the water. He made himself step back, so that he stood on the smooth rounded rocks and the ocean no longer touched him.

The three merrows each took a step forward. "Our home is the sea. It is always peaceful and beautiful there—so different from the harshness of the land, with its hard and painful surfaces and its ever-changing heat and cold and storms. Will you not join us here?" They began to sing to him again, that welcoming song no man could resist.

Parlan blinked water from his eyes as the cold rain drenched his face and body. He made himself step back until he stood on the wet grass at the edge of the rocky beach, and spoke quickly. "I am sorry, but your storm has made me too cold to step into the sea. Perhaps if you would loan me your cloaks, I could warm myself, and then I could join you in your underwater home."

Their voices fell silent. "You would make a prize like no other, High King Parlan," said the merrow farthest from him. "I will give you my cloak." She unfastened the pearl brooch, dropped it into the storm-driven waves, and walked out across the rocks and the grass. Her sweeping gown left a little trail of white foam on the sand. She placed her wet sealskin cloak on Parlan's right shoulder, and draped it down his arm.

"I thank you, beautiful lady of the sea," Parlan said to her. To his relief, the rain began to slow. "But I am still cold from your storm, and your cloak is too small for me. Would not another of you come out to join me here, and loan me your cloak as well?"

"My sister is right," said the second of the merrows, standing behind the first and tallest. "One such as you must not be allowed to escape. I will loan you my cloak."

And she, too, walked out of the ocean with her long sea-foam gown leaving bright white traces behind her on the rocks. She stood beside Parlan on the grass, placing her sealskin cloak over his left shoulder and arranging it on his arm.

The rain had all but stopped. Only the wind continued to blow. "And you, third sister," Parlan called to the remaining merrow—the first, the tallest. "Will you not join us, too, and help ease the chill that the storm has brought?"

"I suppose you want my cloak as well, do you, King Parlan?"

"I do . . . but oh, there is one thing I want even more."

"And what is that?"

Even her speaking voice was alluring and beautiful, like harp notes. Parlan shut his eyes. "Why, a drink of wine, my lady of the sea, to help warm me. But I have no cup. I do not wish to be so rude as to drink from a wine-skin in front of ladies like yourselves. Have you a cup that you would loan me?"

The tallest merrow, still standing in the sea, gazed out at him and her lips curved in a smile. "I will bring you a cup for your wine. But make no mistake—you will be ours, for whether we are on land or sea, once we sing to you again you will not want to escape." She turned away and dove beneath the waves.

Parlan held his breath. He did his best to ignore the two merrows who stood beside him with their Otherworldly beauty, stroking his arms with cool wet hands and murmuring soothing sounds that sounded like gentle waves rushing across a sandy beach.

Finally the first and tallest of the merrow sisters reappeared from beneath the water. She came striding up out of the waves, stepped lightly over the rocks and walked up to Parlan. The rain stopped entirely and the wind eased, until once again there was only a gentle breeze. She took off her cloak and draped it over both of her hands.

"I, too, will give you my cloak," she said sweetly, and held out the garment. "Take it."

Her voice was like drops of water falling onto harp strings. Parlan shut his eyes briefly, drew on his most iron resolve, and took the sealskin cloak from the merrow's hands.

He caught his breath.

The creature also held out a shining, gleaming gold cup in the shape of a small cauldron. The mouth of the cup was as wide as both of Parlan's hands side-by-side, and its curving sides were covered with images of plenty—sheaves of wheat, cups filled to overflowing, bees and their hives, and prized game animals such as red deer and boar and leaping salmon. As Parlan reached out to touch it, the cup gleamed even brighter, for the storm-clouds drifted away and the starlight cast a soft glow over all the world.

If they can be coaxed out of the sea and onto the land, they become most timid and submissive. . . .

Parlan cleared his throat. "Give me the cup," he said, and placed both his hands on it. To his surprise, he took it easily.

"You have your cup, King Parlan," she said. "Now, will you come with us? Listen to our song . . . just close your eyes and listen, for surely there is nothing you desire more than to join us in our home beneath the waves."

The three tried to sing, but the only sound Parlan heard was a dry whisper. It sounded like the dead leaves of autumn blown on a cold wind.

"Oh!" cried the first merrow, covering her mouth with her hand. "We must return to the sea, where we can sing again! Hurry! He must not leave!"

All three of the merrows picked up the hems of their

sea-foam gowns and hurried to the starlit water, but they got no farther than ankle-deep before running straight back out again to stand trembling on the rocks.

"Oh, it is so cold!"

"Too cold for us to ever return!"

"What have we done? Why will the sea not accept us?"

Parlan set down the golden cauldron. He pulled the two soft wet sealskin cloaks from his shoulders and draped them over his arm, and then picked up the third from the grass. "Perhaps you need these," he called, holding out his arm.

"Oh—oh!"

"Our cloaks!"

"It is our cloaks that keep us warm in the sea!"

They all ran up to Parlan and reached out for their cloaks, but at the last moment he turned away and raised his arm up high.

The three merrows collapsed to the grass. "Please!" they begged. "Give us back our cloaks! We can never return to our homes without them, but neither can we live on the land! Oh, look, look . . . look at my gown!"

And even as they stood beneath the starlight, Parlan could see that the sea-foam gowns of the merrows were drying up, leaving little more than salty streaks on the scales of their skin. Even the seaweed trim and belts were beginning to shrivel and fade.

Parlan's eyes narrowed as he looked down at the three sisters. "Why should I return your cloaks to you? You are capricious and cruel. You bring terrible storms just to drown men at sea and keep them with you."

"We keep only those men who allow themselves to fall in love with us through our songs! Any man can resist if he truly wishes. *You* resisted!"

Parlan lowered his arm. "So I did," he whispered. "I resisted because I have one that I truly love, and if I went away with you I could not be with her."

"Then let us go back to our home, and we will not trouble you again," the merrows pleaded. "We have given you the cup you asked for. Please, give us our cloaks, and let us go!"

"Go, then," Parlan said, handing each of them her cloak. "Go and leave men in peace, unless they truly do love you and no other."

The merrows got to their feet, snatched up their sealskin cloaks, threw them about their shoulders and dashed into the sea. In an instant they dove beneath the surface and were gone. There was a brief rush of wind and a few high waves, and then all was quiet once more.

Parlan sighed, and looked down at the gleaming gold Cauldron of the Daghda where it rested in the grass at his feet. "Well, Lady Eriu," he said, "there is only one more sacred artifact that I must gain. May I put my clothes back on now?"

CHAPTER THIRTY-ONE

For another three fortnights, Parlan and his men traveled at a slow pace through the long days and warm nights of high summer. Eriu rode with them, silent and pale, beneath thick canopies of dense green leaves of the oaks and hazel trees, and past white and purple violets in the forest shade, and the little yellow marsh flowers that lined the banks of every waterway.

They were in a region that seemed more river and lake than dry land, and it should have been as lush and green and vital as any place in all of Eire. Yet the burnt and ravaged sections where the Black Dragon continued to hunt and feed became more and more frequent. The riders encountered more groups of displaced farmers and herdsmen, on the move as they searched for any place safe from the deadly cold breath of the beast. Parlan and his men would hunt deer and boar for them, and provide whatever they could, but always the frightened people would accept what was offered and be on their way as quickly as possible. Parlan knew there was no place they

248

could go to escape the dragon, but he gave them what he could and wished them well as they went.

Then, one evening, Parlan's men made their camp near the shores of a tranquil lake, well away from the last they had seen of the dragon's rampages, and sat down to eat their trout and flatbread and honey.

Eriu sat beside Parlan, and ate little, and finally she set aside her plate. "Walk with me, King Parlan," she said, and led him through the twilight around the lake toward the high cliffs and thick forest on the far side. She moved slowly, deliberately, always keeping her dark green cloak pulled close around her, the top of it pulled up over her head and falling down over her face even in the warm air of summer. When they reached the base of the cliff, she took Parlan's arm and walked with him up the narrow winding path until they reached the tree-covered top.

Eriu walked to the edge of the cliff, looking down on the shoreline of the lake far below, and soon Parlan could hear the sweet singing sound of rushing, falling water. He could feel the mist before he saw it. It rose up from where the water fell over the cliff to the lake below, behind a little curving finger of land whose tall thick trees hid the waterfall from sight of the camp far across the lake.

"This is one of my favorite places," Eriu said. "So peaceful and secluded, with the voice of the falls to mask any sound and sheltering trees to protect one from sight. It is almost as beautiful here as it is in the Otherworld." She walked to the very edge of the cliff and looked down into the pool far below. Parlan guessed that nine good men would have had to stand on one another's shoulders to reach from the pool to the cliff where they stood.

After a moment she turned away. "But I did not bring you here to see this—at least, not from up here. Come with me."

She walked on another faint path, this one leading

away from the lake and across the top of the jutting cliff. They reached the connecting hillside and could see the other side. There the dusk deepened until it was blue-black, and Parlan could see yet another familiar outline of low rolling hills dotted with thick forest near the lowlands, and covered with open grass for grazing cattle at the tops. A soft glow behind him caught his eye, and he turned to see the moon, full and yellow and enormous, rising up over the forests to shine down on the lake.

"Do you know what night this is, King Parlan?"

He smiled at her hooded face. "Of course I do. It is the night of the second full moon past the summer solstice. This is the night of *Lughnasa*."

"So it is. It is perhaps my favorite of the festivals, for it is a celebration not of lust and license, as at Bealtaine, but of the harvest and of companionship and bounty, and of finding partners for long-term love and for marriage."

He stood close behind her and placed his hands on her shoulders—and was startled to plainly feel the bones beneath the fine wool of her cloak. He cleared his throat. "Would you like to visit a Lughnasa celebration, Lady Eriu? I am sure there will be one near here, with as many herding and farming folk as there are in these hills. Oh, look! There—*there* is a bonfire!"

As they watched, a small glowing dot on one of the nearby hills flared up into brilliant orange light just as the last light of dusk faded away and the full moon took command of the eastern sky. "Some of the men will no doubt go and join that celebration—at least, those who do not choose to simply stay in the camp and drink beer to celebrate the grain harvest. But we could go and get the horses, and ride out. It is not far—"

She turned to face him. "I thank you, but I must preserve what strength I have. I think I would prefer to celebrate Lughnasa down at my favorite place, down in the shelter beneath the trees and the waterfall."

"Then I will take you there, my lady," Parlan said, and together they started down the narrow path.

Darkness had fallen completely by the time Parlan and Eriu reached the foot of the cliff, and they stood beside the lake with the delicate mist of the falls drifting over them. The soft light of the moon played over the water and left a gleam on the wet grass of the shore. Tall trees and bushes protected them from the sight of any who might pass by, and the steady roar of the waterfall drowned out any sound or voice. As Parlan stood near the trees and watched, Eriu stepped to a place beside the shore, right beside the base of the falls. She pulled the heavy golden brooch from her dark green cloak, which she allowed to fall from her shoulders to the grass.

Parlan watched, fascinated, as the mist from the falls left tiny drops of water in Eriu's long, rippling, dark brown hair, that the moon caught and lit up like tiny stars. As he continued to watch, she lifted up her finely woven gown and drew it off over her head, leaving her standing only in a cream-colored linen undergown. She bent down, untied and stripped away her soft leather boots, then took off her linen gown and dropped it atop her cloak.

It was not often that Parlan had seen her in all her natural beauty. Most often when Eriu came to him, she lay close beside him within their cloaks; and though his body ached at the thought of how she felt in his arms, pressed up against him in all her slender curving softness, he had rarely seen her naked. Now, watching her as she stood with her back to him in the moonlight, he drank in the sight of her body and felt certain he could never get enough.

But his greedy delight quickly turned to deep concern.

Her skin, always fair, now seemed deathly white . . . so white it was almost grey. Her hair was limp and straight, as though pulled down by its own weight. Worst of all, her always-slender body was so terribly thin that every rib showed, and the sharp bones of her hips and shoulders were clearly defined. As she turned to one side and lifted her tired hair from her neck, he could see how small her breasts had become and how flat and sunken her belly.

A dreadful thought made his blood run cold: *She is dying.*

He wanted to go to her and shelter her fragile form in his arms. He wanted to drape her cloak over her even though the summer night was quite warm. But before he could move, she walked to the edge of the shore, stepped into the shallow water and made her way through the knee-deep pool toward the waterfall.

Quickly Parlan stripped away his clothes and leather boots. "Eriu! The water is so cold! Let me take you back to the shore—wait, wait!" He threw his boots aside and dashed into the water, catching hold of Eriu from behind just as she reached the edge of the falls and let the heavy spray cascade over her.

Parlan gasped from the shock of the cold water and tried to pull Eriu close, but she only spread her arms wide, leaned her head back and closed her eyes, apparently welcoming the freezing deluge.

"This water comes straight from the heart of the earth," she gasped, her eyes fluttering in the heavy spray of the falls. "It will awaken me, revive me, for a time—but only for a time. I only hope that it will be long enough."

Parlan let her lean back against him and tried to hold her steady and close, even as her skin rippled into tiny bumps from the cold. Her entire body began a violent shivering.

"Long enough, my lady," Parlan repeated, and he lifted her up and carried her back to shore.

The water streamed from her hair as he carried her across the grass. He set her down on her fine wool cloak, and pulled it close around her, then searched out her shining gold brooch in the grass and used it to pin the cloak snugly.

He let go of her to reach for his own heavy cloak, and she sank slowly to earth and lay very still. He lay beside her and wrapped his cloak around both of them, willing whatever warmth he possessed to envelop her and take away the chill that seemed to go all the way to her bones.

After what seemed like a very long time, her shivering began to quiet, and at last she lay peaceful and still beside him. Parlan reached up and stroked her wet hair. "Sleep, now, dear Eriu," her murmured. "I will do no more than lie here beside you this night and share with you whatever warmth I have. In the morning, we will . . ."

But she cut him off by rolling over beneath the cloaks and pulling him close to her, pushing the front of her cloak aside so that she pressed up against him with the full length of her body. Her skin was dry and a little warmer, and Parlan could clearly feel the pulse of life beating strong and steady throughout her body.

She got her arms up around his neck and pulled herself close. "I am here for you now, King Parlan, if you are here for me," she whispered. "I want to be here with you this night, while I can, no matter what happens to me in the days to come."

There was no doubt that she felt stronger, and warmer than she had, and so once again Parlan claimed the goddess as his own. As they made love, the full yellow moon of Lughnasa shone down on them both, and the voice of the waterfall sang out into the night.

After a time, Parlan held Eriu close and drifted off to sleep, as warm and comfortable and content as he had ever been. And yet his dreams were troubled, for he thought he heard the strong and insistent voice of a strange man calling Eriu's name, over and over, calling her away so that she might never again be seen in the natural world.

CHAPTER THIRTY-TWO

"Eriu . . . Eriu!"

She raised her head. Parlan slept soundly. He was not the one who had called her. That voice belonged to—

"Ogma," she said, slowly sitting up. Parlan stirred, but Eriu placed her hand on his forehead for a moment, and once again he relaxed and slept peacefully. She pulled her cloak around herself and carefully got to her feet. Ogma stood with his back to the waterfall, his tall broad-shouldered form silhouetted against the bright water in the darkness.

"Why have you come?" she asked, picking up her gowns and walking over to him. "Is something wrong?"

"There is indeed," Ogma said, his voice very deep. "Walk with me, my sister, and I will show you."

He waited while she drew her gowns over her head, and then took her hand, laid it on his arm, and walked her along the edge of the bank where it led behind the waterfall. They strolled beneath the misty arc, and when they came out on the other side, the world lightened into sunshine.

Eriu stood for a moment beside the pool and let her cloak hood fall back from her face. She closed her eyes as the sunlight of the Otherworld brought a flush of heat and life back into her face.

"You look better already," Ogma said, with a broad smile on his handsome face. He placed his large hand over her own. "We have not failed to notice what has become of you. So thin, so pale, growing ever weaker . . . what can that king do to protect you from wasting away?"

"He is the one I truly love. There is nothing he would not do to help me—to protect me. He proves himself with each day."

"He has not proven it yet," Ogma warned. "He will not prove it until he defeats the Black Dragon, and you will not be safe unless and until he does."

"Ogma is right," said a warm feminine voice. "His love alone is not enough to protect you."

Eriu turned to see Brighid walking along the shore of the sparkling lake, dressed in a deep red gown with her long red-gold hair shining in the sun. Ogma stepped back to let Brighid embrace her. "Dear, dear, Eriu," she murmured. "I asked Ogma to go and bring you here, to bring you home before it is too late." She stepped back. "Look at you—oh, look . . . you are hardly more than a pale and fading shadow of what you were. The land is dying and so are you . . . and no matter how your mortal king loves you, the task is too great for him."

"He will never be able to accomplish this thing," Ogma agreed. "He will never be able to defeat the Black Dragon, not even with your help—and what help can you give him now? The beast is too strong, and has already done terrible damage to the land. We have only to look upon you to know this. Parlan cannot gain the last of the artifacts without you, and he cannot hope to face the beast without the artifacts."

From somewhere within the forest, Eriu heard a horse's

footsteps coming toward them, along with the sound of a woman's high flirtatious laugh. In a moment a powerful stallion, its coat iron-grey with youth, appeared at the forest's edge. On its broad back, holding the reins to the braided black leather bridle, was a tall and beautiful woman with long coppery braids. Sitting behind her on the stallion, leaning his head against her shoulder and holding on to her waist, was a strong young man with half-closed eyes and a peaceful, dreamy expression on his face.

"Flidais," whispered Eriu. "And—oh, that is Prince Daithi. He was one of King Parlan's hostages to peace, the son of King Morrissey of Dun Farriaghe, and she stole him away at the Bealtaine fires. . . ." She watched as Flidais glanced at her, gave a sly smile, then turned the young stallion back to the forest again. "And she will never give him up—not until years from now, when she grows tired of him and sends him back an aged and weary man to find that generations of his kin have been born and grown and died while he was gone. And while he is here, he will remain under her spell, so besotted that he remembers nothing else—not until it is too late."

"Eriu, it is done," said Brighid. Her warm hazel eyes shone with tears. "If you leave the Otherworld again, you might well not have the strength to return—not even if we help you."

Eriu withdrew her hand from Brighid's grasp and walked over to the lush greenery near the lake. She breathed deep of the warm sweet air, and the soft springy grass under her bare feet made her feel a little more alive. She turned to look at Ogma and Brighid, and could not help but smile at the genuine love and concern in their eyes. "I feel a little stronger here already, just from coming back to the Otherworld. If I stay until I am myself again, I could return to the natural world and be able to help Parlan in the final stages of his quest."

Ogma shook his head. "The moment you set foot in the natural world again, you will instantly become the same way the land has become—ravaged, and in danger of dying. You know this to be true, Lady Eriu. You and the land are as one. It cannot be any other way."

She looked into their eyes, and then gazed again toward the sun-dappled forest.

"How wonderful it would be to stay in a place where the forest is always strong and healthy," said Brighid. "Where the land is always lush and life-giving. Would you not like to do this again, my sister Eriu?"

"You *can* do this, dear sister," said Ogma. "The land here needs you, too."

"For so long, you did all you could for the world of Men," continued Brighid. "You found the best of them to be their kings. You set aside the desires of your own heart in order to serve the people and the land. You taught them to love and care for the earth the way they would love and care for a beloved wife—and still they wasted those gifts and let their lands go to ruin."

"The Time of Men is over," Ogma said, "and it is through no one's doing but their own. Come home to where you belong. Turn your strength toward helping to restore and renew the Otherworld before it, too, fades away and is lost forever."

Tears burned Eriu's eyes, and she closed them tight. "I do not know what to do," she whispered. "I swore to help Parlan, the king I made, but I cannot help him if I fade away to nothing the moment I return to his world."

Brighid and Ogma came over to stand on either side of her, and gratefully she held Brighid's hands and rested her head on Ogma's strong shoulder.

"Stay with us for a time," Brighid said. "You need not decide what to do at this moment. Just stay here and rest for a time, here in your home where you are always loved and welcome."

Eriu sighed deeply. "The Otherworld may yet work its magic on me, and persuade me to stay here forever and no longer open myself to the dangers of the world of Men. But if I do return to their world, even for a short time, you must promise me that you will not come for me again. If I choose to return, my fate must be my own. Will you promise?"

Brighid and Ogma hesitated. "Dear sister—" Brighid began, but Eriu stopped her.

"Will you promise?"

After a short pause, her two friends sighed. "We promise," they said together, and Eriu closed her eyes.

Deep in the forest, Flidais's merry laughter echoed through the trees.

Parlan awoke to the cool damp morning, the wind blowing the mist of the waterfall over his face. He blinked and sat up, and felt a cold emptiness wash through him at the sight of his cloak lying flat on the grass instead of being draped over Eriu.

As fast as he could, he grabbed his tunic and trews and boots and pulled them on. Cold fear kept rising in him, even as he grabbed his cloak and ran all the way back to the campsite at the other end of the lake.

Rian was the first to greet him.

"Have you seen her?" Parlan gasped, catching hold of the man's shoulders. "Is she here?"

Rian tried to smile, but could only shake his head. "Is who here?"

"Eriu! The goddess! Is she here? Is she waiting for me?"

"She is not here. We have not seen her. We never see her unless she is with you."

Parlan let him go and started running along the edge of the lake, toward the deep forest. "Eriu! Eriu!" he cried, trying to look in all directions at once. "Where are you? Come back to me! Come back!"

A strong hand grabbed Parlan's arm and turned him around. "King Parlan, why do you search for her?" asked Rian. "Always she comes to you for a time, and then is gone for many days or weeks. But always she comes back to you when you have need. That is her way, is it not?"

"It is," Parlan gasped, his eyes still searching the forest. "She has always done so," he agreed.

"Then why are you so troubled by her absence now? Did she say she would not return?"

Parlan finally looked back at Rian. "She said nothing at all. She is simply gone. It is true that she has been gone before . . . but this is different, now, from all the other times that she has left."

"Different—how?"

"I do not know. I cannot explain it! I can only tell you that each time she has left before, I still had some sense of her presence. I could feel her always nearby, even when I could not see her. I always knew for certain that she would return in her own time—and so she always did. But this time . . ."

He swallowed hard and looked at the forest again. "This time, there is naught but a cold and empty place in my heart where she has lived for all these many months— and a terrible feeling that she has abandoned this world, for it is destroying her, and that I will never see her again."

Rian, too, glanced into the forest, and then looked at Parlan again. "If she is truly gone, do you mean to abandon your quest?"

Parlan tightened his jaw. "I do not. I swore an oath to her and to all the people of Eire."

"But how can you hope to complete it without her? How can you ever get the fourth object, the Stone of Destiny, without the goddess to show you where it is and help you defeat its guardian?"

Parlan could only stare at him—and then he almost

laughed. "I do not know how I could possibly do such a thing," he said, shrugging his shoulders. "I would not even know where to start. But I know that I swore an oath and I have to try, and that, mercifully, I may well die in the attempt."

"Then let me do what I can to help you, my king, no matter how little, and perhaps it will not come to that."

Parlan gave him a wan smile. Then he looked up over Rian's shoulder and saw the campsite, and nearly every man there looking his way, with Cillian and Gavin standing at their head.

Clearly they had heard every word.

Late that night, as the full moon rode low in the western sky, Gavin and Cillian led their horses far to the rear of the camp where their saddles were waiting—and also three other men.

"Well, now," Cillian said, in a low voice. "Lorcan, Niall and Seamus. Are you here to stop us? Or to ride with us?"

"We are here to ride with you," said Niall. "There are others who would also, but they feel they must wait out their journey to the bitter end, one way or the other. But we feel as you do: This king is false, and another must be found."

"We can be back at Teamhair Breagh in a fortnight or less, if we ride straight through. We can begin the search for another king right away," said Lorcan.

"We don't want to wait another day," added Seamus. "A new king must be found immediately."

"I agree that a new king is needed," said Cillian, swinging his saddle onto the back of his horse. "But we are not riding for Teamhair Breagh."

Niall stepped forward. "Then where are you going?"

Cillian finished tightening the girth on the saddle and turned back to the three men. He began a speech: "You were there last Samhain night at Teamhair Breagh, when Parlan was made high king by the goddess herself, and then, in his foolishness and arrogance, decided that he would have none other but that very same goddess for his queen. He said he would even give up the kingship she had just granted him, if it meant she would stay with him as his wife. His careless rejection infuriated her—and rightly so, for it brought down the Curse of the Dragon on the land." He looked up at the men. "Now this king has been abandoned by that same goddess who vowed to help him on his quest, for surely she knows that he cannot hope to defeat the dragon, no matter how many magicked items he is able to gather."

"She has gone, before it is too late for her to go—and we must do the same," spoke up Lorcan, nodding.

"So we should," agreed Cillian. "But what we really need now is a new king, an unsullied king, a king with the strength and courage to face a horror like that dragon, face it and defeat it. But how can there be a new king when the old king yet lives?"

A silence fell over the group.

"That is why we are not going to Teamhair Breagh—not yet," said Gavin. "We have one other place to go first, to clear the way for a new high king."

"Are you with us?" asked Cillian.

The three men glanced at one another. "We are with you," said Seamus. A short time later, the five riders walked their horses quietly into the night, heading north.

V

THE NORTH

CHAPTER THIRTY-THREE

Parlan and his men continued their slow journey north to the fortress of Dun Orga, though each day his blood fairly burned at the defection of his men.

"You are so sure that they have abandoned the party?" asked Rian, on the day after the five disappeared. "Could they not have gone off on a hunt, and got lost?"

"There is none better at tracking than Cillian. He would be the last man to get lost anywhere in Eire."

"Suppose they did go off for a hunt, but were injured and could not return?"

Parlan snorted. "Of five riders and five horses, not one man and not one beast could find its way back to the campsite? Well, perhaps they all rode off a cliff and vanished into the air. It seems about as likely." He ground his teeth. "You know as well as I where they have gone. They've gone back to Teamhair Breagh, abandoning their king who was himself abandoned by the goddess he swore to serve. They've gone back to find a king, a true king this time, before it is too late."

"If that is true," Rian said, "then we had best move as

quickly as possible to find the last artifact—especially if the Lady Eriu does not return to help us find it. We will have to make a careful search, and consult the druids and the oldest tales, and search everywhere and—"

"We will never find it without her," Parlan said. "No mortal man could ever hope to find the sacred objects of the gods, or those things would have been discovered long ago." He sighed, and looked out at the distant clouds. "All I can do, Rian, is be in the north on Samhain Eve and wait for the dragon to come for me. I will not have the means to defeat it, but once it has destroyed me and I am gone, I will have done the best I could and a new king can come and lift the curse. A rightful king."

He tried to smile. "Surely the dragon will be satisfied for a time with the death of the one who brought it, and give the new king a little time to learn to meet it."

"But how can a new king do this if he still does not have the Stone of Destiny?"

"Surely Eriu will return to create the new king, and help him finish the quest where I failed. He will have her aid as a true king should, unlike me, whom she was forced to abandon because I did not cherish her and her gifts as she deserved."

"Please, King Parlan," Rian whispered, "let us see that it does not come to that."

Parlan shrugged. "As I said, all I can do is be in the northern lands on Samhain night and hope that the goddess will choose to return to me and help me lift this curse—and that she does not simply remain safe in the Otherworld forever, as well she might, and leave Men to their fate."

Many nights later, late in the afternoon of the autumn equinox—a day when darkness and light held equal time over the world—Parlan and Rian and his remaining warriors rode up the last of the hills leading to the oceanside fortress of Dun Orga. They could hear the pounding and roar of the waves, though in this place the sea lay far, far below them at the foot of towering cliffs.

"It will be good to stay in the comfort of Dun Orga," Rian said. "The men have talked of little else save how it is known for its hospitality. I, for one, will admit that after living so long as a beast, I do love the comforts that a roof and a hearth and a warm straw bed provide."

Parlan hardly spared him a glance. "We have no time for the pleasures of food and home. We are here to get our hostages and go on. We must be in the northernmost part of the land well before Samhain night—and there we will wait, and search for what knowledge we can find, and hope against hope that either the goddess takes pity on us or we are able to find the Stone of Destiny on our own. And you can be certain, Rian, that one is about as likely as the other."

Rian smiled at him, patient as ever. "Then I will simply enjoy each night as it comes at Dun Orga, my king, for we shall be sleeping out on the ground again soon enough."

They climbed to the very top of the hill. Just beyond, in a little valley between the hills and the seaside cliffs, the straw-thatched rooftops and massive earth-and-stone walls of Dun Orga rose into view—and just below those walls, lined up outside the tightly closed wooden gates, were several hundred men on horseback, far more than could have come from Dun Orga alone.

Warrior men. Fighting men. Men wearing leather armor and holding iron swords and tall wooden shields and bronze-tipped javelins. Men who surrounded their own kings, Ros of Dun Ghee and Morrissey of Dun Farriaghe and Diarmaid of Abhainn Aille, each of whom stood behind his driver in a two-wheeled chariot drawn by a pair of fiery horses. All of them were shouting and eager for the battle to begin.

Instantly Parlan halted Maorga. His men stopped

where they were. Gesturing to Rian to stay where he was, Parlan rode out to meet the men of Dun Orga.

"Parlan, wait!" Rian cried. "I will go! Let me ride out as your champion and meet them in your name!"

But Parlan ignored him and took Maorga out alone.

He expected to see another man, the kings' champion, ride out to meet him. They would discuss terms, and exchange demands and insults, and possibly engage in single ritual combat. No one would die and honor would be satisfied, with Dun Orga and all the rest getting justice for whatever it was that had offended them.

But as soon as Maorga jogged forward, every last man at Dun Orga set up a tremendous roar and shouting. Their horses shied and danced, but still the men hurled insults and abuse and hammered their wooden shields with their swords and aimed their javelins at Parlan's men.

Maorga threw his head up and turned away from the sudden eruption of noise. Parlan forced the horse back around—and as he did, Parlan caught sight of a familiar face near the far end of the enemy line.

Cillian. Beside him was Gavin. And beside him were Lorcan, Niall and Seamus, every last one shouting right along with the rest of the warrior men of the four kingdoms.

"What do you want?" Parlan shouted, looking toward King Mactire in his wicker-sided chariot. "What do you want? I am Parlan, high king of all Eire, and I am here to collect your hostages to peace! Why do you meet me with swords and threats and insults?"

The noise subsided somewhat as King Mactire's wicker-sided chariot moved forward a few steps. "You are no high king to us, Parlan," said Mactire. He was an aged man with rough white hair and cold blue eyes. "You are an arrogant man whose dragon has brought the curse of death and destruction to my lands and my people. It has also brought about the loss of four of the sons of these other kingdoms, all of them good men who did not deserve such a fate.

"Your goddess has abandoned you. Your most trusted men have abandoned you. Now your kingdoms abandon you, too, for I will give no hostages to a failed and cursed king. If you want hostages from me, you will have to fight for them."

Parlan allowed his stallion to jog back and forth along the hillside. "If I cannot gain the last three hostages to peace, I will have truly failed as high king, curse or no, and there will then be no reason at all for Eriu to come back to me. Even that tiny chance will be gone. Without her, I cannot hope to complete the quest. So, King Mactire, ready your men and ready your allies, and I will do battle for your hostages to peace."

"They remain inside the fortress," shouted Mactire so that all could hear. "If you or your men can reach the gates and hold them before sundown, the hostages are yours."

"Agreed!" shouted Parlan, and galloped Maorga back up the hill to his own force. Rian quickly rode out to meet him.

"You heard what he said," Parlan snapped. "He does not want an all-out battle with too many of his own men lost. If we can get to those gates before nightfall, the hostages are ours."

"You see who has brought this about, King Parlan," Rian cried, swinging his sword in the direction of Cillian and Galvin. "Two traitors who are blind to the fact that they have the most accomplished high king since the days of Lugh—and if anyone knows this, I am that man!"

Parlan just shook his head. He shouted to the men on the hill. "Send the servants far to the rear! The rest of you, draw your swords and come with me! We must get through their lines and take those gates before the sun goes down."

For the span of a heartbeat, none of his warriors moved.

Parlan could only stand in the lengthening shadows and wonder if they had abandoned him, too, and if it would all end here with nothing left for him to do but walk into the sea over the steep cliff. Then, in the next heartbeat, the men drew their swords and began surging forward.

"Let's go, then!" they shouted. "Such poor hospitality, to make us beat upon their gates! If battle is what they want, then battle is what they will have! Let's go!"

Parlan did not know if the men rode with him out of loyalty, or if they just relished the thought of good rough battle after the tension of the many days of their long journey, but at this moment he did not care. He drew the Sword of Nuadha from its bloodred scabbard, raised the weapon high, and swung Maorga around to gallop with his men into the valley where the shouting, swearing warriors of Dun Orga awaited.

The peaceful afternoon quickly gave way to wild destructive chaos—a battle that was perhaps half ritual. The mere sight of the massive, gleaming Sword of Nuadha, larger than any of the bronze or iron weapons the other warriors carried, and imbued with a fearsome legend, was enough to make many of the men of Dun Orga fall away lest it so much as touch them. Parlan had to do little more than wave the sword about and shout.

He quickly worked his way through the lines and began to push Maorga toward the gates. The battle raged all around him. He knew that at first the men would bluff and shout and hurl insults and strike glancing blows, in an effort to see who would back down and who would not, but if things went on this way too long, blood would begin to flow more and more freely.

At last he reached the massive, thick wooden gates of the fortress, now in shadow as the sun began to set behind the cliff. The gates were twice as tall as he was, and closed, he knew, with a heavy oak timber run through enormous iron rings on the other side. There was no way his men could open those gates from the outside, but they did not have to; all they had to do was get between the gates and the warrior men of Dun Orga, and the day was theirs.

Parlan turned Maorga to stand and prance in place right alongside the enormous gates, and he used the heavy bronze hilt of the Sword of Nuadha to hammer on the oak timbers. "Look here! Look here!" he shouted, pulling Maorga up so that the stallion crouched back on its hind legs, lifted its front end off the ground and raised Parlan up above the battle. "I have the gate! I have it! Come and join me and we will cut them off! We will triumph! Come and join me!"

Finally some of them did push through and get close to him—at least, those who could hear and who were not already preoccupied with their own one-on-one fighting. Several riders brought their horses in close, some in front of Maorga and some behind, and the rest between Maorga and the others.

"Drive them back! Drive them back! Let the rest of our men get in!" Parlan shouted. Maorga reared up high as more horses pressed in close. "Drive them—"

And then Parlan saw who it was who crowded in so hard around him. It was Cillian at Maorga's head and Gavin at his tail, with Lorcan, Niall and Seamus pushing in hard alongside him.

"Back away from me!" Parlan shouted. "Back away! I hold the Sword of Nuadha, which none can escape once it is drawn! Will you dare to face such a weapon, no matter how much you despise your cursed king?"

"It is a great sword, but a poor shield," Cillian said. "Give it to us, that we might give it to a worthy king and let him lift your curse!"

"Never," said Parlan. "It was entrusted to me by its guardian. I will keep it in my care until the curse is lifted. Do not force me to kill you with it!"

"You are the one who has forced us to kill you!" shouted Gavin from behind him, and he swung his iron sword at Parlan's head.

Parlan half twisted in the saddle and raised the Sword of Nuadha high behind him to stop the blow—and stop it he did. Gavin's sword was deflected and fell straight into the mud beneath the stomping hooves of the horses, and he quickly retreated by forcing his horse away from the gates.

But Seamus took his place behind Maorga, keeping Parlan's stallion trapped between the other riders and the gates.

"You will not escape us this time. It ends here!" Cillian shouted, and he swung his sword at Parlan.

Parlan blocked that blow also with the Sword of Nuadha. But when he heard the air whistling as Niall and Lorcan slashed at him, he turned in a rage and cut straight across the two of them as hard as he could.

Both men fell from their horses. Parlan caught sight of one man with his head half gone, while the other dropped in a motionless heap atop him. Their horses bolted, followed closely by Seamus, who was kicking his own horse to ride away from the carnage as fast as he could.

Now only Cillian was left. As Maorga half reared and charged forward, Parlan used his sword to knock Cillian's weapon loose and send it flying. Without hesitation, Parlan turned the blade and struck Cillian with the flat of it so hard that the man was knocked from his terrified horse as the animal whirled to escape the attack.

Parlan leapt down from Maorga's back and stood over Cillian before Cillian could get up. His foe lay in the mud near the massive wooden gate; he shook his head, dazed, and started to get up—but stopped when he saw the heavy blade of the Sword of Nuadha aimed at his throat.

"You are a traitor, Cillian," Parlan said, his breathing hard and ragged. He stared down at the man through the deepening twilight. "You threw the sling-stone that caused poor Maorga to throw me into the flooded river. You cut the girth on my saddle so I would fall on the rocks—either you did those things or you ordered Gavin to do them for you."

Cillian looked away.

"But I know for certain that this last treachery—this riding ahead to have the army of Dun Orga ready and waiting to fight me to the death—that was your doing and yours alone."

Parlan moved his sword until it touched the man's grimy, sweat-streaked neck. "I may be a failed and cursed king, but I am still *your* king while I draw breath—and I trusted you as I have trusted few others. For such treachery, any man would deserve to die."

"Go ahead and kill him. I would do no less."

Parlan glanced up. King Mactire stood over him, gazing down from his chariot with cold contempt for Cillian. "It may well be true," the king said, "that the land does need a new high king—but to try to destroy the old one by luring him into a trap, instead of letting him prepare for honorable combat, is hardly the way of a decent man."

Parlan suddenly realized that the battle had stopped. Quiet had fallen along with the deepening twilight, and both his own men and the men of Dun Orga were gathered around him and King Mactire. Beside them as well were the Kings Ros, Morrissey and Diarmaid.

"The day is yours, Parlan," Mactire went on. "Your enemy lies at your feet, here at the very gates of Dun Orga. I will keep my word. You may have your hostages to peace. Just kill your enemy and drag him out of the way, and we will open the gates and let you in."

Parlan looked down at Cillian. The light of the first

stars reflected off the bright bronze surface of the Sword of Nuadha. He pointed the weapon again at the fallen man's throat.

"You are a traitor," Parlan whispered, "but perhaps I would have felt the same, had I been in your place."

He lowered his sword and placed it back in its scabbard. "You were loyal to me once. I will earn your loyalty again, as a high king should earn the loyalty of all his subjects. Get up, Cillian. Go back to camp. If you truly want to kill me, you have only to stab me in my sleep. No need to make it complicated."

Parlan turned around then as the massive gates of Dun Orga were dragged open from the inside. He walked into the fortress with King Mactire and all of the other warrior men, leaving Cillian lying outside in the mud.

CHAPTER THIRTY-FOUR

The days grew shorter, greyer, and darker, as Parlan and his men left Dun Orga to begin making their way through the heavy forests of the north and climbing up into the mountains. Parlan knew that Rian kept a wary eye on the remaining men, ever concerned that Gavin and Cillian might try to start another rebellion, but Parlan also knew they had far greater worries than a few malcontents who could, as he said, easily stab him in his sleep.

Cillian and Gavin remained far in the rear of the party among the servants and pack animals, caring for the horses and hauling wood and water. They would not dare show their faces among the other warriors after the humiliation they had suffered at the hands of Parlan with everyone looking on.

The party rode at a steady pace for seven days, making only a temporary camp each night and going right out again the next day at dawn. On the seventh night, as the moon rose behind drifting veils of cloud, Parlan found himself unable to sleep. Restless and troubled, he got up and walked away from the quiet camp with its few scattered torches and firepits.

The light of the moon soon showed him a faint path that led toward the very top of the mountain where they camped. He followed it, grateful to simply be alone in quiet darkness. Parlan stopped at the top of the mountain and looked out over the range of mountains, watching their outlines turn to silver as the clouds parted and the moonlight shone down.

Such a beautiful sight . . . and yet, even from here, Parlan could see wide swaths of the forest that had been blackened and withered by the cursed foul breath of the dragon. It was plain that the beast was growing stronger by the day. The dark of the moon following Samhain night was now only some three fortnights away.

He placed one foot upon a large stone beside the path, held the heavy hilt of the Sword of Nuadha in one hand, and gazed out over the shining black mountains. "By the love I have for you this night, Lady Eriu, and the love I shall always have for you, whether I see you again or no, I swear that I will continue this quest as long as I have breath and strength and the beat of my heart. If I can do nothing else, I can continue on in your name until it is ended one way or another."

He set his foot back down on the path and continued gazing at the mountains, even as they became shadowed and dim as the clouds passed once more over the moon. He did not know why, but he felt somewhat at peace. At least he knew that he would do all he could, and that no matter what else happened, he would end with his honor in place.

Parlan looked down and was about to go back the way he had come, when a small movement in the forest on one side caught his eye. He stood very still. Most likely it was just a small animal, a hare or some such . . . but then he heard it again. It was not an animal. It was a footstep, and another, and another.

His hand tightened on the heavy hilt of the sword. "Who is there?" he asked, keeping his voice low. "Who is there?"

As though in answer, he heard footsteps on the other side of the path. Parlan drew the sword and held it out. "Show yourselves!" he demanded. "Gavin! Cillian! You are cowards to the last, sneaking around in dead of night! I did not think you would have the courage to try me again, but if you have, come out and fight like men!"

A small figure, deep in shadow, stepped out in front of him on the path. "My name is not Gavin," it said.

"And my name is not Cillian," said another voice behind him. Parlan turned to see a second shadowed form standing on the path.

"In fact, there is not one among us who has such a name," said a third voice from off the path. Parlan found himself surrounded by soft laughing voices in the darkness, voices that were as delicate and as musical as the notes of a harp.

The clouds flew by and the moon shone down again. Parlan saw, outlined in faint silver just as the mountains had been, the large eyes and delicate features of dark-haired people whose heads were scarcely chest high on him. The men were dressed in leather trews and linen tunics, and the women wore long gowns of the softest leather trimmed with lines of fur. All had finely spun wool cloaks with golden brooches, and as the little group gathered around him on the path, he could see that all of them wore finger-rings and wristbands and even dress-fasteners of gleaming and beautifully worked gold.

Very slowly and deliberately, Parlan lowered the Sword of Nuadha, placed its tip back into the scabbard, and slowly slid it home. "I am done a great honor this night," he said. "I am visited by the Sidhe, whom some say left this world long ago . . . yet it is clear to me that you are still here."

"My name is Fallon," said the one who had shown himself first. "We were drawn by your words to the Goddess Eriu. And it is true that we are still in this world, but not for long."

"Not for long," repeated Parlan. He glanced out over the mountains, looking again at the wide damaged strips of ancient forest. "You leave because of the curse that lies on this land. You are going to the Otherworld, where you will be safe forever."

"You are right," said Fallon. "We have come here to the high mountains on the night of the full moon, bringing all our gold with us, to call upon the gods and goddesses to allow us entry into the Otherworld."

"And surely they will grant you entry," Parlan said. "The Sidhe are the most ancient inhabitants of the land, and its most careful guardians. It is no fault of yours that the land is dying. If any deserve the reward of the Otherworld, it is the Sidhe." Parlan cocked his head. "You say you bring all your gold. What need do you have of gold in the Otherworld?"

The man smiled. "We do love beautiful things as much as any man. Gold, the most beautiful of all things of the earth, is very dear to us."

"It is also true," said the other Sidhe on the path, "that we have no wish to leave our precious gold behind for the men who allowed the land to fall into ruin."

Parlan could only nod in agreement.

"And so," said the woman just off the path, "we thought that to offer our gold to the gods and goddesses might serve us better than to leave it for uncaring mortals."

Parlan stood very straight, and he looked around him at the small and secretive people who surrounded him now in the moonlit forest—people who were also being forced out of their home by the curse that lay over the land.

"I do understand why you feel you must go," he said quietly, "and yet it saddens me greatly to see such a thing. The Fair Folk helped create this world, and their magic and knowledge will always be needed here. The natural world will be greatly diminished if you are gone."

He reached up and took hold of the heavy gold torque that rested on his neck, pulled it slightly open at its spiral-capped ends, and slid it off. "The Lady Eriu placed this round my neck on the night she made me a king. I will remain a king to her and to my people until I die; she knows this well. Yet if this piece of gold will help you gain your admittance to the Otherworld, I will give it to you gladly."

He held the golden torque out to Fallon, who took it with the utmost care. "I would only ask," Parlan said, "that if you do see the Lady Eriu once you make your way to the Otherworld, you give this torque to her, for she is to whom my kingship will always belong."

"We shall do this for you, King Parlan," said Fallon, and he bowed deeply. Then the entire group of Sidhe continued on their way down the path, following it along the curve of the mountainside until their faint shadows and gleaming gold were lost to sight.

Parlan quickly followed and looked out where they had gone, hoping to catch one last glimpse of a people he would never see again; but all he saw was the moonlight shining down on the mountains, dimmed here and there by the shadows of passing clouds.

For another fortnight Parlan and his men rode steadily through the shortening grey days, trying to take advantage of all the daylight they could in order to travel as far as possible. A few days were spent in camp, so that the men might have a chance to hunt for deer, riding hard after the huge, thick-necked bucks that were just beginning the mating season. The animals would sometimes turn and face the men, shaking their enormous sharp antlers and snorting and pawing in defiance, but even the powerful bucks were no match for the deerhounds who leapt at their throats and for the men who impaled them with spears. Soon there was venison turning all night on the spits over the campfires; and in the morning, the party was traveling again.

They continued on through the mountains and finally turned south, following for a time the shoreline of a lake so large it seemed as endless as the sea. They eventually came to the end of it, and rode inland for several more days until at last they came to the hills overlooking the plain known as Magh Sleacht.

"This is all I know of where to find the Stone of Destiny," Parlan said to Rian, as they stood looking down on the plain in the fading light. "Eriu said this is where it is hidden, guarded by some beast known as the dullahan. But the plain is vast, and I do not know where to look for just one stone—or even how to recognize it."

Rian became very still. "The dullahan? What do you know of him?"

Parlan shrugged. "Not much. There is little to be heard about him, even in the oldest tales of the druids." He tried to smile. "Whatever he is, he can hardly be worse than the Wild Hunt, or the firedrake, or even the merrows—and since I have no chance against him anyway without Eriu, why should I worry?"

"My memories are . . . different," whispered Rian, looking away. "Before I spent countless years as the firedrake guardian, I was a companion and servant of the gods—and though I never saw the dullahan with my own eyes, I heard much about him, for he was the worst of all

280

the gods, and was feared even by his own brothers and sisters."

"A god? Feared by the other gods?"

"Indeed." Rian paused, and shook his head. "Almost from birth, this one was different. He had nothing of the height and glowing beauty of the others. Some trick of chance, which can happen even amongst the gods, left him ugly and misshapen instead, with rough reddened skin and one dead eye. But far worse than such afflictions was the resentment that grew in him with each day, resentment of the gifts of beauty and grace the others had which he did not—or so he felt.

"The others called him Crom, for he was bent and crooked. And he let his anger and jealousy fall onto the heads of those he was given to rule, right down to the fine horses that willingly served the other gods but refused to go near him and his cruelty. He became a punishing god whom all Men feared and could not love."

"A cruel god is worse than no god at all," said Parlan quietly.

Rian nodded. "Crom decided that he would be the only god that Men would ever know. He began gathering vast armies made up of the dead, and he forced his smiths and craftsmen to forge terrible weapons. The other gods had no choice but to do the same so that he would not overthrow them, and it all ended in the terrible war and dreadful flood that destroyed so much of mankind and so many of the gods."

"Crom did not die with them?"

Rian shook his head. "He did not die. When the end was near and the other gods knew that all was lost, they used the last of their power to bind Crom and behead him."

"Behead him? And that did not kill him?"

"They believed it would. But such hatred and malevolence is difficult to kill, especially in the divine. The other

281

gods could not destroy him entirely, so instead they cursed him for eternity to stay in the natural world, to ride forever on one of the horses he so despised, and to guard the Stone of Destiny—the stone that cries out when a true king stands upon it—knowing that he had proven himself least worthy as a ruler of Men, and thus that the stone would never cry out for him."

"A dreadful story," Parlan said. "Do you have any knowledge of how such a monster might be persuaded to give up the object he guards? Or perhaps he cares nothing for the treasures of gods and Men, and so cares nothing if the stone is taken away."

"One might think so . . . but Crom was always horrifically jealous of the beautiful gods, and of the Men who sought to emulate them. He will give up no treasure that would confirm any man to be a king, for if he cannot be a king no one else will be one, either. He is a cursed god, no longer called Crom but the dullahan, trapped here forever to do the things he hates most—ride a horse, be a servant, and be ignored and shunned by Men and gods alike."

"I can see why he would make the perfect guardian for such a powerful artifact. He could never be charmed or tricked or persuaded—and what man could hope to kill a god?"

Parlan glanced over at the setting sun, and then down at the vast grassy plain dotted with trees. "Have the servants make the camp up here, just behind the hills. That will keep them safe from whatever is to come. Tomorrow at sundown, Rian, you and I will be down there on the plain of Magh Sleacht, hoping that somehow we can find the Stone of Destiny and get it past the dullahan to Teamhair Breagh."

CHAPTER THIRTY-FIVE

On the cold damp evening that was Samhain night, with the full moon rising over the campsite behind them, Parlan and Rian walked down the hillside to the floor of the plain. "This place is strewn with rocks and boulders and stones. I could spend the rest of my days looking at them one by one and still not know if it was the Stone of Destiny. Unless Eriu returns and shows me how to find its guardian, my quest will end here. I do not know what else I can do."

Rian smiled, looking over at Parlan in the deep twilight. "Then do what all men do when they fear they have reached the end. Call upon your goddess one last time, and ask her to help you if she will."

Parlan took a step forward, looking around him at the thinning grass and the tall black pine and holly trees disappearing into the darkness. One day soon, he knew, it would all disappear beneath the cold breath of the Black Dragon and would not reappear with the dawn.

"Lady Eriu," he whispered, closing his eyes, "I will ask you one last time to help me complete my quest. I have come here to the final place to win the final artifact, but this plain is as far as I can go. I have no power to search any farther. Only one such as you can know where to find the possessions of the gods.

"If I cannot find the Stone of Destiny, I will return to where I began. I will await the dragon there at the dark of the moon and do battle with it as best I can. But I ask you to help me one last time, not just for myself but for all of my people, and for you, and for the land that all of us cherish."

He opened his eyes and saw only darkness. He was aware that Rian still waited a few steps away, but except for that silent presence Parlan felt as though he stood alone in some eternal darkness where light might never return.

A wind began to rise, a wind cold with winter. It seemed to drive the clouds away from the moon, and in a moment a soft white glow lit the plain. The trees moved in that same wind, and Parlan found himself watching a grove of very tall pines out toward the center of the grassy plain. The wind blew much harder there, it seemed, for the branches of the great tall pines were forced down so hard they nearly touched the earth, springing back up while the wind caught its breath and then being violently pushed down once again until it seemed that they must snap.

And as the moon shone ever brighter, Parlan realized that each time the wind pushed the trees down it forced them to reveal what stood within the grove—a tall slab of stone, shaped and upright, with another slab just a few steps beside it.

"There!" Parlan said, catching Rian by the arm. He walked at a rapid pace toward the pine grove, even as the wind eased and the tall trees gradually returned to their normal positions, with only the tips of their long, needle-covered branches still moving in the last of the cold night breeze. Parlan worked his way past the pines and then stood with his hand on the rough bark of the last of them, staring at the sight before him.

The enormous pine trees thickly surrounded a wide clearing, one that had been well hidden until the sudden wind pushed the tree limbs aside. In the great circular clearing was not just one standing stone, or two, as Parlan had seen; there were twelve standing stones, each one taller and wider than a man, standing in a perfect circle in the clearing.

"See what your goddess has shown you," said Rian, coming to stand beside him.

Parlan pushed away from the tree, drew a deep breath, and walked slowly toward the edge of the stone circle. The standing stones seemed to move aside as he approached, revealing the very center of the circle—and there, glowing faintly in the light of the full moon, was a flat, rectangular, blue-grey stone.

He paused between two of the standing stones, almost afraid to believe what he was seeing. "Could this . . . could this be the Stone of Destiny?" he whispered, staring at it.

"Go, King Parlan," Rian said from a few steps behind him. "If it cries out when you stand upon it, as legend says it does, there can be no doubt of what it is."

Parlan glanced at him, more grateful than he could say for Rian's calm loyalty. He gave the younger man a quick nod, then strode out onto the grass.

The stone lay shining in the moonlight, a blue-grey slab that would be about chest high on a man if it were stood on end. Parlan stopped beside it. It looked almost alive in the soft glow of the moon, right down to the faint tracing of thin red lines that ran through its sandstone core. He clenched his fists and tried not to think about what he would do if he stepped upon the stone and nothing happened.

Before he could ràise his foot, there came a terrible crashing in the trees directly across from him.

For a heartbeat, Parlan froze. It sounded like some huge army had suddenly materialized amongst the thick pines and was galloping straight for him. He took a step back from the stone, drawing the Sword of Nuadha as he did, and almost tripped over Rian. Together they stood up to face whatever it was that was coming through the trees.

At first all Parlan saw was a horse coming straight at him—a tall black horse, thin and shaggy and rough coated, with a cruelly sharp bit half out of its mouth that left its jaw shining wet with blood. The beast threw its head up high as it galloped toward him, and Parlan could see no rider in the darkness.

"Is this the dullahan?" he whispered to Rian. "Just some terrible horse, set to guard the stone?"

But as the horse came into the stone circle, it suddenly swung hard to one side and stopped—and Parlan saw, at last, what the dullahan really was.

The terrible bony black horse, with its painful bridle and galling broken saddle, did indeed bear a rider—a huge broad-shouldered man dressed in layers of heavy grey cloaks, each one shorter than the one beneath. His cloaks were heaped up high over his head so that Parlan could not see his face. He held his reins in one hand and seemed to be carrying something else in the other.

Then the rider raised his free hand, and Parlan found himself staring into a face—a horrible, hideous, one-eyed face on a severed head that hung by its hair. This rider had no head on his own shoulders, but only one gripped in his hand.

The skin on that contorted face was the sickening grey-white of death, as was the hand that held it. One eye was nothing but a black and tortured socket, but the other held a baleful, malevolent, bulging and bloodshot eye that flicked from one side of the circle to the other, and then glared straight at Parlan. The lips on the severed head moved, and the night was filled with the sound of a growling, hate-filled voice.

"Go from here," said the hideous head. "You are an intruder. Go, or I will take your head as I have taken so many others."

Parlan stood openly between two of the standing stones, though he could hear blood pounding in his ears. "Dullahan, I have need of the Stone of Destiny. I shall return it to your care when I am done. But I will not leave here without it."

The horrible rider raised its head high. His horse half reared as the ugly sharp bit dug into its bleeding mouth and forced it to turn and face Parlan. "Then I shall enjoy the only pleasure I still know—killing men." The dullahan dropped the reins. From a scabbard at the back of his saddle he took a long thin iron bar with a heavy knot at one end. Then, holding up the head in one hand and the iron bar in the other, he gouged the horse's sides with his rough iron spurs and drove it into a gallop straight toward Parlan.

Behind him, Parlan heard Rian draw his sword, but he shouted over his shoulder to his companion, "Get back. Get back! This is for me to face! I've lost enough men already!" Parlan raised the gleaming Sword of Nuadha, gripping its hilt in two hands, and braced himself for the onslaught of the dullahan.

The god's black horse lumbered across the circle, forced on by cruel raking spurs. But just as the beast crossed the center, striding over the Stone of Destiny, a small figure darted into the circle and ran right in front of the horse.

The startled beast threw its head up and slid to a stop— and then the small cloaked figure flung a handful of sparkling golden dust directly into the severed head's hideous face. A moment later the figure rushed back into the darkness of the forest.

The dullahan screeched in fury as his horse reared in fright, and his face shut its eye tight against the dust. For an instant Parlan saw the dead face glittering with gold in the moonlight, and then the headless rider forced the horse around again and retreated to the other side of the circle.

Parlan looked toward the spot where the small darting figure had disappeared. "Who is there? Who are you? Come out! Show yourself to me!"

"King Parlan!" cried Rian from behind him. "Come here! The one you seek is here!"

Parlan hesitated, still watching the dullahan; but the monster had ridden almost to the edge of the pine trees and was trying to wipe the gold dust from the eye of its severed head with the edge of its layered grey cloaks. Parlan lowered the Sword of Nuadha and looked behind him—and thought his heart would leap out of his chest.

In the moonlit shadows at the edge of the pine forest, Rian stood closely surrounded by six . . . seven . . . nine of the Sidhe-folk. And directly behind him stood a tall hooded figure in a dark green cloak that was fastened by a gold brooch in the shape of a circle of oak leaves. The figure raised her head, and Parlan found himself looking into the pale face and green eyes of Eriu.

He started to go to her, but the way was blocked by Rian and the Sidhe and by the thick wide trunks of the pine trees. "Eriu!" he cried, trying to keep the desperate urgency out of his voice. "With the help of your storm and windblown trees, I have found the Stone of Destiny and the dullahan. Now, if I only had some idea of what to do with him now that I have him, perhaps this coming battle would not be so short!"

"Gold," Eriu called.

Parlan frowned and glanced quickly over his shoulder. The monstrous rider had turned his horse toward the circle again. He held his head up high, turning it this way and that as the baleful eye searched the darkness.

"The dullahan despises gold, and it in turn despises him," Eriu continued, her voice softer. "Gold is the most beautiful thing to be found in the earth, and it is the mark of a king like nothing else."

"So one of the Sidhe-folk flung gold dust into his face, to burn and blind him," Parlan said. "Is that how I can defeat him, and get the stone? With gold?"

"The three things that the dullahan hates above all else—the earth to which he was exiled, the kingship that he will never have, and the kindness that he will never know and never give. Those are the things that can defeat him. And those three things have been made into a weapon for you by the Sidhe-folk whom you met one night upon the road to the Otherworld and showed an act of kindness."

"Kindness?" Parlan glanced back again. The dullahan sat very still on the black horse, holding up the severed head so that it stared directly at the gathering under the pines. "Lady Eriu—what is this weapon?"

She brushed aside her cloak and held out both hands to Parlan. Across her palms rested a dagger—a sharp, slender, solid gold dagger.

"Put your sword away, King Parlan," Eriu said. "It is of no use against the armor of hatred that the dullahan wears." Quickly he shoved the Sword of Nuadha back into its scabbard as Eriu continued speaking. "A dagger made only of gold has no strength to cut through armor or bone. It is made for one target alone—the terrible single eye of the dullahan."

Hoofbeats sounded across the circle. "Give me the weapon! There is no time!" Parlan cried. "I will do what I can!"

Eriu flung the golden dagger to Parlan over the heads of the Sidhe. He grabbed it out of the air and turned back to face the stone circle.

CHAPTER THIRTY-SIX

A fine spray of blood flew from the bony black horse's mouth as the dullahan reined it hard around and forced it into a lumbering gallop across the open grass of the stone circle. The rider drew his monstrous iron club once more and held his severed head high, and as the head fixed its gaze on him and roared in rage, for a moment Parlan's blood ran cold.

Parlan hefted the golden dagger in his hand. It was heavy, and it would be slow. Yet he had no choice but to focus hard on the hideous eye, raise the dagger and throw it with all his strength.

As he feared, the dagger flew slowly, end-over-end, gleaming and glittering brightly in the moonlight. The grisly rider simply moved the head in front of his chest to dodge the shining missile.

Parlan ground his teeth. He could see the dagger lying on the grass beside the stone, the gold shining bright in the moonlight, but he could only throw himself down behind the trunk of the nearest pine as the dullahan galloped straight for him and attacked—his iron club smashed the ancient tree nearly in half.

The dullahan had galloped past, and as he struggled to halt his tortured horse and get it turned around again, Parlan dashed across the circle, caught up the heavy gold dagger and kept on going into the darkness at the edge of the forest. The dullahan wasted no more time. With his shrieking head in one hand and his iron club in the other, the grisly rider sent the horse straight at Parlan again.

Parlan gripped his dagger hard. If he threw the thing again, the monster would only see it coming and easily move out of the way, as he had done before. Yet this was the only weapon he had against the dullahan.

Suddenly, from right alongside him, a small figure raced out into the clearing, right for the horse. Parlan could see the glitter of gold in its hands, and knew it was again one of the Sidhe-folk, meaning to try the same trick of blinding the dullahan with gold dust—but this time the beast had his iron club in his hand, and was ready for any attack. He would not be surprised again.

"Wait! Wait! Do not approach him! Go back into the forest!" Parlan called. But the nimble Sidhe continued to fling the dust, keeping a careful distance from the rider's iron club.

Suddenly the dullahan gave the horse a sharp jab on the bridle, and the tormented beast threw its head hard to one side. The unexpected move struck the Sidhe and sent him flying. He landed hard on the grass near the Stone of Destiny, prone.

"Here! Look over here!" Parlan shouted, running out into the circle. He had to keep the dullahan's attention so that it would not go back and crush the fallen Sidhe with his club. As the monstrous rider turned back to him, he dashed into the forest and hid himself in the deepest shadows.

The dullahan turned his horse and began to canter it around the circle just inside the standing stones, looking into the forest for Parlan. The head continued to shout in wordless rage, while the rider swung the iron club viciously through the air. The Sidhe lay where it had fallen, but the dullahan showed no further interest. Clearly Parlan was its only target—and just as clearly, Parlan would have to face the headless rider alone.

He had the weapon he needed, just as he had always had what he needed each time he faced one of the guardians—and each foe, he realized, was connected to one of the four elements.

The Master of the Hunt had come by way of the air.

The firedrake was a beast of flame.

The merrows were creatures of the water.

Which left the earth. The earth, ruled by a goddess, the Lady Eriu. Earth would defeat the dullahan. Gold—and the earth itself.

Quickly he crouched down at the base of a pine and pushed aside the heaps of dry fallen needles. His fingers ripped at the sparse grass and dug down to the damp ground below.

Taking handfuls of earth, he smeared it all over his face and arms and hands, until not even the moonlight would be able to find him. More handfuls were used to coat the dagger until it, too, was as dark and dull as a mud-covered stick.

The dullahan still cantered his horse round the circle, and his cruel voice now growled out one word, over and over: "Parlan!"

Parlan stood up and moved to the deepest shadows on the edge of the circle. He gripped the hilt of his dagger tightly in his right hand. Just as the dullahan came round again, his head lifted high but looking the other way, Parlan shouted out, "Dullahan! Look here! Look this way!"

The headless rider dragged his horse to a stop, forced it around, and raised his head high to see from where the cry had come—and as he glanced around, searching, Parlan flung the golden dagger as hard as he could. It flew directly into the monster's hideous eye.

The head shrieked and roared so loudly that it seemed the very trees and standing stones shook. The rider threw up both arms, letting go of both his iron club and his severed head, and sending both horrible relics flying across the open ground. Then the rider fell backward off the lunging, terrified horse, and he lay in a heap on the earth, the many folds and layers of his heavy grey cloaks settling down around him. His broken and bleeding horse lumbered off into the forest and disappeared.

From across the circle, three of the Sidhe raced out, lifted their fallen companion and carried him back into the darkness of the forest. Then Eriu came striding into the circle, followed by Rian and several of the Sidhe, and she went straight to Parlan.

"Is it over?" he asked, staring at the body of the rider and at the back of the head where it had rolled across the grass. "Is it dead? Can I take the stone and go?"

"It is not over. The dullahan cannot be killed, at least not by any power that I know. He must be bound, which will hold him for a time. But you must hurry!"

"Oh, I am happy to hurry," Parlan said, trying to wipe the drying mud from his eyes. "Just tell me what I must do!"

Eriu and the Sidhe formed a circle around the body of the headless dullahan. "Bring the head," she commanded. "Hurry!"

Parlan turned away. "Oh, of course. Bring the head," he muttered, walking across the circle. He felt dizzy, almost giddy, at the thought that he was so close to actually getting all four of the sacred artifacts. "Bring the head, Parlan. Just bring the head. That's all you have to do. Just bring the foul, rotted, already-severed living head of a monster, and then you can go home . . ."

He stopped. Just on the other side of the Stone of Destiny, the dullahan's severed head lay facing him. One eye was still a scarred and blackened socket, and the other had his heavy gold dagger buried right in the center of it, all the way up to the hilt. Blackened streams of something that might have been blood poured down over the sickly grey–white flesh, and the whole thing gave off a foul and sickening stench.

"Just bring the head, Parlan," Parlan muttered again, and with an iron resolve he forced himself to lock his fingers in the rank greasy hair.

His nerve almost failed him when the head sneered and curled its lip, showing black and rotted teeth; but he kept his hold on the terrible foul thing and carried it over to the body.

Eriu stood near the Dullahan's shoulders, watching as Rian and the Sidhe worked quickly to cover the headless body with damp earth hand-carried from the forest. "Place the head above the shoulders, where it should be. Quickly, now. The rest of you, cover him well. Hurry. Hurry!"

In moments the huge, grey-cloaked body of the dullahan was covered in a thick layer of damp earth, as was its hideous head. "Now," Eriu said, "gather close around. Take out the gold that you have brought with you, and use it to cover this earthen mound."

From beneath their cloaks the Sidhe brought out small bags of soft leather, and from the bags they sprinkled a fine gold powder over the mound of earth. Eriu looked up toward the moon. As she did, the wind picked up and moved the drifting clouds away so that the bright white light of the full Samhain moon shone straight down on the gold-covered mound.

As Parlan watched, it seemed that the gold powder began to melt in the cold light. It flowed down and over and beneath the earth-covered body until it formed a smooth flawless coating in the shape of a solid pillar.

"Bound," Eriu whispered. "Not dead, but bound . . . though for how long, I do not know. Long enough for you to take the stone and go to Teamhair Breagh, Parlan, and for a good number of years after that." She glanced toward the center of the circle. "King Parlan—take your companion Rian and two of the Sidhe, and carry the Stone of Destiny to the edge of the forest."

Parlan glanced at Rian, and together they walked to where the stone rested in the moonlight. With the help of the two Sidhe, they lifted it up from the earth and carried it—easily, for all its weight—to a spot between two great pines, and let it rest there while they returned to the gold-covered, earthbound body of the Dullahan.

Eriu stood at its head, while Parlan and Rian and seven of the Sidhe surrounded the golden pillar. "Now," Eriu said, "while the light of the Samhain moon shines full on it, you nine will be able to lift this pillar and raise it up in the center of this circle—raise it up in the same place that the Stone of Destiny rested. Do so now, before the clouds return."

And so they did, lifting the enormous pillar as easily as they might the fallen limb of a slender tree. They carried it to the center of the stone circle, set it down on one end, and watched it settle into the ground until it was held upright as firmly as the twelve standing stones that surrounded it.

The seven Sidhe and two men gathered near Eriu before the enormous gleaming pillar. Parlan moved to stand beside her hooded form. "I almost dare to believe the quest is over," he whispered. "That I have all four of the sacred objects, and that tomorrow we can begin our journey back to Teamhair Breagh."

Eriu glanced at him and gave a small smile. He supposed it was only the moonlight, or the shine from the pillar, that made her cheeks and lips look so pale. "Your quest is not over yet, King Parlan. There is still the matter of the Black Dragon a fortnight from now, at the dark of the moon."

"I know, I know," he answered. "I feared to think of it, for I had so much doubt that I would ever get all four objects. But I did get them, with your help, Lady Eriu, and even after facing this most terrible of all the guardians no one has—" His eyes widened. "Oh, the man of the Sidhe who was struck by the dullahan's horse—I saw his companions carry him away. Does he live?"

"He does. And he will recover."

Parlan breathed a sigh of relief, and he looked back at the gleaming gold pillar. "Of all the strange, terrible and wonderful things that I have seen on this journey, none seems stranger to me than how such a monster could be subdued and bound by nothing more than gold—soft, shining gold, whose strength is in beauty and not in battle, and certainly not in battle against the most horrible and powerful of monsters."

Eriu smiled. "I told you that the Sidhe had made three things into a weapon for you—a weapon strong enough to defeat the dullahan. Those three things were gold, and kingship, and kindness."

"Kindness. I remember that. You spoke of an act of kindness. What did you mean?"

"When you met the Sidhe that night as they traveled to the Otherworld, you gave them your most precious material thing—your own golden torque of kingship, made for you as one is made for every king."

"I told them it was not the kingship itself I was giving up," he said quickly, "but only the gold. If I failed in my quest I would have no further need of it, and if by the wildest chance I succeeded, I supposed someone might offer to make me another. And either way, if it would help assure the Sidhe their place in the Otherworld, I was glad enough to give them anything I had."

"It was those same Sidhe who are here with me this night, to help you in whatever way they could. It was their finest craftsman, Fallon, who took your king's torque and melted it down with the rest of their gold. Some he fashioned into a dagger, while the rest was made into powder and brought here to bind the dullahan."

"Fallon." Parlan glanced at the small cloaked figures surrounding him. "Where is he, that I may thank him? I could never have done this without his help."

"He rests in the trees with a companion. He is the one who was struck while battling the dullahan."

Parlan closed his eyes. "But you say he will recover?"

"He will indeed, and is quite pleased at being of help to the high king in defeating such an enemy. He will tell the tale of it many times, no doubt, and enjoy the telling more each time."

"Yet the gold they hoped to use to assure their place in the Otherworld is all gone—used to bind a monster they would never have to fear if they were, indeed, in the Otherworld."

"Do not worry, Parlan. The Sidhe will always have a place in the Otherworld, with or without their gold." She paused and turned to Parlan, and then looked down at the ground. She seemed about to say something, but there was only silence.

"Lady Eriu? What is it?"

She collapsed to the earth and lay unmoving, her green cloak floating down around her.

CHAPTER THIRTY-SEVEN

Parlan carried Eriu back to camp. She lay pale and still as death in his arms all the way there. When they finally climbed up out of the plain and topped the hill where the welcoming campfires burned, he shouted for servants to bring the warmest cloaks and furs, and to make a pallet near the trees. He lay Eriu down with the utmost care and covered her with the warm wool cloaks. Her eyes were closed and her face was as white as the dragon's breath, but a faint pulse did beat at her throat and her chest continued its slow and regular rise and fall.

Rian and three of the Sidhe carried the heavy Stone of Destiny to the campsite and placed it on the ground beside Eriu. Then the Sidhe stepped back into the forest and were gone, just as the eastern sky lightened and another day began.

The day proved colder and greyer, and shorter, than any Parlan could remember. He slept only a short time, but Eriu continued to lie unmoving on the warm pallet as though she had no strength left at all.

Parlan spent the day ordering the servants to prepare

298

everything for the fastest possible journey home to Teamhair Breagh. "In barely a fortnight, Rian, the dragon will be there," he said to his companion as they stood at the edge of the campsite. "Yet my only thought now is to get Eriu back there as soon as I can, in the hope that she can rest and regain some of her strength. I cannot take her to the Otherworld, but I can take her to my home in the very heart of the land and hope it is not too late."

"Everything is packed and ready to go at dawn," Rian said. "Save one thing."

Parlan frowned. "What is that? What is not ready?"

"The stone, my king. How will you get it back to Teamhair Breagh?"

"Back . . . to Teamhair Breagh?" He frowned. "What do you mean?"

"Well, think of it. The stone is not so large, but it is so heavy that the four of us who carried it to this campsite knew we had done a bit of work. Men cannot struggle to carry it all the way back to Teamhair Breagh in their hands. It is far too heavy a load for the back of a single pony. Surely you cannot simply drag it over the ground with flax rope, to be battered or even broken. How will you transport it?"

"A chariot," Parlan said. "It could lie in the floor of a chariot."

"It could—but you have no chariot. Your serving men said you did not wish for one on such a long and difficult journey."

"Of course I did not. The mountains would tear them to pieces. But you are right—we will need a chariot to get the Stone of Destiny back to Teamhair Breagh. A chariot drawn by horses. An oxcart would be too slow. The terrain is not so rough here and we do not have far to go. Now . . . where to get one?"

Rian shook his head. "I already asked your men. There is no large fortress within two days ride from here; there are only the scattered raths of farmers and herders, and none of those would have a chariot."

"They would not. But they would have an oxcart, and such a cart could easily be cut down to serve as a chariot for two of our horses." Parlan looked up at the distant hills that ringed the plain. "We will ride to the top of that hill, look for the nearest rath, and then go to them and make them a trade for an oxcart. A good trade—we'll give them a fine young mare. That's how we'll get the Stone of Destiny home to Teamhair Breagh."

He glanced up at the hilltop again. "We still have a bit of time before the sun sets. Go and find the best mare among the pack ponies and bring her here, along with two more who can serve as a team. "I will get Maorga and your own mount. Go! There is no time to waste."

Parlan turned and walked to the open space of grass where the hobbled horses had been left to graze. He searched for Maorga, but did not see him.

Frowning, he started to go to the horseboys and ask them where the stallion was, but as soon as he turned around, he saw Eriu holding both the saddled Maorga near the trees and Rian's bay horse saddled and ready right beside him.

"Eriu, I am glad to see you well—though your face is still pale," he said, walking up to her. "Why have you left your bed? You should stay and rest. I will have you home to Teamhair Breagh very soon."

"I will go with you to make your trade. I will ride the young mare, and then return with you on Maorga."

"Lady Eriu, you are kind to offer, but there is no need. You can stay here and rest in as much comfort as we can provide. The servants will—"

"King Parlan," she said, her voice little more than a whisper, "what strength I have, I draw from you. It is too late for me to find my way back to the Otherworld now. I will not have the power to go back as long as the Curse of the Dragon remains."

She held up her hand as he started to speak. "Please," she whispered. "I knew this before I left the Otherworld for the last time. Please do not deny me my last source of strength and comfort in this world."

He went to her and took her thin form in his arms, and she dropped the two sets of reins and rested her head against his chest. "Of course I would never deny you," he said softly, stroking her long hair. "We will go as soon as you are ready."

The sun was still well above the horizon when Parlan and Eriu and Rian rode up the side of the near hill, the tallest one for some distance. Rian led a pair of harnessed brown geldings on either side of his own bay, while Eriu sat on the bare back of a little gold mare with a cream-colored mane and tail, guiding it only by a single rope twisted round the animal's head. Parlan kept a close watch on Eriu as she rode beside him, but she sat quietly on the mare and looked straight ahead as the horses began the rough climb up the steep sides of the hill.

At last, they reached the broad summit. Parlan halted Maorga and turned him so that the sun was at his back. Looking to the east and then to the north, Parlan stared out at the countryside in silence.

Not one of the three said a word as they gazed at the scarred and blackened land. Some grass and trees and bushes still grew in spots, but more land was ruined than was green.

There was no sign of a farmer's rath anywhere to the north or east. Parlan reined his stallion around to face the lowering sun, and saw at last the familiar form of a small circular earth-and-stone wall in a valley not far away—but the valley, and the rath within it, were both black-

ened and ruined just like much of the surrounding countryside.

"No doubt the beast has learned to target any such
place for the easy meat to be found within," Rian said.
"There will be no cart for us to trade for—not without going much too far out of our way, if we are to return to
Teamhair Breagh before the dark of the moon."

Parlan turned to face the south, where Teamhair
Breagh lay—the direction they would be riding in the
days to come. Most of it was still green and alive, like the
country they had been traveling to; but the death and destruction of the Black Dragon was fast closing in.

Then he saw it. "Look, there!" Parlan cried. "There on
the edge of that southwestern valley—there is another
rath, there behind that grove of trees."

"So there is," Rian said, riding up with the harnessed
team. On the other side of Parlan, he peered down into
the valley. "It is close to that blackened swath, but still
surrounded by living grass and trees."

"Let us go, then," Eriu said quietly. "The beast closes in
even now, it seems. I can feel its breath, even as the ashes
it has left blow over us."

"We will lose no time," Parlan agreed, and together the
three urged their horses down the hillside.

Down in the shadowed valley, the three rode along the
edge of the cold-blackened land with Eriu keeping her
mare as far away from the destruction as possible. The
wind blew even colder here, it seemed to Parlan, though
perhaps it was simply because the low valley already lay
in shadow as the sun slipped behind the surrounding
hills.

"We will have to make our trade quickly, and then go,"
Rian said. "The sun—"

"We can ride for a little in the dark," Parlan inter-
rupted, sliding down from Maorga's back and handing
the reins to Eriu. "Now, wait here. I will go and see who is

here. Eriu—please give me the mare. Rest for a little on the grass, if you will, while Rian watches over you. I will be back as quickly as I can."

Eriu slid down from the mare and handed the rope to Parlan. "Please do not be long," she whispered. When she went to stand alongside Maorga, the stallion lowered its head to her in greeting.

Parlan took the golden mare's lead rope and led it toward the rath. The circular stone-and-earth wall sat up on a small rise between two much larger hills, and its solid wooden gate closed the gap. Yet as he approached, Parlan saw that the gate stood partly open, pushed in from the outside.

He frowned. Normally the gate would stand well open during the day, so that the family could come and go as needed for their work. It would be closed and barred at night to keep out any thieves, but especially to protect the milk cows and oxen from marauding wolves that might think to feed on easy sources of meat.

He started to go to the gate, but suddenly the little mare stopped dead in her tracks and refused to budge. She snorted and tried to turn away from the rath, seeking to rejoin the other horses.

"Come now, pretty one," Parlan said. He tried to turn the horse, to get it moving again, but it was no use. "Come now. This family will value you highly. They will treat you even better than—"

But the terrified mare stood high on it hind legs and threw itself backward, crashing down onto the thick grass and ripping the lead rope out of Parlan's hands. In an instant the mare rolled over, got to its feet and raced back to the other horses, flagging its cream-colored tail high over its back as it ran.

Parlan started after the horse, but he was stopped by Rian's frantic shouting. "Behind you! There! Behind you!"

Parlan turned back to face the rath—and there, standing and looking at him from the half-open gate, was an enormous grey-black wolf.

Parlan drew the Sword of Nuadha. In a moment Rian was beside him on foot, his own sword in his hands. Parlan could hear the pounding hoofbeats of all five of their horses as they galloped away.

Parlan kept his eyes fastened on the gate. "Eriu! Take cover where you can," he called. "We will protect you! We can only hope the family is still—"

But to Parlan's astonishment, Eriu appeared and walked past him toward the rath, even as a second huge wolf joined the first. "Eriu!" Parlan started to run after her, but she turned and held up both hands.

"Stay here, Parlan. They will not harm me, but I cannot stop them from attacking you. I will go and see what has befallen the family. Keep your swords at the ready."

She turned and walked to the gates of the rath, and stepped past the wolves as casually as though they were her own dogs. Parlan could only hold his breath as she disappeared behind the dwelling's high solid walls.

For endless moments, nothing happened except the lengthening of the shadows. The wolves barely glanced after Eriu, but went on staring at Parlan and Rian. And then Eriu returned, striding past the wolves to stand with Parlan once more.

"The wolves would normally stay in the deep forest and do their hunting there," she said, "but you have seen what has happened to the forest."

"Of course. The dragon is destroying more of it each night."

"And so the wolves are starving and forced to take meat where they can find it—as in farmers' raths."

"And the family who lives here? Are they—"

"They are not here. I saw no sign of them. But the milk cows and the few sheep they kept inside have long been food for these wolves."

"And now the beasts are hungry again, gnawing the bones of what is left and hoping the family will return."

"They are."

Parlan set his jaw. "We cannot let that happen. We cannot simply go from here and allow the family to come back, as they surely must, and find the wolves still here."

Eriu shook her head. "Parlan, you must return to Teamhair Breagh and prepare for the ritual at the dark of the moon. These people are not fools. They survived the wolves once. They will—"

She stopped as Parlan took her arm and tried to pull her behind him. Both he and Rian drew their swords and stood side-by-side as the last of the sun disappeared into dusk, and a pack of some twenty wolves poured out through the gates of the rath. The creatures came running straight for them, growling and slavering and baring their teeth.

The wolves were so tall that their heads were nearly as high as Parlan's chest. Eriu stepped away as the beasts surrounded the two men.

"Eriu!" Parlan cried, as he and Rian slashed at the starving animals with their swords and tried to force them away. "We cannot hold them forever! Please—try to go back to the campsite for help. We cannot let it end this way!"

Parlan and Rian pressed together back-to-back and kept swinging their swords at the desperate wolves, sometimes slashing one and sending it into a shrieking retreat, but always the beasts came back. "Try to get inside the rath walls!" Parlan shouted to Rian. "If we can get in there with only a few of the beasts, perhaps we can kill them and protect ourselves!"

He tried to steal a glance at Eriu, but he did not see her. She was gone.

VI

THE QUEEN

CHAPTER THIRTY-EIGHT

The sky was nearly dark. The two men crept along the wide grassy path that led to the rath and continued to hold off the wolves until, after what seemed like a lifetime, they finally reached the partly open gate.

There was barely enough room for one man to slip through. Parlan pushed Rian behind him and shoved him inside, even as one fierce wolf leapt past Parlan's sword and pushed its way in as well. A second wolf managed to do the same before Parlan could get himself inside. Four more of the snarling creatures forced their way past each other, through the gates and into the rath, before Parlan and Rian finally slammed the gate shut.

Now that they were trapped inside with their quarry, the wolves eased back and spread out. The six beasts formed a wide half circle, and the two men stood with swords in their hands and their backs to the gate. As the deep darkness of night descended, with clouds so thick they would still hide the moon even when it did rise, the wolves settled in to watch their prey—prey whom they could easily see in the darkness, but who could hardly seen them in return. The animals knew that all they had to do was wait a little while longer to let their quarry tire before closing in.

"We cannot let it end like this," Parlan repeated through gritted teeth, as he tried to follow the shadowy forms of the wolves in the blackness. "After so much, after such terrible and powerful and magicked guardians, I cannot let it all end in the jaws of a hungry wolf, as though I were nothing after all but a bolting hare or a frightened deer!"

"Then use that great magicked sword of yours, and I will use mine, ordinary as it is, and we will fight back like the men we truly are! We can take them one at a time. They are beasts, and we are—"

"We are blind, is what we are," Parlan growled. "Even when there is moonlight, they can hide in the shadows and still see us. We will never know where they are until they come leaping at our throats."

"Then we have only to hold out until daylight," Rian said, as though it were the simplest thing in the world.

"Indeed," Parlan agreed, as he held the Sword of Nuadha with two hands on the hilt and scanned the newly fallen darkness. "Only until daylight. . . ."

Time stretched on and on. The sky was a solid mass of cloud, and even though Parlan knew the moon must surely have risen by now, the world remained a haze of darkness. Parlan and Rian remained back-to-back, with their sides against the gate, and slashed whenever the wolves grew bold enough to come close. Occasionally they had the satisfaction of striking a wolf and hearing it shriek, but always the wolves crept closer.

"They know we are tiring," Parlan said. "They tease us into swinging at them uselessly."

"Only until daylight," Rian replied. But daylight was still a long time off.

Parlan suddenly blinked, and he looked up over the walls of the rath into the east. Was he only imagining the glow there in the sky? "Rian—look! Can it be morning?"

He could feel Rian trying to look. "I would say that it can't be, it's too soon, much as I would like the dawn to come—but who knows how long we've really been out here?"

The glow grew steadily brighter. It went from a soft pale light to a red-yellow glare, illuminating the thin cover of black smoke just above.

"That's not morning," Parlan said, pushing away from Rian. "Those are torches. Torches!"

He took a few steps into the rath as torchlight filled the walled grounds, and could see the wolves slinking into the remaining shadows behind the round house and the low sheds and pens.

"Here!" Parlan shouted to the lights on the hill, which now showed him the silhouetted forms of men. "We are here! Beware of the wolves, both in the rath and outside the gate!"

"Step back, King Parlan," said a deep voice from the hilltop. "We will take care of the wolves." Parlan and Rian pressed themselves against the gate, and in the light of the torches, a rain of stones flew down hard into the grounds of the rath.

Wolves ran yelping across the grounds and tried to hide behind the houses and pens and the shelters for the animals, but the glaring torchlight picked them out and the deadly stones struck. Parlan and Rian moved quickly to destroy any injured wolves with their swords. In moments, all six of the fierce invading wolves lay dead or dying at their feet.

Just outside the gate there was the sound of more stones whizzing through the air and striking the earth and yelping wolves. Parlan could hear the rest of the beasts tearing away over the grass . . . and then all was quiet. He found himself straining to hear the panting or growling of lurking foes, as he had done for so long throughout the night; but there was only the soothing sound of the breeze far off in the trees, and the faint snapping of the torches high up on the hill.

Parlan put away the Sword of Nuadha and dragged open the gate of the rath. Rian followed him outside, and together they turned to face the torchlit gathering moving toward them down the hill.

Parlan frowned as the group approached. He had assumed they were his own warriors, had thought that Eriu had been able to catch one of the horses and ride back to the campsite to fetch them, but these men were very different from his own. There were perhaps thirty, about half bearing torches. All were dressed in the poorest of dark brown woolen clothing. They were dirty and ragged, and looked as though they had not eaten well in months, if ever. But they all stood and watched Parlan quietly, some with their crude leather slings in their hands, and waited while a tall pale woman in a dark green cloak walked through their ranks.

"Eriu," Parlan said, as relief flooded him. "Where did you go? Who are these men?"

"These are the lowest and poorest of all your subjects, King Parlan," she said. "They are the outcasts, the petty criminals, the lowborn, the ones who wish to live off the land rather than labor as servants in the great duns. They, and a few women and children, live as nomads where they can and try to avoid the king's warriors who want them only as extra shields when there is a battle to be fought."

Parlan looked carefully at the silent gathering. "Rockmen," he said. "You are a group of rockmen. Eriu is right. You are outcast, criminals, even escaped slaves." He frowned. "Why would you face down a pack of hungry wolves for the high king? I may well have been the one who exiled some of you, or took back some of the cattle you stole, in the days when I was the chief of my own dun before being named high king. Of course, you will be rewarded with food and perhaps with a horse or two for saving me this night—but why would you risk your lives in such a way?"

One of the rough-looking men stepped forward. "You did indeed steal back our small and miserable herd of cattle, and not so long ago. It was one of your most daring raids, and I am sure it helped convince the others to name you high king.

"Then why—"

"Even we, the lowest born, know the tales of the gods and the goddesses and how they do sometimes walk among ordinary men. The Lady Eriu came to us, so silently that we heard nothing at all, and told us how you are determined to lift this Curse of the Dragon—if you are not devoured by wolves like a cornered stag."

Parlan's lip half-curled into a smile. "I am the one who brought about this curse," he said. "I am the one who has brought ruin to what little any of you had. Did Eriu not tell you this?"

"She did," the man said. "You are a king who is trying to right a great wrong, a wrong of his own doing. Even men such as we can understand that sort of honor—and if you will have us, we will serve you now at the end of your quest in whatever way we can. If you fail, the dragon will ruin us all. We have little to lose."

Parlan closed his eyes for a moment. "I thank you," he said. "Are you sure you will not accept a fine horse or two?"

The rockmen shrugged. "We have little use for horses, unless it is to slaughter and eat them."

Parlan blanched. "I see. Well, perhaps some gold brooches or armbands—"

"We cannot eat gold. King Parlan, we came here in hopes of saving the land. We did not come for a reward."

"Though we would not walk away for a nice side of venison, or a few loaves of good wheat bread and butter," one man spoke up, and all of them laughed.

"Come back to our camp, and we will feed you all as well as I have ever eaten myself," said Parlan. He smiled, looking at the group of thirty men. "And now that I think of it, I do have a task for you—a very important task. . . ."

"Only a nine-day to go until we reach home," Parlan said, twisting in his saddle to glance over his shoulder. Eriu sat behind him on Maorga's broad rump, holding on as best she could to his waist and leaning her head against his back. She nodded, but kept silent.

To Parlan she seemed to weigh almost nothing at all, and her arms were so weak that he did not know how she held on—but hold on she did, and he kept the stallion to a walk as his men and servants and pack ponies followed behind.

It was not only for Eriu's sake that the party kept to its slow pace. The pack animals could go no faster than a walk, of course, as could the servants who led them; but now, in the center of the party, following the warriors and ahead of the servants, six rockmen carried a crude platform made of stout oak branches lashed together with flax rope and leather straps, and resting in the center of the rough wooden platform was the Stone of Destiny. This stone that proclaimed the rightful king was now carried by those of the lowest station, but it was carried willingly and even proudly.

Parlan glanced back at Eriu again. "We are on the last stretch of our journey, and I know the worst is yet to come . . . and yet I feel better in spirit than I have for a long time. I am not sure why, but I almost dare to hope—now that we have all of the artifacts, and now that we are so near to Teamhair Breagh, so near to home."

Slowly Eriu raised her head. "You have gained far more

314

than just the artifacts," she said, as Maorga carried them with long, sure strides. "Do you not see this?"

Parlan frowned. "What do you mean?"

He could feel her smile in his stomach. "Look at those who come with you now on this final part of your journey.

"You have those of the very highest station—the hostage-princes of each dun you visited, and your companion, Rian, who was once a trusted friend of the gods themselves. You have the people of the land, the farmers and herders, whom you helped by giving them the deer you hunted for yourself. You have the Sidhe, the land's oldest inhabitants, who follow us now unseen in the shadows of the forest. And you have those of the lowest and roughest station, the rockmen, who even now carry the Stone of Destiny willingly and proudly for the high king.

"You have them all, Parlan, from the highest to the lowest, from the newest to the oldest. *That* is why your journey feels complete."

She rested her head against his shoulder once more. Parlan smiled, and reached down to cover her hand with his own.

On the final night of the journey, the party pushed through the darkness and kept on going. At dawn, King Parlan and his warriors, and the groups of farmers, servants, rockmen and Sidhe, all arrived together at the hill of Teamhair Breagh.

Parlan threw his leg over Maorga's neck and jumped down to the earth, turning quickly to catch Eriu as she slid down from the stallion's back for the last time. He lifted her up and held her close to his chest as he carried her inside the great round house of Eire's high king, where the central hearth blazed with warmth against the damp winter chill. At the back of the house, hidden behind tall leather screens brightly painted with red horses and green bulls and yellow eagles, was the wide sleeping ledge. It was piled with clean straw and covered with stacks of soft thick wolf pelts. He placed Eriu on the furs and covered her, and as she turned and burrowed deeply into them, he thought he saw a touch of color return to her cheeks.

He unpinned his heavy, bright-colored cloak and laid it over top of Eriu, over the furs, and then quickly stripped away his boots and woolen tunic. Then he crept in beneath the furs and pulled Eriu close, willing his own strength and heat and life into her with every beat of his heart. She eased close to him and seemed to draw his offer of his life deep within herself, just as she had drawn him within herself a year ago at his kingmaking in a very different way. . . . Yet this was no less intimate or lifegiving, for now it involved great love and care, and a lifetime's worth of shared experiences, in a way that their first encounter never could have done.

Parlan held her close and closed his eyes, and then he fell asleep for what he knew might be the last time in his life.

Sometime later, Parlan became aware that the light within the house had become filtered and dim, and he knew the sun was approaching the western horizon. Eriu still lay peacefully in his arms, and he could feel her featherlight breathing and the faint beat of her heart. He eased out from beneath the furs and swung his feet down to the straw-covered floor, quickly tying on his fur-lined leather boots and pulling on his tunic.

Stepping from behind the screen, he walked to the central stone hearth and found a tall golden cup of honey wine sitting beside a large golden plate piled high with sliced beef in drippings, fresh bread with butter, and boiled apples with honey. He carried the plate back behind the leather screen and found Eriu sitting up on the sleeping ledge, pinning her green cloak around her shoulders with her golden brooch of heavy gold oak leaves.

He sat down beside her, and together they shared the food on the plate and the honey wine in the cup. Eriu took only a few bits of the apples and honey, while Parlan ate heartily; and at last he set the plate and cup aside, pinned his cloak around his shoulder and strapped on the Sword of Nuadha. He stood before Eriu, took her face in his hands, and kissed her gently on the forehead. Then he turned and walked away, out into the newly fallen night.

Not one word passed between them.

Chapter Thirty-nine

In the darkness, with the sky swept clear by the winter winds and the stars shining bright against the blackness, Parlan walked at the head of a silent procession on their way toward the highest point of the hill of Teamhair Breagh. He wore the Sword of Nuadha strapped to his hip. Directly behind him walked Rian, arms outstretched before him and the Spear of Lugh resting across his open hands. Rian was followed by Fallon, the brave goldsmith of the Sidhe, and two other Sidhe who carried the shining Cauldron of the Daghda brimming with clear rainwater. Last of all came seven men bearing the Stone of Destiny in their hands—two of the hostage-princes, two of Parlan's own warriors, and three rockmen.

These were followed at some distance by the rest of Parlan's warriors, and by the remaining herders and farmers and rockmen, and by the rest of the men and women of Teamhair Breagh. The Sidhe watched from the shadows, and Eriu remained in the house of King Parlan within the walls of Teamhair Breagh.

All that any of them could do now was wait.

At the peak of the hill, surrounded by the starry night and by some of the last living countryside in Eire, Parlan stood in the very center of the hill and watched as the seven men placed the Stone of Destiny on the earth at his feet. They stepped back, and Parlan closed his eyes and spread his arms wide. The night winds swept freely over them all with no other hills to block its way.

With silent footsteps, the three men of the Sidhe placed the Cauldron of the Daghda on the surface of the stone. Parlan lowered his arms as he watched starlight glittering in the clear water within.

Next came two of the men of the land, one a farmer and one a herder, one holding a leather bag and a torchstick, and the other man an armload of clean dry wood. From the bag Parlan took a few handfuls of dry twigs and leaves, and arranged them in a neat pile on the other end of the stone. Also in the bag were two small pieces of flint, and Parlan struck them together over the pile of kindling until a few good sparks took hold and began to glow with life. He added three pieces of wood, and in a moment a small fire blazed on the stone.

Parlan stood up and took the Spear of Lugh from Rian, holding it in his left hand. With his right hand, he drew the Sword of Nuadha and turned to face the west.

"Dragon!" he shouted, as the others stepped back from the hilltop. "Cursed Black Dragon! I stand here at the dark of the moon, the first after Samhain.

"I stand here with the Sword of Nuadha, carried to me on the winds by the Master of the Wild Hunt.

"I stand here with the Spear of Lugh, yielded to me against the flames of the firedrake.

"I stand here with the Cauldron of the Daghda, brought to me out of the sea by the merrows.

"And I stand here with the Stone of Destiny, wrested out of the earth from the terrible dullahan.

"And I stand here now in the presence of earth, air, fire

and water, and with the most powerful of all elements—mine own spirit, nurtured and strengthened by the love I bear for Eriu, Goddess of the Land and Goddess of Sovereignty, in whose name I became high king."

He raised the sword and spear high overhead. "Come to me now, dragon!" he shouted, his heart pounding in his chest. "Come to me with your foul breath and hideous wings, that I might end this curse or die in the attempt—die this night and never see another sunrise!"

He stared hard into the west, looking for any movement against the stars and listening for the sound of monstrous leathery wings. But for long moments he saw only the soft waving of the distant trees, and heard only the rushing of the night wind.

Then something made him look up.

He could see nothing but stars and blackness, but could have sworn something came toward him—a piece of the black night sky had detached itself and was moving straight for him.

Then came the beat of those terrible wings, sending a forceful gust of wind across the hilltop. "So, you came gliding in high on the west wind so I would not hear your wings!" Parlan shouted. "Show yourself! Do your worst! I have naught to lose, so I do not fear you! Show yourself!"

The blackness wheeled above him, and as the starlight caught it, Parlan made out the form of the beast. The Black Dragon was as hideous as he remembered, with glaring small eyes and huge claws and long sharp teeth; but it seemed even larger now, and more malevolent, and even more terrifying and evil in appearance, scarred as it was from the damage Parlan had done to it a year ago at Samhain.

"Grown fat and slow from devouring creatures of the land, I see," Parlan growled. "But where is your foul breath? Where is the cold that burns?"

The dragon beat its wings and hovered; then it raised

its head, opened its jaws and forcefully exhaled a torrent of white frost at Parlan. But Parlan was ready, and he crossed the Sword of Nuadha with the Spear of Lugh and held them up to ward off the beast's terrible breath.

Any other weapons would have been shattered by such cold, but the weapons of the gods deflected the stream of frost and sent it straight back into the face of the Black Dragon. The monster screamed in rage, flew up high and circled around.

"Is that all you have? Surely there is more!" Parlan cried. "Come back! Come back! Give me all you have!"

Twice more the dragon hovered over Parlan, and twice more it blasted him with its breath. Both times, as before, his magicked weapons sent the spray of killing cold back up the beast.

Finally, in rage, the dragon tried to breathe a fourth time on its tormentor—but this time there was nothing but a faint white vapor. Parlan knew he must act fast. He did not know how long the beast would be without its killing breath. He placed the Spear of Lugh down on the earth at his feet and held the Sword of Nuadha over his right shoulder, both hands gripping the hilt. "Come back!" he cried. "You must be hungry after such work. Surely I would make a fine morsel for you. Come back! Here I am!"

He waved the bright sword in the starlight, knowing it would not fail to catch the eye of the beast. And sure enough, the dragon wheeled and dove straight down at him. Ready, Parlan braced his legs and raised the Sword of Nuadha high, welcoming the sight of the monster as it soared straight for him, wings outstretched and jaws wide open.

He knew he would only get one chance. With all the strength he possessed, Parlan leapt back and swung the great sword across the throat of the dragon. Any normal sword would have hardly scratched such a beast, but the bronze Sword of Nuadha—the sword that no creature could escape—tore a great gash.

The dragon screamed again, this time from pain. It twisted away and flew upward, showering the earth with a spray of red-black blood, and circled once again.

Parlan dropped the sword to the earth and grabbed up the Spear of Lugh. "Surely it is not so easy!" he taunted. "Come back for me, and I will give you a taste of this as well! Come back! Here I am!"

He gripped the heavy three-pronged spear and hefted it above his shoulder as the dragon dove at him again. When the beast was nearly on him, he threw the spear straight for the gash he had made with the sword. The spear hit its mark, and it lodged deep within the open bleeding throat of the beast.

Again, the monster screamed and tried to fly up into the sky—but this time its effort failed. It fell hard to earth on the hill of Teamhair Breagh, clawing at the terrible spear lodged in its bleeding throat, and choking and gasping.

Yet the beast was not dead; Parlan knew it could still recover, even from such terrible weapons as the Sword of Nuadha and the Spear of Lugh. His task was not over yet.

He caught up the torchstick and thrust the end of it into the fire burning on the Stone of Destiny. As soon as the torch caught, he turned and flung it at the beast. It landed on the creature's chest, just below the wavering shaft of the Spear of Lugh, and began to smolder and glow. Smoke rose along the lines of the dragon's heavy black scales.

The creature screeched again, clawing repeatedly at the spear and now at the flames. It tried to beat its wings and rise into the air, but weakness was rapidly overtaking it—as were the flames that grew on the scales of its neck and chest.

Parlan picked up the Sword of Nuadha and placed it

back in the scabbard at his hip. He straightened up, breathing deeply of the cold night air, and gazed at the writhing dragon once more.

"I never thought that I could do this thing," he said, breathing deep with the exertion and excitement of the battle. "I will be the first to tell you that. And yet with the help of a goddess, and the help and sacrifice of many good people of Eire, I have done it, and it seems the curse I brought upon the land should be truly lifted."

He caught his breath, and took a step toward the dying dragon. "I never thought to do the things that I have done in this past year. I never had thought to be anything but a good king who might win a few cattle raids and ritual melees. Instead, I battled the fiercest of the guardians of the gods and won their weapons from them. I hoped simply to find a fair woman to be my queen. Instead, I loved and won a goddess. And I feared that I would turn out to be the worst of kings, but instead I was forced to lift a curse and become the strongest of kings—and all because of you."

Parlan blinked, and he watched the feebly thrashing creature as it clawed at the spear in its throat and the flame on its chest.

"All because of you . . ."

The wind blew cold and clean over the hilltop, and seemed to roar in his ears.

"Because of you, I was forced to become a far better king than I ever would have been, for I would be dead by now if I had not been forced to my limits, and beyond. If not for you, Black Dragon, I would have remained a shallow and arrogant man to the end of my days, all the while thinking I was good enough as I was—and who knows what irreparable harm I might have done to my kingdom, to my world? Yet because of you . . . because of you . . . because . . ."

His words trailed off into silence. The only sounds were the tortured keening of the dragon and the slow, weak flapping of its leathery wings.

Parlan turned away from the beast and ran back to the Stone of Destiny. He picked up the shining Cauldron of the Daghda and carried it as quickly as he could to the beast, mindful of the pure rainwater brimming it. In one quick move, he dashed the water of the cauldron onto the smoldering, glowing neck and chest of the dragon, stepping back as the beast cried out, and a great cloud of smoke and steam rose up from it into the cold night air.

"I thought you a curse, Black Dragon, but I see now that you are anything but. You are the fifth and final guardian set by the gods, and it is your task to keep unworthy kings from being allowed to ruin the land for eternity. That is why the gods never destroyed you. That is why they placed you here, before they themselves were destroyed so long ago."

He set down the cauldron and walked to the slowly writhing beast, unafraid. Setting one foot firmly against the monster's still-smoldering chest, he grabbed hold of the shaft of the Spear of Lugh and leaned back hard to pull it out, twisting it as he did in order to free the barbs from the flesh in which they were embedded, and trying not to hear the agonized cries of the dragon. At last Parlan got it out, and he staggered back a little with the newly freed spear in his hands, even as the dragon threw its head back with a final cry and fell over on its side.

Parlan walked back to the Stone of Destiny. The small fire still burned at one end, and he added another stick of wood to keep it going. He took the cauldron and placed it back on the other end of the stone. Finally he took the spear in his left hand, drew the sword with his right and crossed the two weapons above his head as he stepped up onto the Stone of Destiny facing west—facing the dragon.

"Hear me now, Black Dragon!" Parlan cried. "I am the

high king of all Eire and I have broken your curse! I hold dominion over you now. Go back where you belong. Go back to the west, beneath the waves. Go back until you are needed once again!"

The dragon keened and lifted its head. It rolled over until its clawed feet were underneath it once again. Raising its wings, it beat them down once, twice, and then slowly rose into the night sky. It flew straight away into the west until it was lost among the blackness and was gone. Parlan knew he would not see it again.

He closed his eyes . . . and then became aware of a deep and powerful vibration rising up from beneath his feet. But wait—it was not from the earth, but from the stone he stood on, from the Stone of Destiny, the stone charged by the gods to cry out when a true king stood upon it.

The low vibration surged up through his legs and body and seemed to go right out to the stars, ending in a high ringing note that seemed to bind every element and every creature together in a single harmonious sound. The vibration faded, but just as quickly it rose up and sang out again, and then a third time, that none might have any doubt as to what they were hearing.

Parlan stepped down from the stone. He set the sword and spear crossed over one another on the center of the stone, between the fire and the cauldron, and as he set them down he felt, at long last, the past year's terrible tension begin to leave his body. For a moment it seemed to sap his strength as well, and he dropped to his knees on the grass. Closing his eyes, he lay down to rest on the comforting earth, knowing that neither he nor his beloved land would ever again be troubled by a dragon.

The quest was over.

VII

THE GODDESS

CHAPTER FORTY

After a time, Parlan raised his head, and he saw a soft pale glow in the east. The sun was rising. He had lived through the night, had lived to see one more sunrise.

Slowly he got to his feet. The stone still rested where he had left it, with the Sword of Nuadha and the Spear of Lugh resting crosswise upon its center. The cauldron remained empty, and the fire at the other end of the stone had burned down to cold dark ash. A few clouds drifted by in the newly brightening sky, carried on the soft wind. Larks called in the distant forest. All was calm, and normal, and ordinary.

From all around the hilltop, Parlan's people began climbing into view. His druids and servants and warriors were there, as were all the men and women who had remained here during his yearlong journey. He saw the farmers and the herders who had come with him, as well as the silent rockmen.

Then the rockmen stepped aside, and through their ranks walked a somber group of Sidhe, all of them cloaked in grey. And then the Sidhe parted ranks to reveal Eriu standing among them.

She stood tall and strong in the morning light, her dark green cloak thrown back from her head and blowing gently in the wind. Her golden brooch shaped like a circle of oak leaves gleamed in the newly rising sun, and as he walked toward her, Parlan could see a touch of color in the fair skin of her face, a shine in her deep green eyes, and the lustre of her long dark brown hair as the wind brushed it back from her smiling face.

"Eriu," he whispered, and took her in his arms.

She returned his embrace with all the gentle strength of a goddess, and stepped back to smile at him. "You have succeeded in your quest, King Parlan," she said. "The dragon is gone—sent back where it belongs—and the land is whole and alive once more."

"I am only glad to see you well again," he said. "And the dragon is indeed gone." He shook his head. "I wonder how many other kings were faced with this same task—and how many found the courage to send the dragon away to remain a guardian instead of trying to kill it."

"I can only tell you that you are not the first. And, like my appearance at your kingmaking—at all king makings—it is not something that the bards will ever sing poetry about. Some things all men must learn for themselves."

"So they must," he agreed.

She reached up and touched his hair, and a slight frown crossed her brow. Parlan was about to ask her what was wrong, when she withdrew her hand and smiled again.

"There is one task left," she said. "The sacred artifacts must be returned to their guardians, should they ever be needed again. All must go back, save the Stone of Destiny. That can remain here, a gift from High King Parlan to all future kings, and especially to the people they mean to rule."

He nodded. "I will gladly give the others back. If I might . . . if I might have a day or two to rest, I will start another journey to return them."

Eriu smiled. "No need for that, Parlan. You have loyal messengers who will see to this task for you."

She turned to the west, spread her arms wide, and sang out a high, clear note.

In the space of three heartbeats, there came the sound of wild hoofbeats galloping up the side of the hill. And then, rising into view, came a herd of nine white and grey horses, all of them wet and dripping with water, their hooves caked with sand and their manes and tails beribboned with lengths of red and green and purple seaweed.

The horses halted near the Stone of Destiny and stood close together, watching Eriu. "They look like they just galloped out of the sea," Parlan marveled.

"So they did. It is their favorite door to the Otherworld." Eriu walked to the horses and touched the nearest one on the shoulder. "This mare, and the one beside her, will take two of your men and the Sword of Nuadha back to the plains of the east, where the Master of the Hunt will take back the sword."

Parlan looked to his warriors. After only a moment's hesitation, two of his men, Oran and Gill, stepped forward and approached the mares. As they swung up and settled themselves on the mares' broad white backs, Parlan took the sword from its place on the stone and carried it to Oran. "Safe journey," he said, and handed over the beautiful bronze sword in its red-jeweled scabbard. The horses turned and galloped down the eastern side of the hill, and the men were gone.

Eriu stood between two other mares. "These will take three of the Sidhe and the Cauldron of the Daghda back

331

to the seashore of the west, where the merrows will once again safeguard the cauldron." Three of the Sidhe came forward, and even in the hooded grey cloak Parlan recognized Fallon as he swung up alone on the nearest horse. As the other two Sidhe got up on the second mare, Parlan brought the gleaming gold cauldron to Fallon and placed it in his outstretched hands.

"Thank you," he said, and with a quick nod the Sidhe and his two companions galloped away down the hill to the west and vanished.

Five mares were left. "For this final journey," Eriu said, "three of the hostage-princes are needed—as are two of your men. The two called Gavin and Cillian."

"The princes are hostages no more," Parlan said. "I hereby discharge them and thank them for their service. They are all free to go." Then Parlan glanced at Eriu and at his waiting men. "Bring Gavin and Cillian here," he ordered, and went to get the Spear of Lugh from its place at the Stone of Destiny.

When he returned, he found Gavin, Cillian, and three of the hostage-princes waiting for him on the five mares. Eriu stood before them as the mares gathered around her.

"Hear me now, Gavin and Cillian," she said. "The Spear of Lugh has no guardian any longer. It is the will of the goddess that as payment for your treachery in trying to bring about the death of the high king, both of you shall return to the mountains of the south and become, yourselves, a pair of firedrakes to watch over the spear. When these three princes have buried it once more, the enchantment will take place. If you refuse, the mares will take you instead to the Master of the Hunt, where you will join his terrible undead followers. A firedrake guardian is, after all, not without honor, and it does carry the possibility of one day becoming a man again. Just ask Rian."

Neither of the warriors made any answer, or even

looked up. In an instant the mares bore them away to the south, closely followed by the three hostage-princes, and were gone.

Eriu turned and raised her arms, beckoning to the gathered people who surrounded them on the hilltop. "Come closer," she said. "Come here. Listen to the offer that I make to your high king and to his people—to *all* of his people."

When the people stood in a great circle around them, Eriu turned to Parlan. She reached up and gently touched his hair. "You cannot know this, Parlan, but now that your quest is over, its ravages show on your body. Your hair has gone iron-grey this morning. Your face is aged and lined like that of a man far beyond your years. And your eyes— your eyes hold all the worry and fear and terrible concern of a man charged with lifting the most terrible of curses. And I can tell you that these marks will never leave you— not as long as you live."

"As long as I live." He tried to smile at her, even while touching his hair and glancing at one of his outstretched hands—which, though still strong, seemed to belong to a much older man. "I take it that will not be for much longer."

She gazed up at him, and he could see that her eyes were bright with tears. "A year, Parlan. Perhaps two. But no more. The quest has taken so much from you, you have no more left."

"But it was worth it," he said quickly. "I have no regrets. I am amazed that I am alive at all. I only wish that mine was the only life lost." He smiled. "If I know that I will see you, my goddess, from time to time, then the length of my life makes no difference to me. I will never take another queen. I will serve my people and you to the end of my days, no matter how great or small their number."

"You no longer wish to have me as your queen, King Parlan?"

He took a swift breath. "Oh, Lady Eriu, there is nothing I would love more—yet I know, for you have told me well, that a goddess who dares to love a man would only be condemned to a long and terrible decline when he dies, as all men must die—and the land would then decline with her. I would not ever have that happen to you, and I would not ever want to be the cause of it. I understand, dear Eriu, that a goddess cannot love a mortal man."

"And no mortal man can love a goddess and survive."

He smiled at her, once again feeling the great weariness that had descended upon him when the quest finally ended. "Yet I would choose this shortened life again, for you are in it, over the longest life without you. I am only trying to prepare myself, now, for your leaving for the Otherworld, for that is your home and you are needed there. A goddess cannot abandon her place any more than a king can abandon his. I will miss you every moment, but I love you truly, and because I love you I understand that you must go." He took both her hands in his own and kissed them, and then he rested his forehead on her hands so that none might see his face.

"Yet there might be another way."

Parlan looked up. Never had she seemed so beautiful, with her green eyes shining in the morning light and her lips curved into a gentle smile. "What do you mean?"

She lowered her hands and slowly withdrew them. "A goddess cannot live in the world of men—but a man can live in the Otherworld with a goddess who loves him, if he is willing to stay there with her forever."

Parlan looked up at her, hardly able to believe what he was hearing. "Eriu, is this true? Do you mean to invite me to the Otherworld with you, as your consort?"

"I do, Parlan. You, who have done so much for your people and for the remaining gods, have earned your place there if you wish. And I would like to think that perhaps I, who have served the world of Men for so long, have also earned the right to love and companionship of my own—now that I have found the best of all Men."

He tried to think, barely able to breathe. "Yet you told me that if you allowed yourself to love a mortal man, you could never again lie with a king and confer sovereignty upon him."

She nodded. "That is true."

"Then how will Eire gain its new kings—especially its high kings?"

"If a woman will stand in for me—a worthy woman, one who asks for my blessing on the ritual—then I will grant sovereignty through her." She smiled. "And if there is any doubt of her choice, the Stone of Destiny rests now at Teamhair Breagh for any would-be king to stand upon."

Parlan drew a deep breath, and he looked at the people who surrounded him—people from every station of life in Eire, from the highest to the lowest. "Yet how can I leave my place as king, a place I swore to keep and protect for all of my life?" He tried to smile. "I know rather well what happened the last time I thought to set aside my kingship."

Eriu took him by the arm and turned him so that they both faced the west. "Look there," she said, and Parlan caught his breath.

The day was clear, and he could see across the midlands all the way to the distant mountains, brightly lit with the morning sun shining on them. But much closer, right at the edge of the hill of Teamhair Breagh, the air just above the grass began to shimmer. It looked as though it had become liquid and wavering, but then Parlan realized he was seeing an altogether different view through the haze.

He could see a vast open field surrounded by trees bearing the new green leaves of spring. The field was filled with lush grass, and dotted with bright yellow primroses, and as Parlan gazed at it a herd of white and grey-white mares cantered past with their heads up and their tails held high, some with little black foals at their sides.

The crowd around him all stared in fascinated silence at the shimmering air and the vision it contained. As they watched, three figures appeared at the front—a tall, smiling and very powerful man; a woman with red-gold hair and great peace and wisdom in her face; and a second woman, very tall and slender and beautiful, with long coppery braids and a lazy smile.

"These are Ogma and Brighid and Flidais," said Eriu. "They are holding open this doorway to the Otherworld for you, to show you that you are indeed welcome there."

Parlan felt that he could barely breathe. "My kingship," he whispered, still staring at the deities before him, and at the perfect springtime scene. "My kingship . . ."

"Have you a tanist, Parlan? Have you a successor? Is there anyone worthy of taking your place as high king?"

He swallowed, and made himself look away to search the faces of the crowd—and there he was, very close by as always. "Rian," Parlan said. "Rian is worthy to be a king, if ever any man was."

Eriu nodded. "He has served gods and men alike. I have no doubt he will be found to be a true king, when the people hold his own kingmaking ritual."

She turned to Parlan and touched his face, and smiled. "Come home now, my love. Come home to life and beauty everlasting, both given and received. Come home with me."

He took her hand and placed it on his arm, and as his people knelt on either side he and Eriu walked together to the shimmering door and crossed over to the Otherworld, where the warmth and life and color of eternal springtime enveloped and filled them with the life and strength of youth that would be with them always.

And just before the shimmering doorway closed, Parlan saw a few white mares and a few grey-cloaked Sidhe step through and go from the Otherworld to the hill of Teamhair Breagh. He felt peace and joy at knowing that a few otherworldly creatures would still remain in Eire, not quite ready to leave it just yet.

PRONUNCIATION GUIDE

Abhainn—AWH-ihn
Aisling—ASH-ling
Aille—AY-leh
Amhranai—AW-rahn-ee
Anluan—AN-lahn
Baur—barr
Bealtaine—BEL-tin
Bearach—BAR-akh
Bhoireann—BUR-rehn
Brighid—BREE-yid
Calvagh—CAL-vakh
Cillian—KILL-ee-an
Daghda—DOY-dah
Daithi—DAH-hee
Diarmaid—DAHR-mid
Dullahan—DOOL-ah-han
Dun—doon
Ebhear—AY-vahr
Eire—AIR-eh
Eriu—AIR-yuh
Farraighe—ARR-ih-geh
Flidais—FLEE-ish
Gavin—GAV-in
Ghee—gee (hard g)
Glamyr—GLAM-er
Imbolc—IM-bolk
Lugh—loo
Maeve—mayv
Mactire—MAC-teer-eh
Magh Sleacht—moy slot

Maorga—MAYR-gah
Niall—neel
Nuadha—NOO-ah
Ogma—OH-mah
Ona—OH-nah
Rath—rah
Ri—ree
Rian—REE-an
Riona—REE-nah *or* REE-ah-nah
Ronan—ROH-nan
Ros—rahsh
Ruirthech—ROO-irh-heh
Samhain—SOW-ehn
Seamus—SHAY-mus
Seanan—SHAH-nan
Siadhal—sheel
Sidhe—shee
Slaine—SLAH-neh
Solasta—SAH-lass-tah
Tadghe—tygh
Tanist—TAN-ist
Teamhair Breagh—TAH-wer *or* TAH-rah, bray
Uaine—OO-ih-neh

SPIRIT OF THE MIST

JANEEN O'KERRY

An early summer storm rages off the coast of western Ireland, and Muriel watches. From inside the protective walls of Dun Farraige, she can see nothing, yet her water mirror shows all. The moonlight reveals the face of a man—one struggling to overcome the sea.

He is an exile, of course. By clan law, exiles are to be made slaves. Yet something ennobles this man. The stranger's face makes Muriel yearn for both his safety and his freedom. She, who was raised as the daughter of a nobleman, has a terrible secret. And she can't help but believe that this handsome visitor—swaddled in mist and delivered to the rain-swept shores beneath her Dun—will be her salvation.